The FIRST Traitor

If you purchased this book without a cover, you should be aware this book is stolen property. It was reported as "unsold and destroyed" to the publisher.

No part of this production may be reproduced, stored in a retrieval system, or transmitted in any form or by any means, electronic, mechanical, photocopying, recording or otherwise.

Copyright © 2015 Laura Campbell

The First Traitor
The 27th Protector Series

Author: Laura Campbell
ISBN: 978-0-9861382-3-2

To the girls who call me mother, who chased moths and dandelion fuzz the summer I wrote this book.

-Summer-

CHAPTER 1

The clouds were teasing me.

It felt silly to say, but it also felt true.

There would be a star, splitting the black, one beautiful shot of light raging through a dark and breathless universe, sending its beam as a reminder that the darkness could not always win.

But then a cloud would block it, mocking all its effort as one gentle breeze propelled the cloud to hide the light. Only it didn't feel hidden; it felt stolen. It was meant to be, but was lost.

A weight fell on my chest and my ears seemed blocked, hearing only an unrelenting scream from an unknown source. In the midst of the lies and despair, there came a shattering truth that summarized the tragedy I felt.

Nothing that was meant to be should ever be lost.

Wasn't that why we saved the Unnecessaries? Or the Vessels who dared to have a child of their own? The Republic stole the permission to live away from those they couldn't control or didn't see as valuable. That included me.

I moved to get up, my wounded arm still protesting as I put weight on it, and leaned up on the mat. I grabbed my arm, turning towards the doorway of my private room in my Training Circle.

Collin was still sitting there, in the threshold, keeping guard not against intruders to my room, but against the intruders in my mind, that would wake me in the middle of the night. I had struggled to tell him a story tonight; our usual diversion from the terrors we faced. But I had trouble thinking of how the story could end well. He told me the story he had written, that he had told me while I was lying on the shuttle floor with my arm cut open.

Now my arm ached again, just enough to prevent sleep. It created anxiety more than pain. The fear that it could happen again threatened while the doubt cast shadows on any ability I thought I had. The only thing that calmed me was seeing Collin.

He was still with me: protecting the 27th Protector.

Except I wasn't the 27th Protector anymore. They would still call me that, but there were only nineteen of us left. It made me feel like I was lying to say it. Or like I was a lie.

The clouds passed swiftly, blocking the few stars again. This was the tenth time these thoughts had awoken me. I had pushed them away, deep inside me where I would deal with it someday, hoping it wouldn't paralyze me with fear when it caught up with me. I wondered if I'd be back in the Republic within a week, in a situation where I needed to escape and suddenly be struck with all the weight of loss. I wondered if it would crush me, and I wouldn't be able to run or hide. I would risk losing a life.

Not just my life. I thought of Katerina, Amanda, Rachel, and André. I thought of baby Hope and baby Collin. Those Unnecessaries, deemed not alive enough to be human by the Republic, were now my foundation for everything I did, along with the illogical belief that Eldridge, as high counselor, thought I could do this: protect the Unnecessaries, the Vessels, those who opposed the perfection of the Republic.

They were a threat because they might trigger genuine emotion, wrecking plans for domination. The Society needed to make sure everyone in the Republic was comfortable, and true love– love that's real – isn't comfortable.

The proof of how difficult true love could be was now laying in my doorway. Some moments, Collin's presence comforted me. Others…I couldn't help but feel wrecked by it. I had fallen in love with one of the few people I was never supposed to even like.

I had rescued two Unnecessaries in one mission, causing friction with an already control-hungry Council. I had witnessed Tessa lose her Vessel and her chance at a perfect retrieval record, causing a moral and mental breakdown that resulted in a fight to save the baby that nearly killed me. I had helped Cassidy save her Unnecessary, remaining behind in the Republic without either of them. I was handed a baby after faking my way through an Elite level party. I had helped rescue Brie from a spy, only to get myself on a security tape that became propaganda for why every Protector should be murdered. I had let a girl from the woods return to the Republic to tell her caregiver she was alright, only to risk both our lives when every Protector was compromised.

And when I was shot, and had no chance of escape, I trusted the one person I was told never to trust to get out: the man who shot me.

I trusted him still. My arm twinged in argument. It filled me with uncertainty with every sharp sting of my wound.

Alex. The most unexpected piece of the puzzle. The Sentry, who should have killed me, had managed to save my life three times. What stung, along with my arm, was his undetermined fate. I didn't know if his last act of protecting me had gotten him killed. He had gotten me out to the woods, assuring me that his cover story would be enough to convince any of his peers that there was nothing strange about his behavior. While his survival was unknown, at least I finally knew and understood his motive: regret, encased in the tragedy of a sister and her unborn child lost and dead because of his refusal to help her. Except his tiny rebellion of hiding babies and ignoring Unnecessaries had grown into treason by rescuing me– just because he had seen something in me.

My head thudded, the center of the pain and confusion wrapped around his words and generating from his grazed kiss on my forehead. His words echoed: *"I saw you."*

I looked at the stars again, but the clouds swept over, and they looked dim: their light was wasted again. It was like looking in a mirror. And it was not going to help me sleep.

So I abandoned the hope of sleep. I winced as I leaned on my arm. I walked fast, determined to escape the pain I only wished wouldn't follow me.

I stepped out of my Circle. It felt more dangerous than when I left my Circle in the middle of the night, months earlier. I had felt bold, then. Now that the worst that I could have imagined had happened, those memories felt far away, lost with my naïve self who agreed to be the hero.

I was headed for the forest when the sound of footsteps made me slow down in front of one of the towering stone training Circles. It was Lynn's Circle. I had never had a lot of contact with her trainer. I was scared to speak. I might add awkwardness to an already painful moment. He stared at me with striking dark eyes that always looked calm, warm even, but they raged with turmoil.

"Keep walking, 27," his tired voice said. "You won't get what you need by talking with me, or any of us."

He seemed to know what I was thinking. That I couldn't sleep and that I wanted to talk about her. Then suddenly I remembered his name. Will. His name was Will.

"Because if you keep walking," Will continued, with a somewhat deadpan glare, "I won't have to hear you say, 'She's a hero. If she hadn't rigged the EMP, the rest of them might be dead.' Or give me any other reason why saving all of you had to cost Lynn her life and how that's somehow a good thing."

I almost cried, but I swallowed out of determination for him to hear me as I said, "But I wouldn't say that. Honestly. I wish it were me instead."

He breathed out, maybe fighting off more grief. "I figured you would say that, from the way she talked about you."

In fear that I was about to jump into the pain I had tried to avoid, I choked out the question, "She talked about me?"

He leaned up against the Circle, and looked at me curiously as he sighed. "She had a nickname for everyone. She called Brie 'the soldier,' she called Eva 'the heir,' and she called you 'the poet.' She said you saw what was happening, in a way that no one else did. She said that you inspired her, and you didn't even have to try."

Despite all effort to stay contained, regret wrenched my soul, pulling tears down my cheeks. They seared, making me burn with the shame of everything I should have done differently.

I should have talked to her more.

I should've gotten to know her more.

I should have known what motivated her.

He looked lost in thought, and then kept walking around the Circle, surrounding himself with grief again as he swept past me, only a few feet away from where I stood. I stared at him with eyes I thought could offer him hope. I didn't even know my eyes held any. But his eyes never reached mine. He never reached out for my hand only inches away.

He continued, lost in sorrow too heavy for me to lift, until he had walked past me, leaving me to run away, releasing the breath I didn't realize I was holding.

The garden.

I was hoping for some isolation. It usually was dark and empty at this time of night. But it was neither. There were just enough lanterns to see someone: a person I hadn't expected to be grieving.

"Sam?"

He froze mid-step, continuing to stare at the walk-way where his eyes were fixed. His shoulders shook slightly, enough to worry me. He had never shown this much emotion in the entire time I had known him, and was fairly balanced at the funeral compared to some. And out of all of the handlers, he hadn't lost a Protector.

But I couldn't mistake the pain I saw in the brief flash of his eyes. I couldn't even make sense of it. He swiftly ran, not saying anything as he made his way down to Central, most likely to relieve Liam, his assistant. I reminded myself that I really should thank both of them again, for not giving up on me being alive. The other members of the tech team had all but declared me dead. Sam had been the first to warn Patterson that we were compromised. I questioned how he could feel guilty about anything, and what he was doing wandering the garden alone.

But he hadn't been alone.

Patterson was sitting down by one of the fireplaces with a small book in his hand, deep in thought.

"Sir." I nodded.

"27? Isn't it a little bit late to be wandering around?"

I moved slowly, sat on the stone bench next to him.

"Well, I don't know if you heard, but I kind of have this issue with things I'm not supposed to do."

He scoffed out a laugh, which at least let me know I wasn't going to be in trouble for being outside my Circle so late. I reached for the stick to poke the fire. My attention was drawn to the small book in his hand.

"What is it, sir? The book?" I asked.

"Nothing you can read." He spoke as if the thoughts that had kept him aloof were fading, letting him break through to reality. "I should be reading it, but I can't…"

I had written enough Protector profiles to know why his pain was acute. He was chosen as a Head Trainer because he was so successful. His Protectors had always survived. He had never lost anyone. In avoiding his gaze, I realized that I recognized the leather: the exact leather my journal was made out of.

"It's like mine…only…"

"The 27th and the Head Trainer's journals are about the only ones sacred enough to still be leather-bound. I'm supposed to write in mine, too. But I don't know what to write," he sighed, then asked, "What do you write in yours?"

I pondered that. "Musings on life. What happens. What I feel: jealous of heaven for having their souls now. I drew what Andre's hand looks like. I wrote down the song Katerina sang to baby Collin. I wrote about Alex and secrets no one can know now. Lynn and the EMP."

"Such beautiful things." He stared at the fire, not at me, his voice haunted by what he had just declared beautiful.

"Why don't you open it? Maybe something in there would help it hurt less."

He stared at the place where his finger was placed in between the pages. He opened it up, and then closed it almost instantly.

"I don't want it to hurt less. I want to feel this pain. I want it to be acute, so I don't let this happen again."

I looked down, feeling helpless against my own agony and not sure if I could maybe help him fight his, even as he continued.

"I need this pain. I can't let this happen again. I…"

He bit his lip and closed the book. His hands jolted suddenly, almost as if he was going to throw the book on the fire. I lifted my hands defensively before blocking him, and then reaching out to touch the book, clenching it while closing my eyes, so I didn't see his anger. When I opened them, I didn't see anger. He looked like my father, any father, with the weight of a world on his shoulders. Only his family was much larger and in much more danger than most. He looked as if fifty years rather than thirty had worn on him. He looked back at where Sam had walked. It took almost a full minute, but then he spoke.

"It's not just losing them, Aislyn. It's never that simple. Like any leader, I have my board. I have to make a play, but I hate the pieces in front of me and the way the board is set." He turned to face me, as if he was finally talking to me and not just to himself. "When I move the next piece, I will hate myself. You'll hate me."

"Sir, I don't think..." I said, at first as nervously as I felt, but then chose a more sarcastic tone to lighten the mood. "I've heard enough masochism from Alex. This isn't worth torturing yourself. This isn't what you need from me. From anyone."

"So what do I need?" he said, more hopeless than frustrated.

"Maybe just...what you offered me once? Trust. I am still honored by that, you know? That you trusted me. I am humbled every day by everything I don't know about this world, by everything these girls have gone through together that I didn't experience because I was chosen one day before our final training started. You had no reason to trust me. But you did, and without reason. I will trust you."

He put his hands in his hair, just briefly. He opened up the book, and read the page that he had bookmarked. I couldn't help my curiosity, which he must have known, because he started to answer my question before I asked him.

"Eldridge wrote something years back, when he was Head Trainer for a brief time. He told me the same thing the night he chose me. He said…that I had to count the cost. If you set out to make a change, and you don't count the cost, the reality and horror of the challenge will drown your desire to keep going. And you'll lose."

His head was buried in his hands as he spoke to himself again.

"This costs way too much. And I didn't count on it."

He stood up, gazing at the book briefly but then stepping out onto the garden path. I realized he looked back at where Sam was standing. His footsteps were heavy, as if the stones were somehow pulling each step down with more weight. He wasn't grieving. This weight was heavier.

And the only thing heavier than grief was worry.

What could worry him that shouldn't be terrorizing me? I pondered every possible scenario. I had been fighting sorrow too hard to feel frightened of what was going to happen next. But the second the possibilities flooded in, I realized I would rather be sad than worried.

I wasn't naive enough to pretend that there wouldn't be repercussions on a political scale that shifted power and threatened change. It always seemed to me that true justice would always be lost in such tragedies. No one could punish who was responsible. That was still a mystery. The Council might manufacture a culprit, so blame could be assigned and some form of justice could be simulated. Someone needed to be labeled guilty, and their lives ripped apart so the Council looked competent.

And a politician's appearance of passion for justice might just be the end of me, Collin, or Alex. Even as I stood in the garden, trying to calm my mind, I felt buried by the anxiety Patterson had left there. I stepped out, only to see Sarah's trainer in tears by a flowerbed. She was huddled in a ball by the wall, eyes closed, probably praying something away. Even as I wondered if I should talk to her, George came up swiftly behind me, turning me around by my elbow as he whispered, "Get back in your Circle. Now."

"But I…"

He was still holding my elbow, and turned me to look directly at him. "You think she wants to see one of you right now? You're alive. You're everything she wishes she had: a Protector breathing. I didn't lose anyone this time, and I'm still jealous. Just go."

The urgency in his voice made his message clear without cruelty. I turned to go, but I could hear George behind me. I turned briefly to see him crouched down next to her, his one arm leaned onto her as he started to speak in a sympathetic tone.

I was far enough away that they couldn't see me, and I was mesmerized by them. There was beauty even in the grief of two legendary trainers. And I was jealous of it.

I already missed the sorrow.

Because I knew I couldn't cry anymore.

The worry would push out any tears I had left.

I had to move forward as if there was a hope that I could barely feel. I saw more clearly what the new normal was going to be: a shadow of our dreams. I didn't want to go back to the Republic. I didn't want to go back to my Circle. I didn't even want to go home.

I just wanted to feel something I could never feel again.

I heard the distant sobs from Lynn's trainer. I hurried into my Circle, only to see Collin there, pacing with his eyes closed, murmuring prayers. Even as he opened my eyes, and began to say my name, I silenced him as I crashed into his arms once again. His arms might have been the last place on the dwindling list of where I felt safe.

CHAPTER 2

A headache fought my desire to be awake, creating a longing for my eyes to remain closed for another hour. But curiosity was stronger. My eyelids blinked open against the blinding light. They felt tired and weary, most likely because Collin had allowed me to release tears and worries all over him, soaking his clothes in tears, finding some solace in his words spoken through his hands pressed hard against my head. He kept repeating "I'm with you" over and over again. He finally insisted on me getting some sleep, kissed my hand, and then remained standing on the threshold. I turned now, hoping to find him there, but the doorway was empty. It jolted me for a second, and then I noticed him pacing, talking on his MCU.

He always used his watch.

He never used an MCU.

As my thoughts stirred in confusion, my brain screamed in pain. I reached for my meds, but subtly. I was about to call for him and ask what was going on that was making him upset until I realized I might be able to discover more from my current position.

I felt a little guilty as I settled in to eavesdrop. He looked stressed, but in a way that was making him angry, not scared. His hands where clenching his dirty blonde hair. His brow creased, clouding his blue eyes. He rubbed his hand down to his neck. He held it there while breathing heavily. His broad shoulders jolted as if some invisible weight was crushing him.

I heard Sam's name, then Liam's. "Patterson, are they sure?"

There was some more intense dialogue and then….

"No, Patterson, you can't make me…I can't…" he said defiantly, but then trailed off. "This is what I didn't sign up for, this is what will escalate things, and this is why…"

He stopped dead in the middle of the sentence, inhaling quickly. He pushed the tension in his shoulders away as he exhaled. He turned his head to look directly at me.

"This is why I should make sure Aislyn is *actually* asleep when having important conversations." He raised one eyebrow knowingly. I felt instantly vulnerable yet proud of myself for remaining almost enough to hear some of the conversation.

"I'll be down in ten. Yes, sir. Okay, five."

I was standing to meet him as he turned off his phone, anxiety still etched on his face.

"I have to go, Aislyn. You'll see on your MCU that there's a meeting in the council room in an hour. Have a meal bar and go down. And try…to remember that we are all on the same side."

He inhaled. He might have wanted to say something more, but he turned and began to walk away. His pace was almost a jog as he got to the archway. If last night was confusing, I supposed this morning wouldn't be any different. I felt blind again, like the first month I had arrived. There were so few people to help me then.

But one of them instantly came to mind.

As I grabbed my white jacket and a meal bar, I messaged Eva to ask her where she was. She replied: "*In medical. Don't bother coming down to ask me what's going on. I have no idea. Everyone's asking. I had no clue how infuriating ignorance was."*

I almost laughed, just because I knew how annoyed she must be, but her message made the air seem thinner as my dread heightened.

As I walked to the garden outside of the door to Central, I turned around to see Lynn's Circle in the distance. The archway was now covered over with a single black cloth. I had a sinking feeling that no one would be allowed in eight Circles for the remainder of the 188th generation.

As I entered the large circle that encompassed the upper level of Central, I glanced down into the chasm three stories down, leading to the five tech stations known as the Hand. I was hoping to see Sam or Liam, but they weren't there.

No one was.

There were assistants standing around, but no one at the stations. I shook the confusion away and rationalized their need to be somewhere else, tracking down the intelligence leak that had led to the massacre. Maybe they were all in the secondary Hub, trying to decide who had tipped the Republic off to our synchronized messages. Our communication to the Territory from inside the Republic had been the way the Republic had tracked us down. It was usually fool-proof: we would send a message from a Republic phone to someone within the Republic at a certain time. It was always benign, like "hey" or "see you at the party." These messages had a totally different meaning to the personnel in Central. Those who received the messages within the Republic were unaware they meant anything, either because of their high message volume or their number of casual acquaintances.

The message time of day 43 was compromised the day Lynn, Sarah, and six others died. I wondered where they would even begin to track down the person who had betrayed us.

But if I was suspected, for talking to Alex...

My worst fear had finally materialized. If that was the case, would Patterson or Sam have a choice to defend me? Even Collin? Collin's last words to me, meant to reassure me, now frightened me terribly. Was I about to be sacrificed to save everyone else the time and effort of finding who was responsible? And even though Alex was far away, I felt instantly defensive of him. The thought of him being blamed filled me with a rage I couldn't explain, even as my wound twinged and the voice in my head said, "*He's dangerous.*"

That sentence in my head usually had Collin's voice. He was still livid, even though he conceded that shooting me was the only viable option Alex had to keep me alive. He said he could have found a better way. Collin probably could have.

Collin's proficiency in everything he did both exhilarated and made me feel an overwhelming guilt. I often wondered if he would leave it all behind for me, sacrifice his career for me, give up being a trainer for me. Or if he should.

As a trainer, he wasn't banned from loving me, but would have to retire after my year of service was over. I didn't think that was much of a sacrifice a month ago. I even resented Collin for not wanting to make it. But now that I had felt the weight of responsibility he held and how well he handled it, I felt a pang of guilt every time I longed for him.

I was jealous of his purpose, and felt like a villain for even thinking about stealing it away from him.

I had finally reached the Med wing. Eva must have misjudged my confused look as a reaction to the pain in my arm.

"I thought the painkillers should be doing their thing."

Eva was leaning against a glass window down a slight inset in the wall. I joined her, leaning against the other side.

"They are. Well, to my arm. They are causing me…"

"Let me guess– massive headache?" she smiled, as if she knew something I didn't. It wasn't until she offered me two bottles of water that I realized that I had ignored a huge component of the doctor's instructions.

"Water," I remembered suddenly, a little embarrassed.

"Yep. Your choice: headaches or frequent bathroom breaks. Choose this one," she nodded as she threw the bottles. "I told you I didn't know anything, by the way. Why are you down here?"

"Just to talk," I said, casually. But she looked suspicious, and so I added, "Seriously, I don't want intel. I just wanted to see you."

She pondered that for a moment, and said, "Oh," eventually. It pained me how hard it was for her to imagine a reality where someone just wanted to talk to her or see how she was feeling.

Even though I didn't particularly feel thirsty, I tried to drink the whole bottle within a few minutes. We observed the ultrasound of Eva's Vessel through the window.

"Did they tell her it was a girl?" I asked, losing myself in the beauty of her moment, thankful she was letting me share it.

Eva smiled, flipping her short hair, and said, "No. They told her she could be surprised– whether it was a boy or a girl. She looked confused. The whole order of things had been reversed. The labs in the Republic usually order the DNA around, to make humans into what they want them to be, and if the little cells don't comply, it's considered a failure. She was even shocked she could name the baby whatever she chose. She wanted to be surprised. So she will be."

I let her words sink in, one piece of humanity rescuing hope from the back of my mind, almost flooding my eyes with the wonder in the Vessel's face. The Vessel turned to face the glass to see Eva and me. I felt for the first time that I was imposing on a moment that wasn't mine to share, but as she smiled at Eva and waved at me, the awkwardness vanished.

"The father?" I asked.

Eva said, "Didn't believe her. He was a Citizen, though, so she thinks that he assumed that she was lying to trying to force him to marry her. That would be essential for him to become an Elite."

"That and five million dollars," I said, meaning to be witty but also thinking of Alex's bank account, just under that amount.

"Yeah, not sure which is harder to attain. Well, I can see you had a nutritious, balanced, and yet nauseating lunch," she said as she nodded at my meal bar wrapper. "I hate them. But I especially hate eating them when I'm not running for my life."

Eva had successfully diverted us away from the serious conversation to her usual playful tone. But it still came with a bit of a shadow. I wondered if she would ever be the same after losing so many of us on one night. Especially Lynn.

"Well, I needed to be quick, you know…so I could sit and watch people who have no idea what we are really up against decide my future. Are you going?"

"Yep, even if only to mourn that there will be one less person making those decisions than before."

I turned to look at her, pausing mid-step as we began to walk beside each other down the hall. She sounded tired as she continued, "You know that after this happens, whoever is in charge has to resign and someone with drastically, or even with slightly different views, will take their place?"

"They wouldn't…" I almost couldn't speak. "Eldridge–"

"Eldridge is safe," she said, smiling reassuringly, which made my feet able to move again. "Mostly because he is still elected directly. They'll most likely dethrone Matheson. You see, the Secretary of the Council is who directs us, our training, and more menial, yet really influential decisions. Eldridge was granted more power because Matheson gave it to him. I'm terrified Zander will be chosen. Others might be worse, but her… I'm sure you can tell from a few debriefs where some of them stand."

"So, if Matheson isn't there when we go down…"

"He's never going to be there again," she said, somewhat resolute and sad. "And our fate is in the hands of whoever is sitting in his seat."

She looked at me, knowing the weight of her words as she opened the door to the Council room mezzanine.

It was like most of the rooms in Central, only the theater-seating faced a half circle desk, with the Council placed on the other side. When I had entered before, it had been on the floor level below them, which I told myself should have been the more intimidating place to be. But seeing it from the mezzanine gave more scope to the grandeur and scale of the room, making their power seem absolute and unchangeable. As we slowly moved to the front, more people started to move past us. All I wanted to see was the chair at the center and Matheson sitting on it.

But I didn't. And the person who was sitting in it didn't bring me any comfort at all.

Eva said, "So it will be Zander."

Then she cursed under her breath, letting me know it didn't bring her any comfort either, just as Brie came up between us as she said, "We'll all be dead by the end of summer."

We saw the room fill with people who looked much too distracted to notice us sitting down in our strange, silent vigil. I had never appreciated Matheson, not thinking that his removal was ever a possibility. He was the one who had rallied support when I had rescued two Unnecessaries on a single mission, despite Zander's and others' objections.

Even as I stared at Margaret Zander, both Eva and Brie looked stoic, looking at each other as if they knew something I didn't. I knew the glares hidden under their cool exteriors meant something they weren't going to tell me, even if because of who they were.

The veteran Protector of three years: "the soldier."

The girl whose mother was Head Trainer, the ninth Protector to claim her family name over the centuries: "the heir."

"What don't I know?" I asked, then adding the disclaimer that was probably necessary, "I mean, something that you'll tell me."

Eva leaned forward to look around Brie as she whispered, "Do you know when I told you that Collin had a philosophy about training? That it was old-school and there were people who had abandoned it for a decade to move into a more militaristic or a different direction? Pretend there are people like that, only they think that no one has gone far enough yet."

Collin was one of the few believers in keeping with the traditions that the Protectors were based on, that blending the quadrants in training should be essential, not forbidden, and that prayer and motivation were just as important as endless physical drills, medical knowledge, and combat expertise. Avery and other trainers felt that the old style training was too weak to face the current dangers. Collin was already fighting a losing battle.

This change in leadership was like losing a war.

I shook as a chill went down my spine. Brie and Eva took on a neutral, blank gaze. I tried to mimic it. An instant later, Zander stood up and asked for silence. A hushed silence fell, by those who wanted to hear or wanted to hate what she was going to say.

"Many of you at the heart of this sacred mission know what responsibility has been placed on me. For the first time in our history, or perhaps not the first, we have had a massive intelligence breach. We have a system— and because there are media here, I cannot elaborate— for communicating with Protectors at all status points in their mission. This system was compromised, leading to their deaths. What our former Secretary told me, what others have only guessed at, is true. One of our Protectors took initiative when she realized the breach. You should know, Protectors, that you are all alive because of the 3rd Protector of your generation. Our team is proud that she was selected to be as highly ranked as the 3rd Protector to show our recognition of her talent."

It was hard to listen to the cold, calculating tone of her voice, not only because she wasn't saying Lynn's name. But she seemed to be missing the whole point of what Lynn did. Zander wasn't talking about Lynn's heart and sacrifice. And what was almost disgusting is that Zander was trying to make this into an opportunity to mention Lynn's ranking as she was chosen as a credit not to her character, but to the team that chose them, even though Eldridge chose all of us independently, without the Council's approval.

I scanned quickly to see Eldridge was on the end of the panel. She seemed to pull away from him, somehow, with her body language, as if she sneered at the powers he held and grasped at the powers she wielded. She bragged about spending endless hours discovering the cause of the leak, but never mentioned the Hand.

"Just so you know," Eva whispered, "you need to work a little on that neutral look."

I breathed out slowly, letting go of the annoyance that my attempts to remain calm and collected had failed. I then slowly pushed my shoulders down and blinked to soften my eyes.

Brie whispered, "Better."

I decided to look at someone else, glancing at Eldridge and then at Downhower, who was irritated and not hiding it. I focused on them and tried to be a little more aloof as Zander continued to talk.

"That is why we are going to focus on combat for the next few weeks, re-entering our Protectors into a vigorous week of training in combat and evasive maneuvers. During this time, they will pair up with a trainer who is most qualified for the type of combat. We are…redistributing trainers."

She was doing the one thing I hadn't expected but couldn't have dreaded more. She was taking away Collin. Even now, as he sat staring blankly ahead as many of us did, I wondered if Zander could feel my eyes burning into her.

"You will no longer be exclusively trained by one trainer. George will be teaching physical defense. Avery and Emily, physical combat. With that and weaponry covered–" I cursed in my head. I had missed who was teaching weaponry.

"We had some debate concerning knife throwing. Emily?"

Emily stood. I had never noticed her much before. She was Adrienne's trainer. Adrienne had not been the only one who had died but taken out two officers first. Her skills were unmatched by anyone. Or so we thought.

Emily stood and said so respectfully it almost seemed fake, "Mrs. Secretary, I don't rank the highest score on a knife throwing test. Collin does. I cannot evaluate more than nine Protectors at a time. I am requesting Collin train the top ten. They'll require minimal instruction due to their existing skill level."

Behind me, someone whispered, "That's what she was freaking out about last night. She was screaming she didn't want to do it."

Although I had never known her, I was instantly inclined to give her a hug the next time I saw her. Or I would have, if I hadn't thought that she was one of those people who would stare blankly or hit me if I dared to hug her. Even as Zander was obviously struggling to find a political way to object, Patterson stood up and said, "This would work well, Margaret. Your plan is great, but one alteration is normal, especially since everything has gone so smoothly. Two groups would work better. Collin agreed this morning. So, you mandate it, and we'll have the best solution."

Patterson sounded almost unnatural as he made his point. He was pandering, and I discovered that I hated it. I also hated the way Zander kept glancing at Collin as if he was expendable; or worse, a threat.

"Well, only if he's given the Protector's that rank the highest. That would be the only acceptable group."

Patterson nodded, even as I struggled to discover the meaning behind her last comment. I presumed that the "acceptable" group did not include me. She glared at Collin while continuing to speak about some new policies, as if he was a pest she wanted to squash.

Then she stared right at me.

I barely had time to hide my anger.

What Zander knew was uncertain, but she knew something.

I smiled slightly, hiding my fear. She looked away, not satisfied by my lack of reaction, but continued with a smug grin that unnerved me, as if she would get what she wanted in the end.

I could tell both Brie and Eva thought, as I had, that the worst was over. These changes were enough to satisfy their need for us to fight back, to be soldiers.

They were enough to tear us and our purpose apart.

But Zander continued, and in a much harsher tone.

"It's also my sad responsibility to dispense justice for the breach that finally proved these changes were needed. I want to make this clear: it was not a Protector. No one suspects this."

She stated this as if there was no room for opinion. Or even evidence, for that matter.

"And it is, therefore, our prerogative to see who did betray you. There were few who could have caused this disaster, and I appreciate the leadership of our Head Trainer Patterson, who quickly took action against these individuals. He made a bold choice that might make us uncomfortable, but will ensure safety. The time for our sorrow has come and gone; the fight for tomorrow has begun. Today is the first step in that fight."

I wondered briefly if the entire Hand was somewhere, maybe in the other Hub, trying to find the leak. I wondered if maybe they were being pulled off of missions, with us in additional training.

And then a horror filled my mind. A panicked question screamed. Where was the Hand?

"It is by this council's decree that the entire Hand, and their assistants, have been placed under arrest for suspicion of espionage, and will be held as enemies of the state until proven innocent."

They didn't order the Hand to track down the leak.

They were convinced that the Hand *was* the leak.

There was a scream that couldn't escape my lips, because I couldn't breathe. There was a reaction from the crowd that couldn't be more polar. There were screams of protest, fighting for the freedom of the hand. There were calls to maintain their imprisonment. I was frozen, and though I wanted to join them, I found I still couldn't scream.

"The arrests have already been made, with the help of the trainers, who all agreed *unanimously*, and additional security..."

Unanimous meant Collin. Collin had betrayed them.

Two people who were his friends, who had saved my life.

All of my body froze, telling myself to sit still so I didn't betray myself by letting an emotion escape that would endanger me, even as others bolted up out of their seats in rage. Brie held me down, placing her hand on my leg. She was squeezing it slightly in anger.

In my head, the picture forming sickened me. Sam and Liam. Joel and the others, locked in cells. Sam's words, spoken months ago, now echoed in my mind: *"We don't matter."*

Even as my composure dropped, I glared at Patterson, who was trying to be heard among the many people asking questions. I think he was speaking to me, but I didn't want to hear what he had to say.

Agreeing that we should all be militarized and trained as soldiers was one thing…but this? He knew Sam. He had sacrificed Sam for what? The chance to save political face by having someone to blame? So instead of shouting like I wanted to, or bursting in to save Sam and Liam, I turned and left the chaos behind me. I passed Eva and her mother in a heated debate a few seats over from us. But as I left, I thought with horror that I didn't know where I was going at all. I couldn't talk to Patterson. I couldn't go to combat classes. I couldn't talk to Collin. Every stone surrounding me seemed to be crumbling and everything I was beginning to cherish was fading away just as I had begun to love it.

Sam and Liam were now enemies of the state.

They would be imprisoned; they would be held in solitary.

They would be tortured.

I couldn't think past that horror as I passed Patterson, who had dodged out of the room. He moved towards me.

I stopped only briefly, the anger in my eyes enough to tell him everything I thought without a word. He began to speak as if there was more, but I couldn't hear an excuse for this. I assumed it would just make me hate him more if he could rationalize betraying his friends. So I kept walking.

He didn't call after me or order me back. I looked back in a second to see him still standing there, facing the wall but with his eyes closed. I tried to remember my words, but no matter of hope or faith could compel me to trust Patterson now.

I could no longer stand to be in the same place, breathing the same air as Zander and her lackeys, or even Patterson. I was walking back to my Circle when Brie and Eva caught up with me.

"I saw that, you know, although most people didn't. Did you seriously just ignore Patterson?" Eva asked surprised.

"You were yelling at your mom!" I said defensively.

"I always yell at my mom! I'm almost the same rank, finally," Eva said offhandedly. "They can't do this to Sam. Or Liam."

Brie said, "I bet George is furious. He hates being manipulated."

"What do you think they have against Collin?" I asked. "And what– are we not going to see our trainers anymore?"

Eva rolled her eyes as she said, "You aren't seeing me whine. Just because you have such a– how should we call it?– unique relationship with your trainer doesn't mean the rest of us are going to fake being heartbroken."

"And this is a friendly warning, if you haven't already considered it." Brie turned to gaze intensely at me.
"Be cautious about the 'unique' relationship with your trainer. It might be more dangerous than you think. Be careful. For his sake."

They both peeled off, and I kept walking back to my Circle. I had wondered if after seeing Collin's reaction to my near death had revealed some things, or many things, that I didn't want Brie to know.

And if Zander wanted to discredit me as a Protector, I realized I had one more thing I needed to protect: all the secrets I should have never known.

CHAPTER 3

I was already pummeling the punching bag when Collin's cautious voice called my name.

"Aislyn?"

"Leave me alone. I can't talk to you right now."

"Aislyn, please. Just look at me."

I stopped where I stood, still facing the bag.

"Unanimous! You didn't find anything wrong –"

"Of course, I did!" he shot back defensively.

"Then why not speak out? You are always afraid to do what you believe in! Even in the beginning, you tortured me so that you could fit in with the other trainers, when everyone told you it was the only way to save me. So, with your career on the line once again, you made the same cowardly decision to save yourself..."

I trailed off. I knew I was lying. I wanted him to burn under the heat of those lies., but the truth was powerful enough to hurt.

"Firstly," he started, his breath uneven, "I didn't have a choice. I want you to know I believe in Sam, but there is a chance someone else in the Hand leaked the intel, and we couldn't separate them out. I...there was nothing else we could do," he sighed as his hand wrung through his hair.

"But you carried it out, Collin. And you..."

I trailed off again as I remembered the phone call this morning.

"You arrested them, didn't you? That's what the phone call was about. Were you there?"

"Aislyn, it was the order—"

"But you...Collin, who did you arrest?"

I fumed as I stood there, a fire that must have been in my eyes ready to consume everything in my rage, including his words.

"Liam. I arrested Liam."

He said it, his voice cracking. He blinked rapidly, biting his lip. But he didn't say anything else. I stood, leaning my hands against the bag and looking down at the ground.

"What do you need, Aislyn?"

"I need you to leave. I love you, but I can't understand this. And I'm afraid of that. Just leave, Collin."

He took a step towards me, but I didn't look at him and backed away. He turned quickly on his heel and left, his head hanging low.

I kept punching the bag. The clouds had formed over the sun, creating a haze. I tried to tell myself, an hour later, that I didn't care where he was. But with a tinge of guilt, I realized I hadn't given him a chance to explain. The last time I was this mad at him, I should have asked him more questions, though he might not have given me any. I shouldn't be shutting him out. I should care where he was.

Where was he?

I was wondering where he would be if I wanted to talk to him. Would he hide in his room? I couldn't go there.

I grimaced as I looked at my schedule and saw "Meditation."

As I sat down against the concrete, I began trying to push the question out of my mind as I tried to pray on my own, not sure if it was going to be prayer or throwing accusations. I was annoyed that the question was still interrupting me. I felt too incompetent to concentrate. It irritated me. I pulled out my journal, flipping through it for some explanation or inspiration to make today bearable.

And it was then that I saw the word, "sacrifice."

For some reason, it stood out. I saw the margin, written by the second of the 27th Protectors.

"It doesn't sound like much of a plan. It doesn't sound like much of a strategy, but I've already bet my soul that sacrifice wins. Sacrifice won me. I should probably give it a try."

I touched the words, trying not to think about her fate. She had died saving a Vessel, but it couldn't have been too tragic if she believed she'd live forever. I envied her resolve, her commitment to a God whose plan was to die to win. No one saw it because–

I jolted. A single breath lurched out of me. I was frantically circling through all the information in my head as a new story began writing itself. I was blinded by what I had seen in the council room, assuming it was all true.

Someone did have a plan.

It wasn't Patterson. It wasn't Collin.

It wasn't even Zander.

It was Sam.

It made sense, as horrible and sickening as it made me feel.

Sam wanted Patterson to be preserved, to have a good standing with the council.

But why?

I searched my mind for every new change made today, even considering that us all being questioned might have motivated him to martyr himself.

We were to be trained in serious combat.

That was still very controversial. I was guessing based on Augustus Miller's face and the glares that came from Downhower and some other members of the council.

Patterson argued about who our trainers would be, who—

I interrupted my thought. Patterson must have chosen the replacements for the Hand. This plan was all about the Hand.

And if I was right, I knew where Collin was.

I walked slowly, even though my legs felt spring-loaded and I wanted to run. I went out to the woods surrounding the complex first, and then walked along the edge a few hundred yards.

I hit the code, and within seconds was flying down the staircase to the secondary Central hub. I jumped from under the second-floor walkway onto the main level to where Sam usually sat.

"Michael?"

He turned to face me, calling out, "She's here already."

Collin came out first, looking as if he might kiss me. Instead, he ran to me, hugged me, and then spun me once around. I realized how much I had missed him in just a few hours. Whatever act had been going on from this morning was over.

"I knew it," he said, sounding relieved. "We weren't sure if anyone was listening, so I had to trust you'd figure it out."

I turned around to see Patterson shaking his head.

"About time, too. Were you followed?" Patterson asked.

I shook my head, and said, "Not that I know of."

Michael rolled his eyes. "So what am I doing here?"

"It was Sam's plan, wasn't it?" I asked, urgent to know.

Patterson nodded, "Sam begged me to do this. Even with the added risk of you punching me and Zander going power-crazy."

Patterson sounded defeated, even as he was defending himself.

My anger was still burning as I said, "I know there's a few that are warmongers; there always have been. But if Collin's getting heat for how he's training me, and we're saving more Unnecessaries than ever, we're dying for a cause that is pure. The warmongers lost."

"That's the point," Patterson said, in a tone that frightened me. "They're losing. That makes them more defensive, and dangerous, than ever before. You didn't hear the accusations that he was too soft on you, or when Council members forgave you for bringing home two Unnecessaries. Soldiers are not trained like that."

"But we aren't soldiers!"

Michael shifted uneasily in his chair, at which point I turned to Collin and found him staring at the floor as if someone had died. In that moment, I remembered what Eva had said the day I had first realized Collin's struggle. I repeated it, almost to no one specifically.

"An idea died, didn't it? This whole shift in leadership…it's more than that. She's going to order us to kill them, isn't she?"

Patterson nodded solemnly. "Your objective in a month may not be to save children clinging to you or scared mothers hoping to escape. It will be to take out Sentries and police, even labs, where anyone– even Unnecessaries and innocent civilians– will be seen as collateral damage. They are, after all, not really alive."

"And that makes us no better than the Society!" I yelled. "This is why I hate politics."

"This isn't about politics; it's about power and targets. And they want to use their power to change your target. I played the game of politics. So did Sam and Liam. For you," Patterson said.

I was about to argue, protest, and even ask, "*Why me?*"

But instead, I took a breath, letting it out slowly as I realized the truth. "But this isn't about me, is it?"

"No," Patterson sighed, shifting as he continued, "Sam knew that you wouldn't have the handler you needed unless I could pick them. A hardened, combat-driven handler that Zander might appoint would never trust you, or be able the truth of what you've truly experienced. They would never let you pursue your target."

Patterson let the silence completely permeate the room before he continued.

"And you, Aislyn, have a unique target."

My arm burned. The arm that my target had shot. The arm he held while dancing. The arm that held the baby the first time I had looked at him intently enough to convince him not to shoot me.

"Alex."

"Who's Alex?" Michael asked, maybe feeling a little forgotten.

I wanted to protest that I couldn't trust Michael, but as Sam had bet his life on his abilities, it seemed rude to argue. Patterson nodded. I sat down in the chair facing a very confused Michael.

And I began my story. The one that everyone knew. I told him about Katerina and the child she had saved. I explained how I had saved the baby Tessa had abandoned in the woods. I told him how afraid I was in the ballroom before I was handed a baby to save. I tried to express the pain of a bullet tearing through my arm.

But then, I shared the details that no one else knew.

That a Sentry didn't fire at me while I clung to a baby.

That the same Sentry had committed open treason in a room of Elites and Citizens by helping me maintain my cover, and then handed me a baby that he had promised to kill.

That the same man had shot me to maintain his cover and stop the Sentry next to him from taking a shot that would have killed me.

That the same person had led me to safety in the aftermath.

The only thing I couldn't tell Michael was the last words Alex had spoken. I couldn't believe them enough to be uttered out loud. But I touched my forehead, where he had kissed me, keeping my secret that the feelings he had for me were escalating his rebellion.

Still, it was enough information to send Michael into a state of shock– but something was different than what I had expected. Even as he stood and covered his mouth, he wasn't drained or confused. He was full of energry. I was beginning to doubt Patterson's choice, wondering if he could handle the shock, or if he was about to run to Zander to spill everything I had just told him.

But then he said the phrase I had least expected.

"Patterson, I was right. Was I right?"

I looked at Patterson, who looked proud as he said, "It appears so," with warmth in his eyes I rarely saw

I looked back at Michael, who had turned to us again to lean on the desk. He was holding his tightened fist to his mouth as he smiled. And then he jumped up, gave a loud "Yes!" and sat back down. As he apologized, I almost lost myself in his joy as I found myself quoting Patterson out loud.

"I remember now. Patterson told Sam, 'I see you've spoken to Michael before, because that's always been his theory: that it would take someone close to them to start to hate them.'"

I could tell Michael was honored that Patterson had quoted him, as Patterson continued. "There were no fans of Michael's theory. He buried it for any chance at a career. While paying his dues– extra years of training– he perfected his tech skills past anything any other trainer has ever achieved, making him a perfect candidate for a Handler. Sam knew that if I pandered to Zander a bit, I would hold the roster to choose new Handlers. I did. Now, we need a plan. Quickly."

Michael breathed in deeply, "First thing. Is he alive?"

"I don't know," I said, somewhat weakly.

"We need to make sure that no one saw him helping her escape, after…" Patterson trailed off, but Collin interrupted.

"After he shot her, drugged her, and left her to hide alone in a warehouse for hours?"

Collin's tone was enough to tell me that his opinion about Alex was still shaky, but his eyes were livid as images of Alex started appearing on the screen.

I thought Michael missed the tension, furiously typing, until he said sarcastically, "I can tell someone is a fan."

We were all silent as Michael continued to work for the next minute. He made a "shh" noise even though none of us were talking. Patterson and Collin simply ignored that, and stared at him more intently. Collin closed his eyes, waiting or perhaps praying.

"I'm in."

"It's only been two minutes!" I said in surprise.

"That's why Sam picked him. Okay, you want to go to…"

"Way ahead of you," Michael said as five screens popped up with different images and information on other Sentries.

"What's that?" Patterson asked.

"We only have one minute. I have to look up every Sentry, just in case they discover my hack. Otherwise, they'd be suspicious as to why I just looked up Alex. I'm covering my tracks."

All of the other stations' screens started to open other profiles. I tried not to look at Hydech's picture as I passed it. We went to the station with Alex's picture and began scrolling.

"Alive. Looks like he was tested after he got back."

"Tested for what?"

"Drugs," Michael said. "Maybe they thought he was under the influence and that's why he missed. Hydech put in his report that he could have taken you out from where they were standing."

Patterson continued, "Hydech's killed more Protectors in three years than all other Sentries combined."

"Well, Alex, on the other hand, seems intent on avoiding it, and on avoiding being an Elite. He does rack up local fines for them, which is why they love him as a Sentry. If Aislyn is right, he has to spend a lot of money to avoid hitting the five million mark when he'd be able to buy his commission to become an Elite."

"How does he spend his money?" I asked.

"Well, looks like he escapes his life through drug-induced comas," Collin said cruelly. "Probably why they tested him."

While I wanted to defend Alex, the numbers on the screen were concrete: a long list of psychotropic drugs and painkillers.

"He never seems disoriented," I said, wondering to myself more than shielding Alex's actions.

"Of course not," Michael said. Then he began to type again, without explaining. We all stared at him, then there was a glitch on all the screens except his went to static as he explained.

"He doesn't take them all."

"What?" Collin asked.

Michael continued to explain, "Well, for one, there's only trace amounts in the test they took. Even if he took a recharge, which he does order, there'd be more of a trace. And he does have to spend his money on something. Once he has all the money to buy his commission, he would retire as a Sentry to a higher posting or a political position."

"He said the only way he could save anyone is if he's close enough to kill them," I said, echoing Alex's words.

"Sad, but true," Michael said, continuing to type.

"How does he get away with that at all?" Collin asked. "He is a Sentry, for heaven's sake. Don't they have any rules?"

"They'd allow it if he's telling the truth about his sister."

That was true. The Republic would accept that he would be upset over her death, but would expect him to hide his emotion with pleasure and happiness, like any good Citizen would. They would applaud him for hiding his pain.

I looked at Patterson, feeling nervous seeing the uncertainty on his face. "You can't find any record of the sister, can you?"

"Well, I can, but no record that a Protector ever knew her. She died, the poor infant died, and they were ejected from the Party publicly. The dates are all in the same month. But it doesn't match up with his story that both the sister and the baby died with a Protector. It sounds like that's why he's trying to help you."

"Regret is a powerful motive," Collin said, almost eerily.

"Yes, but I'm not sure it's enough," Michael was looking at me oddly. "But then again, there's always more than one secret, and he could be hiding the truth under the secret he chose to share."

There was a silence. Michael's glanced at me warningly. I could only hope he didn't think I was hiding something. He finally turned to Collin and asked, "What do you need from me?"

"You need to learn the new codes," Collin answered as he was typing. "She uses different phrases at the scheduled check-in time. We always knew if she saw Alex, was with Alex, if she was with Alex and compromised, or if she knew she was in danger."

"But that won't work anymore," Michael argued. "Even as a handler, I can't control what Zander or her people will see. She can't send completely different messages without suspicion of the rest of the team. Joel may not have asked questions before, or–"

"Sam asked Joel to trust him," Collin deflated, and all of a sudden very upset. Then he hit the back of the computer table with his hand while cursing.

"What if I send two messages?" I suggested. "And the second one was the message about Alex. And if someone was watching…"

"It's too risky," Michael answered.

Collin shook his head and took a step towards Michael. "We need to know she's safe."

"We can't have more, Collin, or we open it up to suspicion," Michael argued.

"We need it!" Collin's voice was stern.

Michael sighed, sounding more confrontational. "We can't–"

I started to reach out for Collin when he finally erupted.

"We need to know you're safe! I care about you too much to not know! I'd rather die than not know."

Michael looked from me to Collin, and then back to me, just as the hand I had reached out had touched Collin's forearm. His muscles shifted as his fist relaxed.

Patterson coughed awkwardly, and said, "Collin?"

"Sorry, Michael. I…"

Michael had one eyebrow up, and a slightly skewed smile as he said, "No, I get it. There's always more than one secret. Right?"

Collin looked at Michael as I slowly removed my hand from his forearm, turning to face the wall across from me as Collin glared at Michael. He closed his eyes for a second, breathing out his anger before meeting my hand and holding it briefly.

"Yeah, I guess so," he answered, squeezing my hand before turning to me. "I just want to know what you're going through. It's one of the ways I can still be with you, when I'm not with you."

Patterson said, "Michael, I'm also going to need more intel on Alex, his daily schedule, maybe his itinerary for the each day to see if he deviates from– Michael, are you listening?"

"Ummm…yeah, sorry. I need a few seconds to process…this." He quickly pointed to the space between Collin and me. "Is this–?"

"None of your business." Patterson looked at Michael sternly. Then he looked at Collin just as sternly. "Although we'll talk about how we deal with this," Patterson made the same waving motions between us, "a little better in the future. Collin?"

"Yes, sir. Sorry, sir."

Patterson stared at Collin, the pressure mounting. Maybe it was because I was desperate to escape the tension that I thought of the solution to the problem.

"I've got it! Michael, what if I used a normal code to check in, but I'll misspelled it? I'll spell one word incorrectly, or add an extra coma…something like that?"

"That's brilliant!" Michael said. It was enough to enable him to dive completely into his work again. Patterson nodded in affirmation, and then nodded up the stairs. "Aislyn, come up with me. We should all leave at different times to avoid suspicion."

As I walked up the stairs with Patterson, I asked the question of the person I knew would give me the most honest answer.

Collin would try to spare me pain, and not give me the truth.

"Sam. Is he okay? I mean…"

"I know what you mean. And the answer is yes and no. He will endure pain and torture. They already have been. Having to see it has –" He trailed off, not able to continue.

"Did Sam tell all the techs that you would arrest them?"

"Aislyn, they all knew they might be under suspicion anyway. Sam told them that there was a way they could help you. He didn't have to tell them the details; it was enough for them to agree to his plan. You are the 27th, after all. They'd do anything for you."

I stopped walking. Their pure devotion to me made me feel appreciative and sick at the same time, not only because I hardly knew them and could hardly believe how committed they were, but because I was desperately afraid of letting them down.

Patterson continued. "Aislyn, you don't know what is at risk. I think you are catching on. If we are not careful, we risk making the same mistakes that have been made through ages of human history. We dishonor their sacrifice by ignoring the pain they've endured. Liam knew that, too. He said at this point, we need a miracle. And however you spin it, even if none of us know how this will end, you have to admit: Alex is a miracle."

As we reached the top of the stairs, I heard Michael yell from the bottom of the cylinder, "That's not the point. You weren't supposed to fall in love with her! We need you here!"

I looked down briefly, but Patterson pushed me up the last stair. He stared at me warningly, and told me. "Keep going. Just look like you were out for a run. Like nothing happened."

"Like hoping that the man who shot me is alive and safe?"

He smirked. "Yes, try to avoid looking like that."

I left before he asked anything else, worried I'd hear more of Collin and Michael's conversation.

And I ran, thinking of things I probably shouldn't.

I shouldn't have kept what Alex had said about me a secret.

I shouldn't have put Alex in a position where he had to shoot me in the first place.

I shouldn't have gone back with Amanda into the Republic.

I shouldn't have…

"Stop!" I spoke to myself, out loud. It was only when I stopped that I noticed Zander was there, between two Circles.

She glowered at me in a way that made my breath leave me.

"Oh, please, my dear," she said coldly, "continue. You were at a good pace for recovering from a wound. Where is your trainer? They tell me he usually runs with you. To encourage you, or does he just keep you from talking to yourself?"

Without wanting to debate why encouraging someone was better than demeaning them, I told her the truth; well, one truth.

"I like to run alone as I'm going through the past mission in my head. Looking for mistakes I made."

"So, you said 'stop' because…?"

I was honest, just to gauge her reaction.

"I was regretting something. I wanted to stop regretting it."

"Oh, my dear," she said, with fake compassion that sent a shiver up my spine, "Why ever would you do that?"

An eerie silence followed her voice before I could speak.

"After looking at your files, Aislyn, some regret is advisable, if not required. You should've gone straight out into the woods with Amanda. You should've killed Brie's attacker. You should've decided to be stronger. You shouldn't have fought Tessa. One mistake after another. But the first mistake with your name on it wasn't your fault. It was Eldridge's."

"I don't understand," I said, my voice betraying me by shaking.

"You should have never walked into your Circle. I'm surprised you have even come back to it. You should ponder all the reasons why you've barely made it back, as much as possible."

I paused, wondering if she meant what I thought she implied, but with one look in her eyes, I knew she would rather be looking at the air behind me than having me standing there alive.

I took a breath, and spoke as confidently as I could manage.

"I suppose then that the five Unnecessaries I saved would– what? Regret that they allowed themselves to be saved by me?"

"Oh, Aislyn, don't you see where this is headed?" she said as she turned around, looking at me with faux sympathy for being so naive. "Saving them doesn't matter anymore."

She left me there, the fear running through me shattering my desire to respond. Not only because she implied I should've died, but because she implied an Unnecessary would.

And she couldn't care less.

I ran, away from the regret and her, to hit my pillow and to find solace in solitude. I opened up my journal for just one piece of wisdom that would sound like Eldridge's.

I opened to the wrong page.

It was the same phrase that Patterson said was in his journal. There was a crudely written "Count the Cost" in large quotations.

"If you set out to make a change, and you don't count the cost, the reality of the challenge will drown your desire for change."

Underneath that: a blank space. But as I picked up my pen to write the words in my mind, I felt emboldened by the challenge I had just issued to myself.

"When someone pays the cost, don't forget it."

"Keep breathing." I said it out loud a few times until I heard his voice jokingly interrupt.

"Such a simple goal. It's so hard sometimes; breathing."

I smiled, seeing Collin in the threshold.

"You okay?"

I nodded. I hardly wanted to tell him what Zander had said. I didn't want to complain relentlessly about people who didn't like me. I didn't want to make him worry anymore. Besides, I instantly was more curious about his conversation with Michael.

"Codes?"

"Yeah, um…duress during a mission is 'Hey you' but with a period afterward. The other two, you can misspell it randomly. So you'd message 'Got anything going on tonight?' with 'tonight' misspelled if you are with him, and 'anything' misspelled if you think that he's compromised and you're in danger."

"And no one will suspect a thing," I said, tired with anxiety.

He must have sensed my urgency or my search for a question, because he said, "Don't worry about anything now, okay? We found out the Circles aren't being bugged. And there's tomorrow, however grim it might be; it will, at least, hold more answers."

I nodded, but without thinking, I asked one question.

"Michael and you— You were friends, weren't you?"

Collin sighed. "Yes. We still are. Despite his shock that you and I… He just knows how dangerous this is; how dangerous…"

He trailed off, but I finished the sentence. "We are."

He reached out for me, and I found myself not reaching for him at first, but stepping closer. Slowly I stepped until his arms, circling around me, pulling my head into his chest as he cradled it. After a little while, he let go. I moved back to my bed as he slid down the doorway, laying down on the threshold.

"What did Patterson say?" he asked, breaking away slightly.

"Storm is coming, danger, blah, blah, blah," I said somewhat sarcastically as I backed up again.

"And that Alex is a miracle."

"That's one way to look at it," Collin asked as he slid down the doorway to the floor. "Do you think he's a miracle?"

I stared at the glass separating me from the rest of my Circle. The slight gleam of the reflection of the lights made it impossible to see my reflection. It felt impossible to try to grasp who Alex was, as if I was only viewing a tiny bit of who he was.

"Yes, I do. I always have," I said, resolved.

Tiredness pulled me down to my pillow, leaving me unable to react to the last thing Collin spoke before sleep entrapped me.

"It worries me, Aislyn, more than you know. Because I do trust him. But it just feels like a miracle should be more… safe. He's not, though, is he?"

He took a shuddered breath, and after a few moments, he whispered, "This is such a dangerous miracle."

CHAPTER 4

The blur of emotional and physical pain in the next few days was more excruciating and nauseating than I had expected.

Wake. Run. Train with George. Rejected to see baby Hope. Spar with Brie. Climb the wall four times. Peel off blisters.

Train with Emily. Spar with Emily. See Emily tower over me as I lay defeated on the mat.

See Collin in the hallway. Ignore the feelings I could never express when his fingers would brush over mine. Bury the impulse that wanted to run away with him. Find a reason to keep going.

I wished it was a bad dream. But in the instant I woke, the pain in the blisters, the bruises left by Emily, and the desire to see Collin all stung like only reality could.

The alarm on my MCU was beeping. I reached over to pick it up as I read, "*Wake up call. Training required 30 minutes before morning announcements and breakfast.*"

I looked up, but was unable to move. All messages came like this for the past few days. "*Running required 1 hour before noon.*" "*Further training required in understanding the moral depravity of Sub-Terras.*" "*Training required in medical room.*" But then I remembered today was knife throwing testing. I jolted awake, the previous day's events flooding my thoughts and leaving behind a rush of adrenaline. As if to emphasize that, I heard a knock on the frame of the door.

"Hey," Collin stood, seemingly bold, although before it was just normal to see him standing there. "We're going for a run."

"Together?" I said, perhaps a little too shocked.

"Yeah, well, I know that's 'scandalous' and all, but it hasn't been 'required' that you run alone yet. We might as well spend some time together before she bans it."

Realizing I was wearing my running clothes from the previous night, I got up. I regretted not taking the time to shower, but scolded myself for being so needy or girly. Within the first mile, there was silence until he finally answered the question he must have known I had tried to ask. My throat was dry, so it came out as a cracked, incomplete, "Why this morning?"

"I need to tell you…Palmer made another speech last night. More like his first, that the Society Party needed to rally behind him, as their leader, and end the threat of…protecting life, I supposed."

"I guess The Society's attempt to vilify us has expanded?"

He nodded, "You were all labeled evil, worthless, and that it was worth the effort to exterminate you to ensure The Society's success."

I paused for a second. "Isn't that already assumed?"

He was running in place at this point, looking as tired as I felt.

"Yes, it's weird. The media already covered the initial attacks of the Protectors on their broadcasts when it happened, although they aren't sharing numbers, especially because some Terras died as collateral damage. It was just Terra's and Sub-Terra's, but if it were a Citizen or Elite, they would have had to apologize. Palmer usually wouldn't go through that much trouble to defend himself."

I heard a message on my MCU. *"Protectors 23-27 are required to attend a simulation in the tech room at 9:30."*

"But Zander doesn't see it that way, I'm guessing? Just more fuel for her fire."

He scoffed. "What she thinks is fuel is water. If Palmer is trying to convince the Republic that we're all evil, it implies that people aren't assuming we're evil anymore. I don't know why she can't see that!"

"Well, that would *require* her to think," I said sarcastically, which made Collin smile despite the seriousness of the situation.

I had finally caught on to what had Collin so unnerved. It was scary, because no one would talk about Zander directly. Just whispers, like the shadow of a problem no one would recognize.

As we began to run into the woods, to a place we could finally talk freely, Collin turned, to change the subject almost too quickly.

"I know what…what you're going through. Well, no, I don't, because I've barely talked to you in the past few days. I just wanted to make sure you were holding up okay."

"You mean since I've been training to kill people?"

He nodded, looking a little more concerned. My tone was blank, probably because I was repressing what was happening. "I'm fine…just, tired. I'm tired of being yelled at and compared to others, as I try to scale walls and try to win at least one sparring session with Emily. I hate the way we talk about missions now. But I…." I trailed off, wondering how to put it into words.

He must have thought I was going to have a breakdown when I stopped running. He reached out, holding my arms.

"Collin, I appreciate that you are worried about me. I value your love far more than you may know. And I know how emotional I was the first month here. But I'm not who I was three months ago. That even scares me, sometimes. But I don't need anyone to convince me to do this anymore. I've seen enough. I've felt the pain of their struggle and their desperation. I will never need another reason to go back out there and protect them."

He placed his hand on my head, his thumb grazing my cheek.

"I had hoped that. I kept holding my breath for you, worrying about you, but I realized I just needed to trust you. Trust that you weren't becoming anyone else but you."

He was staring into my eyes, as if to make sure the hope was really there. He reached out his other hand, his palm resting just along my jawline.

I had stopped running, but my pulse was still racing as if I was sprinting.

"I'll always be holding my breath for you."

He took my chin and leaned it up until my lips met his. Gently, softly, and yet with an undefined, powerful magnetism; pushing us together despite everything pulling us apart.

As he backed away, a part of me protested, because I knew the truth. We had stolen a moment, but we probably could not steal another one.

"This may be one of the last times I see you before you leave." He held my head with both hands, his fingers grazing my hair.

"I know. I'll be fine," I said. But I couldn't lie, even after I just had said it. "I don't know if I will be okay…when Zander gives the order to kill him."

He didn't have to ask what I meant. Or who I meant.

His face contorted in pain a bit. Enough to make me worry. "Collin? What is it?"

"Let's keep running, or you'll be late."

He was avoiding telling me, but I ran with him. We were a minute later when he finally reacted to my many glances.

"The vote is in three days, Aislyn, before you all go back out. Then they will tell you if your goal is to save or to destroy."

I kept running, from something I couldn't escape. He sensed my tension as he continued. "Patterson wants to see us all tonight, in our little spot. I'm sorry Zander rigged knife throwing training to keep us two apart by giving me the top ten."

I bit my lip, smiling, and laughing at his confusion.

"You forget, Collin, that while you know me, you don't know everything about me," I said. "And neither does Zander."

"I– wait, are you saying…What?" He had started three times, only to stop. I rolled my eyes and started to run away at his now-frozen figure. I winked at him and kept running.

My secret helped me endure a lot that day. It helped me remain silent through breakfast, watching a bored Cassidy move her eggs around her plate and Lydia try to stay awake.

My secret helped me keep my composure while watching Palmer's fabricated, hateful broadcast.

My secret helped me endure each of Zander's comments.

My secret made me smile when I saw the message that I was "*required to attend the test for placement in knife throwing.*"

And my secret gave me confidence right up until the instant it was revealed: when all three knives hit the center circle and I turned around to give Zander an unforgiving, smug smile.

"Try again!" Zander yelled with a strained voice. "That was just beginner's luck."

Patterson removed his grin to look more calculating as he said, "Ma'am, I'm afraid that's not possible. Everyone is scored on a scale of 3. It can't be unfair or–"

"It's obviously just beginner's luck!" she almost screamed.

They were still arguing while I walked up to George, who was still looking at me with one eyebrow up. I grabbed three more knives from him as he bowed jokingly, smirking at me.

"They're all yours, 27. I have to admit, I didn't know."

"No one knew," I whispered. That made him smile again.

Patterson was still talking as I stepped back up to the line. I nodded to Michael, who winked as he removed the last of the knives from the target I had previously mastered.

"Patterson, this is non-negotiable," Zander all but yelled. "She cannot…we'll just change the parameters."

"She is a hunter's daughter. This talent is unexpected, but…"

She interrupted him, her eyes burning with anger as she turned to me, "I want Aislyn to try again!"

I spared a moment to see Collin suppress a grin.

"It's no problem, sir. My pleasure," I interrupted.

As I turned, I began to throw the first, my shoulder lurching forward. I had just turned to face the target completely when the first one hit almost dead center. The thud gave me the confidence to hit the next two close to the first, all in the red-center circle. Within a few seconds, I was turning around to face her again, as she stared at the knives. Those knives had torn apart her plan to separate Collin and me, make me feel inferior, and create a prejudice towards me. I felt a pride and a pain, missing my father's voice correcting me. I would have done anything to hear him, even if he was criticizing my technique.

But no one else had any critique to offer. Patterson called out nonchalantly, "I need rank, please. George? Avery?"

"Based on her second attempt, she would rank right after Brie. Based on the first attempt, she would have been ranked before Brie." George looked at me with a bit more respect, which I never expected from him.

Avery was behind him, shaking his head as he responded almost angrily, "That would put her in 2nd, and in Collin's group."

Zander sighed. "Well, I hope you can hit the real target, then."

Maybe it was because I was offended that she didn't acknowledge my ability at all. Perhaps it was because I saw the vicious look in her eyes when Brie and Eva had gotten their scores, or maybe it was the fear growing in Patterson's demeanor. Now I heard my father's voice, echoing a warning I was about to ignore.

Never poke a bear.

"And what target would that be?" I asked.

Collin shot me a look of shock, almost warning me to apologize while shaking his head slightly.

"I am sorry, young lady, if you do not understand your target."

"My target was clear the day I started. It was saving them."

She looked bitterly at me, and then said, "The Republic is a gigantic puzzle being put together by monsters who throw away pieces that they decide don't fit. They throw away hundreds at a time, and you think that saving a few will redeem you? Or them?"

Even though she was far away, her glare and her anger made her feel uncomfortably close.

"It's time we take out the monster before it puts another piece of the puzzle in or throws another piece out. It's all that matters."

Collin remained frozen, but there was a twitch in his hand.

Patterson's look of warning to me disappeared, now only focused on Zander and her words. That was my intent, so I quickly succeeded the best way I knew how.

I faked a smile. "Thank you! That makes complete sense."

I could tell she was instantly thrown off by my compliance, which is what I intended. She turned to leave.

Collin went up to Avery, grabbed the list, scanned it, and then held it out to return it. Avery didn't take it back right away, but stood with his arms crossed. There was hidden tension between them I couldn't quite make out, but it seemed to be growing stronger by the minute. Finally, Avery took the clipboard. He leaned in and whispered something that completely unnerved Collin. Collin shut his eyes for a second as Avery walked past him, bumping into Collin's shoulder. By the time I had reached Collin, he had opened his eyes, smiling, and hiding any anxiety he felt.

We walked back to our Circle, away from Zander, Avery, and Patterson. Collin spoke into his watch, "The trainer of the 27th Protector requires entry into the 27th Circle for…" He paused, closing his eyes before saying their names. "Brie, Eva, Cassidy, Tessa, Abigail, Maria, Alice, Megan, Erica, and Lydia."

He opened his eyes, and continued, "You weren't kidding! What other secrets do you have up your sleeve? Any mutations I should know about? Can you pick locks? You can, can't you?"

"Yeah, well, our locks that aren't electronic. A lot of good that skill will get me in the Republic."

I decided to ask while it was fresh in my mind.

"What was Avery's problem?"

"'Sir Avery' doesn't have problems," Collin responded. "Just opinions on everything. It's just him being him. Ignore it."

I decided not to push it, even as he laughed again. "You should have seen the fist forming behind Zander's back. It took everything in me not to burst, Aislyn. She didn't see that coming."

"Yeah, well, that was kind of the idea, wasn't it?" I pulled a knife from the pile in my Circle and hit against the board. "Bet she didn't see the other thing I said coming either."

"What were you thinking, by the way?" he asked, almost scolding me. "You can't talk to her like that. You didn't even prove a point."

I sighed, looking at the target board and the knife I had just thrown at the center.

"I wasn't aiming to prove a point." I threw the last knife, saw it hit center, and then turned. I thought he was going to ask another question when a familiar voice echoed through my circle.

"Oi, does she still have to let us in? Like, every day?"

I turned to see nine girls standing in the archway of my Circle.

He turned to me. "You technically have to give them permission…for every day. You might want to–" He shrugged.

"Got it," I said quickly to him before yelling out, "I, the 27th Protector, allow those who have ranked in the standings of top ten to enter the 27th Circle today, and during any scheduled times for knife throwing. Just…announce yourself. So I know."

"Eva, 26th Protector, knower of all secrets, entering Circle! That was fun." Eva said in a sarcastic tone as she took a step.

"But not today," Collin said, almost directly after she said it.

Eva turned on her heel, headed back out, and then turned to face Collin as she said, "And that killed the moment."

"We're going on a field trip first," Collin started confidently. "We'll be in here a little bit over the next few days, which is why I have the board set up, but I have something a little more interesting planned."

"Of course you do," Abigail said, unimpressed and annoyed.

It didn't affect Collin at all, though. He smiled and said, "Woods. Out by the wall."

"What, we're going to throw at the taller wall?" Alice asked.

"You'll see. Abby, less attitude please."

Collin ran with us out to the other side of the courtyard, by the wall. But it wasn't the wall that was drawing our interest. Within a few seconds, I could tell what we were going to do.

"Are those…the hologram projectors? Hanging from the trees?" Erica asked, seemingly disapproving and yet impressed.

"Yes," he answered. "And there are panels scattered to catch them. There are going to be some targets that pop out, and then there are going to be a few moving targets."

"Brilliant!" Eva said, easing his tension with genuine enthusiasm.

"Thank you," he said. "Look, the thing is, you all are great already. But I feel that facing a plastic wall with outlines won't help you as you challenge yourself."

Abby stepped out and said, "So you created your odd backyard version of a game that we usually play inside because…?"

"It is more realistic, surrounding yourself in the atmosphere you would be in so you can imagine an intense situation. This is—"

She cut him off to say, "Weird. This is weird, even for you."

Brie stepped out a bit as she said, "Well, maybe if you weren't so busy worrying about avoiding being weird, you wouldn't be in danger of having accidentally missed what was most important."

Brie glared at Tessa, who glanced from Brie to Abigail. Megan gave me a look that conveyed the growing tension between them.

Then, unexpectedly, Tessa was the first to grab a knife.

"Run it." She gave Collin a single nod. He nodded, happy to ignore whatever pressure was mounting.

The holograms were sporadic, but they appeared: not glowing, but more like shadows. It wasn't lit up like in the hologram room.

They were different colors.

"Now, the monitor will let me know when the knife hits the hologram. And I've also made it simpler just for today by having the images in only blue and green. Green for Sentries and Police, blue for innocents. And remember to keep your shoulders down a bit, okay Tessa? You tend to tense up before you throw."

She rolled her eyes, then lowered her shoulders. He counted down until the lights started appearing. They would flash on in a second, and then off in just three seconds. She was pretty quick, and despite the fact that there was still a part of me that hated her, I had to admit to being immensely impressed at her speed. She finished with an almost perfect score.

"Okay, that was a great job. I'm sure you noticed this simulates the barriers in a space with wind resistance as well as branches and leaves. I also wanted you to notice that Tessa turns with the target she's facing. It's not always vital, but it is always more accurate. Watch where your toe is pointing, too."

Tessa finished up, then Brie, and eventually everyone. Collin continued to give us personalized attention, sharing any technique problems and touting their strengths.

"Okay, good start! Now, I want you to think of a Republic phrase while you throw it, and repeat it to me."

"What?" Abby said, as if he had just let out a curse word.

"Oh, just do it." Eva took the knife, threw it, and a few Republic slang and curse words. "We've been in the field for weeks. Quadrants really don't matter at this point."

"That's one way to think about it," said a deep voice.

I turned to see a very disapproving Avery, and he stared at me directly, as if letting me know I was the one he hated the most.

"Don't you have something to do, Avery?" I asked.

"No, not really, since my Protector should be out in the field, with the rest of you right now. And by you, I don't mean *you*."

He was staring at me directly when he said that, and I was praying Collin would remain where he was as I saw his leg jolt.

Avery continued, "I'm not thrilled we have to do this, but I suppose it matters. We're finally getting our priorities straight."

"So you're here to what?" Brie asked confrontationally. "Talk priorities? That's ironic coming from the man who trained her!"

Brie nodded to Tessa. But Tessa focused on the holograms as she threw her first knife, seemingly ignoring the debate behind her.

"Like you've never made a mistake, Brie? None at all your first year?" Avery faked a compassion that made him sound cruel. "Tell me again, how your third Vessel died? For no reason?"

"Tell me again," Brie growled, "how you fell from a respectable position to become Zander's dirty, little spy."

He was about to interrupt, even as Megan looked at me, scared, and Eva jumped at the sounding of the loud buzz. Everyone froze.

"What does the buzz mean?" Alice asked.

"It means she accidentally threw a knife through a blue beam," Eva said, going forward to retrieve the knives.

"Yeah, because that would be the end of the world," Avery said sarcastically. Brie had turned to look at me, containing her anger as he continued. "You're all way too obsessed with one blue. You want to save the blue? You need to kill the green, and get over it when you make a mistake," Avery said and he began to walk away. He looked back at Tessa, who still wasn't looking at him.

Avery turned to leave, glaring at Collin, who was ignoring him. Eva stopped and pulled out the knife that had gone through the blue beam out of the trunk of the tree. She turned to lean against the trunk and stared at the blade, holding it as if she held every dangerous idea causing this revolution in her hand. As Avery's last words echoed in my mind, I wondered at Tessa's strained expression as she stared at the knife Eva held with a regret I never thought she was capable of feeling. She turned away from Brie.

"Collin, I'm done. I'm sorry."

He nodded, walking in front of her to look in her eyes.

"Go for a run, Tessa. 25 minutes, and I don't want you anywhere near Avery, do you understand?"

"Or her, I'm guessing?" Tessa glared at Brie.

"I was attacking him, not you!" Brie lashed out defensively.

"Yeah?! Well, clarify that the next time you bring up the biggest, soul-crushing mistake of my life. Why would I take that personally?" She didn't yell, but the intensity of it shook me; her anger only stopped the moment one tear fell from her eyes.

She got her MCU and started walking past us. She saw me. I couldn't work up any anger towards her, for the first time in my life. Instead, she just whispered quietly, almost seeming surprised by my silence.

"I'll never be the perfect one now. I never had a chance."

Then her face turned unresponsive as she ran away from us. It shook me that she still might be missing the point of all this, but I couldn't critique her regret. Collin yelled back, "Make it 45 minutes, Tess!" before glaring knowingly at Brie.

"You're not helping," he said to her, scolding slightly.

She rolled her eyes and said, "I'll apologize later."

Collin was still staring at Brie as he yelled out, "You're up next, Eva."

Eva was still in the shadow of the strobing blue hologram, looking strange in the light, like the child she sometimes appeared to be: scared and vulnerable.

Somehow, she repressed it instantly, and then for long enough to hit every target and finish up the morning with a run an hour after as we had completed filleting the targets stuck on the trees.

As we were stretching, I finally went over to talk to Brie.

"Ugh, you're going to ask what's going on with Tessa and Avery, aren't you?"

"Maybe," I started. "But I'll guess first. I'm thinking that he's mad his golden child is on probation for what he thinks isn't a big deal, and her conscience has finally caught up with her, and the both of them don't know how to handle it."

"Excellent deduction, 27th, and while it hurt her to have it thrown in her face, I'm afraid that her regret is the only thing that will paralyze her, making sure this situation doesn't happen again this year. With her probation, at least I won't have to put up with her next year."

There was a pause, and while I processed what she had said, something came spilling out. "What do you mean, next year?"

"Well, there's no way she can go back out next year now that–"

"No, Brie, I mean…why would *you* have to put up with her next year?" I asked. "I thought you were done after this year!"

Her gaze met mine, deflated as she answered back.

"What else would I do, Aislyn?"

The silence permeated the air as I tried to confront her choice.

"Brie, you know…there are…I know…"

"You're stuttering," she said, matter-of-factly. "You, of all people, know what condition I'm in. I have nothing else to live for. Nothing. I will never get married, I will never have a child, and I will never know love. But you are fighting me right now because you are so irritatingly innocent. You want to say something that'll change it, but the facts are running so fast you can't fight them. You're stuttering. Don't stutter. Just accept the facts."

She thought she had won, looking back down at her MCU. Out of anger in her assumption, I fought back.

"Okay. I won't stutter." I continued with a confidence that I could tell scared her a bit. "You have saved countless lives, you have looked into the eyes of mothers and gave them their lives. You can't do this; this is a life mission, not a way for you to commit suicide."

I got as close to her as I felt comfortable being, not entirely believing that I had to confront her about this.

What she had implied was heart-breaking, and couldn't stand.

"Brie, you know the purpose and the beauty of life, too much for you to throw it away. You can't…you can't throw away yours."

"And you know too much about what we do to call this throwing my life away. This is the purest, most breathtaking mission in the world. I have nothing better to do with my life than this, until I die."

She wasn't looking at me anymore. I could already tell by her tone, her body language, and by her phrases that she had fought this argument before, and she was confident enough to fight my attempt to persuade her.

"What about…can't you adopt the one girl? Hope?"

"Hope got placed already. There was someone available who was able to nurse her, so she was out within a week." Her voice was unsteady in the end. She was very protective of Hope, and considering Hope's mother was a traitor who would have rather had the chance to kill Brie than save herself, I couldn't really blame her.

"What about…" I was straining to remember the conversational details of when we had brought André and Hope home. I screamed at my mind, feeling as if I was jabbing it like a punching bag until I had what I wanted to remember.

"Caleigh? Right? And she'll be three soon, able to leave the shelter to get placed."

She looked torn, but then shook her head, shaking the idea away as she said, "And Avery just referred to her mother as my mistake."

I strained to remember our lessons in the med room and Brie's countless stories. Caleigh had been born to a dying mother, only being able to hold her baby for moments before leaving this earth behind. Brie had blamed herself, but in the end, almost everyone else said the mother had felt too betrayed to find a reason to live.

After the long silence of me recollecting, I heard her say, "I don't need you to fix this for me, and I don't need your input. Just because you're the 27th Protector doesn't mean you know how to fix every problem. You're a writer; that doesn't mean you get to write a happy ending to every story. This is the only good ending; I make this pain worth something."

I was a little offended, enough to stop talking for a second– that was all she needed. Her glares from there and her rigidity ensured that the silence continued, until Eva walked in between us.

"Hello there. Is Brie playing nice, or is she continuing her streak today of deciding to rile her friends and push them away so no one will know how tired, hurt, or vulnerable she is?"

Brie scowled at Eva. I still was shaking off the feelings Brie's words had exposed in me, but not quickly enough. Eva noticed.

"Apparently, we're continuing the streak. Well, Brie, what's the score, three for three?"

"If you don't want to be four, you'll shut up. And how do you—"

"My mom. Your little rebellion has all but broken her heart. We're equally disappointing her now."

"Ugh," Brie sighed, and then walked away as Eva said, "Nice chat!" and dropped to do sit-ups.

Even as Brie left, I felt there was more I should have said or done differently. The need to convince Brie to retire overwhelmed me until I realized there was nothing I could do—not because I didn't care, but I quickly realized, as Collin said we were all going on a run together, Brie's decision was months away.

Since we were all running together, I would think it would be different. That we'd talk. That we'd look at each other. But while we would sometimes glance around to see if someone tripped, or as a sign of encouragement, we mostly all found a strange solace in the fact that we were all alive, breathing the same air, and running. But we were all running for different reasons.

I didn't know why Eva was always running away from her mom.

I didn't know why Brie was running toward danger.

I didn't know why Megan kept looking behind her as she ran.

I knew I was running away from Zander, but didn't know if I was running toward Collin, or towards the Republic.

I was running to save the pieces of the puzzle– the few people– about to be dropped from the table.

That mission wasn't good enough for Zander, apparently, and it shook me to my core that in the process of saving these people, they had become equally expendable and unnecessary to us.

CHAPTER 5

It was many hours and a few spars with Emily before my feet had hit the bottom floor of secondary Central. They hit for only a second before I was lifted up, leaning on the person who had crashed into me and was lifting me up into his arms. Collin had me, and I was safe again. His hands rubbed my tired back.

"You were amazing today! But seriously? How many intense conversations can you have in one day?"

"I was trying to determine something," I said defensively, "and I did, because I get under Zander's skin as much as she gets under mine."

I looked over at Patterson. "It was good target practice."

"What?" Collin asked, staring at Patterson.

"I knew Patterson wasn't going to believe how far she'd go. She said something to me, the other night. It's like she doesn't care about saving them at all anymore. I'm not sure you would've believed me, so I had to get her to say it again. But now–"

"I know," Patterson said from behind Collin, straightening out his back to point at me. "I'm starting to see it, more each day. But it's clear now, and I really do appreciate that, Aislyn."

"What are you saying?" Collin asked.

Patterson said, sounding winded and out of breath, "I thought this was just about making you more effective killers, but she's been a lot more dangerous than I could've imagined. I thought if I complied with some things, I'd be strong enough to fight her before some mistakes are made, but I'm not going to be. She's too ruthless. At this rate, the law will pass."

Collin looked down at the floor, even as Michael said, "For those of us in a tech-cave all day, can you elaborate?"

"She's changing the primary objective. Aislyn will be ordered to destroy a Sentry if she's see one. Zander's training next year's recruits at the Academy to work in teams to bring down larger clusters of enemies, and it's quite clear at this point that she isn't concerned with collateral damage."

"Speaking of killing Sentries…" Collin started.

"Ah, yes…Alex," Michael said nonchalantly. "Just a huge, monstrous complication and occasional good guy."

"What?" I asked, confused. But instead of answering, Michael nodded at the screen, which showed Alex leaving a coffee cup on the ground.

"What is he doing?" Collin asked.

"He just left his coffee and food near an alleyway after he had breakfast. He's done this every day for three days. Then, by the time the camera comes back around, it's gone. This happens four times a day, different locations, since I've been watching him."

"What? Did it just disappear?"

"No," I said, realizing what Alex was doing.

"He must have given it to a Sub-Terra who's smart enough to take it when the camera pans the other way," Patterson said.

Collin leaned in on the desk, and despite his apprehension, he seemed enamored. "He's like a messed-up, tortured Robin Hood."

Patterson and Michael both confusedly asked, "Who's that?"

"Doesn't matter, I'll tell you later. What's the complication?"

Michael started narrating the footage as he showed it. "Okay, so, sorry to depress everyone now that we're all hopeful, but about twenty minutes later... Boy is caught, Sentries are called in, boy is put in vehicle with the Semsiol police, and carted off to death."

Patterson cursed, and Collin covered his mouth. What I felt I couldn't express without cursing or yelling, so I just didn't bother to show it. I just wanted to know, "Did Alex get there to try–"

"He was late to the call, on the other side of town. But he tried," Michael said. "I think...I think he probably feels guilty. Because we have another issue."

"What?"

"He went to a party and got loaded. He locked himself in a room a few hours ago. I was monitoring the footage. I thought he was going to disappoint us all, you know, morally. But it's just him, I think. I don't have video access to the individual rooms."

Patterson sighed, leaning his head down as Michael continued.

"You know how we said we weren't sure if he just flushed the drugs? Well, we know that on occasion, he uses them. He took a range of anti-depressants. No recharge this time."

"What is that? It's the second time you've mentioned it." I hoped my simple curiosity made me sound calmer than I felt.

"It gets any drugs out of your system: quickly. Elites and Citizens use it so they can get wasted, but go to work the next day. They get all the pleasure of being high or drunk without suffering any of the ill effects."

"Is he still at the party?" Patterson asked.

"I wish," Michael said, with a controlled emotion.

The next screen displayed Alex sitting in the same alley, staring at some stones the Unnecessary had probably piled on each other.

Michael said, "I know he's upset, but–"

"He's not upset, Michael. He's broken. And there's nothing worse than seeing good that you've worked hard for just slip through your fingers." Patterson spoke while looking at the screen, but no one moved for fear he would react. He had been so harsh on himself lately, as I was sure Michael or Collin were aware, maybe even more aware than me. Collin was the first to ask Michael where his weapon was. Michael answered in a shaky voice.

"He didn't check it in after work. He, umm…unholstered it a little while ago, and stared at it for about an hour. The way he was staring at it…had me worried."

"He wouldn't–? He wouldn't." I trailed off, then tried to fight my own uncertainty, sounding more desperate than I wanted to.

"Patterson, if he's considering suicide, we have to–"

"We can't." Patterson shook his head, looking pained.

Collin touched my hand as he spoke, just over a whisper.

"I'll pray for him tonight, the way I pray for you. That's all we can do. I promise I'll stay awake all night. As long as I can."

That struck me, even as I nodded. I had to keep that fear out of my mind. "Anything else we need to discuss?"

"Well, nothing new. Just that everything just became more dangerous," Michael glanced at Patterson knowingly.

"I thought things were already as dangerous as they could get. What's worse than getting caught with Alex by the Society?"

Even as I had uttered the question, Collin looked tormented, even as Patterson answered.

"You, getting caught with Alex by the Territory."

I stopped, struggling to understand Patterson. And when I finally did, I realized just how vital Michael was going to be.

"In 48 hours, you will be under orders to kill this man the next time you are with him. They will be monitoring you. That means if you are caught talking with him, being with him, even rescuing someone with him, you'll be…"

"A traitor." I said the word breathlessly as the final implications of Zander's reign flooded over me.

"You'll be locked up, on probation, or…"

It was Collin who said it, maybe because he feared it the most.

"Sentenced to death."

There was a silence that followed, awkward and still, which was probably why Michael broke it.

"So don't get caught."

I wanted to throw something at Michael, because having my life on the line deserved an additional few seconds of silence to ponder, but then I caught my breath and decided to let it go.

After all, I had risked my life before. I would again.

"He's right. It's simple. I won't get caught." All three looked at me, almost as if they were concerned that the tone in my voice showed my sanity diminishing.

"And I'm sure my handles could help me, especially if he knew what area I was going to be in, and what streets to target."

"There's too many variables. Protectors never talk to handlers anyway…Oh!" Michael said as my implication became clear.

"Yeah, they never talk to handlers." I couldn't help but be sarcastic and enjoy the moment a little. "If you can follow me…"

"While I'm keeping an eye on Alex at the same time…"

"You can hopefully kill the data before it reaches anyone."

"Brilliant! So just let me know by tomorrow where you want to go, which sector you'll be in. That way…you know, you won't be…"

"Sentenced to death."

Again, it was Collin who said it, his arms on the rail, hunched over, staring as if the space behind the railing was an abyss. And the silence returned, and I realized I had been stupid to try to fight it.

"I need to…I can't believe I'm saying this, but I need a run."

"Let's go," Collin said as if running away from the room would be running away from the sense of fate that just fell. Moments later, I was happy that my tired muscles and skin were running through the warm, summer night wind that screamed of a million recollections I tried to suppress. All of them were a blur of beauty, but all I could see was the blur. I had erased the details of nights in the woods with family and friends so I could make room to store more vital information. I had never dreamed of holding these fears when I made those memories on those summer nights.

It was when I felt the full weight of that, of the choices I had to make, that I finally stopped on the trail. Maybe Collin was expecting this, but he instantly reached out and held me, as if it was all he had wanted to do for days.

"I feel like I'm starting all over again, only I can't even remember what I'm going to regret missing. I can barely remember things I swore I would never forget."

He sounded strained. "You're not alone. That's different than months ago, isn't it? Focus on that: on us. I'm with you."

He reached out, grasping my neck and bringing my forehead to rest on his. He didn't kiss me. I didn't need him to kiss me. I needed to escape my fear. With each moment he stared at me, the calm of his presence seemed to draw out every fear as if he were draining poison. He continued to press his forehead against mine, his gaze changing slightly as if he understood each fear as it came flooding into my mind, and he pulled it out. I felt the minutes slip away, my breath steadying as the soft wind surrounded me.

He finally spoke. "In any prayer I scream and whisper, it always starts with you not feeling alone. Even when we first met, when I couldn't tell you how I felt, even as I was the stupid coward yelling at you– trying to save you instead of admitting that I loved you– I wanted you to know you weren't alone. I made decisions in fear, not love. To love you, I had to be your friend. To love you, I had to let you be you. Which is why I want to beg you to stay away from Alex, but I know I can't. Fear always leads to the worst decision. The day you said you loved me, the fear disappeared."

It was only when I felt free from the worries he had obliterated that I leaned into him as he kissed my forehead, sealing my mind, now calm and clear.

But it was then that I heard it: a single footstep. No, it was more than that. As if someone just leaped. And it was way too close to have missed anything that Collin had just said.

I quickly turned to see George leaning against the tree.

"What are you doing?" Collin asked, still holding my head.

"Night climbing. Helps me focus only on the feel of the branches. Plus, you know, it's more discreet," George said, raising his eyebrows. "Not that anyone worries about being discreet."

I was blushing, or the rush might have been a tinge of anger.

"Collin, maybe we should have a little chat? Grab the rope."

I could tell George wasn't angry. Not like Michael or even Patterson had seemed sometimes. Collin whispered, "I'll see you later," as he winked at me, and then quickly stepped out to grab the rope that George threw at him.

I turned to run, already hearing George laugh at something Collin said. I had never quite worked out the dynamic between those two, but I had almost stopped trying. There were only so many stories I could write in my head. Instead, I kept running, past the Circles and right to the forest. I sprinted to the entrance and touched the stone with the engraving of the angel, leaning on the wing to catch my breath. It wasn't until I was about to turn that I thought I should at least take a walk to cool down. My heart ached a little like so many other nights– when Eldridge would be there. When I could ask endless questions, and found a little confidence. The garden was always empty now. I went in an idle search of him, just to mourn the void for a moment.

Except that despite all odds and probabilities, Eldridge was there.

"Sir?"

He smiled softly, his grey eyes shaking off the shadow of worry that had glinted just an instant before.

"You looked."

"What?"

"I haven't been up for days; I haven't seen or talked to you, and at this point, you would have no reason to even search for me. But you did anyway. That means something."

I slowly took my seat, ignoring his strange comment to sit by his side as he said, "So, do you have a question?"

I scoffed, and said, "You sure you wanted trouble?"

"Indeed. Actually I'm quite sure that trouble is needed now more than ever. I'm very happy you're making what you can of it."

I sighed, staring at him even as I sat next to him, realizing I wanted to know something else. "Where have you been?"

He looked at me, knowing it would perhaps cause more questions. "I've been down with the Hand, helping to conduct the inquiries. Helping them. In whispers. In prayers. I keep telling them you're okay, especially Sam and Liam."

I leaned in, catching my head as it fell into my hands.

"Am I okay?" I said, feeling lost in grief.

"Well of course you are."

I glared at him, instantly infuriated at his assumption.

"You ladies are going to be able to go out, in just two days. And you're going to realize something. It's not going to feel very different than it did, weeks ago. All of this drama will fade the second you hit the border. Soon, you will be free to make every decision you need to make to save who you were meant to save."

I stared at him, my expression softening even as I heard his words seeping in as he continued.

"You have the courage the Council does not. You get to decide who you live and die for. Your courage will free you, because they are not brave enough to step outside these walls with you. They can't tell you how to save the world. That's up to you."

He stood up, signaling that we were almost done. "And the more you fight, the more ammunition we have to end this."

He paused for a second, not smiling or hiding his fear like he usually did.

"In the end, I suppose that's one more thing to be praying for."

I smiled, "Well, between you and Collin praying, I suppose I'm all set."

Eldridge smiled. "Ah, and what is Collin praying for?"

I smiled, but then bit my lip, "That I won't feel alone. And that…Alex…won't feel alone."

Eldridge sat down again, waiting in silence for an explanation.

"He tried to save a boy, in an alley. The boy died yesterday."

"Poor boy. Poor man," he said, and then said, "But I can't pray he won't feel alone. Or that you won't."

"Why is that?" I asked, almost irritated again.

"You are alone. So is he. You will be in this mess of a world, in unthinkable places, and you, Alex, even Collin, will be very alone. But if you have hope– irrational hope– you'll keep going."

He got up again then, and disappeared down the stairs. I walked back to my Circle in a trance, digesting his words. As my MCU buzzed once more, I felt my hands reach out for it, hoping to read some silly message about another thing I was required to do.

"You are required to get ready for your first mission, and exit for the first mission in two days."

Even as I read it, wrecked by confusion, I saw Patterson run by.

"This law can't be an executive order placed without a vote. She's only doing this because she knows she'll lose the majority!"

He looked at me, confused more than scared. Which, for some reason, scared me more than it would if he had looked terrified.

I walked back into the Circle, heading to the mats to pull them over to the center, wondering about Collin just as I heard his voice.

"You need to climb that tree sometime. The view is amazing!" He said it with all sincerity, making me smile, thinking there was a little 12-year-old boy in every man who loved to climb trees. And then wondered if that was what George was doing. Just taking an instant to be a 12-year old boy, or lecturing Collin.

"What did George say?"

"Nothing much. It might surprise you, but he almost has no qualms against us being together. He has issues about us not being…what word did he use…discreet."

"Can I ask a question?" I sounded unsure, even though I was determined to get an answer no matter what.

"Shoot."

"Well, George. George has a long wait for Head Trainer. Why doesn't he just give this up and train at the Academy?"

"A few reasons. One reason is Brie, just to try to get her out of this alive. Maybe he can keep her alive long enough…"

I answered as he trailed off, "to change her mind?"

"So, she told you," Collin sighed, "that she's doing this 'til she–"

"She's not going to die!" I don't know why I said it so urgently. I'm sure Collin didn't support it, but I almost yelled it just the same.

"It's okay, Aislyn. I yell that a lot… in my head, when she isn't looking. Funnily enough, she always knows when you're thinking it."

I tried to not even think about it as I tried to slow my breathing so I could sleep, but it was very distracting. Maybe that's why Collin kept talking.

"To answer your question, George…has other reasons." Collin got very quiet all of a sudden, and then said, "It's a secret."

"Like us?" I smiled. He nodded, but then I found myself suspiciously thinking.

"Wait, Collin. Like we're a secret, or a secret that's like us?"

He looked at me, knowingly, and he said with a solemnness that was rare even for him, "I can't. I promised a long time ago."

My day seemed to be filled with discovering Collin in a new way, in a way that I had never seen him in his earlier life as a trainer. I was straining to discover who George could love even as Collin set up the mats in the center of the Circle. But George was keeping our secret as if it was sacred. I was just as responsible for keeping his secret, so I didn't want to know what it was.

Instead I was going to try to save Alex. I felt frustrated that it was all I could do– sit on a mat all night and beg.

But if this was the only thing, I was going to do it.

I walked over to where Collin had placed the mats. He was already sitting, eyes closed, pleading with God to save the miracle he called dangerous. For us. For the future of every Protector. For everything he held dear. And that gave me what Eldridge thought I needed so badly.

Hope.

CHAPTER 6

After waking several times in the night to wade through the fog of emotional, physical, and mental exhaustion, I fell back asleep. To dream. To have nightmares which jolted me back awake. To pray until they faded, to remember that souls never really die. I had dreams of climbing trees, of meadows, and of other memories I had pushed away earlier. It was as if they had returned to give me a glint of happiness, but they made me burn with jealousy instead.

I was staring at Collin, eating my eggs while getting my pack ready. "This morning– Council meeting, sparring with Emily, lessons on how brainwashed Citizens are, and knife-throwing. So, not all bad."

I laughed, sighed, and then bit my lip. He nodded to the doorway. We began our morning run. At first, we enjoyed the summer sun. I felt like maybe a summer sun could erase the dark, and thought of one of the memories of summer.

"What?" he said, noticing a small laugh I had released.

"Nothing," I said, my smile wiped clean by the judgmental face of one of Zander's assistants. After we had passed, the next moments were tense with silence. Until curiosity became more powerful again, and I remembered the limited time we had.

"Has Michael called you yet? What exactly happened?"

Collin looked at me, knowing I didn't want to continue.

"Michael was there almost all night. He did say Alex went into his office, and eventually crashed in the officers' dorm quarters. He slept for about four hours and woke up this morning." Collin sighed again, before continuing.

I breathed out relief, but still found myself thinking about Alex. And Michael. "I don't know Michael very well. I can't tell how he is holding up."

I was waiting for an answer when there was an unexpected voice.

"Probably no better than the rest of us."

I jumped a bit, but continued to run at the pace I was at. And while I was upset that Collin and I would have to hold off our conversation until later, I was glad to see Eva.

"Eva, aren't you supposed to be…"

"Oh, no, you forget I'm 'required' to run," she said, cursing under her breath. "So, I'm running."

She flowed into the conversation, turning to Collin.

"Michael's mad that you are ditching him and all this for her, isn't he? Is that why we're all tense and secretive here?"

I turned, shooting him a warning look.

"Maybe a little," he said, not wanting to tell her the real reason.

I realized that if Patterson had said the same thing about Collin as he had about Michael "resisting the trends," that they were probably good friends. If Collin chose me, he would have to leave all of this behind.

"He hates me, doesn't he?" I had finished my thought out loud.

"No, I don't think so," Eva said. "I feel like he doesn't hold any animosity towards you. Collin is the one considered a little weak."

"Thanks for that, Eva. The next time…" He stopped, looking at his watch, then behind him. He halted, and looked livid.

"What?" I asked him, just as a message came up on the MCU.

"In the future, morning workouts will require no interaction with the trainer or other Protectors."

I showed the message to Eva, who sighed and cursed.

"This is getting ridiculous, even if you two being in love is horribly inconvenient yet charming. Zander is such a—"

Collin elbowed her before she cursed again. We ran, not talking about anything, as if they were afraid to tell me what I already knew.

I should've known when Emily pinned me yesterday, her knee on my back, and said, "They will kill you if you don't kill them."

I should've known when George was clenching his jaw when we watched a video describing all the Citizens and Elites as expendable.

I should've known when Alex's face was put up in the tech room, and my injuries were explained, when he said that he needed to be taken out, not just avoided, because he had shot at a Protector.

I was surprised by that, if only because Zander had probably wished he had succeeded in taking me out.

"Anyway, as an alternative to us all being worried about a certain vote we can't control, the real reason I'm running into you is because I ran into some friends yesterday."

"Who?" I asked, a little annoyed at her forced nonchalant tone.

"Around ten other people whose lives the Council destroyed."

I opened my eyes wider as I realized what she meant. Collin was the one to speak first.

"You saw Sam? How did you get down there?"

"Do you…really? Are you still asking me that? No one asks—"

"Fine, whatever," I said. "Eldridge said he was down there, but he didn't want to tell me…what are they doing to them?"

She sighed. "Not a lot, actually. They are trying to break them down a little slower now. They aren't feeding them a lot. But they are all hanging in there. Sam…"

She paused. "Sam made me promise to ask you something."

"What? What did he say?"

"He wanted to ask you, 'Did it work?'"

I felt like saying no, I felt like objecting, because we were only days away from sentencing Alex to death and hours away from becoming a soldier and not a Protector. But Michael was going to be there, taking every chance to see if Alex was okay.

"Yes, tell him it worked." Even as I said the words, I hated them, or hated myself. Maybe both.

"I'm guessing you aren't going to elaborate?" she accused.

"Nope." My eyes were set, as concrete as I could be.

"And I wouldn't have it any other way," she said, winking.

I was expecting for her to be just a little betrayed.

Instead, she smiled mischievously.

"As much as I love you as an ally and a friend, I love a good challenge. And I'm going to enjoy unraveling this."

She ran off ahead of me. I shared a nervous glance with Collin as we separated. I headed downstairs to the Council room to be attacked by the subtle weapons of politics. Only it didn't feel subtle; it felt brutal.

Zander didn't say anything about the upcoming vote. She didn't say the thing that all nineteen Protectors knew was coming.

She hinted. It was more annoying than her confessing it.

I had a headache that followed me all the way to Emily's Circle, or her former Protector's Circle. I was a little surprised to see Patterson there, but even more surprised that Emily was arguing with him.

"This has gone on far enough," Emily said in a tense tone. "I only agreed to do this because you said you could fight Zander."

"What would you propose I do? I can't fight it! It's going to pass and I am not on the council. And I can't defy her–"

"Why not? Who are you protecting?"

At that moment, Patterson caught me in his eye, and so did Emily. Perhaps I looked guilty. Perhaps Patterson looked too pained. But in the second that followed, Emily looked at me in a way that made me feel exposed.

"Right. Her." Emily's words weren't full of anger, but regret.

"Remember," Patterson whispered, thinking I couldn't hear, "She is not the only one with a secret I'm protecting."

"Like that's my fault. I've pushed him away more than…"

It seemed like she was going to continue, but then she didn't, as if there was really nothing more to say.

Patterson left, and instead of my brain filling with the previous moves she had taught me and every possible meaning of what secret she was keeping, I was already focusing in on one possible secret she could hold.

I looked at her, the same age as George.

Just like George, who also had a secret.

A secret like us.

"What?" She looked about to be confrontational.

"Nothing," I lied, as my memory strained to recall every moment I had ever seen them together, when I had seen them stare at each other knowingly across the room, that I had seen him gaze when she had turned away, looking guilty somehow. How they had always climbed together. How he had gone to her the night she was crying.

"What is it?" she said again, more emphatically, maybe worried that I heard the last thing she had said to Patterson. More memories flooded. Him reaching out to help her, her pulling away. I didn't want to confront her. I couldn't mask that I was confused.

"You don't approve of making us all soldiers. So why are you training us, saying the things you've been saying, and quoting Zander, if it's all a lie?"

She sighed, looked at the mat, and then back at me.

"Grow up, Aislyn. Just because you're right doesn't mean you get to be right. Even you know that by now." I could still sense her eyes on me in a strange way, and I stopped.

"So you're saying…"

"Just because you think you may have just discovered something about me right now doesn't mean you get to use it against me."

I looked in shock as she continued, "What? You don't think I've been hiding this for years and I don't know the look on someone's face when they figure it out? I know. Besides, it's not like it's all my secret. Just because he feels that way about me…"

She moved to the side as she nodded at the gloves on the mat. My eyes turned to meet hers, only this time she was the one averting my gaze, staring at the edge of the mat. It almost seemed as if she was fixated, and I wondered if, like me, she saw a line she couldn't cross. It didn't seem so much of a line as a cliff.

I stared at her, wondering if I should ask what I was desperate to know. She didn't look up right away, but followed the line of the mat from where I stood. She paused as her eyes finally hit mine, piercing and burning with an intensity I had never seen before.

"Ready?"

Six moves later, I was on the mat, my breath knocked out of me.

She got up from her crouching position and stood up, back to me. I was wondering if she was upset when she turned slightly, wrapping up her wrist brace tighter. My body ached as

I got up. I wondered if I was going to pay for my curiosity in more ways than one. But I suppressed any expression even as my knee objected to my first step. I knew the only reason she respected me was my persistence. So I got up. I persisted.

"Do you love him?" I asked.

Three moves later, I was on the mat. She grunted.

And I was up again. Before she could say, "Hands up, cover your face," I was jabbing at her. I added a kick she barely blocked.

"Pathetic. Completely pathetic," she smiled as she slid out of the way of three jabs, even as I ducked and rolled past her. I had gotten used to her verbal abuse the past few days, but found that as I improved, she still said the same words. She said them jokingly.

She punched.

I blocked again.

I jabbed at her stomach, pushing her back.

She smiled while insulting me again. I attempted a lower leg kick, spinning, crunching my knee. She jumped. I missed entirely, but instead kept spinning, so that by the time she had stood up from her jump, I had swung my leg around, hitting her torso and sending her hurtling back on the mat.

But she instantly threw her hands behind her and pushed herself back up to rush me. I willed my body to duck and slide away, and found myself rolling under her kick.

She winked and said, "Completely pathetic."

I was pulling up from my roll when I asked, "Does that mean you'll answer my question?"

In every moment I maneuvered around her, I felt empowered. I was almost about to pin her when she tried one new move I didn't see coming. I saw the mat again, laying on my belly, staring at it from inches away.

I breathing hard against the mat, getting up as my sweaty skin stuck to it. I peeled myself back up.

She jabbed again.

Duck. Jab. Lunge. Drop.

I got a kick in at her ankle. She fell to one knee when I lunged at her, spinning my body around her as my arms squeezed, pulling her down. She tried to roll, but I pushed against her back with my foot.

My foot pressed harder when I felt her shoulders tense.

"Do you love him?" I asked in panted breaths.

"Still missing the point, Aislyn."

Then she turned quickly, grabbing my foot as she twisted out of my hold, pulling my leg out from under me. I face planted on the mat, feeling her knee between my shoulder blades, making them scream in protest.

"Use your knee to pin. Not your foot."

I got up when she released, now out of breath from missing oxygen while gasping.

But she was putting her hands up again.

I almost protested, but I didn't have time before she lunged toward me.

Jab. Hook. Duck. One answer.

"I don't know if I love him, because I never even allowed myself to even let that question exist, let alone ask myself it."

I punched, only to have her grab my arm and wrench it to the side. I rolled with it, continuing to wrestle until free.

"But George has asked you?"

Within a second, her leg was swinging around to hit my torso. Instead of blocking, I ducked, pushing it up slightly but still using her initial momentum to slide it over me and force it onto the ground. I lunged at her torso. She pushed back with one leg until I remembered what she had said earlier and quickly kicked it out from underneath her before she could get her bearings. She fell back on the mat with a thud almost right underneath me. And this time, I used my knee to pin her down.

Feeling more confident than I should have been, I decided not to ask again. I was going to pin, and see her reaction.

"And you lied when you answered, didn't you?"

Her eyes answered the question, even as they looked away at the wall in uncertainty. But then she looked determined.

"Getting your attacker to slip up using an emotional dilemma is a good strategy, but you should remember one thing."

The fear and any other emotions left her at once. Within a second, her eyes glared at me, cold and calculating. She pushed up quickly, while stretching her leg back to kick my arm. I winced as she threw me off, as her leg swung to hit my shin, and then she pinned me down, her knee on my one arm. I could feel my blood pumping harder, my artery cut off for only seconds. As I lay winded on the mat, ashamed that I had lost again, she glowered.

"A few things."

"Which are?"

"One, you should've put –"

"More pressure on the knee. Yeah, got that."

She then moved her other knee to my chest, pushing it down as her face hovered only inches from mine. She flicked my temple with her finger.

"Two, when you've distracted their mind enough to attack their body, make the next move count."

I closed my eyes, still trying to breathe, and not focus on the black specks taking over.

"Got it. Anything else?"

"Three," she continued slowly and with a smug smile, "when you are 'distracting them,' be sure that you're not being played."

I stopped the breath I was about to take, wondering why I suddenly felt so vulnerable, so naked, as she spoke each word.

"While you were trying to figure out what was in my mind, I guessed at what was in yours. Who, after all, could think that anyone could fall in love in this place? Perhaps, someone in love."

She knew. She had seen right through me even as I thought I was unraveling her. She continued, "You get some free advice, 27. Because you did, finally, pin me down once."

"And what's that?" I said, barely able to speak.

"I've already given it to you. But let's put it in different terms. Just because you love someone doesn't mean you get to be in love."

There was something haunted in her eyes, something that scared and fascinated me, but in the end, I felt nothing but pity.

All the hope I had for Collin and I left me.

"So we're doomed?" I said, still pinned underneath her, defeated in every possible way.

It felt strange to be comparing myself to her. But the words, finite and horrible, were piercing through the barriers she had built up against them.

She scoffed, but then looked behind me, at the mat.

"Yeah, we're doomed."

I was about to speak when her watch buzzed. Only it hurt.

"Ouch!" I said in response not to her words, but to the slight electric shock that went off in her arm. I continued, trying to keep it light now that she had let me go to stare at the watch.

"I didn't even know they buzzed like–"

"You need to get up."

It was fast, and her voice was muted emotionally. It was a few tones deeper than normal. I realized there was no display on the watch. It just buzzed two more times, I was only just realizing that it was a pattern.

She didn't look scared, if you were to look at her, but the fear in her voice was unmistakable.

"What is it? Is it–"

"Aislyn, you are going to die one day, because you ask too many questions. Just go! Lockers. Now!"

"I'm going," I said, surprised, as she helped me up. She pushed me forward. I didn't look back.

I think she was one of the individuals who would've thought that a sign of weakness.

I was completely confused as I entered the garden, not sure of what I was supposed to find. Or who. But then I saw Megan walking towards the same door. Then Cassidy, in the distance.

Even as I held the door open, I glanced back at Tessa's Circle. No movement. And I could see Abigail doing combat moves through the doorway in hers.

Megan came up to the door, "What's going on?"

"Just go! I think I just figured it out."

"Who buzzed the comms? And why…"

"Hang on, Megan, I'm sure she's not going to want to explain it more than once."

"Who?"

I opened the door to the locker room, seeing nothing but the backs of the long rows on either side. I paused for a second.

"Eva?"

Within a second, Eva leaned back from on the bench, popping into view.

"Aislyn. And Megan. And…Cassidy," she said finally as Cassidy came up behind us, and then she looked away, cursed, and said, "How much do I owe you?"

"Hundred," Brie said, just as we walked into view. "And I want Republic money. I need coffee when I get there."

"Ugh…I can't believe you can drink that stuff!" Eva said, and then turned to us again while handing Brie money. "Sorry to lack faith in all of you, but I didn't think all of you would show up."

"All of us?" Cassidy asked, looking back at the door. It closed as I looked at Lydia and Erica. "Who are 'us'?"

"You were listening in on the council," I said, starting it as a question, but then realizing I knew the answer. Her one eyebrow raised, as if to say, "obviously," before her face dropped.

"And they voted, didn't they?" Megan said behind me.

"Yeah. It's done. It was about five minutes ago. They are still in deliberation, but we only have a few minutes."

"To what?"

"To try to make sense of this? Decide if we want to protest?"

"So we all are what? The revolution within the revolution?"

"Yeah, sort of, I don't know, I don't like that name," Eva said offhandedly. "We need one that makes us sound more awesome."

"We just…wanted a chance to make a promise, even to each other," Brie started nervously. "I know I'm going to have to go up there in a few minutes and get new orders from Patterson. But if I know that we're on the same page, that we're still going to try to save them, it'll help. And to know we can go out together…"

"Hey, whenever the Hand can clear us, we're with you," Megan said, even as Cassidy said, "The second it's noon, we can go."

Eva shook her head. "Zander is going to want to make a big deal about it, have us all on media, drill it into us, have three more days of training, maybe even give us missions…"

And suddenly, I felt something: a need to escape and rebel in any possible way, to feel the only revenge we could ever have on her.

"Now. Let's go now!" I said, permeating the air with the energy I could feel seeping through my mind. "Just message our trainers; they'll message our go-codes, and we'll be gone. Let's just get out of here!"

"I knew I liked you 27," Cassidy winked at me as she and everyone else punched numbers in their MCU.

"Our trainers are all in the meeting? Can they even send–?"

"Mine just did," Eva said, and then held her breath. "And Michael just approved me. And I've been advised of new orders...blah blah blah..."

"Are our trainers going to get flack for this?" Megan asked.

"Probably, but in all honestly, Patterson will spin it some way that will make everyone unsure. He'll spout off how eager and dedicated we all are or something," I answered.

Megan said, "Sorrinson cleared me. Advised of new orders."

I looked at my MCU just as she finished talking. I had a message from Michael that said, "Cleared. Get out of here. Now."

And one from Collin: "I can't leave. You should see Patterson trying to hide his smirk, though. By the time Zander is done with the meeting I'm in, half of you will be gone."

The reality that I wouldn't see him before I went was sinking in quickly. I might not even see him again before I died. I asked myself if I should stay, but I already knew I shouldn't. There was more to us than what a kiss goodbye or one last hug meant.

Just as I thought that, I saw his other message. "Don't be sorry. Don't message me. You don't need to. Just keep going, so you can be free from all this. I need you to go as much as I once thought I needed you to stay. No matter what happens, I'm with you."

I touched the screen, but all of a sudden was aware that I wasn't alone when I heard Cassidy slam her locker behind me as she said, "I don't care if it's the new color in the Republic, that green is just…"

Megan and Lydia laughed as Erica said, "It's horrid, isn't it!?" They all joked behind me, opening lockers and feeling the crazy energy. Eva just stared at me, her knee pulled up under her chin. She looked worried for me. Brie watched me carefully as she zipped up and then froze to see me staring at the MCU.

"You going to be okay?" Eva asked. "You can always just… Maybe you can call him…"

"No, she can't." Brie looked at me, almost as a warning.

"I can't, Eva," I said, opening my locker, pulling out two outfits.

Eva pulled her other knee in, looking almost as injured as I felt as the other girls continued to comment on the new atrocious green that had become the fashion craze. Slowly, the energy of rebelling took over, and as I felt the rush I had felt minutes ago. I pulled out my pack, my hand shaking for a second as I held it.

"It's okay, Eva. There's nothing you can do. And besides, haven't you heard?"

I said it with all the anger and hurt I felt, letting it go as I slammed the locker door.

"We're doomed."

CHAPTER 7

"Say you are on 8th Street, the café with the cake—" Eva started

"Because it's all about cake," Cassidy sighed.

"Well, isn't it?" Eva was trying to improve her meal bar by warming it over the heating rod. It wasn't working, but we were all eating them just the same. "Okay, by 8th…Go!"

"South on 8th, alley on Lauriel down to 20th, bus to 42nd, alley to business district, past labs, and home free." Megan was quick.

"Okay, Cassidy, who would leave the café without cake, go!" Eva said as she pointed to her.

"North on 8th, bus to 32nd where I could grab a cheaper cab, out to business district, and then past labs and home free."

"Survey says…" Eva turned to me.

"No go for story, Cassidy, you can't take a friend or a kid into the business district. It doesn't make sense, although it's faster."

"It is cheaper to take the bus from 32nd Street by $100, so I'd do a mixture of the two," Brie said. "So Megan, 8 points. Cassidy, 4 points."

"Ugh," Cassidy whined, watching Megan smile and wink at her. "Can we pick new judges?"

"No," Eva said, "Brie and Aislyn are the first and last Protectors. It's poetic. Okay, Megan, your turn to call it."

"Um….4th Street, Elite's house, Sub-Terra Vessel."

"Whoa! There's a good one, okay…" Lydia looked as if she was concentrating on the invisible map we all had engraved in our heads. "Taxi up to 10th, even though it would cost a fortune, sewer line up to Oak Street, alleys and buses to the west until we hit the warehouse district, to the border, then home."

Eva already had somewhat of a game face on, and didn't hesitate as she said, "Taxi to 20th, then bus onto Elm, alleys under the warehouse district, and then home."

Brie looked at me, winked and said, "I say 7 for Eva's."

"8 for Lydia." I nodded in response.

"What?" Eva said, shocked.

"Your plan is four times more expensive," I said, adding on, "And bus onto Elm? It's crowded. This is a Vessel, and it's likely someone might see her or recognize her, even as a Sub-Terra in that area. And there's no need to go underground in warehouses."

Eva glared at me. "Forget poetry. Can we pick new judges?"

That made even Brie laugh, and Eva winked at me a second later to confirm she was joking. There were eight more turns after that, in which I learned where and where not to go case by case. With each story, however grim the circumstances, I felt the weight lift off of me. Hopefully, these would be our stories. Stories of hope and survival. Stories of them being worth so much more than us.

And in the seconds that followed, I forged a memory in my mind, and told myself I needed to remember to thank Eldridge for giving me hope. He was right. The second we were away, we were good. No one could touch us here.

It wasn't until I pulled myself out of my reverie that I found Eva was reveling in our freedom from the Council as well.

"Just think. We all get to be out here, roasting meal bars, instead of–" Eva paused. "What do normal people do in summer?"

I smiled, even as Megan said, "They camp out here. For fun. And they usually roast other things, like meat or marshmallows or something that tastes amazing with some flame on it."

Eva poked the leaves. "So, they aren't sitting around pondering how to evade enemy soldiers through the streets of a dystopian world because they all suffer from a mass psychosis that makes them think the lives of certain individuals don't matter? What a shame."

"I wish we didn't have to grow up," Lydia said, gazing at the flames.

"Well, no one really wants to grow up…" Megan trailed off.

"Never growing up. Maybe that could be it," Cassidy said. "Just think, if we had something more seductive to offer the Society, something to make them feel just as comfortable, they'd follow us instead. Never growing up. That's attractive."

"But money and sex is sexier," Brie said dead-panned, looking at the meal bar she was eating. "So we'll always lose."

In an instant all of our MCUs went off. I was so thankful for the distraction, I hardly realized what was happening.

Eva cursed. I heard the shuttle, even as Eva got up.

"It's fine. I was expecting this to happen."

The shuttle that we heard was about twenty yards away when it slowed down, shifting to a stop. Within two seconds, the door slid open and Avery and Michael jumped out. They had barely stood up and Avery barely had a chance to scowl when Eva put out her hand.

"Here's my wrist just in case you want to slap it."

Avery rolled his eyes. Even I wanted Eva to be quiet. I wasn't in the mood to be dragged back because she wanted to annoy Avery.

"You're not taking us back, are you?" Brie asked, and stood in a way that would make anyone afraid to take her anywhere against her will.

Erica looked equally scary as she said, "I'd like to see you try."

Michael started to say, sounding rehearsed, "No, we know you are very dedicated people who just couldn't wait to fulfill the new objective, and are just wanting to do what you do best–"

"Shut up, Michael," Avery said, without even moving his glare off of Brie. "We're here to give you your new orders, just to make sure you didn't leave without the memo."

"No," Brie said. "You're here to make sure we know that we can't escape our new orders and guilt us–which is impossible–into thinking that we are a bit traitorous for disagreeing with them."

"And that you are all under review. Not probation, but review. And for what?" Avery began to sound more annoyed and angry. "A statement? A small act of rebellion that will never be remembered?"

"If it was no big deal, why are you here?" I asked.

I wished I had thought to say something more, but in the end, the silence and Michael's smirk confirmed it was the perfect thing to say.

Brie finally spoke. "Well, are you going to give us the orders?"

Avery looked at us in disgust, shaking his head as he said, "No. Michael is."

Michael looked surprised, like he might protest, as Avery threatened, "Now."

Maybe it was just that he clearly knew Michael disagreed with the decision, but it made me hate Avery for making Michael say it. Michael looked at me in that moment, feeling powerless and outranked. I mouthed the opposite of what I felt: "It's okay."

He took a deep breath, "To the 1st through 27th Protector of the 188th Generation, you are now charged with killing any enemy of the Territory that is seemingly vulnerable, in any circumstances and not limited to self-defense."

He took a breath, and I could see the pain in his eyes. "Should you encounter an Unnecessary or a Vessel, you are to retrieve them. But no longer save them at the cost of your first objective, if you must make a choice. They will be seen as collateral damage if necessary. Do you promise to adhere to this new directive, as much as possible, without risking your life?"

I wanted to say, "No!" a million times, but I didn't. I just nodded and said, "Yes," along with everyone else.

"There," Avery said, with a smug voice. "Was that so hard?"

It was Brie who spoke, her eyes hard as she continued to walk forward with each step.

"This wasn't an act of rebellion. It was desperation. Now you know what we would have given for one more mission where our goal was pure – that one life could be saved without taking another one. And this was worth it."

She was almost right on top of him, making him flinch as she said, "Because now you know how desperate we are."

She turned quickly away from him, even as he glared back. But he didn't respond. He turned to return to the shuttle, calling out for Michael as he went.

Everyone else retreated, back to the fire circle we had formed earlier. Michael stood still for a second, and I wondered if he was waiting to speak with me.

"Is Collin…"

"He's fine. I volunteered to come because…well, reasons."

Someone behind me burst into laughter, then someone else. I turned around to find Erica throwing something at Eva.

Michael nodded at them, and then said, "I hope we didn't interrupt anything."

"Just know that you can answer honestly when Collin asks. Because I'll be over there laughing with them soon. And I'll be alright," I said. "You got the agenda I'm going to follow this time? Was there anything else?"

"Something…" he looked like he was struggling to say it. "I didn't tell Collin, or Patterson. I don't even know if I should tell you. It's just a theory, a crazy one, really. But it can wait. It feels like the wrong time." He looked down at his feet.

"It all feels wrong, Aislyn. I just ordered you to kill someone who saved your life."

"Yeah, well…It's a good thing that I'm an incompetent newbie who can't follow orders."

He smiled, got back on the shuttle, and left.

Left me to laugh at Eva's jokes.

Left me to guess with the others at Zander's backstory.

Left me to hike, talking about what "normal" school was like.

Left me to see Brie stare at pictures of Caleigh on her MCU.

Left me to pray in the middle of the night that I would see him.

Left me to think of how badly I wanted to keep Alex alive.

For the first time, I felt like I was going into the Republic with someone I was protecting. Only Alex didn't know how far I'd go to protect him. But that wasn't what scared me the most.

I didn't know how far I'd go to protect him.

A hundred miles away and two hundred hours later, I felt the depth of all of my promises to myself. Only they crushed me.

Because I realized that in four days, I hadn't seen anyone who needed me.

I felt the shame of nearly losing my chill exterior, not in a dangerous situation, but rather in a café. I was staring at a cup, and for some reason was overcome by anxiety. I felt as if I had a target on my back, as if I was marked for death and should just surrender and yell, "I'm a Protector" right there in the café. I'd read stories from other Protectors and in my journal about this strange urge, when you've been undercover so long without leads that you just feel so desperate. My vulnerability increased the longer I went without a target, with nowhere to go and no one to pretend to be. If I just had one, I could go home before running into someone I was supposed to kill. I had promised Michael to stay in this sector, but it was more confining than I imagined.

"You are you." I said it to myself over and over again. I tried to identify with every strength I had, and every confidence I had ever felt. I had to find a way to stand stronger than I felt right now, just because there would be a moment I might miss someone who needed me to save them. I tried to simply listen, hearing random comments, when I heard one that stood out.

"Your painting, sir, as requested." My eyes perked up to see a man bring a beautiful drawing to the café manager. Everyone began to notice. Some even clapped as he unveiled it.

I wasn't clapping because everyone else was, but I was clapping. I was genuinely impressed; lost in the piece almost instantly taken with its beauty. It was illuminating. He held his hand over the piece, hovering, as if it was heat or power he was absorbing as he discussed it. His pale hand stood inches from it, silhouetted under all of the color that had somehow made me forget my worries. He made a few more announcements, and then left with an assistant behind him to grab some food. At least that was what I assumed.

I finally took a sip of my drink. I was still not accustomed to the taste, but swallowed it down. I turned to look at the painting again. I felt an urgency to look more closely. I was only a foot away when the assistant passed in front of me, taking a bag of food as he left.

Follow him.

I froze as I heard the voice, thinking as I did the first time I heard it that I must be mistaken. Why would I want to follow this bratty celebrity artist?

But then, why did the painting seem so different?

Even glancing at it, there was something...

What couldn't I figure out about it? I didn't know. To that response, the voice answered, *Don't you want to know? Follow him.*

I had acted illogically on faith once before, and decided to risk faith again. But this time, I felt that risk more acutely. Walking into a store was harmless, untraceable, and unsuspicious. This was more deliberate, which made it more unnerving. And in the split second I think the anxiety reached my face, someone looked at me.

"I know, right? He almost never comes to this part of town! He's so down to earth! No wonder he's a genius."

I was trying to get a better view of the assistant trying to catch a taxi in my peripheral vision, while pretending to continue to stare at the painting for a few more seconds until I saw a taxi slow down. I slowly exited, looking as disinterested as possible. I was straining to hear him say the address over the hovering of the taxi.

"206 Fif–," the voice said before the shuttle door closed.

I then turned, as if I had responded to something on my phone. Even with my small triumph, I didn't know if it was 206

Fifth or Fifteenth Street, and I didn't know if it was North or South. I though back to HistCulture though, and even though he was an artist, and most likely a lucrative one, there was no way he lived on Fifteenth, as it was all commercial properties.

To go to Fifth, I would need a private shuttle or a taxi.

Both were massively expensive, but I didn't hesitate. I saw a taxi and hailed it. I gave the driver the address and settled in for the twenty minute drive.

I thought it would be a good time to use my digital ear pieces, so the driver wouldn't start a conversation with me, but it only made my fear heighten. Every breath I took echoed in my ears, sending shivers down my spine.

These were not the leads we were supposed to follow.

Why in the world was I following an Elite artist?

Why was I blowing what little money we had been given?

The shuttle stopped at the address I gave him.

245 South 5th Street.

I had realized very quickly that in such a high-profile neighborhood, it would be strange if I was outside too long or targeted the artists address. Instead, I was staring at the storefront of a popular boutique, which I glanced at for a minute before wandering off in search of 206. There was very little foot traffic on the street, so hoping no one would see me, I quickly ducked down the alley. I quickly found the back of the yellow house, labeled 206 for deliveries.

I didn't need to see the number, though. It was obvious that a painter lived here.

There were canvases in the alley, half-painted but all beautiful. It was the most ethereal and surreal alley ever seen.

All of the discarded pieces were beautiful and bold, yet innocent.

That word struck me: *innocent*.

It echoed if only because in the world I was in, that word was never spoken, never thought, never pondered while in the Republic. Art is supposed to make you feel emotion, but no artist here in the Republic that could feel "innocent."

Unless…

The word that had first struck me was now piercing me repeatedly. I took a step back, taking a deep breath before I lunged forward. I found the door, and without hesitating anymore, I opened it. I quickly thought of several different reasons I could be in the house if someone on the other side of the door discovered me, but I hoped that there was only security for the main sections of the house, not the service area.

It was not well lit, with worn and used canvases strewn along the dark hallway. I saw a few more things that confirmed my theory, building my urgency with every breath.

"Innocent."

I turned toward the entrance of the next door when I noticed the panel next to it. It was at the end of the hallway I had just traversed. I quickly scanned for cameras. There were none. I quickly looked at the security panel again. It was a card entry and number entry.

I needed a card.

I thought of the simplest tactic: attack the next person who I saw, get a card so I can escape...

I stopped myself. Maybe I was too cautious, but I cringed at the thought of tackling or possibly killing the person who walked through the door. They didn't deserve that. Another part of me wondered at the tactical advantage I would lose if I lost a fight. But I couldn't think of another way until I saw the canvases.

The person who came out of the door next would just be moving down the hallway, probably with a bulky painting. They would be cautious about not damaging the art, but have no reason to look behind them. I weighed the risk of waiting in the corner, for a chance to sneak in the door after it opened, and that there would be no one on the other side.

Even as I calculated that risk, something beeped on the other side of the door. Hearing the keypad confirmed my worst fear.

A two-way lock. They were locking someone in the house.

And if getting inside this house was hard, getting out was going to be impossible.

I heard someone continue to enter the code, and panicked until I finally bolted for behind the door, holding my breath and freezing every muscle in my body as the door opened.

It almost hit me, but then remained inches away, slowing as it approached my face. A person walked past with their back turned towards me as they maneuvered a canvas through the door. They were intently focused on their task, as I had hoped. I could tell from the sliver that I could see around the side of the door that it was signed. It was a completed work.

I instantly breathed relief. It was worth thousands. No one carrying it was ever going to worry about checking behind doors.

I hated my rashness. I didn't know what my next step was. I only hoped that the story in my head might play out in reality as I saw him move a few steps down the hallway. Still focused on the painting, he didn't see me move from behind the door. I had two seconds to check to see from my limited field of view, but there was nothing there. Just a huge marble floor. As his feet shuffled through a tight spot, I quickly moved through the doorway.

My mind strained as each step I took on the marble echoed slightly. The door began to close just as I heard an engine in the alley. The painting would be loaded in a shuttle after just a few seconds, and then the man who was loading it would return....

I chose a direction and hoped it was the right one, wondering where the voice in my head was now. I felt blind. I needed something. All I had was my story, built on one word. Innocence.

But even as I said it, I realized that innocence needed inspiration.

I quickly moved up the stairs. I was hoping the owner was eating his lunch somewhere, giving me minutes to choose a room.

The entire hall was marble, with all the doors around the square and with a wide open rail looking down to the center. If I went the wrong way, or entered the wrong double doors, I was dead.

I was already running through everything I had done wrong.

I shouldn't have just jumped in the house.

I shouldn't have just guessed who was in here.

I shouldn't have…

I was one more mistake and moment away from getting caught. I ran up, not worrying that my feet weren't completely silent.

Half of these rooms, if not almost all of them, were empty. I thought about how rarely they were used– probably for parties, only holding people that barely mattered to him. Never leaving an impression, just going by. I thought back to when Collin and I were talking about their feet. They walked so lazily, never leaving an impression with their soft steps.

But they would, I thought to myself. Their feet would leave an impression on a polished floor like this. I looked down the hall, looking at each small space before the entrance to each room.

Only one spot was duller than the other clean, polished areas. The traffic of shoes rubbing against it had made the floor less shiny.

I sprinted, opened the door, and turned to shut it.

There was no movement as I first entered. No sign that anyone was there. There were paintings scattered in the room, probably meant as a muse for the artist. They all emanated with feelings of purity, innocence, and simplicity. I took a few steps when I first heard his small voice.

"Who are you?"

I looked toward the voice, behind the easel.

I couldn't see him yet, but then that's what I had expected to find: A person smaller than an easel.

When his eyes crept from behind the canvas, they did not look as surprised as I thought. They looked with wonder, not something I could have imagined was possible from a boy who was being held prisoner. Perpetual blamelessness in its true form: a child.

"Are you my model?" he asked. "For the portrait? I thought that was tomorrow, but I sometimes lose track of days in here."

I shook my head, not even certain what I could say to make him follow me. His eyes locked onto mine. The light seemed to reflect off their dark aqua shade. From his golden hair and perfect features, I could tell he was lab-made, but not a SubTerra.

"That's a shame. You have the most intriguing look about you. Like you have an amazing story," he said.

I breathed out a laugh, smiled as I stepped forward, and said, "It's funny you should say that. I'm a writer."

"What do you write? Is that why you're here? To write a story?"

My lip quivered for an instant, before I swallowed. I took a small breath, but it felt like a gust of wind entering my chest. The room felt as if it were moving, with the strokes of color in it. Everything felt thick, laced with meaning.

"I came to write a different ending for a story," I whispered.

"How does it start?"

"It starts with a Protector, actually."

"You're brave," he scoffed. As sheltered as he was, he must have known it was a touchy subject. "What's the Protector doing?"

"She's having a coffee. She sees someone. A man. There are many admirers. His works are legend. But then she sees one of his works. She is listening to the crazy voices in her head, hoping they are divine. She follows him home. And then she sees another painting. And she knows that the artist...didn't paint them."

He stopped mid-stoke, freezing while pulling back the brush only slightly, leaving the longest bristles hover over the canvas.

"You see, where she is from, she was one of the few children in a program to develop creativity. She was a writer. She knew many artists, though they weren't many. And they had different strokes, when they were younger, because they couldn't reach as high. They had to reach sometimes, because they were short. There was always a little more paint on the top of the strokes. They pushed it upwards, as they stood on their toes, reaching for what they were creating. It was so beautiful. She promised she'd never forget it."

His eyes reflected a strange mixture of fear and awe.

"But it wasn't just that. She knew only a child could convey what was in that painting, wild and free but leaving you with a sense of breathless innocence so pure it could hardly be human. But most definitely one that comes from a soul lost in his own beautiful kingdom where he must be hiding. And she thought of a story. An artist who agreed to take on a Sub-Terra, and who maybe noticed when that Sub-Terra picked up a brush, what he could do. Once the Protector figured it out, she was resolved. She snuck in, without much of a plan for getting out. She thought at least if she died, she wanted to let the child know."

"Know what?" he asked confidently, even though a tear fell.

"That someone saw you. Locked in here. In your work. I didn't know who you were. But I know you painted it."

His eyes dropped to his work as he blinked tears away rapidly.

"The backstory seems a little off, but I think so far, that is an amazing story. But someone would be crazy or brave to be in it."

"A little of both," I admitted with almost an embarrassed smile. "But I feel bad. I don't even know the main character's name."

"They don't know he has a name, like the paintings he is not allowed to name. But if they were to ask, he would say he remembers being called Gabriel."

"Gabriel." I spoke his name, and then allowed the silence to make it sacred before I asked, "So, my backstory was off?"

He smiled. "A little. But it's all good."

He moved to face me, almost drawing me down to his level as he whispered, "Because it's the part of the story you didn't see that's going to give you hope."

I looked confused, until I registered what hope meant. The one hope we needed.

"Are you saying…is there a way out?"

He smirked mischievously as he whispered.

"There's a way out."

CHAPTER 8

"The artist didn't find me," the boy said. "The cook did. One day, after school. I was 7…" He stopped and looked up at me for the first time, scared– or showing a memory of fear.

"I couldn't go home."

"Your parents would have killed you?"

"They were Citizens. And sometimes…I don't even know how we think of people as our parents. I didn't. Anyway, while I was creative, I think I always showed more attachment than they would like. But believe it or not, I wasn't the one who was too emotionally attached than they would have liked. She was."

I stared at him curiously.

"She was in my class. She was beautiful. She was a writer, like you. Like I was an artist. She was so attached to everything. She once wrote a poem about birds after seeing two huddle together in the rain under a branch. I told her to hide it. One morning, they asked to see her in the office. I still remember I was nervous for her, even then. She giggled. Her cheeks glowed. I remember when her hair caught the light. It wove through it. That was the last thing I remember. She didn't come back after five minutes. She didn't come back after an hour. By lunch time I knew. She was never coming back. I couldn't go home. I just…didn't want to. I realized that there was more…but I knew I would be next. So I ran."

I tried not to cry, but I didn't quite know why. Maybe too much emotion would scare him.

"What was her name?"

"Kieri. Isn't that a beautiful name? Kieri."

"So…what happened then?"

"I was outside of the school, walking down the alley, on the third day. The school cook saw me. She kept me eating. Then she told me…well, she told me where she was going. She was getting a better job. She was going to get her debts paid off faster. She helped me out. I was waiting for her the evening of a party the artist was having. I found a sketchbook and some pencils in the alley, and sketched for the first time in ages. He came in and was about to yell at her, but then she…she's smart, you know. She showed him the notebook. Within days, I was here, in this room. Within months, my quota was one painting every few weeks."

"Was it difficult?"

"Well, yes. Just because I was trying to mimic his style at first. I refused. It was too hard. Then he locked me in the room."

"Why did you paint for him?" I asked, disgusted, but at the same time angry that he felt like he had no choice. "You had to know what he was doing, that he was taking advantage of you."

"Well, I kind of did. I remember the day I yelled that I would never paint again. I remember it was right over there. I…"

His eyes fell on the marble floor. I couldn't imagine what his punishment had been. I had begun to push vomit back when the boy sheepishly said, "He took it all away."

"What?" I said, genuinely confused at how that was a penalty.

"He took it away. Every color, every easel. He fed me every day, but…he just left me alone. It was so idle. I held my breath a few times just so that regaining my breath would become something to do. I tried to dance to songs in my head. I made lines in the dust forming on the floor. But in the end, I begged to have it back. I am a slave. I know I am. But I get to do something I love. I'm just…alone."

I stared at him, even as I panicked gauging his age. But there was no turning back now.

"That's where I come in."

"Guess so," he sighed, staring at the last brush stroke he had placed on the canvas, bold and striking. "It's a shame, though. This would have been beautiful. I already did the first part. It's not complete. The first one had gold in it, instead of yellow."

I stared at the red lines shooting out from the sun, already carrying a beautiful line of light.

"You can finish it when you get there," I smiled measuredly.

"Can you even promise that we'll get there?"

I stared at the red on the canvas and felt a sinking fear. Out of my other Unnecessaries, this was the first not in mortal danger.

Going with me was almost more of a risk than staying here.

"No," I answered truthfully. "I can only promise I'll die trying."

He looked up, and surprised me by reaching up for my cheek.

"Now who wouldn't want to be that loved?" he said, smiling.

He picked up one brush, and put it in a bag off to the side. He carefully placed it on his shoulder. I realized he hadn't gone many places. I carefully took note because I realized that if we had to run or move quickly, it would be difficult.

"You don't leave this room much, then?" I asked. Maybe he sensed my thoughts, because he answered the question I didn't ask.

"I'll be alright. He lets me go for a run on that machine over there once in a while. I'm not great. I do have this thing. I have medicine for it. I breathe it in. I don't know what it's called."

"It's called asthma. I have an inhaler in my med bag, just in case we run into an Unnecessary with the condition. So when—"

Just then, the door opened. I hit the ground, making my wrists burn as I tried to make my landing soft, like a cat landing silently.

"Hello, dear. Talking to yourself again?" She was around forty. She sounded so sweet, even from the first word. I felt a tinge of guilt for stealing away what she thought was almost a son. Just as I felt it, she continued, "Well, good news. He's super busy this afternoon selling another one of your pieces. He is going to be gone all night, so I can get out the chess board and try to…Darling, what's wrong?"

He shuddered a little. I could tell he was about to cry. He swallowed, "I can't play chess tonight, Darla."

"Oh, I see. Big artists never rest, right, dear?"

There was no easy way to tell her. And then I decided that I should. So I stood up from where I was hiding, slowly.

I startled her, but not enough to make her scream, and in the instant when she was about to ask who I was, she stopped short.

"He thought maybe we'd play a different game," I said, my eyes filling with instant sympathy for her.

"What game did you have in mind?" she asked, slightly shaky.

I smiled as I said it. "Hide and seek?"

She smiled, looking at Gabriel with her warm brown eyes. "I always had hoped you would get to play that game one day."

He smiled as she grabbed him.

"He'll know it was you," Gabriel said, hugging her as she grasped him tighter.

"No, dear. He won't. I'll be fine. Remember, he can't punish me too much. He can't accuse me. No one knows that you exist, so how can you go missing?"

That seemed to calm Gabriel down, but I could tell she was lying. Her look of challenge hit me. The look said, *"I'm about to die for him, so you had better save him."*

I knew she couldn't say anything aloud, so I mouthed, "I will."

I told myself to etch this moment in my memory. I wanted to remember her holding him, kissing the top of his head, and making sure his medicine was in his bag. Her movements reminded me so much of my mother, it made me feel sick for the need of her and jealous of him for a moment. She pulled him close one more time before opening the door to the alley.

We moved past all the paintings, this time running past the beauty.

By the time we had reached the alley, the tears had dried.

Mortal danger pushed out the grief. And I needed it to.

We had traveled down the alley. Dusk was falling around us, but I realized as we traveled nearly ten blocks, anonymity didn't matter. No one had ever seen him. They had always seen what he could do, but had no idea who he was. His eyes met mine and I could tell what he was thinking.

He was invisible to them, as was I. There was no reason to skulk around corners and alleys when you were hidden much better in plain sight. All the same, even as we walked on the open streets, every time the media report came on or Palmer's face appeared on a screen, my heart drove punches into my chest and I found it hard to breathe.

We were on 20th Street when he stopped. Unexplainably. Without indication. I almost reached into his bag for his medicine when I saw what had drawn his gaze to the store window.

His work.

His soul in water and color, on a canvas that told a story no one saw. I saw it, through the reflection of the glass, our figures cast against his work: our reflections surrounded by the art.

"You know what's funny?" he choked out. "I didn't name it."

I looked to the left corner, and quickly tried to hide my shuddered breath as he continued.

"That whole time I was locked up there, thinking I was invisible. Not only did anyone never see me, but they never knew what I saw in my paintings. They couldn't know why I painted them. But I guess I wasn't as invisible as I thought."

I kept staring, hopefully still without suspicion, at the name of the piece painted in the right-hand corner.

Release me.

Three days later, I lurched awake for the third time that night, only to find him asleep. He was sleeping. I was awake thinking of Darla. Thinking of the consequences she would face if she was found out. I even remembered the code, not that there would be much need for the code– not with Gabriel stolen.

I felt horrible for leaving her there, wondering at her lonely days and lonelier nights. All for the sake of saving him, so he would be...

I panicked for a moment. Safe? Free? I wondered at what parents he would have, and if they would understand him. I wondered at how long he would be at the shelter.

I briefly thought about my own consequences. He was well over the age limit. He was ten. I wondered if I could use his innocent eyes and younger figure to pull off a younger age. I hoped I wouldn't have to pay for that. That it wouldn't hurt. But that wasn't what hurt most right now.

I couldn't quite escape the feeling that I had left something behind. That was when I realized that this had been my first mission where I hadn't seen Alex, although I was thankful in a way for its simplicity. But I missed not being able to ask Alex the flurry of questions I had for him. I found my mind yearning for an answer to at least one question, so the ghosts of uncertainty wouldn't haunt me. They woke me up from another nightmare about ten minutes before dawn.

I stared at the blanket below me, feeling the pine needles and dirt hit my hand as I reached out to stabilize myself. I glanced back at Gabriel, hoping to get a quick check on him, still sleeping in his sleeping bag.

But he wasn't sleeping.

"What's wrong?" I asked. I felt out of breath.

"Nothing. What were you dreaming about?" He didn't look at me. He was still watching the stars, even as they disappeared into the sky, swallowed up by the light of the rising sun.

"A nightmare I sometimes have. It's never that I die. It's that I'm alive, but I'm not able to see anyone."

"Like Collin?" he asked.

I paused with fear, even as I tried to create a cover story.

"He's my trainer. He'd feel like he failed if I didn't come home, or if I died…He's a friend, in a way."

"So…you're not supposed to love him, then?"

I felt embarrassed for getting called out by a ten-year-old I had barely known. Maybe it was because some thoughts about Collin in the café had almost distracted me from ever noticing the artist, which meant I had almost missed Gabriel. But he deserved the truth I couldn't give to anyone else.

"No. No, I'm not."

He gazed at me, like he understood something I didn't.

"It's okay. I can keep a secret," he said with a mischievous grin. "I've been one long enough. Feels like I should be good at it."

"Thank you."

I laid back down, curling up. He kept staring up at the stars, not wanting to miss anything. And I realized for a few seconds that I was in danger of selfish thoughts, or at least it felt that way.

"So, when do we have to leave?" he said, looking up at where the stars were now fading fast.

"Well, we don't have to leave now. Why do you ask?"

"I wish I didn't have to go anywhere. It's funny, because I always had to stay in the same room. But I feel like I could stay here forever."

I mentally cursed at the Republic for making such a beautiful soul and then emotionally draining him.

But I wasn't going to drain him anymore.

"You know, Gabriel, we have the tents. It's clear weather. How would you like to be free? For just a little bit longer?"

There was a smile from him that would mesmerize me for the days that followed. It captured me as we saw each sunrise. It grew as he watched bugs crawl. He pulled the petals off of flowers. He spent our rest time sketching in the dirt and making shapes out of pine needles.

I was ruined some hours, thinking through doubts and regrets. Thinking about Collin. Thinking about how Zander would punish Gabriel for being saved by me. I was destroyed by impatient worry, thinking I should be rushing back, calling for an EE so I could go save someone else. I needed to save someone else.

But I realized that in a strange way, I was still saving him.

Days passed, and I let them become memories instead of regrets.

We had checked in the fourth day. It had hurt to not hear Sam or Liam on the other side. Michael had been off duty when I had called, so it felt like it wasn't coming home as it had been before. It felt like home was missing something– not just me.

So when I finally did hear Michael's voice days later, it took me a second to respond. I was breathing out in relief and yet, in that moment, I agonized about how to tell them that Gabriel was ten. I had debated telling the truth for days.

"Aislyn, you there?" Michael asked, sounding a little rushed.

"Yeah, why?" Without even telling him what I was supposed to tell him, I worried for the many reasons he may be hurried.

"No worries. There's a few shuttles picking up Megan and Tessa already. I'd like to get you in the same group."

"Well, I have a nine-year-old, so if he'll fit, we can make it work."

There was silence.

I was in trouble.

There was a sigh followed by "umm" and more anxious sounds, then a gradually intense whisper, "Pick up, pick up, pick up."

"You're thinking Patterson isn't going to be happy?"

"Not exactly; he's already knee-deep in something else from Tessa's report, so no, but…"

"Patterson here, I am not…"

"It's Michael. I have…a….227-4C."

There was a pause, and then an exhausted tone: "Aislyn?"

"Sir, he's nine-years-old. That's all."

"Aislyn, don't lie," he sounded like he didn't want to be messed with at all today.

"Okay, he's about to be ten."

"Aislyn, that is almost two year–"

"He's been locked up for three of them anyway! The Society couldn't have influenced him if he was stuck in a room working all day. It's not like he's their biggest fan."

There was silence. Then Patterson said, "Wait, what are you saying? Why was he was locked in a room for three years?"

"He's a painter. Someone found him about to be disappeared, and stuck him in a room to paint for him. Made a fortune."

There was a horrible moment when I was scared the silence that followed my logic meant they weren't going to take him.

But then Michael said, "That is sick. That is so…"

"Sick is the nice word," Patterson said. "Alright, you bring him in. I'll have hell to pay again, but I'll pay it…again. Oh, and you don't talk to Tessa. Period. I'm working on it."

I unhooked my MCU and earpiece, retracted it, and stood up, the silence of the woods seeming so strange after the intensity of the call. I didn't even realize that Gabriel had moved only a few feet away from me.

"So, I'm nine again. That's fun."

"Sorry. We have a rule."

"I get it."

But all of a sudden he seemed nervous. He asked a few more questions he had already asked. And I think we both realized that we were avoiding the real issue.

"I'm too old. You're afraid no one will want to take me home, aren't you?"

His lower lip trembled for a second, and he began to blink rapidly. I moved to sit next to him, and stared at him until he was ready to look at me. But the moment wasn't coming. So I thought of what I could say.

"You know, there are some people who will not take you even though they can. But I think what matters most…is that one family will. You only need one family to give you all the love you need."

He looked at me then. He was nodding, but then he began to cry softly. I put my arm around him until the tears faded into short spurts. He started breathing more evenly, although I did have to give him the inhaler once. He slowly kicked the dandelions at his feet, the small fuzzes flying and then disappearing, looking as invisible as he felt.

We reached the rendezvous point for the shuttle. I felt the urgency to give him one more piece of advice. "You know, Gabriel, you shouldn't discount or ignore the people who do value you just because not everyone does. I made that mistake once. I thought I was invisible. One of the girls who saw me…" I had to swallow for a second, "Her name was Lynn. I was so busy trying to be noticed or praised by other people, I didn't appreciate the way she saw me. I'd give anything to have her see me again."

Just then the shuttle came up. I held my breath, but to my relief, Will got out with Eric, who I didn't know well.

"Didn't catch the name, young man," Will was smiling as he reached us, and held out his hand.

"Gabriel," he said, holding Will's hand.

"Awesome name." Will continued, even as Eric hung back a bit. "Just a second, we're shuffling a bit."

There was a second shuttle. Will explained, "We quickly realized not everyone was going to fit, so Protectors on one, Unnecessaries and Vessels on the other. Gabriel, you're going to meet a new friend or two, okay? And I want to hear about this art! I love art."

"Okay," he nodded, remembering what I said would happen. He gave me a quick hug and said a quick goodbye.

"So, have you ever ridden in one of these?" Eric asked.

"I haven't been outside since I was six, so…a long time ago."

To my relief Eric said, "That's okay! You'll catch on quick."

As Cassidy and Tessa exited, I knew something was wrong. And I was willing to bet that Tessa not meeting my eyes had nothing to do with me, and everything to do with her.

Will nodded for Eric to go with us. We quickly got in, strapped in the seats. I was facing Cassidy, letting Eric have the job of facing off with Tessa on the way home, dealing with whatever issue she currently was steaming over.

To my relief, Will kept talking to Gabriel, and the last thing we had heard before the door sealed was, "That's a baby? It has hair!"

I grinned, and Cassidy laughed as Eric shook his head. Even Emily smiled, which I noticed as she looked back. It wasn't until after she yelled, "Moving" that I thought to ask.

"Are they going straight…"

"To the shelter, yeah. They want to get him settled, and they have a few questions. You already said enough goodbyes, and the babies just need to be placed– well along with the Vessel."

Tessa was still staring at some random splotch on the floor. It wasn't until I was staring at it that I realized what it was. And even as the thought made me want to ask whose blood it was, I recognized the placement of it.

Eric leaned in towards me. "Emily, I think you might have picked the wrong shuttle to put the Protectors in."

"I'm not going to get all bent out of shape. I know what my own blood looks like," I said, even though I was slightly nauseous.

Then a tension rose as Eric said calmly, "And blood's okay, right? We should all be calm and collected about spilling it."

He stared at Tessa, as if they were continuing a conversation.

"I understand killing the one, but why the second?"

"I don't know; at that point it didn't seem to matter, and I knew I couldn't get caught."

"So what happened after they were down?" Emily asked as I was frantically trying to catch a greater hint of what was going on.

"The one came in to help, found them dead, and then called for a medic. He left quickly. Maybe he'd never seen anyone die before, or at least not someone he considered to be alive."

I was now getting a clearer picture of what had happened, and Tessa still wasn't meeting my glaze as I addressed her.

"You killed two officers?" I asked, not taking the time to filter who on the shuttle agreed or disagreed with Zander.

"I should've known you'd have an opinion about that, 27, but no one is going to tell me what I should or shouldn't have done. I had a newborn and a mother who was dying and... I made a choice, and it doesn't matter to me that yours might have been different."

It wasn't what I was expecting from her, but I was inclined to be a bit more understanding. If I was protecting a newborn...

"And I already feel like I messed up again," she said, grief saturating her words.

She had a look in her eyes that I hadn't seen since that night in the forest. She seemed terrified, and yet all her anger boiled.

"Then why did you do it?" I asked, hoping those words weren't the trigger that would set her off.

"I'm not like you. I still need to be on Zander's good side."

"What– after all that we went through that night, and after all of that…" I wanted to say 'hell,' but kept going. "You didn't learn that what they– Avery, the council, Hannah– think doesn't matter? Why are you still chasing this illusive, perfect version of–"

She interrupted me, half angry and half exasperated.

"I learned too late! But now…" She paused, as if she wasn't sure she wanted to tell me. "Don't you get it? I'm on probation. I don't have the luxury of ignoring them and irritating them. I have to listen to everything they have to say, or I don't get to do this anymore– redeeming myself or saving just a few lives so I can sleep at night. Not that I thought you'd understand. You're too immature to know what I'm dealing with."

"They're using you?" I asked her, more from a concern for our situation than for her, but as I saw her jaw shudder, and her breath stagger for just a moment, she answered.

"I know they are. And there's nothing I can do about it."

She looked as if she didn't want to argue, or even say another word. Maybe because I still annoyed her or somehow infuriated her, I felt a guilt, a heaviness press on my chest. Emily was the one who finally spoke to stop the awkward silence.

"Okay, look. I know where both of you stand, but frankly, I don't care. Facts are facts; besides, Tessa did save a baby and mother, Aislyn, who deserve to live much more than a few Sentries."

"Sentries?" I asked, and then quickly retracted anything but a look of surprise and tried to fake a look of confusion. "I thought you said police?"

"Nope, you said police. Sentries. What, are you going to shock me by pretending to be impressed now?" Tessa said.

I willed my face to stay calm. My heart was screaming, bleeding, crying. There were only 40 Sentries. If she had killed two...

The only hope we had to break through an enemy line could be dead.

The boy who saved my life could be dead.

Someone who dared to kiss me could be dead.

"Maybe," I said. I had to pretend to be something, because falling over myself in panic was not an option.

For a moment, I wished I were Gabriel and could be locked in a room alone. If I were locked away from anyone, I could scream as loud as I wanted to.

But instead, I was free.

And being free meant I had to hide everything I felt.

CHAPTER 9

I was thankful for the little time I was allowed to be in a room alone. I had time to panic, shaking as I waited for 30 minutes in my room for my debrief. I thought back to the first time I was in this room, when Collin was there. But the door didn't open this time. I realized there was almost no way it was going to. I spent the long minutes looking at the floor. With every second, it seemed less likely Collin would make it in before Patterson. The room became loud with silence, the air seeming thicker as the minutes crept by until finally the door jostled. It opened an inch, and I was expecting Patterson, but instead, Michael stepped in.

"Michael?"

"Hey, 27. So, the other girls are taking a while. He thought you should recharge with some food after the journey since much of yours was on foot."

One of Zander's assistants held a tray with milk and toast with jam, as well as yogurt and eggs.

"Thank you, Michael. Thank Patterson, too." I didn't mention Collin. I think that was why we were playing the pronoun game.

"He's quite relieved that you are back safely. We good?"

"Well, I was talking to Tessa, about the Sentries she took down…you know…I probably shouldn't be talking about it."

Michael looked at me. He looked scared, but said nonchalantly, "Good call, 27. We shouldn't discuss the Sentries."

He hadn't known either. I could tell by his face, as he backed up looking at me, nodding slowly. He turned to leave the room slowly, almost too obviously controlling his actions.

I moved to the tray. I quickly lifted one of the plates to find a single rose petal underneath. I felt it as I lifted up, fighting off the regret that I couldn't hold Collin yet. I swallowed the regret to hold the petal, remembering love was real and that would be enough.

Despite the fact that the meal was a gesture to hide a sign of affection, it was a sign of affection in and of itself. I had eaten most of it when Patterson entered. His expression was strained, different, and within a few more steps, I knew why.

His steps were followed by Zander's.

"Sir. Ma'am." I decided I should be extremely respectful, not knowing how to address this new development, and feeling a little uneasy for having another breach in protocol to report.

"Ah, looks like Michael brought you your food. Sorry, Margaret, couldn't have her starving in here for an hour. Please, sit Aislyn."

I moved slowly to the chair, my eyes on Zander, but keeping Patterson in view. I was looking for any sign of reassurance, finding my thoughts lost in an abyss of uncertainty, because no proof of reassurance was on Patterson's face. Instead, he began to explain.

"Aislyn, Secretary Zander is going to be interviewing everyone for debrief. Every time. She is very interested in your first reactions, first facts, all that....What's most important is that I want the facts from you without fear of repercussion for your violation of code. We discuss that after the debrief."

Zander looked interested as Patterson spoke, and said, "Indeed." But even as she agreed and I started, I was thankful for the cryptic warning underneath.

There was nothing to hide, despite the fact that I continued to lie about Gabriel's age. With his short stature, no one seemed to be questioning that. Zander looked at me once in a while and took notes. I added very little emotion, but shared what I felt at the time.

"Well," Zander started. "I do want you to realize that this is a breach in protocol, bringing back someone so old."

I started, "But considering the root of the meaning in the law… how is saving someone who has been locked up since seven different than saving someone who is seven? They haven't been influenced by the Society Party."

"Yes, well, you can't pity everyone. And you are not up to interpreting the meaning of the laws. You follow them. Clear?"

She shuffled some papers as Patterson said, "But Margaret, maybe you can look past her mistake and use this story, focusing on the real issue at hand, which is the Republic using children as slave workers even if they aren't SubTerra."

Zander, for once, looked annoyed at being pandered to, but her mind was also working. "Yes, perhaps. Let's focus the press conference on that, and not on Aislyn's…unnecessary bravery."

"You would rather I have less bravery, ma'am?" I asked, despite a warning look from Patterson.

"There's no need to pursue such strange cases or difficult circumstances. If you were less brave, you'd probably have a

Vessel, as you are the only one without one right now. Don't be so caught up in being a legend that you forget who you are."

She left the room. Something about her words bothered me, even though I didn't know if I would change a thing about who I rescued or why. Patterson nodded towards the door, and even I got the sense that we couldn't talk openly.

I got the hint I think he was sending as I said, "So I'd rather go for a run, if I could. And then clean up. Is that okay?"

"Great idea; it's a way to ensure you're pushing yourself." And then he nodded to one of Zander's assistants, "Done. I'm going to be out of Central for a while, running interference…"

I didn't hear the rest. I left out the other door. I was in the central hallway when I saw him with George and the others.

I already knew he had been kept from me, and I already had an idea of what was supposed to happen next.

"Collin?"

His hands reached out to me to grab my shoulders, but stayed rigid, not pulling me in closer. There he stood, an arm's length away. He was reaching out only to block me from hugging him, which I knew I couldn't do. I felt his hands shaking on my shoulders as I started, "I need to know…"

"Not now…whatever it is, it'll have to wait. Gabriel…"

"He's amazing, Collin," I told him as his eyes lit up. Despite everything, there was no reason to hide his excitement about my return with an Unnecessary, and I found myself lost in that moment of celebrating the soul we knew had survived.

"I'm going for a run, actually, so I will have to see you later," I said very matter-of-factly, my eyes hopefully communicating what urgency and hint were needed.

"Okay, great idea. I'll hang out until you're done."

He nodded, as I ran off. And I ran. I enjoyed feeling like I could be free from everyone, think anything, as long as I was out here. But when I was in my second mile, I stopped, as if my thoughts held too much weight for me to continue. I felt as if everything that had just happened should have cost me something, and maybe I shouldn't run from it. It needed to hit me, affect me, so I could have my freak-out when I was alone. But I found myself catching my breath, staying calm, still.

I wondered if I was stronger than I thought. Or maybe I was just getting better at hiding what I felt. But I was shaken by the fact that I was back in the Circles. It made the shift in our objective feel heavier.

I got to the second Central. I ran down the stairs, thinking how odd it was that the real Central had been turned into a battle station, and this one had become the haven: our strange sanctuary.

And there Collin stood, five feet away. So much stood in the space that filled the gap between us, but it was as if he reduced it to ashes in a second with just the few steps it took to reach me. He grasped the back of my head and crushed it into his chest as he whispered into my ear. I'm not sure what he was saying. It was nonsensical affirmations.

But his voice, the very tone and breath hitting my ear as his arms wrapped around me, told me everything I needed to know.

Because eventually, the whispers I couldn't determine all became, "I love you."

I finally felt him release just enough for me to maneuver my arms out to hug him back. He spoke again, leaving me breathless.

"You know, sometimes I think I don't know how we're going to make this work. Sometimes I believe the voices I hear saying we don't have a chance. Any chance for us…is growing impossibly small. But when I'm holding you, I can't imagine not taking it. I'll always take it."

My heart was pounding, but I didn't speak. I didn't have to. I leaned in, until his breath was close enough to hit my lips. Even as his forehead grazed mine, even as he pulled me in, even as his lips hovered for a second before pressing mine, I realized how small the chance was. But this was just another chance. We took it.

It could have been minutes or forever until he let go. Not that it felt like he was letting go. He was still looking at me, the calm blue of his eyes keeping me feeling close to him.

"It was a brilliant tactic," he smiled, almost laughing, "leaving in the middle of the meeting." But then he looked somber, biting his lip before continuing, "Only…you can't break the rules again. Zander will have your head. Or mine."

"Well, I don't try to break the rules. It's just that my trainer was in his first year and isn't experienced," I said, feeling like I had succeeded in making him smile.

But I couldn't smile back.

"I need to know…was it Alex?"

I thought he would know, but his confusion unnerved me. Then, Michael burst through the door, jumping down the stairs.

"We were told it was police, not Sentries, and then when you said that… I finally got Tessa's dumb handler to talk and then I had to find an excuse to get away."

"What are you talking about?" Collin asked, looking back at me.

I answered, even though I wished my voice was steadier. "It was two Sentries that she killed, not police."

"Are you serious?" Collin responded, and then looked at me in terror. "Who were they?"

"I don't know," Michel started, "but it was warehouse district–"

"Was he still stationed there?" Collin asked.

"Yes," he said, glancing over at me. "I'm checking now…"

He was concentrating all of his energy on hacking in, I knew it. I also knew panicking now wouldn't help, but I felt vomit rise and my heart beat louder. I ran my fingers through my hair, thinking of how I had done that when I was nervous as a child. Collin moved to hold me my hand so Michael couldn't see it was shaking. It jolted as the door opened.

I heard Patterson's voice an instant after the door closed.

"Tell me he's alive."

"Working on it," Michael said. "I've got the first name. Not him. I'm checking the other records now."

"Just check the field report, not the coroner's office," Patterson ordered, looking at the screen. He then came over to us. I didn't even bother letting go of Collin's hand, as it didn't seem to matter and was the only thing holding it still.

Collin was about to talk when Michael said, "Aislyn?"

I couldn't decipher his tone. But then he smiled.

"He's alive. It wasn't him."

I breathed out relief, though confusion quickly took hold.

"We do know why Tessa probably wasn't caught. He was the Sentry who found the downed agents. He reported they had been dead for ten minutes when he combed the area. He must have known otherwise. He might have even saw Tessa, if she caught a glimpse of him, but he let her go."

We had all jumped down to the middle level to look at several of the screens displaying surveillance from the incident.

"There is no footage of the incident directly, or the whole Republic would have seen it by now as the Society would have continued to warn its subjects that Protectors are dangerous, horrible people who kill Sentries and steal babies…"

But I had already turned from the screen. I didn't want them to see my relief, although I didn't know why. Maybe I just didn't want Collin to see how much I cared. But he saw. The look on his face wasn't that much different.

"It still should bring an interesting response from them. I'm surprised there hasn't been a broadcast yet."

"There is going to be. There's chatter to suggest it's going to be tonight, and rumor is Palmer was at the studio earlier. Bet Zander's going to love that, or hate it. But she has a response already recorded, too. So the two teams have prepared for their scrimmage, and all we can do is watch."

Collin asked, "What are you thinking. Aislyn?"

"Something Zander said…I just was wondering…"

"Look, don't listen to a word Zander said," Patterson said.

"How did Zander see her already?" Collin sounded shocked.

"Starting today, she's in debriefs with me. New orders."

"What did she say?" Collin asked, as if he knew the one thing that could distract me from worry was anger.

"She said if I wasn't so worried about finding special cases, I'd probably have saved a Vessel by now. And that I was selfish."

I trailed off. Patterson quickly responded, "It doesn't matter, Aislyn. You do overthink. You do make sure you run into special situations. You were meant to be a legend. We wouldn't all be standing here hoping a Sentry was alive if you weren't."

"Speaking of a Sentry…" Michael began. "So, I checked the alley. This is thirty minutes later after the incident with police and Sentries cleaning up, and this is the footage from the café across the street. This is Alex, on a phone, alive and well."

"Stop!" Collin called out.

"What?" Michael stopped typing. "This isn't live, and I'm already out of the hack." Then Michael looked up in panic, as if maybe Collin had heard someone coming.

"No, look." Collin pointed to the screen. "He looks right at the camera and says something."

"Whoa," Michael said, shocked, and then turned to me. "Does Alex know how we do intel?"

"I've held up my deal, Patterson," I said. "I haven't told him anything about operations, but he has to know we'd do intel after an attack like this. Or he guessed that we would." I specifically looked at Patterson, making him sure I wasn't lying.

But then I turned to Collin to ask him, "Why are you asking?"

Collin looked unsure, but then he turned to Michael and said, "I think he tried to send us a message."

We all were still, but then he continued, "Okay, if a Protector killed Sentries, and he assumes we are going to check intel, or check on him, he assumed we would have seen this."

"What did he–?"

"He looks at the camera, then while on the phone, calls it, and…I'm just guessing here…" he paused, looked at the camera, and then zoomed in. "Here. He says your name, I swear."

On the screen, he stared at the camera, said something short into the phone, pocketed the phone and then stared at the camera again.

"What did he say?"

"Visper…Vesper…Vertigo…Wow, I'm bad at this."

"No, there's four syllables for the first word."

Collin was squinting. "Vinalia? The Vinalia Ball?"

Michael shook his head. "That is all kinds of dangerous."

Patterson answered my unspoken question as I turned.

"It's an Elite and Citizens-only party to mark the beginning of the most elaborate month of summer, based on wine festivals centuries ago. It's on the 19th of August. But this…"

Collin said, "We're going to have to find a way to prepare you for every possible dance in the next month."

"Until then, we keep this amongst ourselves. Aislyn, we need you to try to get in contact with him sometime between now and then. We'll have to try to make sure that's what he meant."

Patterson's watch beeped.

"Palmer is on now. Just more warnings. Looks like…"

Michael said, "I got it…"

Palmer's image appeared on the big screen in the room. Patterson yelled, "Don't stay too long, Collin. I'm leaving."

Michael darted a look at Collin as he shut down all but a few monitors. "Later. I'll be done in ten."

Palmer continued, showing the pictures of the two Sentries and describing their deaths as being inhumane and torturous, and then showing a friend of the Vessel, or "third victim."

"You see," her friend said sobbing, "it all started when she got pregnant. She was so concerned about it, and she didn't want to deal with it and move on with her life. I wish someone had been there to talk her out of it. They're gone, but the Sentries are dead. How can someone claim to save us, but kill people like that?"

Palmer continued to emphasize the savageness of the attack, of course completely ignoring the fact that the Republic killed infants and children every day; that somehow killing the Sentries had been more barbaric than killing the mother and baby would have been. Then he was asked by the person interviewing them, "What message would you send these Protectors if you could, sir?"

I stared at him intently, as he was now addressing me.

"To those of you who think you are saving the lives entrusted to us, you forget the most important thing: it's entrusted to us. We know what's best to ensure our happiness and freedom, which is the most vital goal of any people. And since you have stolen that sense of freedom and peace that everyone benefits from, from Elites to Terras, you have given us no choice but to retaliate. As I've stated, it will not be a cost you are able to pay without pain."

The transmission ended. Static replaced the screen's black void within a few seconds. It looked like it was a storm, full of fear and doubt. It felt like a mirror.

I might have felt more emotionally out of control if not for the pictures in my mind of Amanda, Katerina, André, Collin, and Gabriel– without the touch of their little hands in mine, the hopes for their future, the sound of their giggles. And the last tether holding me down from being swept up into the storm was a single hand, reaching out to hold mine, seemingly clasping to the very life in me while I sensed he was about to say words that would propel me to leave again.

My eyes looked to Collin, but returned to the screen as he slipped away. I heard his steps echo up to the door.

It was the first time I had been alone with Michael since he had asked about Alex earlier. Even as he began replaying the message, I caught the intensity of Alex's gaze through the camera feed.

"What are you looking for?" I asked, not wanting to watch.

"It's not what I'm looking for, it's what I think I'm finding. What I think I'm discovering the more I study this. The one thing that never tracked for me."

"What's that?" I asked, nervousness creeping up on me.

"Motive. Even with his sister and his government killing innocents, he shouldn't have enough motive to continue to help you. Yet he does. I had a thought...I think I might know what his motive is, however misplaced and repulsive you may find it. I figured it out. Only I'm afraid to tell you, especially now."

He couldn't have guessed what Alex had said.

"Well, actually, I think you'd hit me if I told you why I think he might be helping you. Well, you specifically." He tried to be light, yet he was still nervous, as if he was trying to work up the courage to tell me his theory. He looked up at me, as if he was about to drop a bomb.

But instantly, his expression changed into a suspicious curiosity as he saw my expression shift from curiosity to vulnerability. And I must have looked vulnerable, because my lip was trembling until I bit down on it.

"And here I thought Alex might still be keeping his secret," he sighed, turning off the monitors. "He didn't keep it, did he?"

"No." I looked at him, feeling exposed, like maybe he was going to see something he didn't like.

Michael shook. "I didn't just order you to kill someone who saved your life; I ordered you to kill a man in love with you."

I looked at him, acknowledging the truth I thought no one could ever guess with a slight nod.

"Yes, you did," I spoke, but then smiled a mischievous grin as I felt the boldness of that statement sink in. "But don't forget what I told you that night, Michael."

He looked at me intriguingly with a skewed smile at my words when I repeated them.

"I'm horrible at following orders."

CHAPTER 10

"What was it like to be in the room of a master artist?"

We were in the woods. It was the only place we could hide. I technically was on a run. Michael had set up Collin's MCU with a slave drive to his CU in his room, so someone would guess he was in there. Michael hadn't been too thrilled about it, but he had agreed. I was wondering if he was 'secret-weary,' if there was such a thing.

"I had never seen so much color or beauty in one place," I finally answered, while at the same time amazed at the colors around me.

"What made you think that he was in there?" Collin asked.

"You know, he asked me the same thing. The truth is, I could tell the instant I saw the paintings that they were made by a child. Everything about them screamed innocence and the brush strokes were made by a child." I was mesmerized then by the promise I made him. "How long do you think before they'll let him paint?"

"Well, don't you think he wants a break?" Collin asked, still typing furiously.

"He got upset when they took it all away even when he was trying to fight for his own basic right to freedom. No, I don't think he wants much of a break."

"If he doesn't get to paint for a few weeks, he'll survive. He has a whole new world to discover before he paints it, doesn't he?"

I smiled, thinking of him on the way home, not bored at all, taking in every piece of natural beauty surrounding him.

"Yeah, I suppose," I said, noticing Collin's calm gaze again.

"There's a lot of the real world to catch up on. He'll be fine. Trust me, I should know," Collin said, stopping typing for a second.

"What do you mean?"

"That's how I felt when I met you. All I knew was this: rules, objectives, following orders, workouts. And while I had a different idea for how training should happen, it was still…only this. No stories, no dreaming, no love."

He stared at me, through the haze in the forest. I was wondering how long this could last despite the moment lengthening.

"And what did you learn from a silly thing called love?"

He sighed, and said, "That it's harder than I thought. It's stronger than I thought, too. It's a storm. A beautiful storm."

The silence deepened, until the slightest breeze broke it. My hair flew in front of my eyes, still glued to his. I feel like I could see that storm more, and before I had a chance to ask, another storm had drawn him back into his work, and he was typing again.

I smiled at that, but wished I could throw his device across the forest. "So, what are you up to?"

"Some data collection and stories. I'm trying to prove something that will convince some members of the council to drop this initiative to attack Zander."

"Why not mention Zander's crazy revenge plot?"

"What?" he said, looking confused.

"Eva seems to think, but isn't telling any of us, why Zander is so angry at them." I said, looking as he shrugged.

"She's always seemed angry, but other than the obvious…"

"What obvious?"

"She's not married. She doesn't have kids. And she doesn't let anyone ask her about it, either."

He looked at me knowingly.

"She can't take the Shield Vaccine, so the serum…"

I found myself unable to answer the sentence, but even as it was difficult to talk about the weapon of infertility the Society had wielded against us, I was defensive.

"That's no excuse. There are healthier ways of dealing with it, isn't there? Look at Brie! She's a Protector who uses her skill and channels her anger into something productive, risking her life and…and she's….she's convinced she'll never have a life that's worth more than her death, and taking unnecessary risks because she doesn't want to live past her pain." I slowly realized I had talked myself into a corner and my argument was defeated.

Collin sighed and said in a weary sarcastic tone, "Yeah, there's a healthy example of coping."

I put my face in my hands, trying not to think about it. "Tell me someone else has talked to Brie about this."

"We've all talked to Brie about this. And we've all promised to keep talking. For the record, though, about Zander, I think it's something more than just another irrational response to a Shield vaccine issue. Whatever it is, Hannah knows. But no one–no one– gets her to talk."

I thought of Hannah briefly, and that brought my thoughts back to Central, to everyone, including her daughter, who might still be on missions. I was more curious about their fates than Zander.

"Who all is back, by the way?"

"Well, Eva is still out. So are Cassidy and Lydia. Both of them have checked in."

He went on, listing names. I was glad to hear Bethany had come back okay, recovering from her near miss with some Police. But I noticed he seemed nervous all of a sudden, and it wasn't until I remembered his first sentence that I said, "Wait."

He looked at me, repeating whatever he had said about Abigail as I interrupted, "No. You said Eva is still out and both Cassidy and Lydia have checked in. You didn't say that Eva did."

I stopped, seeing the look on his face drop, as if he had failed in his strategy to avoid lying, but also avoid the harsh truth.

Eva hadn't checked in. He wouldn't have been setting his jaw so tight if he wasn't stopping it from shaking.

"Two days. She missed today, just ten minutes ago. It's okay, though. You missed two days. You've missed two days twice now. It just…it doesn't mean…"

He stopped, right when I needed him to continue. I had never realized how scared I could be for her until now. Even in the warehouse, I knew there were Protectors dying, but my ignorance allowed me the hope of saying that she might be okay. Now I knew she was in trouble. She was the only one who hadn't checked in.

"You worry about her," I began to ask Collin, but it came out more like a statement.

He raised his eyebrow. "Not a lot of other people do, at least not in the right way. They worry when she doesn't perform or isn't excelling at something. They worry about her being where she shouldn't be. They never worry because they care."

There was a suspicion growing in my mind. He saw it in my eyes, but then he blinked and turned his head away. He became entranced by some shoots of grass by my foot.

"You don't have to talk about it," I said, already recognizing a look of pain I had only seen a few times and confirming a theory that I had guessed a month ago.

She had lost her father on a mission.

He had lost his mother on a mission.

"They, um…" he started, and then paused. "Her dad was actually on the follow-up mission, to try to find out what had happened to her. There was a…um…code word she had left behind. 'The basement,' I think it was, along with the words, 'still alive.' So it was some mixed-up combination of that."

"The basement?" I asked, never hearing the phrase before.

"Yeah. It was those phrases, repeated. They said she was shot and bleeding out…so she was disoriented. She was–"

"Collin, don't…please, don't."

I trailed off my short plea for him to stop describing his mother's death, but he nodded as he continued, "We found out about a decade later that the 'Basement' is a term they use for all of their intel. The Basement moves. It's never at one location. And whichever base hosts the intel, for that month, is called the

Basement. He investigated it, went after it. And that was how…"

"He died."

Collin closed his MCU.

"The first time I ever met Eva, I told her I owed her an apology. The first word I ever said to her was 'Sorry,' and it wasn't enough. Because she didn't remember her dad because she was too young. But I did," he said, running his hands through his hair before starting again. "Because I was seven. He came to see us the day before he left. He looked me in the eye, on one knee, and promised he would find out what happened to my mom. And I begged him to find out what happened. I begged him to…do anything…"

He looked overrun with guilt. I would've hugged him if I didn't think he might push me away. So instead I just said, "You were just a boy. You wanted answers."

He bit his lip. "That's what Eva said. But I knew she hated me for a while. Until one day, she rushed up to me….and punched me."

"Effective," I said, almost laughing through growing tears.

"Apparently," he said, but in a different tone. "She threw in a few more punches before collapsing and crying. I hugged her. We both cried. I congratulated her on beating up a 14-year-old boy. And then, we were friends. Have been ever since."

I looked at him, lost in the story and its strange beauty, but wishing he had happier memories to tell me about.

"That was the first time I was responsible for someone dying. That night when I talked about it, Avery said that meant I would be a great trainer, if I could live with that."

I stared through the pain he was feeling. "Tell me your hot-headed 14-year-old-self punched him in the nose."

He shook his head, smiling.

"No. George held me back, but then he punched him."

"George? Really?"

"Yeah, well Avery apprenticed under him then. When he heard he said that to me…"

"Wait, George mentored Avery?" I said, barely registering the fact that they had all trained together.

"Yeah, I know!" Collin said. "Mentoring doesn't mean he could solve Avery's issues— not that Avery would say he had any. He's fitting in fine now."

I sighed, once again realizing just how vast the world I stood on was, even as he said, "We should head out."

I thought about her, and couldn't help but smile.

"What?" he asked.

"She was 10 years old?" I asked.

He laughed, and nodded. "Well, someone told her afterwards that's how she knew she would make a great Protector. Not because she could beat someone up or because her mother was a Protector, or for any other reason. But she took a swing when it came to who she loved."

I looked at him again, suspicious, but smiling. "But she was 10 years old?"

He sighed, rolled his eyes, and said, "Let her gloat about it when she gets back. She loves telling that story. Let's go. You go to the left, I'll go right," he said, shifting his MCU to the side. "I can't come tonight. It's okay. I'll see you tomorrow, maybe."

Uncertainty was haunting him tonight. I could tell.

"Collin, what's wrong?"

"We're running out of time. I need to try to find a way to fight them, to prove that this is all worth it, to find the right words to say or the right angle…and I'm failing. I'm failing."

He stopped. For the second time tonight, his chest deflated, like it was hard to breathe because of the invisible weight on it.

"Are you going to be okay?" I asked, reaching up to shift his hair.

"That's usually my line, Aislyn," he said, biting his lip.

I looked at him. "It works both ways. And I'm not the only one who needs to know they aren't alone. And you're not."

"I know. But in a few more hours, I'll be back to trying to convince people that we can't win a war so we shouldn't start one. Aislyn, you couldn't imagine what we're up against, and there's only around twelve of us. I'm terrified I'm going to let my mother down; that I won't be able to make the choice she made, to give up everything…even you…to fight for what matters."

The scar where his fear had burned him was being revealed, and I could tell he wasn't feeling good about it. I said the words that had changed everything when he had said them to me.

"You should know that I'm on your side. I'm with you."

With that, I opened my eyes, only to see his glistening. He leaned his head, defeated on my shoulder. He breathed out his anxiety, even as I said over and over, "I'm with you."

A few seconds later, his watch beeped. I glanced down at the small display reading, "*three minutes until a meeting.*"

He reached up to me, holding my head with of both hands as he moved to kiss me, slowly. Something was different. It was more intense, maybe because he had felt scared to lose me maybe because he had let down barriers, but I found myself holding him after the kiss, more intensely than before. In the end, he wrenched himself away, looking back before running off and leaving me in the woods.

To wonder. To worry. To feel my lips burn. To feel flushed.

And to feel more lost than ever before, wondering if I was hurting or helping him. I was his mission and his distraction.

I went back to my Circle. It felt emptier than normal, but I didn't mind. I wanted it to be empty. Because even as I stood in the room, the one thing I needed was there. And it wasn't Collin. It wasn't Eva. And even though it broke my heart to be without them, and even Gabriel or Amanda or Katerina or the babies....

I needed to do the one thing I could do, what Eva had yet to do: find a better title for the revolution within the revolution.

I needed to write it down.

I wrote for hours. I wrote about Collin, Alex, Brie, Eva, and every Unnecessary I had saved. I etched every word to the page finding some solace in the scratch of the pen on paper, so that in any future after those moments writing, no one would ever miss the point of saving these souls. No one would confuse saving them as a mission that wasn't worth it. No one would mistake me for the hero. In the end, I was unsure of everything I had written. Unsure that maybe I had misjudged situations. Maybe out of fear of the future, maybe out of the need to get it all out, I kept writing into the evening until I placed the journal under my pillow, as my eyes closed out of exhaustion.

It felt dishonest to feel so many things to not tell anyone. I found my peace by writing it down, telling someone who didn't even exist yet. It didn't seem logical. It didn't seem like it would help.

But it did.

The dawn was pink, shards of high thin clouds lighting it up. It hurt as I turned my eyes from the sky, away and back to reality full of stone. But he was there on the threshold, which made it better.

"Hey, I brought you breakfast," Collin said, looking down at two plates on the tray inside my room. The one was half empty.

"Peckish?" I asked, as I got up, quickly.

"I only ate some of it, but yeah. Hope you are in the mood for pancakes, because I twisted some rules and got you some with blueberries from the garden."

"Thanks." I stared at him, wondering what I should say to get him to leave for a second. I needed a second.

"Um…I actually wouldn't mind changing first," I blurted out.

"Oh," he said. But he didn't move, as if he was in a trance, staring at me until I cleared my throat.

He jolted. "Oh, I'm leaving, I am definitely…I'm not interested in you…not that…you know." He looked flushed for a second, and then turned around and left, almost dropping the plate. He stomped his foot, and pushed his palm against his forehead.

I wondered if as we got to know each other more, loved each other more, if it would be more difficult for him to walk away, or for me to let him. But as he was in the med room, still embarrassed or ashamed ten minutes later, I thought maybe it was a good time to have a talk that was as awkward for me as it might be for him.

"I'm sorry…I don't know what–"

"Collin, is it okay that I kicked you out of the room?"

"Yes, absolutely, I don't want to be there. I mean, I do. But only if you want me there, and not that way. And I shouldn't have thought about you… someday…" Finally, he stopped, and looked at me. "You've got me more baffled than 13 Council members and the entire staff of trainers combined. I can't get a sentence out."

We both laughed for a second. He was still staring at the med table in front of him, not looking up until I began to speak.

"Collin, I don't need you to pretend that you don't want to stay. I sometimes wish you could, too. I think of that…someday. But I'm going to keep kicking you out when I need to change, and I'm going to admit when it's hard, on the days I wish I could be closer to you. So you can tell me–"

"It's hard." He said it, and then continued. "And when I think about the fact that we only have today, any maybe only a few hours, it's really hard not to want to be near you in every possible way. But yes, keep kicking me out. And we'll fight for the better story with the ending with you in white, and me waiting for you."

I nodded, almost breathless to think that far ahead as he moved forward, grabbing my hand to kiss it gently.

"Okay," he said, biting his lip, looking intently at me. "And I'll smoothly transition our conversation over to your itinerary."

"Good luck with that," I smiled. "Is Brie leaving today? I saw she got back last night, but my MCU is still in for updates."

"Well, you know her. She goes right back out, but maybe you should go by yourself, and…"

"Meet up with her later so Zander doesn't see all of her non-fans leaving together all the time?" I said as I processed it. "When?"

"Well, your debrief with the whole Council is this morning…and after that, you have scheduled time with Emily, but you technically can be discharged. There's nothing keeping you here, but they will keep you busy if you decide to stay."

"Got it." And I did. Staying here didn't mean extra time with Collin. It just meant more time to brainwash me and teach me how to have a better right hook. "Anything else I should know…before I head back out? Sam and Liam?"

"The same. Eldridge says that they're hanging in there."

I nodded solemnly, thinking this was all for Alex, when I thought of what we had just discovered or guessed, "Vinalia Ball. I need to practice, don't I?"

"We have a little time this morning to cover that," he said as he pulled out a memory card. "Dance, Volume 19 through 23."

He nodded for me to look at the screen, even as I was taking my first bite. I picked up my plate to shift over towards the monitor. I slid up against him, accidentally, but he leaned in, putting his arm on the small of my back as he spoke.

"This is going to be a bit difficult. We are going to do some basic moves, and then you'll have to practice a lot on your own."

"Can my body move like that?" I said, watching the screen with horror.

"Yes, you've been great at this so far. Don't doubt yourself now."

"Collin," I said, "I'm not…going to be able to pull this off."

"Every move is the same basic movement with your feet, your hips, and your back. You're just moving your arms in different patterns. And remember, this is only later in the party. In the beginning, they still start with the partner's dances. And we are going to spend our time doing the Latin based, then this…"

"Collin, dancing like this would be worse than me not kicking you out of my room."

"I know. What if you practiced on your own for a while?"

"Well…I guess there's no one to be embarrassed around in the woods."

"Well, if you move your hips like that, I think the squirrels might blush."

I laughed out loud. He slid his hand out of his pocket to reach for the MCU I had just placed on the table. He plugged the memory card in and began downloading as I continued.

"It's not how I'm dancing, it's more that I'll know what every idiot in the room will be thinking of doing to me as I'm dancing."

"Well, imagine me punching them. 'Cause I would be if I were there. And you'll be fine."

I smiled again, before stopping, and almost nervously asking, "You wouldn't punch the person I'm dancing with, though?"

"And interrupt Alex and you trying to save the world? Never."

And then my MCU beeped.

"My debrief," I announced, and then realized I was suddenly more uncertain than I had ever been, I asked, "What do I say?"

"Whatever words you think need to be spoken," he said definitively. "If you want to make a statement, go ahead. But I don't want you to think you have to play a game of politics just because we are. Stick with the facts. You should be fine. If you really don't want to make a scene, then don't."

"But I want to help. I mean, you said you're losing a battle…"

He sighed, and said, "Honestly, the best thing you can do is kind of play along. There's an angle already, about Gabriel."

I nodded. I wasn't sure I could do that: play an angle.

But in twenty minutes, when the question was raised and my probation was mentioned, there were three pairs of eyes that were looking at me cruelly, the mounting pressure forced me to play.

"I saved a boy who had been locked up when he was seven. Not only was he sheltered from all influence of the Society, but he is keenly aware of how barbaric they are, and how callous to any Republic influence. And it seems to me, Council, that a person like him stands as a symbol and example you may point to, to show people what atrocities the Republic are capable of."

One set of eyes stopped looking at me cruelly, and then stared at the wall. Another started calculating. Obviously, they liked that idea more than they had liked telling me how I had broken the rules, or else realized they couldn't argue. As several other members seemed to non-verbally affirm that answer, Zander asked if there were any other questions. And then seemed very annoyed by the prevailing silence after my statement.

"Are you certain that's why you saved the boy?" Zander asked.

"Why else would I have saved him? He was worth saving."

"Really? Not a Vessel? Was it worth the risk when you could have chosen to take out an enemy that would kill Gabriel and others? It seems like a poor move."

I shifted in my seat. I felt anger like I had never felt before, especially because even if I could think of the words to say, I probably couldn't speak them in the room. Her harsh eyes looked over me, and even as she saw me open my mouth, she said, "That will be all, 27th. You would do well to remember that you are the only hope for hundreds, not just for one. We need a person who can see that and become the hero we need; not just you. So you should perhaps think of growing in that area before you appear before us with another sob story and your own personal agenda."

"Yes, I understand," I said, keeping my response short to keep my rage hidden.

"Then I'm guessing you'll want to be leaving right away?"

I must have been unable to hide my confusion, even as I stumbled, "But I have…"

"Work to do, and in case you *confuse* yourself here, you were chosen to work. Not to pursue anything else. You're cleared, and should be gone within the hour. No exceptions or delays."

She banged the gavel. I tried instantly to smile, to nod, to fight the anger– feeling a burning embarrassment raging.

I asked myself the same question I waited to ask Patterson as I met him in the back hallway out of the council room.

"How does she know?"

"She doesn't know, that's the point. You get people in that chair and they reveal anything. Which is why," he turned to face me before continuing, "it was great that you just smiled. Because even if there's a rumor going around, that might have sedated it. For now."

He was already looking at me oddly.

"I need to see him, Patterson. Please."

"I'm trying. But I can only keep you in a debrief room for a minute. And remember, I'm not encouraging this. I'm keeping this under wraps merely because I don't want it to hurt either of your efforts to stop her. And because I know how much it would infuriate her. But I really wish that I didn't have to deal with–"

The door opened. Collin burst in.

Patterson sighed pointing between us as he said, "–this."

"What happened?" Collin said confused.

"You have one minute," Patterson said, "and I can't leave the room to give you any privacy. I'm sorry. I'll be over here."

Patterson went into the corner of the room, and leaned on the one wall, facing the other as Collin came up to me.

"What does he mean we only have–"

"I'm being sent out. That's my punishment, I think, for going off during the meeting. I'm being sent out right away."

I felt my voice crack at the end, closing my eyes for a second to find some bravery. I couldn't cry. He would worry too much.

He was already arguing, "She can't...she can't do this. She..." but then he trailed off, realizing that arguing would only make me staying more suspicious.

"We don't have any time, do we?"

I stood, stopping my lip from shaking by biting it. He reached out, pulling me into him slowly, like each moment he pulled me in would fight each of the thousand moments we were away.

He looked at me, then reached into his pocket, keeping his eyes locked on my face even as I looked down at what he pulled out.

"I transferred the music and Dance 19 through 23. But I also transferred something else. I didn't have time to tell you. I wrote to you. I wrote to you every day you were gone last time. And they are all on your MCU now. Read them, okay?"

I nodded, not speaking for fear of unleashing a flood of emotion I wouldn't be able to control. He placed his hands on my head, his fingers brushing my cheeks gently.

"It's really okay, Aislyn," he said breathlessly. "You love me, but you love them, too. You fall in love with every one you save. I love you for loving them. You have to go, because you already love whoever you're going to save next. Don't you?"

I didn't know who would be next. But I know someone needed me. Their life depended on it. I was battling for more time with Collin, but my desire to stay with him was losing to the sudden urgency of their desperation to live.

"Yes, I do."

He leaned in to kiss me softly. He moved closer, more intense than I expected, which only reminded me more of his fear that every kiss might be our last. I felt his breath hit my lips as he spoke.

"No one you love should die so we can have a few more hours. Go. Love them. Choose them."

His eyes looking sad but resolved, his breath ragged.

I leaned down, burying my head in his shoulder. I felt lost in the static until he finally spoke what I needed to hear to crush my fear-filled abyss.

"I'm with you."

I heard Patterson shift, and turned to see him take his ear phones out. He sighed and said, "You need to be done. Now."

I nodded. I ran my hands through his hair, kissed him on the forehead, and backed away. Collin was still looking at me intensely as he let go and backed up toward the door.

"Collin?" Patterson said warningly.

"Yes, sir?"

"Go for a run, go talk to George, do what you need to do. I want you back in one hour, and I need you here."

"Yes, sir."

He turned around quickly and went out the back door.

He never looked back. Perhaps because he couldn't.

"Try to keep up," Patterson said as he opened the door.

He pulled it open, and then motioned for me to go out as he started to talk, "That's a great idea! I think that's a good focus. Schools in Sector 14 can be monstrous places. And I think some intel on what they are teaching is a great target."

I was walked down the hall as he continued to talk about Sector 14. I couldn't figure out why he was continuing to repeat it until I read the message on my MCU that I was cleared.

It was from Michael, who was supposed to be deleting any evidence of Alex and me, who I hadn't had a chance to speak to yet.

I started to speak as the hall ended and I was about to enter the locker rooms, "That's why I thought Sector 14 was best."

Patterson smiled, glad I had gotten the hint, "Yes, 27th, a very good place. You have everything?"

"I do now," I said, somewhat quieter, even though the nearest people were now more than thirty yards away. "And thank you."

He nodded. "For what? The hint on where Michael wants you to go to monitor you or a second with Collin?"

I smiled. "Both. You know, no matter what…she can't steal away the one thing that matters. I still have a chance. And with that, I opened the door, and said just before it closed, "I still have a chance to save them. And I'm taking it."

CHAPTER 11

Three days later, the words from the notes Collin had written mesmerized my every thought. I was lost in the seeming poetry mixed with the tedious events of his everyday life. He would talk about meetings, trainings, politicians, how much Avery was annoying him, and then me– as if he was falling in love with me even more when I was away. I felt both flattered and in shock that the simple words he used strung together existed to describe feelings for me that I once doubted completely.

I deleted the letter then, like so many of the others after I had read them, and looked out at the city skyline. I missed the words the second they disappeared, but I tried to absorb them.

I had wondered if the note would give me courage before entering the Republic again, but I found myself hiding my pack with less confidence. Maybe it was because I felt drawn back to Collin, Patterson, and Michael.

Sam and Liam used to be on that list. I wanted to run back and free them. I found that didn't help my motivation to enter the Republic either.

One of the few things that did was my destination.

Upon leaving Gabriel, out of the many days we had spent in the forest, he had somehow managed to identify his school's location. It was one of the schools in Sector 14, which meant that I could try to look out for Alex, which is what I finally guessed Patterson's hint was meant to aim me towards. I had enough money to grab a taxi shuttle there, which would have been necessary in that part of town to avoid suspicion, but my outfit stood out. I needed what an Elite or Citizen would wear during the day. I had dug up my old dress from my second mission. After having to leave so quickly because Brie and I both had infants, I had to put it in a bad and bury it so I had a chance to resell it later.

I had been forced to leave Brie days earlier. I had waited in the forest for her after my forced exit that was my punishment for our expedited exit. Megan caught up to us a day later. She had said that we had all gotten some kind of punishment for our little act of rebellion in the beginning. Megan said her punishment was not having downtime from her small injury. She had broken her wrist on the last mission saving her Vessel. Instead of letting it heal, they used the very painful reconstruction meds the Republic used, with no other pain medication.

I didn't discover Brie's punishment until a few days later.

Brie never talked much, but she wasn't talking at all. I tried to ask her a question, but stopped mid-sentence. At that point, we had walked over twenty miles together. Brie was finally speaking, but her tone was scary, as if she was warning me to back off.

"You should be careful with Zander."

"Because of what Megan said?" I guessed, looking at her behind us a few yards. "Zander's dangerous, but…"

"You can't just say that as if it wasn't going to destroy some part of you. It's true, Aislyn. And you shouldn't…" She stopped, as if she was rattled. This alone was a reason for me to stop. Anything that rattled Brie deserved my complete attention.

"What can she do to you?" I asked.

"You know, this is why you are annoying. You create disasters, and you don't even know it."

"What disaster did I create?" I was growing more confused and feeling even more defensive by the second.

"I was fine. Everything was fine. I knew what I was going to do. I was going to do this until I died. But no…you had to put crazy ideas into my head."

I only hoped she meant what I thought as I asked, "Caleigh?"

"I called the shelter and asked what I would need to do…to have her. But…" she shoved her MCU in her pack, "I can't even talk to her right now. Because I'm under suspension."

"What do you mean? Why are you under suspension?"

"You are still asking that?" she said, looking at me expectedly.

"Zander." I said it out loud as the pieces fell in place. She was putting up barriers between Brie and what she wanted. The spark of anger I had towards Zander had now burst into flames. This wasn't just about an agenda, but two beautiful lives, and Brie's only chance to be a mother. I had no reason to hide my anger and disgust, but I realized that I deserved any anger Brie directed at me.

"Brie…I'm so sorry." I was about to try to convince her it wasn't my fault, but then I realized, "It's all my fault."

I dropped the small stick in my hand as it started again.

I shouldn't have said we should go that day.

I shouldn't have suggested that Brie should be striving for something else.

I should've had some leverage over Zander to–

"Stop it!" she said, urgently and suddenly, even though I wasn't speaking out loud.

"What?" I asked, breaking my stare to look up at her.

"I know what you're doing. Hitting off all the ways you messed up. It never helps. We did what we did, and in the end...maybe it will all work out."

I shook my head. "She's a monster. I can't believe she did that."

"Yeah well, you're just as bad. You're probably going to say I shouldn't give up–"

"I am! I mean, for just one of the reasons to not give up, can we please admit that for the last few years, you haven't been fine?"

She smiled, knowingly. "No, we can't admit that. I'm always fine, the same way you're fine right now." She repeated it in a trance-like voice, "You can't have melt-downs and try to save the world." And with that, Brie curled up, and either fell asleep or feigned it so I would leave her alone.

Just after that, we had heard a shuttle. Lydia had an EE. I happened to ask William if there was any news on Eva. He said she hadn't called in, but he didn't have a lot of time to talk. Lydia's Vessel was weak after her C-Section. I had been praying for her, even though that had somehow caused me more anxiety than peace. I found the more I thought about it, even to pray for it, I couldn't let go of the conclusion that there was just too much for God to handle; someone was going to fall away, invisible and forgotten. Dead.

I pulled my thoughts out of the dark as I pulled out the dress from the locker I had left it in outside the club on 28th street the day we escaped with André and Hope. It looked alright for having been placed in the tiny square space. Collin had explained that because of the caliber of the party I had attended, I could never wear the dress again. I was almost sad, even as he joked that he wished he could have seen me in it. I wish he could have.

I placed my survival pack and some of my med pack in the locker, and then the dress in my bag. Collin had said I was to take the dress to one of our few undercover operations, where I could perhaps swap out the dress for some extra spending money. The shop owner would receive more money for the dress than most things other Protectors would bring in, and would then be more willing to give me some extra clothes, or, at least, cash for them.

As I entered the shop hours later, I found myself hesitant to part with it. I wasn't sure if it was because I had survived in it, saved a life in it, or danced in it.

Or danced in it with Alex.

The strange flashes of any memory of Alex had a strange effect on me. They would jolt me, as if the recollection of his touch could stop me where I stood. I got oddly breathless. I told myself I was just flattered because he had said he "saw me"– as strangely vague as that was– but then I thought back to my panic when I had thought he might have been dead. I asked myself if that panic had exploded because we would have missed the opportunity of having an agent of the Republic on our side. And I knew the answer to that question: No.

Because he was more than a pawn. I cared if he lived or died. Because I wanted a chance to be his friend.

The presence of the person behind the counter pushed any other thoughts from my mind. I approached him, cautiously as I was directed.

"Hello, ma'am, how might I assist you?"

"A friend recommended you, and that I might look good in red. Her name was Aislyn. You helped her friend on 27th Street."

I breathed relief as I heard each word come out of my mouth in the correct order. He smiled, and nodded to my backpack. He took it away from me, leaving me feeling strange without it.

As he returned from the back, his eyes were wide, and I had to smile at his reaction, "They weren't exaggerating; that is a dress."

I laughed. He explained as I chose my new outfit that it was made out of satin silk hat was genetically altered to be softer. The fabric itself was worth the cost of two outfits that would be a suitable "fashion" for being above 7th Street.

Within a few minutes, he had something suitable for me, and quickly fitted it as I waited and watched in the window as the victims I couldn't rescue passed me by, oblivious to any real love past a one-night stand and hanging on Palmer's every word. Even as I watched them, shuffling, laughing, gossiping, I found my hate evaporating into pity. I couldn't even tell them what they were missing, and at the same time, wasn't sure if what they were missing was worth the heartache.

I took a taxi to 7th Street, getting off where the school was located. Not wanting to draw attention to myself, I went straight for the café across the street. Teachers who had once instructed Gabriel and Kieri were currently instructing others, one of them was probably not achieving everything that was required of them.

I didn't know who. But that, of course, was why I was here. I drank my last sip of my drink slowly, hoping the buzz would give me enough nerve to do what I needed to do.

I quickly crossed the street, moving toward the front door. Collin and I had prepared the script and walked though it as many times as we could. Collin's hands had wrung through his hair when he when I would get the script wrong, because he knew how it would end if I did.

A knock. A door opened. There was no turning back.

"Hello, my name is Andréa. I would like an extended tour."

Almost immediately, I knew I had said the right thing, was wearing the right attire, and spoke with the authority needed. The Sub-Terra who was at the door whisked me away to a teacher who took me into the office, and explained all the values of a school centered on the talents of certain children. As siblings of Citizens often cared far more for each other than parents, my story was believable.

As we passed, there were features that were very much like the ones in my school. Even the hallways looked very similar. The familiarity shook me to my core. I wanted to see stark differences everywhere, but the pictures looked the same, the letters looked the same, and even the paintings looked the same. And it made me miss the ordinary that was my life before I had been chosen.

It only took a few more seconds to see the disparity that usually caused my indignation. I saw what the stories written under the pictures were about: goals of owning their own Sub-Terra, drawings of endless parties, pictures of them in gowns.

No magical creatures, no friends helping, no families.

Except in one. This one showed a girl holding hands with a smaller child, who appeared to have a bandage on her knee. I looked at the scribbled name on the top of the page.

Maggie.

I told myself to remember that name, even as we were standing in the doorway of another class. Something had just happened, and all of the children had left their desks to rush up to the front.

"As you can see, we have the standard procedures in every classroom as is required by the Society as well, which is the three pleasure centers a day. We measure their ability to stop what they are doing and we also gauge their interest in the distraction as a positive sign of their development. Any child who is not distracted right away is swiftly redirected and encouraged to join the group. They are encouraged to rejoin only after the allotted time is over, which is why so many of our students have the necessary IQ even if artistically talented."

As each child clamored to see the screen, sitting quietly for what looked like a video that was almost hypnotizing them, I saw a girl still at her desk, modeling with the clay like the others.

She was the only one still working, up until the teacher pointed to the screen. The girl replied that she wanted to finish when the teacher took her work, and squished it onto her desk. The girl quickly looked like she was going to cry, but hid her tears, and walked over to the station.

"As you can just see demonstrated, we do not allow any focused time during the scheduled distraction. Children must know that the primary objective is the pleasure of life, not getting caught up in their work, and that when the leader's goals are the same, they need to comply with that leadership. They must work and focus productively, and look to the centers as rewards. Our focus and attention rates are incredible. As you can see, even from the unruly student you just saw, there is an amazing effort in math skills to understand the principles of engineering."

My heart broke as I watched the child hide her defeated step over to the screen that was now showing a funny cartoon character, I answered back, as softly and approving as I could, "Of course. I can only say that while it is discouraging such a student would take so long to responds, I was impressed at the teacher's swift ability to maintain the standard."

"She is a fantastic teacher, although your brother would be…"

Her words faded. Faded into the colors of the videos meant to help kids forget the art of their purpose or how living a fulfilled life could fill. Faded as the teacher gathered the clay off the desk so that I could see the name plate, and her model of a triple-seat shuttle.

Maggie.

I solidified the name and the girl in my head, because she was the next person I was going to risk my life for.

After taking some information and asking some rather pertinent questions, and perhaps some unusual ones, I quickly left. I had to remember not to shake her hand or say thank you. I had to remember not to look at any children as I left. I had to remember that I was only interested in me, and not in the child who may be cowering in fear of being disappeared one day because she didn't fit into their mold.

I breathed out relief in the café a little later, perusing through the brochures as I sipped on another beverage that cost more than my father's monthly salary. While it began to make me wish I had ordered something without caffeine, it was helping me stay alert.

As alert as I was, I was sharply reminded that I couldn't predict everything.

"Aren't you a little old for school?"

I recognized the voice immediately. It had caused me dread once before, and I had to frantically search my head for his name before replying. I had almost taken too long to reply when I finally remembered it, and was able to add it to the end of my sentence.

"Well, I suppose so, but then there's a lot you didn't get to know about me that night, Linden."

He smiled, a somewhat charming smile.

"You remembered, but as you said, there's a lot I didn't get to know about you, like your name," he said.

I decided to play the game I played that night, hoping that flattery would probably work to hide any ignorance on my part.

"Elysian," I said. It was close enough to my own name, but I enjoyed the reference. Something Greek and old to fight their modern Roman hell. "I hope you won't forget it. And I'm afraid as old as I am, it doesn't affect the age of my brother, his need for school, or my parents' desire to make sure he gets in the right one."

"So you can make Elite?"

"That's everyone's goal, right?" I said, and then trying to be a little more witty. "I'm sorry, did I say goal? Did I say my 'parents desire?' Just replace those two phrases with 'unhealthy obsession.'"

He laughed. I laughed, but I realized I was digging myself into a bit of a hole. I now felt trapped, again, as school was about to be let out and I was running out of time. I wouldn't know a quick reason to get away without risking my cover. If my life were the only one at stake, I could perhaps fake a conversation all day. But not today.

"Why don't you take an hour off? Come to my place."

He said it in a way that made me shake my head instantly, even while remembering I had to flirt. I knew what he was implying. He continued, "After all, if your parents are trying to gain the last money for Elite, you must be exhausted of being with people you've been arranged to be with. What if someone just wanted you, for you, and I got to have you for a brief afternoon, with no strings attached? Freedom."

I was careful not to respond in any way that would give away my confusion, even as I was trying to hide my disgust at what he was implying about how I might be "arranged" to be with certain people.

"That would be nice, Linden. Really. Except…"

Story. Think of a story. I felt crushed under the weight of my urgency and the need for him to ignore me. And then a brief chance of getting air came rushing to the surface.

"I think someone else is here to see you."

There were two girls, who had tried to wave him down without success until I nodded. He sighed, winked at them, and then said, "Another time, then." He used an Elite phrase that meant something extremely inappropriate, which forced me to say something equally uncomfortable back. As he left, I laughed and shook my head, waved at him, and then stared at the paper.

I hoped no one else knew I had just swallowed something that was creeping up my throat. Even the word "creeping" made me feel queasy. I was instantly thrown into a search for the meaning of his words. It implied something too horrid, even for them. But as I thought back to the kids in the room, forced to be distracted by the mesmerizing colors and the funny cartoon, I thought that this society was capable of any sin, even trading in their own bodies to be with the right people to ladder climb. It certainly wouldn't be the first time in history, nor the last, people had manipulated someone else to fake love and intimacy to climb a ladder. But I hated it.

The only thing that managed to break me free from my thoughts was Maggie. I was desperate to see her face, even if just to focus me on the mission of saving her, and to forget all about Linden.

But as the minutes passed, I noticed that she hadn't left the building. She hadn't been seen on the porch, waiting for a taxi. She wasn't anywhere, and as the person who gave me my tour closed the door, I panicked.

I quickly smiled, hiding my panic in plain sight. I left my seat, threw an insanely large tip on the table, and moved to the door. While I thought her presence would distract me from other contemplations, her absence had focused my energy more than her presence ever would. The story behind her absence was forming in my mind. She had hesitated to perform as expected during a prospective student tour. That alone would not condemn her, but if it wasn't the first time…

She would be disappeared before the hour.

I walked lazily across the street, a block down, and into the alley. I realized the school most likely had a camera around it, so my presence would be recorded.

I was trying to strategize how to enter without detection when there was a bang of a door opening hard against the alleyway wall.

I dropped low, holding my breath until I saw the little hand appear grasping the outside edge of the door.

Maggie appeared only an instant later with her backpack. Her face was flushed and her eyes red, her auburn hair blowing wildly as she whipped her head around from the school to stare at the alley.

It might as well have been a canyon. She was doomed, and she knew it. She whispered out, "Please." She said it again and again.

I didn't know how she could have guessed that there was a God when I had sometimes doubted Him. Maybe she had hoped that He would save her, by some supernatural miracle. But she wasn't going to get a miracle. She was only going to get me.

"Maggie."

At first, she didn't move. Perhaps she thought it was a voice in her head, but then I said her name again. She caught me in her eyes then, hiding behind the dumpster three buildings down.

She made a step, but I held my hands up, and then pointed to the black square right above her, pointed at the steps she now stood on. She stared at the camera, and looked back at me, nodding. She didn't want to be on one of Palmer's broadcasts either. Or didn't want to get caught on the way to the border.

The border. We both had to make it there.

But not together.

Even as she looked at my eyes, a little curiously as I lifted a box off the ground, I gestured to it again, turned around, and swiftly left. I only turned to look, as I was about to leave the alley, to see her look at the box, but with an expression that told me she was understanding. The last thing I saw as I exited the alley was her quick movement to pick up her bag as she ran to the opposite end.

"Yes," I whispered under my breath, not being able to contain it. Hopefully, if someone heard me, they'd mistake my excitement for something else.

A few more minutes past. She was waiting by the store in the next street– the store with the logo that had been printed on the box I had shown her. I quickly got on my phone, and was talking. She stared at me, I glanced at her, then spoke into my phone.

"I'm on my way to Sharnoff's now. Yeah, I can't wait." At that moment, I caught a taxi. I noticed in my peripherals that she hit the shuttle button on the edge of the sidewalk as I entered my taxi. I turned back, once I was inside, risking a glance. She looked at me briefly, but long enough for her to see me wink. She winked back.

Sharnoff's was closer to the warehouse district. By the time her shuttle had arrived, twenty minutes after I had arrived, I had purchased a small bag and exited when seeing the shuttle through the window. She was on the opposite side of the street. She was staring at the sidewalk, looking so dejected I could hardly stand it.

"Please. God, turn her head. Make her see."

And almost as she was about to turn away, she saw me. I walked out by the warehouse district, and so we walked, twisting and turning down alleys. I would glance across the street several times, but we never made eye contact, until ten blocks down.

I crossed the road one more time, speaking one more location into my phone. After that, it was all alleys to keep off the main road.

It was ten blocks later that I saw her again, from above on the corner of the last few blocks within the border. I didn't know how to tell her that I instantly loved her, not just because I was saving her, but because she had helped me save her.

"They tell you, I suppose," I started, as she instantly froze, "that you aren't supposed to trust me."

She looked up to where I had perched myself on the fire escape, the only sound was the few rocks scraping underneath her feet. "They say a lot of things, but I don't believe them. Not really."

I jumped down, her eyes on me intently. I realized she was perhaps mildly impressed or still scared as she spoke.

"Being told your parents are late and then seeing a Sentry in the hallway doesn't make you want to believe them either."

I gave her a sympathetic look as she continued.

"So I believed what the whispers say, under breaths when they think no one is listening. They say…that you're the hero."

I gazed at her, in wonder of how her words had struck me as I answered, "They say a lot of things. But some days, I don't feel like I'm a hero."

She spoke in a quivering voice. "But you can be mine, right?"

I reached out to hug her. She began to sob. I allowed her the moment to let her fear and sorrow escape before kneeling down, her warm brown eyes only inches from mine.

"Yes, Maggie. I can be yours."

CHAPTER 12

"Did you know you were going to pick me when you saw me?"

As the days went past, we had discussed how I had entered the school. She had said she felt horrible for leaving a boy named Oliver. She answered a few questions. I made her take a lie detector test, although it made her nervous. I hated to put her through it. A few hours in, and I found myself repeating answers to questions.

"Yes, from the second when your teacher took the clay away."

She looked as if she might be upset and then she said, "Is there clay where you come from?"

"Yes," I said, almost laughing at the concept. "You like to design, right? It's for math and design, the school you were in?"

"Yes, although I think I would have preferred computer design, but we can't choose that until we're seven."

I shook my head. I couldn't believe I was having this kind of intelligent conversation with a six-year-old. Due to her intelligence level, however, she would have been in school for four years already, with a lot of the Society's influence already permanently imprinted; however, she seemed fairly confident in her choice to escape her home, except for her nightmares. The previous night had been the worst. She almost ran off to find her parents again. I had to yell the truth to keep her safe, reminding her she couldn't go back. I had to yell, "Your parents will kill you."

We cried back to sleep, and then she was calm again.

I told her stories that she had never heard, about fairies and pirates. I told her about the shelter. I told her that she was safe.

But on the second day that strange things started happening.

She mentioned she missed her medication. Four times.

She would rock back and forth for an hour while singing.

She wouldn't quite look at me, even while staring at me.

She had a strange reaction to certain sounds.

And on the third day, I decided I needed an EE.

"Michael?"

"Hi, 27. Nice to hear from you, but what's up?"

"I still have my Unnecessary. But she's…"

"What? Is she sick?"

"No. But I need an EE. She's fine. And then…she's not."

She seemed to be okay for that moment. I almost doubted my judgement, thinking maybe that I overreacted.

But then the wind blew, and she said, "My hair hurts."

I listened to her eerie statement as Michael was trying to get my attention on the earpiece, asking me if everything was alright.

"Her hair hurts."

There was a silence on the other side of the MCU.

"And there's other things, Michael. She told me something that made me think she was on medication, but I have no clue what. What can I do? How good is the lab in the Q Station?"

"Not that good," he said. "Best bet is to bring her here soon as possible. We're sending out another shuttle for you, because the one with Emily is too far away. She's got Brie. Give us an hour."

So we waited. Some moments, I felt like Maggie was fading, but then she'd say something so lucid and brilliant.

"Hey Maggie, pretty soon, there's going to be a shuttle…"

"Sweet," she said, now very focused. "What are the hover pads like? It's run on an antigravity servos, so what's the power like? Do you have blueprints? Is it propulsion or electromagnetic?"

"I have no idea," I said. She continued to talk, more like Eva did when discussing technology. And it was scary. Even as she was getting more focused, she wasn't looking at my eyes again. She was drawing something in the dirt with a stick: something symmetrical, like a fractal image that was now almost three feet wide. I had to keep reminding myself she was only six-years-old. I was telling myself again after she flailed her arms, sat on them, and then looked up slowly, straining to keep her own eyes focused on mine. Then she repeated what she had said earlier.

"I think something's wrong, Aislyn. You asked me, the other day, if I took something…like medicine. I said that I did, didn't I?"

"Yes," I said softly.

"I did, didn't I? My parents got it for me. It's illegal, because anyone with my condition is destroyed usually. They said it would help me fit in. They didn't want …I'm not right, am I?"

I looked at her, even as I said, it hoping she believed me.

"Yes you are. You're perfect."

"You don't have to lie. It's not like you have to pretend it happened naturally. I know a bunch of computers made me, and somewhere one of the doctors misplaced an amino acid or placed too much or too little hormone producing instructions in my hippocampus or something…and I'm not right. I wasn't created, like you. I was just someone's job. Someone missed their coffee that morning, and I was created, instead of the person that was supposed to be. I'm not even supposed to be…"

"No," I moved to her, not touching her. "You're more than all that. Because I don't think that if you were someone's random, messed-up job that you would have been saved. You were destined to be saved. That should mean something, make you significant. You are so smart! Just…how are you so smart?"

"Oh, well…I think I was like this all the time. The medicine helps, but it…it cuts me off. Like a barrier, from the parts that don't make me work right."

"How did your parents get the medicine?"

"From a friend. Another Citizen."

"That must have been dangerous," I said.

"They didn't do it because they loved me; they did it to fit in."

"Weren't they afraid of getting arrested?" I asked, trying to gauge her reaction. She wasn't looking at me again, but was playing with the pine needles with a stick.

She laughed, "Well, he would have had to arrest himself."

"What?" I said quickly. I held my breath for the answer.

"He's a Sentry."

I was desperate for more answers, but she wasn't looking at me again. Finally, I said, "That's…unexpected."

"Tell me about it. He gave it to them, for free. They'd never be able to afford it on the black market. They were saving to become Citizens, so I would have been a complete embarrassment if I was discovered. And it means you saved me from two horrible fates."

I was about to ask what that meant when I heard the shuttle coming. It was Will driving, and then I saw George come out.

"Hey, we need to go. Quickly," George said.

"What's wrong?" I said, realizing I shouldn't have asked.

"Nothing. Just want to get home as soon as possible, right?"

He was trying to sound innocent, but his panic worried me.

"Oh," she looked despondent at me. "So I am a mess up, and you do need to get medicine into me as soon as possible?"

"No, that's not it at all…it's just…" Will was trying to explain.

George reached out and grabbed me, "We need to go."

"Honestly, it's not about your medicine," I said, kneeling down to meet her eyes. "His hand is shaking, his watch is lit red, and his eyes are dilated. He's trying not to scare you, but something's wrong! There might be a drone. We've got to go!"

George looked at me, as if I had just ruined his efforts to be sensitive. But then she got off the forest floor in a swift motion and jumped in the shuttle with little emotional reaction.

"She's a little different," I said as I moved into the shuttle.

"Yeah, I can tell," he said, and with that, the door closed. We were already moving by the time I was grabbing my seatbelt.

"So, what's up?" I asked, making sure Maggie strapped in.

He didn't look at me at first. He just looked scared.

Just then, I could hear the alarm go through the woods, an echo from the Circles. And an unusual rumble that got louder.

I heard something pass over us.

"I only said that…Is that a…"

He didn't answer. Maggie did. "Class 4 Drone, D-series, meant for tracking and demolition only, no long-term surveillance storage, most likely to carry thermal-seeking missiles."

"Who is she?" Will called from the front.

I looked at George, hoping my eyes were sharing the desperation that I felt. I instantly felt my chest tighten, making the quickened breaths I took more forced. I reached out for her, faking a smile.

"We have the technology to beat it, sweetie."

"To confuse it, maybe, but not stop it. Not if it's tracking us," she said it matter-of-factly, but fighting a fear quaking her voice.

"We'll know when it locks on," George said.

"Why did it go right past us?" I asked.

"If it's not locking on to us, it could be locking onto…" Will said, losing his voice towards the end of his sentence.

"Where's Emily?" George asked, unbuckling his restraints to reach up to the panel in front of Will.

Will was already pushing buttons above him as he yelled, "I'm trying. I'm trying."

He cursed, and then yelled into his headset, "Emily?"

Finally, the speaker came to life. "Will, is that you?"

"Emily, there's a drone coming for you. It didn't see us, which means it has to be locking on to you."

"Will...one just went past us."

George turned to look at Maggie in horror, even as Will cursed and yelled out, "They have a better chance of hitting us from a longer approach, even if we divert."

"Where are you?" George yelled.

They called off coordinates, but I wasn't listening. It was all becoming blurred as I stared at her. Maggie had her hands over her ears and was speaking so softly I could barely hear her.

"What if I was a mistake? What if you weren't supposed to save me? Wouldn't that mean you didn't matter anymore either? What if I cursed you?"

I didn't have a chance to say anything I wanted. George yelled, "Emily, the one that past us is almost to you. It's almost in range."

"We have the one heading for you. We tracked it as it passed. It's about 10 miles out."

"Abandon the shuttle. Now! Head for the Q nearby."

"We have time!" I heard their driver scream.

"No, you don't Parker. You need to get out, do you–"

"They are locked on!" Will screamed. "They're about to fire!"

"Okay, we're out…"

There was a squeal in the speakers, followed by a low buzz.

"Emily? Emily?!"

The only response was a crackling, deafening static. The only interruption was the debris of the forest hitting the shuttle.

Then it cut off. Suddenly. Because the engine sounded louder.

There was a blur of movement as George grabbed four things rapidly with his shaking hands.

"We're getting out. Now!"

The brakes were sudden. I unstrapped her and yelled at her to come with me. Even as I lifted her up, I felt weak, but insistent on carrying her. If she were clinging to me, my fear wouldn't paralyze me, and I would be stronger for it.

I had just enough to make it twenty steps away when I heard a sound I didn't recognize: a high pitched squeal.

The missile had fired.

George yelled Will's name. And before I knew what was happening, George was behind me, wrapping his arms around us. Will had jumped in front of me, his hand tucked my head into his shoulder. They had pressed us both between them, George leaned in on my shoulder as he pushed forward.

My legs gave way as George pushed us forward.

We started to fall.

Then it hit.

We were pushed harder by the hot air and the force of the blast, into the ground we were already falling towards.

It sounded like there was fire burning inside my ears, the heat and force exploding from the bomb in a way that rattled my chest. I barely felt any debris as we fell. I landed on Will, feeling a sickening crack through my back. But none of my joints had cracked. My body shook, as if there was an explosion within me.

No debris had hit me. That was impossible. I felt vomit rising.

I turned to look at George, through the smoke. His face contorted in pain. And I knew why no debris had hit me.

I should have never asked for the EE.

I should have taken a faster route somehow.

I should have chosen another target.

I should have shielded George.

But regrets for the past were pushed aside to feel the more urgent, horrifying present.

Heat.

Pain.

Crying.

Ringing.

I know I was here. I know I was intact. I know I was whole. But I didn't feel it.

I felt shattered, as if the bomb had truly hit me and torn me to shreds. I could feel her sobbing into my shoulder. I could feel the words coming out.

"It's all going to be okay." But all I could hear was the words echo through my crushed mind. Even I didn't believe them.

She leaned back to look up at me, a face glowing with the light of the fire that almost consumed her, and her eyes were mesmerized by mine, as I forced a calm expression.

I repeated over and over again, "It's all going to be okay." I knew she could barely hear me. But even without hearing it, she believed what I said, and buried her head back into my chest.

William pulled me up and asked me to keep moving. He was holding his arm in front of him, with his other hand. I wondered if his shoulder was dislocated.

"George?"

He was unconscious, but stirring.

Cringing. Screaming. Pain.

It wasn't just the debris. He didn't have to tell me.

I swore I saw the words on his lips, "Emily."

My wrist was burning, but I could ignore it because the pain of Brie's death would hurt more. William was motioning to move towards the woods, but I hesitated.

Where would we hide? How could we remain breathing for longer than five minutes with a drone still in the air? How could we remain safe when our every movement was tracked?

But it wasn't our movement the drone could track. It could only track out heat.

I waved furiously, desperate to get his attention. Will was trembling, probably because he didn't know how he was going to get all of us away fast enough to avoid the drone.

I shook my head again, and mouthed the word, "Heat."

He looked confused. George had just started to get up, revealing pieces of glass and plastic embedded in his back. I was trying not to look, instead staring at his face, trying to move my mouth in a way that he understood.

"The fire. The heat."

They both understood it that time.

George pulled me closer, pulling open my bag. He motioned to keep walking as he looked through my pack. I couldn't imagine what he was getting out of there. I started to cough on smoke, and then I got an answer to my question. He pulled me around to place a wet cloth over my mouth.

I quickly nodded, holding it over my nose. I noticed he had the air compressor as well. I forgot it had a built in filter, meant to concentrate and filtrate any oxygen in the air for infant lungs. And while Maggie wasn't an infant, it would work on her. She put it on without hesitating. George wrapped the wires around her ears as best as he could while she was still holding them.

And then we waited near the raging fire; in the shadow of the death they had planned for us so that we could live. The drone passed again, although I barely heard it above the inferno. We all froze, so it didn't detect any movement. I coughed when I took my first breath after holding it.

William nodded. If they hadn't fired a shot, they couldn't have thought we were alive. We stepped out from the fire while William pulled out his MCU only to pocket it as George began to climb the tree. He scaled it quickly, getting half way up a minute later despite his injuries. He began to scan the skies.

There was no sign of anything. On his way down, the other drone shot past, too quickly to be targeting us. It was heading back to the border, cornering sharply to the east.

I could start to hear a ringing in my ear, but I still couldn't hear their voices. George had made a sign language, "Q." and then put up four fingers. Will shook his head, and put up two fingers.

George nodded, and mouthed as he winced, "Good driving."

I looked at Maggie. Her hands were still over her ears. I could tell it was torture for her. I couldn't block out the sound she heard. The ringing was inside of her. I screamed, even though she could barely hear. Will nodded for me to come closer, and then to turn around. He was searching through my pack.

Will pulled out what I hoped he was looking for, and then he knelt down in front of her. She was rocking on her knees, trying to cope from the ringing. He motioned to her, then poured some of the fluid on the cloth. He made the motion to cover his mouth with his other hand, and then to breathe deeply. Then he slowly reached out and closed his eyes with his hands. She looked confused, so he did it again, this time reaching out to her to cover her eyes, the strands of her hair flowing through wildly around her.

I watched him put the cloth over her mouth and her eyes close slowly. I was searching through my bag for the pre-dosed painkiller, and pushed the needle into George's shoulder. He shook for a moment, but then breathed out slowly. I went to pull a shard of glass out of his back, but he shook his head. I strained my memory to remember any medical lessons about puncture wounds. But George pointed to Will, and then to my shoulder.

"No," I said it, and mouthed it.

He looked at me severely, but I shook my head, "I can't."

"You need to," he mouthed out. And then his expression softened, "And yes, you can." He mouthed each word out slowly as he gripped my hand.

Will guided Maggie's sleeping body to the ground. He was staring at her, sleeping quietly and contently among the wreckage of war. The image burned in my head. Will was about to stand when I placed my hand on his dislocated shoulder. He shuddered, stayed on his knees, closing his eyes. He leaned his head back, opening his eyes slowly to reach mine. "I'm sorry," I mouthed.

He nodded. I reached my arms around his shoulder.

"On three," I mouthed as he nodded.

"One."

He shook as I put my knee in his back, clasping my fingers within one another, one over and one under his arm.

"Two."

He winced. I held my breath.

"Three."

I thrust my knee in, pulling back quickly in one swift stroke. I felt it shift back in the socket.

I reached out, but he wrenched away from me, pushing out the leaves underneath him with heaving breaths. He might have screamed, but we wouldn't have heard it.

We had to move. We were moving, but it was labored. I helped George on his feet to lean on a tree as Will pulled himself over to Maggie and picked her up.

We trudged for the two miles. We took turns, having George lean on my shoulder and carrying Maggie.

It took us almost an hour. A long, horrible hour.

The second we got in the Q station, Will motioned for me to put Maggie on the table, which I did. He then pointed at the closet. I had reached the closet just as reached out, grabbed my neck, and pushed a metal device in my ear. I felt a cold substance in the deepest part of my ear, like he was flushing it out with water.

"What is that stuff?" I asked, realizing not only could I hear, but the buzzing and pain had faded. He placed it in my other ear. While it was an amazing result, it gave me a queasy sensation. He replaced the nozzle with what looked like a disposable, and then placed it in his own ears. I saw him shake a little.

"Okay, that's amazing. But that felt weird," he said.

"Yeah, agreed," I said, feeling like I had regained my balance.

"It's a genetically engineered polymer that fills the holes in your ears after an explosion, and then helps them heal with some genetically engineered…awesomeness. I don't know. We stole it from the Republic. I'm going to need your help. You up for that?"

I nodded, going to help George up from the stair where we left him. I pulled him over to the station as Will went up to make sure the door was secure. I heard the three steel doors slam shut gradually as I took George to the ear nozzle. He put it in each of his ears, with me to steady him.

My first question was almost a confrontation, "Why on earth didn't you let me remove the debris?"

"While something is in you, even though it's pierced you, it's stopping you from bleeding out. It's why you should always leave a knife in, if you're stabbed," Will was explaining, even as George tripped and Will reached out to grab him under his arm.

He grabbed his head, too. "Tell me if you're going to faint. And don't fight it. Do you need more pain meds?"

George took a few sharp intakes of breath before answering with what he needed.

"Emily?"

I knew then that no pain killer was going to help.

"Brie?"

Will opened his mouth, and then closed it rapidly.

"Anyone?"

"I haven't pulled up comm, yet, okay? I will after we get you–"

"I got it. You get comm," I said quickly, to fight my own doubt.

"Aislyn, this isn't childbirth," Will said, voicing the uncertainty I felt. "And no offense, I saw your field med record."

"I got him," I said, more confident than I felt.

"Alright. I'll be at that station, right over there. If you need my help, call me."

Will went to the station as George sat down on the op area on the bed. I stared at him, unsure of whether to take off his shirt first or pull the shards out.

He sighed, "I know this is going to be hard. I'm going to walk you through it. And I'm going to trust you to follow my directions. Shirt first. Some shards will come out. Deal with that bleeding first. Then take all the rest out," he said, looking at me.

I bit my lip. He kept reassuring me, even as he winced in pain. Some pieces did come off with the shirt, pulled out of his skin, slicing it, making him wince. I was trying to move slowly, leaving the largest shards still in, including one that was 3 inches long.

"George, I'm going to cut around the shirt, okay?"

"Oh, that's why that one hurts the most then? How big is it?"

"It's…um…going to give you bragging rights for a while," I said, trying to smile. I didn't know if it worked until he bit his lip.

"I'd laugh, 27, if my whole back wouldn't bleed if I did."

"Speaking of that," I asked tentatively as I sprayed the antibacterial spray and put on my gloves, "I wanted to know…can you feel any punctures that are deep."

"The one down there…it's bad, I can tell, and it's in muscle. It means no pull ups for about three months. That's all."

It was painstaking to pull each shard out with the tweezers. George was hoarse from screaming or even trying to subdue screams with groans. I pulled three that were about an inch and stitched him up with body glue after each one.

Twenty minutes later, Will was still at the station. The lack of information was filling the room with dread with each passing minute, as the shards I pulled from his back and laid on the tray became larger and I had a harder time keeping my hands steady with each cry of pain he made. I finally pulled the largest piece, which resulted in me needing to call Will for help.

Will raced over, but he must have decided to get all the worst pain over with. He looked at George, as if helpless.

"George, it looks like they were 5 miles away from a Q station. They were also 5 miles away from another station, where they can ask for backup. So we just don't know. But it's too early...just because no one has heard anything doesn't mean..."

The news hit George just as the bleeding was getting worse. The tears formed, risking to fall with the blood on the table.

"Will? Um...the glue...it's not working."

Will looked at George's back, slightly impressed, which annoyed me only because I felt like I was failing.

"Not bad 27, but no, the glue isn't going to do any good. Real sutures this time. Just hold that one, it's started to seep through, and I'll get that too."

"I want to get it." I said, even as I wasn't sure why, but I felt something rising up in me. It almost felt like anger or loyalty, but it was more compassionate.

"Why? You got most of it, Aislyn. I can get–"

"No!" I yelled, and then not even sure what to say, I just let my thoughts scream. "Because it's my fault. Because you were shielding her! Because you were shielding me! Because saying thank you is never going to be enough unless I do this!"

I took a jagged breath, even as I begged, "Just let me do this."

But the only problem was, by trying to prove I could do it, I was now fighting tears. I blinked them away just as quickly. They both were frozen. Will looked sympathetic, but I couldn't read George's expression. Finally, George held out the needle to me.

"Make them small, 27," he said it, reaching out his hand to my shoulder. "And…'thank you' will always be enough. Always."

I started. I sewed, trying not to think of mending dresses at home with my mother. I would concentrate so hard I would stop breathing, and have to remind myself to take a breath.

"So, what did Central say?" I asked.

"They didn't respond after saying they couldn't find Emily. I've sent them updates though. But nothing has come back. Just like I tried to send a transmission to Emily."

Will went to check Maggie's pulse and put an oxygen tag on her finger as George continued to ask, "Is something wrong…" George paused as I inserted the needle again, "with the receiver?"

"I think, maybe. I'm trying everything. Trust me. Collin should know his Protector is okay. George, you should know your Protector is okay. That you didn't fail her, sending her out to die."

"Will," George said, warningly, "don't go there. There's so much emotional tension, I think we could burst. No use in adding more."

"Done," I said, and I instantly rinsed his back down with the sanitary liquid, making him cringe and shake. Will came over to hold his shoulders still so I could spray the rest of i.

"Well, what do we do?" Will said, pulling out some more pain meds. He gave one pill to George, and then took the other one.

We looked over at Maggie. She was sleeping, softly breathing.

"Sleep. We need sleep," I said, trashing the needle and gloves.

"We can't," George said. "I mean, I can't."

I turned to her as I said, "She only had one dosage. But she's still sleeping. She's found a peace in this madness, and if you think her life is any less emotional or complicated than ours, you're wrong."

Will looked down, and George took a sip of his water.

"She's a kid. She can escape in a way we can't. She can run away from hell. In her mind. We can't."

"Well," I sighed, "maybe it's about time for us to escape through our mind. Just for one night."

They looked at me strangely, even as I started, "Once upon a time, there was a hidden kingdom within the mountains."

I started the well-known fairy tale, and even as Will shook his head in disbelief, George didn't scoff. He didn't mock me, like I thought he would. He slowly sank, lying down on the table as I continued. He was either too weary to complain, or just needed more innocence than reality. His dark eyes stayed glued to mine. Will was quiet, overcoming his disbelief and even laughing at a joke once in a while, as he put a needle in for George's IV. Then he sat down, putting his head on the MCU console.

George spoke softly, staring up at the ceiling.

"When we got to the part with the troll, my mom…she would sing that song. Do you know it?"

I stopped, trying to remember. I think I sang it while in school once, but it made me dizzy to think about that. Bright colors, long recesses, books, fields with blankets strewn over long grass. But I remembered it, with every painful moment, more of it came to me.

> *"Don't you know, when the night winds blow,*
> *The morning sun soon breaking*
> *Don't you see, what dawn could mean,*
> *That every dream's now aching.*
> *For when dawn breaks, every dream aches,*
> *For most die in the night,*
> *They only keep, one more hope of sleep,*
> *Their chance to come back to life.*

I sang until they fell asleep. I stood in the room; amazingly awake, yet drained, singing the song to no one but myself. I went to Maggie's table, pulled in the chair, and put my head on the table by her arm, my eyes memorizing the room, writing images on my brain of the people in this room.

The desperate. The crushed. The lonely. The broken.

"For when dawn breaks, every dream aches…"

There might be no hope in dawn, and so I couldn't sing another word.

And as weariness finally crushed me into sleep, I reached out to the only girl who had dreams that might still come true. I held her head, felt the perfect brokenness of us, and closed my eyes, praying that at least one of us could completely forget this moment.

I knew that it would never be me.

CHAPTER 13

"What is this?"

After being asked a hundred times, a part of me wasn't sure I wanted to answer her. Again.

But then the other part of me cherished each precious breath, every beautiful inquiry. All the sparkles in her eyes needed an answer. I conceded to her curiosity with grace, so that I could see the wonder and joy one more time.

"It's a pine cone, sweetie."

"Wow!" she exclaimed as she slid her fingers across each layer, tracing it with each touch. "What's it do?"

"Well," I said smiling, ignoring George as he began to hit my MCU against a tree trunk, still trying to get a signal, "Mostly they tend to just sit on the forest floor. A lot of them just do that. But they all have seeds. If the conditions are right, one seed will emerge and form a tree."

"Oh, so it's like a system for ensuring the reproduction of the flora necessary for the growth of a pine tree? Does it close when the dispersal of the seed is complete? Are there male and female cones? Do they look different? Do they open when it is dry or humid?"

And then there were questions like that.

"Yes, not sure, I think so, yes depending on the tree, and I think they open when it's dry."

"Disappointing. You should know five for five, forest girl," Will said nonchalantly. His eyes were still closed, trying to get a quick nap. It had been a long day. We had hiked to the place we should have been picked up, but Will's message must not have gotten through.

George had barely slept. He had woken up several times the night before, one of them crying. I held his hand as he fell back to sleep, with mutters of prayers. I know the drugs were helping his pain, but they had made him disoriented. But he seemed focused today, despite everything that had happened. I was about to ask him if we were in the right spot when Maggie took the pine cone and started rubbing it along her arm.

"Sweetie, why are you doing that?"

"I don't know, I feel like I need it. Or I need to feel it."

She said it as she continued to rub the pine cone harder against her arm, not looking at my eyes again, as they were filling with worry. I looked back at George, who was focusing on his MCU again. But it was Will who spoke first, his eyes now wide open.

"George, we need to stop at the next Q station."

"We can't. We're hours away from the normal pick-up spot, and…" He sighed, looking at Maggie. "She'll be scratched, but she'll survive."

"Well, then can we at least guess and give her something?"

George put his MCU in his pocket and nodded towards my bag. He asked me as he rummaged through it again.

"Was she like this? When you picked her up?"

"No, but I think her meds wore off."

We didn't speak our suspicions as to her diagnosis. She was intelligent, but had trouble communicating. She had major sensory issues that only seemed escalated as the ringing in her head was still making her upset. Now she was seeking sensory input. It seemed to fit a pattern. They didn't have a name for it in the Republic. It was all but eradicated in the Territory, so it was rare.

"And yes, we can give her something." George unzipped my bag, and then pulled out a brush.

"A baby's hair brush, what–?"

He moved over to Maggie and gave it to her.

"Just try it."

She started brushing it across her arm where she had been scratching with the pine cone. Her face looked peaceful, maybe finding the sensation she was feeling.

"Maggie," George said tentatively, "I'm going to need you to walk some more, if you can. We have a few hours, but if we aren't in the right spot, they aren't going to see us."

She stopped, and put her hands over her ears as she rocked back and forth. George was quick to respond, moving to his knees to look her in the eye, "I have an idea. How about we carry you for ten minutes, then you walk for ten minutes? You can keep the brush."

She hesitated, then looked at his eyes intently before nodding.

The hours dragged on, exhausting, because there was little hope we were going to make the check-point on time, but we couldn't find the energy to move any faster. There was even less of a hope that someone would find us if we didn't make the station.

"Does she know what medicine she used?" Will asked me as George and Maggie were packing up after lunch.

"No," I said, almost remembering with a sharp pain, "She said a Sentry brought it to her so she didn't know."

"A Sentry? Seriously?" Will said shocked. I shook my head.

"I know, right? He was probably doing it as a favor for the parents, trying to make Elite and all, but…" I felt the need to give Alex some credit, even though Will couldn't know the whole truth. "But it sounds like he just wanted to save them. It doesn't matter. I think it's worth it for them to try to find her a new solution, so she can be more…her."

"You mean freaky-super-genius? That would rock. Did you–"

I wasn't sure what he was going to ask. But at that moment, I didn't care. We both stopped moving and talking, staring at George ahead of us, as we heard a murmuring sound. He froze, too.

"That sounds like a shuttle," he said, seconds before we saw it.

It came through some brush on the right. It was one of the smaller ones for the dense part of the woods. The door opened, and Avery came out. It was the only time in my life that I didn't hate seeing him, and I could tell from his expression the feeling was mutual. He was followed quickly by Dylan, who I hugged upon approaching us, despite barely knowing him. He said, "Good job, 27," a few times. He turned to Will next.

"Well, there you are," Avery said almost irritatingly. But then he nodded knowingly to George, who was smirking. Dylan knelt in front of Maggie. Will and George threw their bags to Avery.

"Hello. Your name is Maggie?" Dylan asked, smiling gently.

"I suppose so," she said, sounding tired and nervous.

"Well, we are going to go back on the shuttle, okay? That might be scary, but there are no drones in the area, and from here, our missiles can take them out. So it's safe. It's safer…"

"What percentage safer?" she said, analytically instead of anxious.

Dylan looked at her strangely, then at us. George whispered something in Avery's ear, and nodded with big eyes, as if to say "answer the girl."

Avery said, "At least 84 percent safer. That, combined with other factors like the weather being clear, we have about a 97 percent chance of reaching our destination without incident."

He said it as if he were saying it to Patterson or Zander, with his usual authoritative tone.

"Okay!" She jumped up, smiling as if nothing could be more thrilling. I laughed at their reaction as she skipped into the shuttle.

"You sure know how to pick them, 27," Dylan said jokingly.

We were still strapping in when Avery grabbed George's shoulder as he sat across from him.

"They're okay, George. Emily and Brie are fine."

"What?" George exclaimed.

"They just found them on a random patrol of the 10-mile mark. All their equipment fried in the blast. They had no way of contacting us. The driver…didn't make it. They jumped from the shuttle only moments before it hit as he was putting on the brakes. And they weren't even sure where they were, because he was driving. I just got confirmation, they're heading back."

"The driver? Parker?" George sounded a little deflated.

"Yeah, Parker. The Vessel is… she's okay, but barely. She was pretty far along, at least 35 weeks. Baby is under severe stress. She's bleeding. I just heard on com that she was going into labor when they found them both minutes ago. Thank goodness Emily and Brie are on it, but they aren't sure if…if the Vessel is going to make it."

No one talked after hearing that. George leaned in, either feeling relief that Emily and Brie were alive, or praying for them in their desperation to keep their Vessel survive. Maggie leaned against Dylan and asked to see his MCU. It was then that he saw the scratches on her arm. I was about to explain when…

"You need a brush?" he asked, once again surprising me.

"George gave me one." She pulled it out. He took it gently and rubbed it against her arm.

"You know, I have a sister who is a few years younger than me. She used to love brushes. She would play on my MCU all day."

"She's like me? I thought you don't make people in labs," Maggie sounded confused. "Why is she messed up?"

Dylan leaned in, and said, "She's not. And neither are you."

I now remembered one of the girls in Olivia's school; one who didn't go to all of her classes that shared Dylan's features and bright red hair. I noticed George and Will were looking at Dylan and Maggie, understanding fully a story I was just putting together. Avery was staring at his MCU, looking as if he was busy, but my guess was he probably didn't want to comment, or knew I would punch him if he did. Maybe both.

By the time we got to the compound, there were half a dozen people outside. Someone was on the ground, and she was screaming. There was only one kind of pain that could cause a woman to scream like she was.

"Well, she's not dead," Avery said casually. But he moved with urgency, jumping out of the shuttle and sprinting over to them.

We ran towards where Emily was cradling the mother's head, trying to keep her calm while Brie was hooking up her vitals. They were telling her to hold on, begging her to fight passing out. The person delivering...

"Collin, what do you got?" Dylan called out.

"She's stabilized, but she's bleeding! A lot!" Collin was yelling, and hadn't even looked up yet as he continued to talk to Dylan. "The girls are staying with her because she doesn't know me. But we're at ten centimeters. I was hoping you had found... I need a Protector."

He trailed off. As if he couldn't say my name.

I was almost behind him when I said, "Would the 27th Protector do?"

He turned to look at me, turning his knee on the ground. He stared at me through bloodshot, but intense eyes, his jaw dropping. As hard as the last days had been for me, it looked as if he had been just as tortured by the uncertainty of my fate.

I realized how much I had built up this moment in my mind. The moment I saw him, first laid eyes on him, I should have been able to hug him, to hold him, to tell him every prayer he had prayed, every effort to keep me alive, had brought me back to him.

But I threw it away so I could find beauty in the moment in front of me.

"Is that sani-powder?" I asked, kneeling beside him.

"Yes, it is. Gloves are next to you," Brie said, before turning back to the mother. "We thought…we weren't sure you made it."

"Trust me, the relief is mutual," I said to Brie, sharing an unapologetic smile. "What do you need?" I turned back to Collin.

"You mean other than knowing you're alive? I just need you to catch. I'll help if you need me. The baby is fine, but the mom…"

I saw what he meant. She was bleeding far too much to survive at this rate. The only reason she had to be hanging on was because of the transfusion Brie and Emily had set up.

"I'm sewing after we deliver–"

"Nope. I am," said a voice from behind me. It was Dr. Swanson, who appeared with a stretcher. "Collin, Aislyn, I want you to stay with the baby after delivery. I don't want to move the mother now. We might as well deliver here. Avery, Dylan, and Will, you're on stretcher. We'll get the mother to Operating Room 310. I'll handle afterbirth as well. Hopefully, we stop the excess bleeding. Looks like she must have ruptured…"

The Vessel screamed.

Brie begged her repeatedly to bear down, to push.

Collin looked at Brie interrupting, "We're close. Really close."

"Selena, so when you feel the next one…"

Her answer came in another scream. Brie kept coaching her through the push. I was about to say it when Collin yelled, "almost!"

"Give me one last good push, Selena," I shouted. "One more!"

Emily was whispering something in Selena's ear as she cried, but whatever it was, it gave her the strength she needed.

"It's coming…" Collin yelled, and yet trailed off into a whisper.

There was more screaming. More blood. More tears.

And then there was a boy.

Collin was holding the baby underneath his head, almost shaking. I held the body, quickly checking the feet for color, and Collins' hands moved to support the head and the chest. I slid my hands to cradle the baby as he cut the cord as quickly as we could, feeling my stomach turn as I noticed the bleeding was horribly accelerated.

"Brie! We need to hurry or we'll lose her," Avery said quickly.

Avery then lifted the mother in seconds, laying her on the stretcher as the others took hold of it. He called for the men to keep the stretcher on the ground, on our level as we kept wiping off the baby.

He pointed at me, and said, "See, the baby is fine. You did great. You'll get to hold him in just a little bit, okay?"

He kept echoing those words as they lifted the stretcher and went with her. Dr. Swanson gave me a wink as he started to speak with her. I kept wiping off the baby after Collin placed the monitors on. He smiled, the joy pushing out the tears he had tried to hold back. George had taken over handing me materials, and he took the blood type prick.

Collin looked in the baby's eyes, as if entranced by him.

"Look at that; you made it." He paused, then repeated "you made it" a few times as he looked up at me, and then down to the baby again. "We were worried about you, you know? You don't know how much we needed you to make it."

I gazed across the inches that separated us. I felt closer to him than I ever had, even though I couldn't obey my impulse to hug him. All I wanted was right there. A breeze came, warm and soft, pushing everything around us, as if to let us know the world was still moving as we stood frozen in space and time.

It felt like forever, because I would have stayed there forever if I could. Maybe a part of me would. But reality screamed, and I came crashing out of the haze of my thoughts.

The baby cried in my arms. I found myself smiling uncontrollably, almost embarrassed. George had pricked him for a sample again, glancing at Emily as she repeated "You did it" to Brie as she clung to her.

Brie looked relieved, but wasn't crying. She seemed like she was shaking off any fear she had felt, and was as confident as ever.

"Last sample," George said. "Brie, I think your arm–"

"I know. It's deep. I hit a branch as we jumped, and it sliced right through. I'm going down to medical. Give me the samples."

She gave George a quick hug, and rushed off.

"Is she okay?" George asked Emily tentatively. He was professional, not even hinting to any of the feelings I knew he held. Concern flooded his eyes, his feet anxious to move closer. But I noticed he took a step back right before she answered.

"Yeah, just a scratch. She's going to be fine. She's…"

She trailed off, and then an instant later lunged into George.

I could hear the breath almost get knocked out of him. Her arm wrapped against him as his hands hovered in front of him, not quite sure how to react to her. He winced slightly. Maybe he wished she wasn't clutching to the new wounds on his back. But then I realized the pain of not having her there, in his arms, would be worse. She could have broken open stitches, and he wouldn't have cared.

"She's going to be fine," Emily finally said, still shaking.

And I wondered if she was still talking about Brie as she repeated it. "George, I thought you died…and I never…told you."

George winced in pain, though his eyes were lit with hope. It was the strangest expression I'd ever seen, but he stopped her from saying perhaps what he had waited years to hear.

"Not now. Just wait. And not…" He winced. "…Too hard."

"Are you injured?"

She took one look at his back, even as I explained how he shielded Maggie and me from the crash. She looked concerned, but spoke boldly. "Let's go. Looks like you need a med room, too."

He didn't argue. He was too exhausted, emotionally and physically. He followed Emily as Maggie knelt beside me, in awe of the baby wrapping his fingers around mine. She knelt down and kissed his forehead. Collin held my other hand, grasping my wrist, as if he needed to feel my pulse as confirmation that his prayers were answered. I was waiting for her to ask a million questions, but she only asked one.

"So…this is where babies come from?"

Collin and I couldn't help but laugh; that question universally feared and so often awkwardly avoided was answered in the midst of the chaos. So much meaning, for one moment.

"Yes," I said, breathlessly, resolving with all my heart to write her words down in my journal, followed by the words I said next.

"This is how life starts. It always starts with fear and hope, fighting against each other."

I stared at Collin, taking a breath before continuing.

"And love makes sure that hope wins."

CHAPTER 14

The wind blew softly. It barely grazed my skin, but it seemed to hold the power to open my eyes. I wanted to see the leaves flutter in the soft breeze. The leaves each turned and spun to grasp the sun for a moment, looking almost transparent. They would float and swirl, and then lay still. And my eyes closed again.

I had been doing this for nearly an hour, barely speaking even though he lay in the grass right next to me.

"Did you read all my letters?" Collin asked quietly.

"Almost all of them. I hope the last three weren't particularly important."

"Why?"

"I deleted them," I said, my voice laced a regret that felt stronger now. "Along with some that I wrote to you. I had to give George my MCU, and I figured he wouldn't approve. Not discreet enough."

"Smart move. Look at you, little spy-soldier," he said, looking at my eyes now. His head was inches away from mine. He was lying just close enough to reach over and touch my hand. Sometimes it felt comforting, other moments it felt electric and made my pulse race. But even the sparks comforted me.

I finally remembered the questions I wanted to ask.

"Did you find out…does Alex know that Maggie's okay? He was bringing her meds, he has to be worried if he doesn't know."

"No. He doesn't know where she went. The details in the report suggest she ran away."

I paused, and felt a spasm down my arm again.

He grabbed my hand, saying for the tenth time, "He um…he took something again. He went in to do physical drills for about…twelve hours. He left this morning. It's going to be okay."

"Sometimes I feel like it's never going to be okay. He's reacted this way before. He thinks she's dead, Collin. I'm sure he feels–"

"I know how he feels, Aislyn. Trust me."

I winced. He reached out and squeezed my hand. I whispered, "So do I. No word on Eva?"

His blue eyes pierced me again. He clenched his jaw before speaking, maybe so he could sound calm. "She still could be fine."

He was trying to hide his own pain, just as he held it in last night when I discovered she still wasn't back.

"You have a worry beard," I said. I reached out to touch his chin and the tiny hairs that had gone unshaven in his anxiety.

"Yeah, I think Will has given up on shaving, too."

"Is Will still with Maggie?"

Collin nodded. "Lydia is there, too. They used the intel Michael hacked to try to find what medication Maggie was on, but they are sure they can improve it so she can be more herself. She's brilliant, by the way, even Avery said it. Lydia said they must have subdued some of her higher brain function with the medication. It cut off a part of her brain…just to cut off a couple weird behaviors."

"Well, I have to admit, I'm having a growing affection for anything called 'weird.' It always seems to make me more…alive," I said, even as the wind blew and I opened my eyes again. But as it slowed, the silence grew as I shut my eyes, asking what I hated the most. "So, is Zander still on the rampage?"

"Yes," Collin said, "But at least your initial debrief was…brief."

"It was barely existent. It was just Patterson and Zander, and she didn't want to hear anything about Maggie. There was too much going on. I heard she had a press conference to tell the world we were alive and she somehow took the credit for that."

He didn't speak, but rolled his eyes.

I continued, "And I don't think she likes Maggie. I could tell by the way she said her name. Then Patterson said something, Zander mentioned I didn't have a Vessel. And that was it. Still…"

I wouldn't dare say she was right, even as I pondered my failure to bring home a Vessel. I wanted to change the subject.

"How's George?"

"Oh, he got discharged today," Collin said as he released my hand. "Looks like Selena and Parker are alright."

"I hope someone explained that Parker is a last name, but I could also understand why she didn't care," I said.

I laid still, but then after a few minutes of silence passed, I jolted again. Collin held my hand firmly. I opened my eyes as the wind brushed against my skin. I stared at the leaves, but found myself at a loss for how to describe them. I could have written about them for hours on a lazy summer day a year ago. Now...

"I can't describe the tree. I wonder if I could even tell you a story now. I feel spent, in a way that I can never get refilled...and yet, I would rather do it again, even if it meant I wasn't...whole."

"So, what? You feel torn?"

"You can't imagine," I said, while knowing it was a lie.

He rolled over on his torso so that I could see his eyes, striking and clear, as if he wanted me to understand completely what he was going to say.

"I don't want you to feel torn. Who you are and who you are becoming are sometimes two different things. What you love...is sometimes two different things. But it's all still you. And I love it."

The breeze stopped, making the world seem still. But this time as the wind died down, I didn't close my eyes. I couldn't have closed my eyes, no matter how hard I tried. I needed to let everything he said saturate into my mind and heart.

"No one should be torn because they love too much. I know it's hard, Aislyn, to love them, and me, and everyone you do. But that doesn't mean you're torn. It might mean that you're whole."

I nodded, resolving to try to believe him. He leaned in to kiss my forehead, and then laid down again on the grass.

And whether to lighten the mood or to make sure I knew, he sarcastically said, "And really? I don't know what it's like to be torn?"

I laughed. "Yeah, sorry. That was a pointless jab to get you to realize how I felt. How adolescent of me."

He scoffed, and then reached down to put an extra blanket out around us. His watch beeped. I caught a glimpse of a message.

"Sam? Liam? Are they okay?"

Collin sighed. "As far as I know, yes. They are out of their isolation, in a group cell now. So, we didn't know this, but there was a program recording all keystrokes and communications from the Command Center. They have all been proven innocent."

"But they're still being held?"

Collin shook his head. "They have to have someone to blame. And they can't blame a Protector."

I closed my eyes again when he said, "Speaking of 'they,' your Council debrief is in an hour. Are you ready?"

"Yes. Well…maybe." I opened my eyes to see his boyish smirk before saying, "Not at all."

He smiled, the world bursting in sunlight as the breeze blew the leaves out of the way so the sunlight could strike us. I tried to write this moment in my head, resolving that during the debrief I would remember it. It would distract me so I could do what Patterson had warned me to do: stick to the details with as little emotion as possible. He made me promise to keep my head down.

In the past, I had dreaded sitting in front the Council. But I had lost any respect for them that made them intimidating. I did notice half of them were suspiciously looking at Zander. I saw Eldridge at the end, looking concerned as a man named Robinson continued to question me.

"It was three days into your journey that you began seeing developmental changes in Maggie?" Robinson all but scowled.

"Yes," I said, wary that they were bringing up her condition.

"Well, I suppose it does happen. We would, however, like to think that you are risking your life for some with more potential."

I almost screamed right there, ready to take Robinson out, but Patterson's eyes got very wide. Still, I knew I wasn't hiding my emotions as well as I could. I breathed out, but it was too late.

"There's no reason to get upset, 27," Zander said as she typed on her MCU. "We are aware that Maggie deserves our compassion and respect, but we are much more likely to make an impression among our people in the Territory and among the people of the Republic when we save a Vessel, which you have yet to do. You have yet to reach your potential. We have trained you with skills you aren't using, for missions you're avoiding. In that light, some may think it was…a waste. Or that your training was wasted."

While realizing how rare it was for me not to have seen a Vessel yet, I was so infuriated by Robinson's and Zander's comments that I had to let my rebuttal fly, despite Patterson's eyes begging me not to talk as I stood to speak.

"Yes, I suppose I haven't used any of my abilities to help a new life into this world. Except for when I got back from my last mission. And delivered a baby. Or when I was in an alley when a mother tried to kill Brie. And delivered a baby. Or when I was in the forest with Tessa. And delivered a baby."

I said the last one loudly, and stronger rather than sarcastic. I now understood what the sensation of freezing a room with a sentence felt like. Patterson's eyes weren't shooting off warnings anymore. They were closed. Eldridge looked like he was trying to suppress a grin. A few of the other council members surprised me by looking impressed. One of them said, "Well, young lady, you certainly are correct. And there is no reason for you to feel inadequate in any way. And Maggie, I think her name is, will be a fantastic addition to our community, I'm sure. She is very smart."

"Yes, but it's still not dealing with the problem at hand," Zander said, enraged. It was only then that I heard a camera snapping pictures. I barely noticed the press, and at this point barely cared. I was staring harshly at Zander as she spoke again.

"You keep running into unique cases and strange sob stories. You keep looking for something, attaching before even thinking if this is the easiest or the best person to bring home. Do you realize there are Unnecessaries and Vessels that are less of a risk?"

I breathed before answering, if only so I could sound as steady as I could. I didn't want the room to hear my fear. I wanted them to hear my words.

"Yes, I do. But I'm choosing to save these children, instead."

"Because you need to be the hero? Yes, legendary 27th Protectors must be heroes." Her voice dripped with sarcasm.

"No," I said in a surprisingly determined tone. "No, I'm not a hero. They are. You know what a hero does? They are called 'Unnecessaries' and survive despite overwhelming fear. They are Vessels who hold life within them as they hold their breath they won't get caught. They save babies and live in sewers with no hope. They paint and create beauty even when they're slaves. They find a light in their darkness. And the only thing I'm guilty of is saving the heroes you ignore."

I suppressed every emotion stirring in me, hoping I had a chance to say it as clearly as possible. "I'm not the hero. They are. That makes it worth risking my life to save them."

There was silence again, save for the uncomfortable shifting in some chairs. I was preparing for another round of insufferable questions from Zander. I felt my anger burn, waiting to talk about the shuttles being hit by the drone.

But it worried me.

Because she was smiling.

"Thank you, 27th Protector, that will be all."

I stopped, openly sharing my shock in my expression. I opened my mouth, gaping at her nonchalant statement.

"What do you mean? I haven't talked about the attack–"

"You, like many others, will attribute your feelings about your shuttle explosion to our change in policy. You see the attack as retaliation for us killing two Sentries. It's clear that you're emotionally charged at this moment– which no one can blame you for having been proven wrong about the recent events of the Society's savage attacks on us—so I think we're done for the day."

Another councilman, I think it was Miller, said, "Ma'am, with all due respect, we shouldn't refuse to listen to testimony because *you* don't agree with it. Many of us feel the consequences of your new policies, which have caused the Society to retaliate, has put our Protectors in more danger than they were already in!"

"I think all the hard details are in the report, and we hardly need to hear again how horrible the attacks were."

"Yes, I agree," I said, talking as solidly as I could, knowing I only had a few seconds. "How horrible it would be for them to learn that because you started a war you can't possibly win, I had to sedate a scared child and pull pieces of debris from a trainer's—"

The gavel hit. Before I knew it, she had yelled, "Dismissed!"

I stopped, stood up, and was a few steps away when someone yelled, "This is unacceptable." I heard another quote Matheson, Miller yell for an injunction, and Robinson curse back. But I was dismissed. I turned, my back to the room as I left the flurry of arguments behind me. I almost didn't care what they said.

I was in the hallway by the time Michael caught up to me. He shook his head. "Way to keep your head down, 27. Subtle."

I was fuming, wondering if I should punch my bag in my Circle, imagining Zander's face in the center.

Zander. She was brilliant. She was a brilliant, evil, genius. But that's not what I called her under my breath. I cursed, just loud enough for Michael to hear.

"Agreed. Could you say that a little louder? I'd love the chance to be more targeted than we already are so that all my effort to keep all your secrets is wasted. That'd be great."

I tilted my head back, closing my eyes briefly. "Sorry. I should've realized that you would have to pay for what I said."

He shrugged. "Well, at least we all got it on camera. Maybe the press will eat it up and public opinion will change enough to dethrone her. Weird way to go about starting a revolution."

I raised my eyebrows. "Please. Let's not add revolutionary to the list that defines me, along with reckless, crazy, delusional, and inconveniently in love with my trainer."

He nodded, "And of course, you didn't even name him." He stopped, looking shaken for a minute. I knew his mind was on Alex, but he didn't dare say it. Even thinking about him made me jump when the door opened. My panic only subsided when I saw it was Patterson, who looked irritated.

"Aislyn, not quite what I was looking for," he said disapprovingly.

"Are they still–"

"Debating. Let's call it debating, Aislyn. Did you prepare that little speech?"

I shook my head, trying to shake the anger that had lit up in me to deliver my "speech."

"No, trust me. I hate this. Why didn't she want me talking about the shuttles?"

"You're a good writer, Aislyn, but a better storyteller. People knowing what happened– through your eyes– is completely different than people knowing the facts. It would have swayed them to push Zander out of power. There are more people advocating for 'peace,' and not that I've ever been a huge advocate for peace, I wish they could understand...this isn't war. This is chaos. War will come, when it's time. And this is ..."

"Not the time."

I turned to see Eldridge. He shifted towards me.

"I'm sure, my dear, that Patterson is going to suggest a hasty exit tomorrow morning, back to the Republic. So that being said, maybe I could relieve him of that task by walking you to your Circle, so that Patterson can go back in the Council room?"

"You shouldn't have," Patterson said sarcastically.

"Michael, I think you'll need the release codes from Collin. And maybe give him a debrief on the debrief," he said, as he opened the door and pointed to the source of the angry voices.

"Yes, sir."

Michael walked quickly past me. Patterson closed his eyes for a second, a look of bravery and nobility overtook him, and he entered the Council room in confident strides.

Eldridge held out his hand: his invitation to walk and talk. But I found I couldn't talk. I was infuriated he wasn't saying anything, or that he hadn't spoken in there in the midst of the chaos. Or that he hadn't stopped any of this from happening.

"Well, are you going to throw a punch, or just yell at me?"

"What?" I asked genuinely confused.

"You're angry at me. And yes, I can tell. You're most likely mad that I've let this get too far, or perhaps because you don't understand my silence, or because you are upset that the task you fought to commit yourself to is suddenly not deemed worthy enough of your time."

I let out a breath through clenched teeth. "All of the above."

"Ah. An honest answer. As a politician, I rarely hear one. It's a shame, for I love answers dripping with clarity. Then let us begin at the beginning. Aislyn, you're allowed to be angry at me. I'm not even going to try to change your mind. Because I want to talk to you. I want to communicate with you. I'll let you be angry."

"Okay," I said, feeling a little relieved and free to speak.

But he cut me off. He turned to say in a scolding tone, "I am affording Zander the same opportunity. She can be angry, as long as she communicates honestly. I haven't sold out. Trust me."

I couldn't think of a response, even as he continued, "I don't need Zander to be proved wrong, Aislyn. I need her to change her mind, or admit she's wrong before she leaves power. These mistakes should not be repeated, but at the same time, these actions may be justified in years to come– under different circumstances, we may have to give the same orders. Do you understand?"

I nodded, almost scared at the seriousness of his tone.

"Secondly," he said, as he continued to walk, "you've misunderstood my silence. Silence is not inaction. I'm still fighting for you. For all of you."

"How?" I asked, more confrontational than I wanted to be.

"I've been praying," he said. I thought he was going to elaborate, and when he didn't, I flared up again.

"That's all you're doing? I thought you'd be meeting with people, with the press, with Patterson. You're…praying?"

"Yes, because approaching the king of the universe to try to save us from ourselves and those bent on killing us, someone who claimed to love all of us so much he would die, does seem like a silly option compared to yelling at people with feigned political power."

I opened my mouth to protest. But not thinking of anything right away, I closed it.

A few steps later, even though I knew it might offend him, I asked, "But what if God's not listening?"

"You have rescued two Unnecessaries in four weeks, despite the five extra days of training tacked on, which might have broken you. Against all odds, you have evaded every Sentry and officer. You have survived an attack on your shuttle and delivered a baby. You have discovered that you have friends here that you didn't even know the names of a month ago, who are risking their lives and freedom for you despite you being a stranger. And Alex is still alive. It may seem like God's not listening if you aren't looking for it, but the second you look for the proof, it couldn't be clearer that He is. Look, Aislyn. Please look."

I swallowed, a little ashamed to admit my doubt, but also feeling convicted to try to see things differently. He continued.

"So, I believe the last issue was that you are struggling with is your identity, most likely because it disorients even the most secure people. Just as you fell in love with the idea of being a Protector, the world shifted. And you feel overwhelmed."

I didn't argue, but said, "And the solution to that problem?"

"Nothing. There isn't one. Identity is an elusive thing, Aislyn. Don't be so self-doubting that you feel you must settle the debate of exactly who you are and your purpose in this moment of your life. You are loved. You love. You write. You ask questions. You have amazing ideas. You believe in something enough to die for it. Don't you remember what I said?"

I stopped, not expecting to have the conversation shift this way. I was beginning to feel like an immature mess when all of a sudden he was addressing me with honor I didn't feel I deserved.

"Be alive enough," I said, echoing his words from months earlier.

"Enough said, then," he said, even as he turned to walk away. "You can be the truest version of yourself if you don't compare or overthink it, and if you believe that someone created you to be you. That requires neither time nor argument: just faith."

He pressed his hand against my shoulder, moving past me.

I walked back to my Circle, processing some of what he said, and pushing away some thoughts to process later. I walked in to find the punching bag in the middle. Collin leaned on the pole holding it up, saying with a skewed smile, "Thought you might need this."

I bit my lip and then released it to smile, not sure why I hid it at first. "You read my mind."

He laughed. I punched. I vented. He talked. There were too many details to remember, but I did get a hold of some names I wanted to keep in mind. Augustus Miller was the one that stuck out the most. I tried to pull my mind back to the million more pressing things. We talked about my agenda for the rest of the day: getting my pack together, meeting with Michael, getting new files on my MCU, and getting ready for Vinalia.

"Are we going to practice Dance?" I asked, catching my breath as I held out my hand for him to take my pulse.

"Yeah, consider this a warm-up," he said, leaning against the bag. "You said you practiced? So, we just have to see how it works."

"Yeah," I said, all of a sudden feeling flushed. Even with everything going on, I couldn't believe how he made me feel, even by touching just my wrist. I was very conscious that I would be near him, close enough to feel his breath, trying to remember moves while feeling his every muscle moved next to mine.

"I'm sorry, if it's going to be uncomfortable. I hope it's not." He stopped, looking at the floor. He was still holding my wrist as he pulled it out towards the wall. I slid my hand down to his waist.

"Alright, lift your back, clear your mind, and drop your shoulders, and reach out your hand a little more. A little more."

I followed his directions, reaching out as far as I could. Then a little more. He pushed down on my shoulder with his other hand.

"Ow!" I said, almost jokingly. It did strain it a little.

"Sorry. Keep your shoulders down. It's an amateur dance mistake, and the fewer mistakes, the more chances of you getting out alive. Now, I'm going to dip you, in the circle. So do two steps, pull your knee up and around me. That's your anchor, so as tight as you can, then just keep your back straight and pull in your abs when I pull you up. We only have a few hours, so we need to…not get distracted. I need you to promise me."

I tried to dance with him while ignoring how I felt about him. It was nearly impossible, and not just for me. He sounded breathless a few times, diverting his eyes away from me. I felt more confident sometimes if only because I was making him lose his usual calm exterior. But as we kept dancing, I lost things, too.

My breath. My focus. My resolve.

I was just about to apologize when a few moves later, his eyes hit me, looking both fascinated and frightened of everything he was feeling. He leaned in close enough to kiss me, his lips almost grazing me as he spoke.

"Keep it together. I don't know how to…if you could just focus on…"

"Dance?" I said, even as he was stepping to the side, trying to see if I could diffuse my feelings before they exploded. "Yes. Maybe." He spun me, pulled me in.

"Not at all."

There were so many breathless moments as the afternoon hours went by. There were moments when I was laughing with him. There were moments I truly felt I couldn't pull this off.

There were moments I sat on the mat without moving for minutes. I yelled at him once for almost dropping me, and then apologized ten times. There were moments when he looked at me as if he was restraining a feeling that he couldn't express, and then would look at the floor rather than at me. He pulled my hand in and kissed it. In a strange way, despite everything I had been through, it was the hardest thing I had ever done: not to kiss him.

By the time I picked up my journal that night, too tired to write, I had decided to keep the breathless moments a secret. Instead of writing, I tried to find some notes I still hadn't paged through. I thought there wouldn't be anything to advise me. Everything seemed way too complicated. But as my mind wandered to those complexities, the words of the 27th Protector of the 125th generation that seemed to rise off the page.

"We don't see it as it is. It's not that complicated. It's simple."

I couldn't find any truth in what she said. I felt as incapable of finding peace as I was next to the inferno of the shuttle wreckage. I wish I could have screamed back at the words in the book. Eventually, every regret and worry tired me until I fell asleep.

Collin came back at 1 A.M. The meeting had confirmed that my anxiety was justified– the agony of regrets that became my lullaby.

I should have never agreed to learn Dance.

I should've looked harder for a Vessel.

I should've trusted Eldridge more.

I should've listened to Patterson and kept my head down.

We had stayed up to see if Eva would check in by 2 A.M. She didn't. I leaned into Collin, who held my head and kept praying for her, just loud enough for me to hear. I found myself praying God would hear him. I didn't care or expect God to hear me, but I just begged him to hear Collin. At 4 A.M., Michael brought my pack up, asking what time I had gone to sleep to be up so early. I had to admit to not sleeping, which made him roll his eyes.

I did get a few hours of sleep, if only to give me the strength to do what I needed to do.

I had to rip myself away again.

I couldn't hug him. I couldn't tell him anything more about how I felt that I hadn't already told him, and yet my silence was suffocating me. I wanted to say it all again.

We both were holding our breath, standing inches away from each other in the elevator. The air felt electrified by the distance between us, like an unseen current trying to draw us together. I felt vulnerable, even as we walked down the hallway stoically. I was worried that even though my love for him was invisible, nothing so strong could be ignored or overlooked by anyone walking by. I could tell he was struggling for words, but he wasn't able to speak. There were no words to use to say goodbye.

Finally, he whispered in my ear, "I'm with you."

When we got up to the field where the shuttles usually take off, our concentration was broken by a tiny laugh.

"Maggie!"

"Hi!" she exclaimed. "I just found this. What is it?"

We both turned to the piece of fuzz she saw, flying through the air, riding a summer breeze.

"It's a pollen fuzz, sweetie." I wanted to tell her to catch it and make a wish. That fairies come from them. That she should blow it apart and let it go, following it until she was too far from home, and then find enough courage to find her way back. Instead, I prepared myself for more technical questions she might ask.

But she didn't ask them.

"I've spent an hour catching these. I love catching them."

"People usually do," I said, surprised. "How did you know that you were supposed to catch it?"

"I just knew," she said, her hair flowing around her making her look as if she was floating. "It looks so lost. So beautiful."

Then she blew it upwards, towards the blue sky, where it all but disappeared in the white glare of the sun hitting the clouds.

She did it again, and again. George and Brie walked up behind us. I half expected George to tell us to keep moving. But he didn't. Instead, he looked deep in thought.

I was thinking out loud, echoing the words in my journal.

"It's simple. You see beauty floating, just out of reach, something that you can't have or be. You see it fall, and urgency hits every nerve in your body. It can't fall. You need to catch it."

I had turned to Collin before I said, "People think what we do is hard. And while it does come with pain, it's just a reflex."

As I finished, Brie had cupped her hand to catch the last of the fuzz floating by, but the wind bounced off her hand. Her fingers wove through the air, following it as it blew upward.

This was our reflex. This was our reaction to the lost souls that would float away unnoticed or lost. We reached out and we caught them.

It was natural. It was as natural as breathing.

Even if it cost us our last breath.

CHAPTER 15

I finally had found enough courage to walk through the warehouse district on a certain street I wasn't sure I'd ever walk down again. I touched the holes made in the door from the Sentries' bullets that had chased me down the alley, wondering which one of them had shot through my arm first. I didn't have the courage to go up the stairs, to where I was hiding after he shot me. I might never be able to go up there again.

I might never see Alex again.

I wondered if that was why I lingered here: because this was the last place I had seen him. I bit my lip, thinking of every clip of him we had seen on surveillance. I found myself wanting more than ever just to assure him of something. Or to be assured.

I lost myself in thoughts as I headed to the streets in-between the warehouse district and the fashion buildings. I was walking on the main street, past people talking about everything and nothing at the same time. It was busy, which was good. I was finding peace in the busy places, because the chances of someone noticing me were less than if I was somewhere exposed. I was watching a broadcast through a window as I checked in for the day.

"In other news tonight," the broadcaster said, "brilliant artist Paul Kalahan is taking a break from his career in the art world. He said the atmosphere of the political state is too distracting, but that the problem was–"

I didn't hear the rest. I smirked as I whispered to myself.

"The problem is that someone stole your indentured servant and you have no real talent."

I was listening to other news, but it wasn't until they mentioned the word "Protector" that I made sure to listen. I forced my head to move up slow enough for no one to notice.

It was another police shooting incident. I knew exactly who was involved, because Tessa had characteristically shared every shred of detail about her latest run-in with the police in her attempt to take them out.

I pulled myself away from the broadcast, left the café, and keep walking. I was wearing my pack, going for a more Sub-Terra look this time, but that meant my cover didn't allow me free time to frequent cafés all day. I had dressed differently, taking Brie's advice. She said it made you more approachable. If I was honest with myself, Zander's urgency not being a factor, I did want to rescue a Vessel. I could save one. I knew it. There was no reason not to want one.

But I had no reason to ignore the movement in the alley.

I was looking ahead, like so many others, when I saw the box tip over and a shadow running. I stopped to look at a window before moving back. I pretended to check my phone.

I saw it again.

It was a boy, small, probably age six.

I stopped myself from heading down the alley. I almost wanted to let him go. I was supposed to be looking for a Vessel.

I hated that thought, with a pang of guilt. I wanted to keep going, if not only to find a Vessel, but to try to find Alex.

But he needed me.

I swallowed my frustration and took the first few steps down the alley, still looking at my phone, until I felt like I was far enough away to look up and try to find him

Except he wasn't there.

I had a moment when I had to remind myself not to panic. I moved quicker, looking around boxes as I ran.

I moved down another alley minutes later, now regretting my hesitancy, saying to the boy I had lost, "I'm sorry." The doubts flooded in again.

I should've moved faster.

I should've looked up from my phone.

I shouldn't have missed out on saving him because I had tried to ignore my reflex for a chance to bring home a Vessel.

But I felt both relief and panic when I heard a small voice.

"Sorry for what?"

I turned, and he stepped out from behind a dumpster.

"For losing you," I said. "What is your name?"

"Oh–" he looked as if he had to think about it. "John."

That was weird. There was a blip on an internal alarm in my mind, but I pushed it aside. If he were trapping me, he wouldn't have made it so hard to find him.

I was getting a queasy feeling that became harder to ignore.

"My name is John. I…left school today. This was the third time I was warned I needed to, you know, just kick it into gear, I guess. I don't have the gear they need me to shift into, you know?"

"Yeah, I get it." It sounded genuine. He couldn't be lying.

But even as I did continue to speak, he didn't seem any more comfortable. He just seemed more uneasy.

"John, if you're scared…"

"I'm not scared of you," he said quickly. "I'm scared of them."

"You don't need to be," I said reassuringly. "You can leave it all behind, and never have to be scared of them ever again."

He glanced to the right of him, at something behind a dumpster. I thought maybe he was just thinking, pondering. His brown eyes were sad.

"I just wanted so badly…to be one of them."

"I know," I said, lying. Not really sure why rejection hadn't convinced him to run for his life, I got on one knee, trying to remember everything from psychology classes to try to talk to him.

"The thing is…I thought, the other day, that maybe…there's a way for you to help me."

"Yes, John. There is." I was wondering if he just needed time to process, so I settled in to give him that, placing my hand on the gravel.

Except there was a glint of something in his eyes.

Something dangerous.

"You see, they don't think I'm one of them. But if I caught a Protector, I would be. If I caught you, if I pulled the alarm…"

My breath caught. I looked at the fire alarm to the right of him, feeling vulnerable with each moment I stared at it.

"They would believe that I'm one of them. They would, right?"

I had the sinking feeling that I was dead and didn't know it yet.

"John?" Panic was already taking over, because I couldn't think of what to say next even though my head was racing. I repeated his name, not even sure if it was his real one. I was very aware that I had my knife.

I dismissed that thought instantly, thinking that killing him would be worse than any pain. It would stay in my pack.

My pack.

He took a step toward the alarm. My breath returned, ragged, matching my heartbeat. I shifted, but almost lost my balance, still one knee with my hand hovering over the street. There were tiny rocks stuck to the sweat on my palm. I felt them, just like I felt everything acutely.

I was still on one knee, so I tried to beg.

"Why would you try to entrap someone willing to save you?"

Another step.

I tried again. "It's not that hard. We just go."

Another step.

I wasn't going to convince him to save me.

But I could slow him down, to give a chance for my plan B to form. In the panic, I didn't know if I could form a plan B, but then it began to take shape. George's words in the Q station echoed. I had told him I was amazed that he had pulled out the cloths so we could breathe by the fiery shuttle and even made a quick fire out of the alcohol and lighter. He had said, *"Everything you'll ever need is in your pack. You just have to see it differently."*

Another step.

"John, if that's your name, please. You just have to come…"

Even if I ran away, he would remember what I looked like.

The next step crunched against the gravel. He hesitated.

I had slipped off my pack, just in case I had to do what I needed to do, thinking through everything I could do. Thoughts raced like my pulse as I pulled on the zipper slowly.

"You just have to trust me. Please don't do this," I pleaded. I knew it would be my last as his hand rested on the alarm, but all I could say was, "Trust me. I will save you."

His hand was still on the alarm as he faced me.

"Yes. You will."

He pulled up his shirt. There was a recorder strapped to his belt.

"The second they hear this, after they catch you, I'll be necessary to them. You still get to Protect me. It's not so bad."

I finally stood up, feeling the rush of adrenaline hit every nerve in my body. I reached for the bottle I needed, even as the revolting sound of the alarm pierced the silence.

The sound forced my mind and body to feel the betrayal and pain that I needed to feel to do what I needed to do.

I poured a drug on the cloth.

Maybe he wasn't expecting me to charge him, but especially not with a rag. He even looked at my knife. But I threw it on the ground to distract him.

I put the cloth over his mouth. He collapsed in my arms, and I slowly lowered him to the ground. I was about to run away when I turned around, the story forming furiously in my mind.

The alarm was still ringing.

They were coming.

They would kill him.

They were going to kill him when he awoke in a few minutes, because he wouldn't remember what I looked like.

There were sounds and screams.

Screams. I thought of a plan.

I needed to make him necessary to them.

I found the largest roll of tools I could find and emptied it, the instruments clanging on the hard road as I wrapped the canvas around my face.

He might be able to prove what I sounded like but not what I looked like.

I took a few seconds, got three vials of the most flammable alcohol and my lighter, some gauze, and then I grabbed the sani-powder packs.

Even as I prayed this would work, feeling wrecked inside as I began to think about what he had just done, I picked the boy up. I finally heard footsteps behind me. I had seconds. I dropped the boy and turned to the footsteps and the officer just as he turned the corner, and released a sani-powder pack straight at his chest.

It exploded, as it usually did with a three-foot radius, flying in his face. He had just reached for his weapon, but was pulling back in shock. He was instantly blinded, trying to scream, yet gagging on the powder. I ran up to the dock and opened the door to the alley.

I squirted the alcohol on the piles of boxes and lit it. I threw the vials on the ground, breaking them on the concrete, then lighting the rag on fire right at the doorway, I dropped it as I opened the door to the building.

As I had hoped, I quickly saw the faces of about fourteen people on the other side, who went from vaguely concerned about noises in the alley to shocked at seeing me, holding the fabric over my face with flames behind me, screaming, "Fire in the alley! There's a little boy! Everyone out, now!"

They all moved, screamed, shouted, and panicked like I had hoped they would. It was an office building of some kind, so there was security already calling the police. One was brave enough to look out and yell, "There's a boy! And an officer!"

Hopefully, the boy wouldn't die if people knew he was there. It was hard to disappear a victim of a fire who police had saved, and some civilians would find him alive. I moved him inside as people were hovering around his coughing body.

In moments, I saw the chaos I had successfully created unfold, with nearly a hundred people in the street to cover my exit. That chaos was going to buy me time. The police in the alley moved towards the boy, but out in front of the building, even as I exited a minute later, pretending to hold my cloth over my face from the fire, I saw Hydech pull up. I had hoped it would be Alex. I cursed in my head.

And in my head, the clock started ticking.

I tied the cloth around my face. I ran. I was half a building away when I began running through events as they would be happening in real time.

By now, the police would have found no real source for a fire.

I was one more building away.

By now, they would have found the tools and the sani-powder.

Two buildings away.

By now, they would have used something to wake up the boy and ask him what happened.

Five buildings away.

I ran faster than I ever had before.

Because next, the boy would answer. He wouldn't remember all of it, but enough. He would have the recorder. They would listen. They'd see the tools, and make the connection.

I was two blocks and twelve buildings away when a very different alarm sounded.

I pushed through to the nearest door that looked unused.

I had realized why. As I took off the cloth, I noticed the whole building seemed to be under construction. It was the perfect place to hide, but then again, they knew that. I turned out the door, walking down the alley. I crossed the street, placing the cloth over my face again. I found the last vial of alcohol and lit the gauze I had jammed in it, and threw it in the air across the street from the building I wanted to hide in.

If they thought I had crossed the street, I had a chance. They needed a place to look, and would hopefully follow the explosions.

It blew within seconds. I didn't see it. I was already running away. I prayed no one had gotten hurt. I swung around the rail of the dumpster to jump inside. I was there, smelling something rotting, feeling something rotting in me.

My faith in every Unnecessary was tainted. How could he have done that? And under that despair, anxiety come creeping in as I asked myself the most urgent question: how would I ever trust anyone again?

I moved back into the building once I heard the police race down the alley. They had taken the bait and ran across the street. I was hoping they would follow their logical plan, assume I had crossed the road, and I would have a window to escape. I was certain the plan had worked when they began sending everyone north of Market, leaving me huddled in a ball buildings away.

But eventually, when their story had a dead end, they'd come looking. They still probably had enough officers combing the area leaving very little hope.

But if they chased down another story, that lead to another dead end, would they give up? Collin's voice broke through my cloudy thoughts. It was a memory of him training me, mixed with his desire to keep me alive.

"The more places you could be, the less chance they'll find you."

I realized that if I led them on again, in a different direction, they'd be more dispersed. More leads for them to follow meant officers would scatter over larger distances, making larger gaps in the perimeter.

I jumped up and out of the dumpster, taking a second to see if the alley was clear. I for reached the sewer grate. Even as I did, I cursed in my head as I realized it had made too much noise.

Someone shouted, "Sewers! I need someone underground."

I slid down the ladder, pulling out a sani-powder packs and throwing both of them forward in the tunnel, hoping it resembled a trail. I knew it was a risk, but I returned back to the ladder, and began to climb up until almost at the top.

I could tell someone was stepping on the grate. It was a tactic, I was sure, to have one officer cover an exit until they all had partners to go underground.

I wasn't getting back out. I'd failed. With my short trail already laid out to convince them I moved in one direction, I wondered if I should just go the opposite way.

No. They'd be thorough this time. I couldn't just run in the opposite direction. The footsteps would echo like crazy and I'd never get far enough to hide in the labyrinth. They'd turn around right after getting off the ladder and see me…

But they wouldn't turn around as they were climbing down the ladder. They would turn around at the bottom, not the top.

I held my breath, scared I wouldn't survive what I was about to do. I felt the fear escalate as I climbed back up the ladder. I kept moving up each ring of the ladder. My head ached more with each quickening heartbeat. Their voices became louder. I had to get closer to the grate with the man standing guard for the plan to work. It made every breath feel strained, fighting the paralysis of dread as I climbed the ladder.

I got to the top, and then turned to look at the ceiling of the cavernous space, leaning back only one leg and leaving one hand on the top rung of the ladder. To my relief, there were pipes about one foot below the ceiling. I tried not to stare at the grate that could open at any second. I was having trouble grasping the pipe. There were three. I reached for the first, pulling my one hand on and planning to swing.

I quickly let go as I felt it begin to drop, spinning back to the ladder as quickly and quietly as I could. The sensation was nauseating, watching the gravel drop from where I had pulled.

I didn't hesitate. If they had heard, I only had one chance.

I took it.

I didn't keep one foot on this time. I leaped up, pushing off from the ladder, and in one fluid motion pulled my stomach in as I wrapped my calves around the pipe to hug it.

And then I froze.

This pipe wasn't loose. I could feel it was steel and it was cold, which meant it must have been a water line. It wouldn't budge.

I slowly used my arms and legs to crawl down the pipe away from the ladder, moving my arms in small movements, sliding across the pipe just like Avery had taught us. My legs were cramping. I looked, upside down now, wondering how long I could hold on. My arms had begun to shake. I pulled up and around the pipe so I was resting on top of it instead of dangling beneath it. I had just adjusted my balance when I heard the grate.

I saw the first officer enter, and he placed his flashlight on the ground below him. He was only a few feet away from me, but couldn't see me in the immediate darkness. There were four officers who followed. They all missed me as I hovered above them. If any of them had turned around on the top of the ladder, they would have seen the white in my eyes. But they all looked at the ground, as I presumed they would. The gestured as they spoke about me in the most unflattering language imaginable. Then they split up, and were out of sight within seconds

I needed to move quickly. I knew that. But I was paralyzed. I screamed at my arms to move, but my muscles were too tired. A drop would risk injury.

An instinct to survive had empowered me to climb up, but it immobilized me. I couldn't stay, because when they came back up, there's no way they would miss me.

One inch. I moved my arm out, my breath drowning out my thoughts. I strained to remember everyone I loved, hoping if fear couldn't push me, maybe love could.

Collin. Another inch. Maggie. Another inch. My sister Olivia. Another inch.

I went through a long list, almost back at the ladder, feeling my legs cringe and cramp as they held me onto the pole. I shifted to swing out, with just my arms holding on as I swung out my legs. I slid off, falling at an angle, making my stomach lurch as I reached out to the rung of the ladder and finally made contact, wrapping my legs around the ladder as I reached it.

There was no time. It made a noise, although the echoing cavern would help cover my exit. I climbed as quickly and quietly as I could. I didn't see anyone in the alley. I just noticed that the building under construction had all the doors open…

Which meant that they had already cleared the building.

I ran to the abandoned building in seconds, fighting my reflex to barricade, or even close, the door. I wanted to leave everything as they had left it. If they had checked it already, there was a chance they wouldn't be back. I had another small chance.

I just needed to hide. I needed to be still.

I couldn't though. All of the running, hiding, plotting, and now I was just standing here, on the other side of the door still open. Minutes later, more police ran past that door, down into the trap I had set. I was aware of every noise I made, each soft step as loud as a clap of thunder in my mind, because even the smallest sound could betray me to my death– and it could strike at any minute.

I finally forced myself up seven flights of stairs, slowly, painfully warry. Luckily there was little residue on the stairs that was noticeable. There were many prints. I found a desk, and laid under it. I felt my legs shaking, almost uncontrollably. I thought of the irony. Maybe Alex would find me now, lost, hiding in an abandoned building, and fighting for my life.

So I waited. The minutes became longer. I searched my pack for anything to calm me. I needed to save battery on the MCU, and they might be able to track it somehow, so I turned it off. It reminded me of Collin's last letter.

Of course he had prayed; he prayed that I would save someone.

He probably hadn't guessed that they would try to kill me.

I found some strange comfort in the fact that at least I believed in a deity who knew betrayal. It was a unique, sharp pain: almost being murdered by the person I was trying to rescue.

I think I dozed off, the adrenaline leaving me with nothing but fatigue. It had been an hour, maybe a little more, when I awoke. I heard a voice yell, ordering men to sweep all the buildings again. I felt tears grow. My muscles burned, as if to protest for causing them so much pain in a vain effort to keep me alive. I found myself paralyzed, yet resolved as I heard a door open.

I stayed still, opening my mouth wide so the air could escape and be drawn in without making the noise of it moving past my lips. I'd been listening. Only one officer was checking each floor.

The door closed. A few footsteps echoed.

Then he spoke into his walkie. I couldn't hear what he said. I didn't care about the specifics. Even as I stood, he said my name. And I didn't even care that it was my name. It didn't matter.

All that mattered was that it was his voice.

"Aislyn?"

Alex was only feet away as I stood up, but I still ran to him. I fell into his arms, emotionally and physically spent, not sure how if I could even follow the plan he had to get me out.

But he didn't share his plan. He kneeled on the floor, cradling me as I fell with him. He kept repeating, "I've got you," over and over again. It was a few seconds before his hands took my shoulders and he pulled me back just a bit, only to lean in and try to meet my eyes. My eyes felt tired. They were either dashing around or closed in panic.

"I wouldn't have gone through the trouble of saving you if I didn't think you could keep going. You've gotta keep going."

He knew what I was thinking. I still didn't know how in a single glance he could know that.

"Hey, look at me," he said. He took my head in his hands. "You can breathe. Breathe. It's easy."

"Easy for you to say," I struggled even to whisper. I had held my breath and my voice for too long, yet my voice sounded hoarse as if I'd been screaming.

"Really?" he said. It was light, sarcastic even, but the tone he ended the question with was horribly pained. "You think that it's easy for me to breathe right now?"

"Alex, I..." I was too tired to continue processing a response, but I saw a mirrored fear in his eyes. "No. It's probably not."

"Then breathe. Don't talk," he said, his voice slightly lower.

I took a breath between words, speaking only as I exhaled.

"But you," breath in, "need to know," breath in, "that I got," breathe in, hold it. "I got Maggie out."

I tried to focus on his eyes, and gained back a little of hope I never thought to hold again as his eyes widened in shock, as he pulled me in again quickly. He held me, saying "Thank you" over and over again into my shoulder. He pulled me away to look into my eyes again.

"I can't believe it! I thought maybe..."

And then his expression dropped. He looked to the side, and went from holding my shoulders to cradling my forearm.

"She's fine, Alex. What is it?"

He was looking at my arm. My sleeve only covered half of the scar, and he was pulling it back to see it.

"I'll never forgive myself," he whispered. "I'll never...what happened? The scar is huge. I thought it might be infected, but–"

"Compartment syndrome, and now is not the time."

Even as I finished saying it, I heard the latch on the door. We froze. I heard someone say, "Alex got that one."

Alex yelled out, "I'm still checking."

I almost jolted when the door slammed again.

Despite me saying he shouldn't worry about it, he was still staring at my arm, tracing the outline of my scar. I couldn't argue or tell him not to worry because I couldn't talk. I could feel my breath was still too labored. He finally looked at my eyes as I pleaded in a whisper, "Please. It's okay."

He said, "We're probably good to whisper again."

"How long have you been trying to find me?"

"They played the recording of you talking to the boy. I heard your voice. I asked to come over since I was on duty. Here."

He pulled out a vial from his pouch.

"It'll help re-oxidate your body and your muscles, and it'll give you a little adrenaline boost. And, here's one for the road."

I looked at the vial, wary of taking it. He almost instantly saw my hesitation as he downed his vial.

"It's fine. What's wrong?"

"Nothing," I said not convincingly. "I guess it shouldn't surprise me that you would have access to this."

I told myself I probably shouldn't be so harsh in a moment like this, but more afraid he would return with a response that it was no big deal. He closed his eyes, instantly making me regret my words.

"So…your people are doing their homework, I see."

The regret faded. I knew had to confront him about it.

"How can you even think about risking everything, even your own life, to take that stuff all the time? And how are you–"

He cut me off, "I don't take it, Aislyn. I'm sure they know that by now, too. And if you took a look at my bank account, which I'm sure you did, you've noticed–"

"You're loaded. Yeah, we know. This is about the other night, when the boy who you left the cup for…"

I trailed off, feeling miserable again that I had accused him of something, while at the same time wanting to comfort him.

He looked directly at me as he continued, "I know what you must think of me, but you do realize that I am responsible for killing my sister. I am responsible for killing children, or capturing them for others to kill. I try so hard to do one good thing, or many good things, and all I see is death. I have to stay in a position I hate…just so I can let a few of them go, or so I can ignore your friend when she killed two Sentries. Or so I can be in Central command to listen to recordings of you trying to save a boy who'd rather entrap you, and volunteer to kill you."

He sighed, now looking at the ground. "And yes, sometimes…I need to escape it. I use a dose or two. I expected your trainers to judge me. I didn't expect it from you."

"I'm not. I just…care. I don't want you to be…not you."

He looked at me curiously. "Well, that's a first."

255

I looked at him, hoping I could convince him. "If you think you are the only person ever to have unhealthy ideas for dealing with remorse, you should talk to someone who just lost most of their team. You know how many of us died that night. I know it's hard, but you can get through it. I believe in you."

He looked at me after pushing his forehead with his hand. "You're different. You know that, right?"

I sighed, almost annoyed he might be missing the point. "So I've heard."

But he continued, in a more serious tone of voice. "I wasn't joking. You see me. You get it. The others don't. I can tell, even by the way you speak about them. Did you spend a lot of time with Unnecessaries growing up over there, and just learned to love and respect them instead of pity them? "

"No," I responded. "Nearly all of them stay in the shelter in the woods, even to go to school, until they are older. I just…"

"Oh," he interrupted, "if you were doing your homework, then do you know about the Vinalia ball?"

"Yes, but I have no clue why–?"

"Someone sent me a message that, while a little cryptic, indicated that they need help from one of you."

I whispered, "Wait. A Vessel?"

"Yeah, she's going to be there. She promised. She wants out."

I breathed some relief. I was glad I finally knew the answer to one mystery. "I'll be there, Alex. No matter what."

I don't know why I added the last part, maybe just to boost my own confidence that I would keep breathing until then.

At the moment I felt more confident, I was bold enough to ask.

"Alex, you have to promise me." It was ridiculous, but I was determined to get a response out of him. "Don't take anything again. Please. Not even the pain meds. For any reason."

As my eyes pierced his, he closed them, and said, "I really wish I could promise you that, but seeing as the plan I have right now would end with the need of medication, I would have to break that promise within the hour."

"What do you mean, Alex?"

"You know we're boxed in, right?"

"Yeah, and I have no way down."

"Yes, you do." As he spoke, he reached out with a metal device that from a glance looked like a zip line runner.

"Use it on the cable for the elevator. It's shut down while we look for you. It will give you a good hold for the descent down the cable, squeeze for the brake," he said as he showed me all the parts.

"Someone will be there at the bottom, covering the exit," I said in response to his plan. It wasn't even the objection to the height that I wanted to make. That would make me sound like a coward. Then I repeated the most obvious fault in the plan again.

"Someone will be there."

"No. They won't." His voice cut off at the end. It sounded strained, disturbed somehow.

I was getting a bad feeling that he was going to tell me to take the officer out, or that Alex would.

"Where will they be?" I asked cautiously.

He took a deep breath before answering.

"Racing up to this floor, where the Sentry will report that he's found a Protector. And then they'll all be busy for two minutes. That's the window I can give you."

"But they won't be up here for two minutes, and they'll know you lied when they sweep the floor and can't find me."

"No, they'll know you were here. They'll be attending to a Sentry…with an acute abdominal wound."

At that moment, he pulled the knife out of my boot, flipped it over to hold the blade, and reached out the handle to me.

It was the perfect distraction. If he ordered them all to come, they would. The authority of his rank ensured that. They would search the room and other floors thoroughly once they saw he was injured. Half would be stopping his bleeding until a med team arrived.

The boost from the medicine was starting to work, but my breath was jagged, and my heart was racing as I answered him.

"No."

"Aislyn–"

"No!" I had to remind myself to speak softly, but I wanted to yell it. Surely he could see the scream hidden inside my whisper.

"Aislyn, please. I'm a Citizen and a Sentry. I won't die; they won't let me. They'll see that this is your knife, so the cover story will be complete. I'll survive."

"I have no doubt they could save you, Alex. But if letting you die would cause more of a political play to prove their point…"

"They can't. They can't afford to lose me. I know it won't be easy, Aislyn, but you need to do it."

"I can't, Alex."

"I shot you, you know; this really should be easy."

I took a moment to process that, but it didn't help. I continued to shake my head slowly, staring at the knife through tears.

"Aislyn, just take it. Just…"

"I can't."

He dropped his hand and then looked down at it. He slowly reached the blade up to look at it, staring at it ominously.

"I was afraid you'd say that."

His hand shook a little. The change in his voice scared me until something scared me more: his plan B forming in his mind.

"Alex?"

He wasn't meeting my eyes when I called his name. He wouldn't meet my eyes if he was gong to…

"Alex, please! Give me my knife."

He looked up at me, but only for an instant. His hand jolted again, and his jaw shook as his shuddered breath left him.

"I will…I just need it real quick, and then I'll get it back to you," he said, his voice shaky while he forced it to be calm.

"Please…" I think there were tears escaping, but I cursed them for getting in the way of making him see that he didn't need to do this, all the while knowing what he was going to do.

He flipped the blade once, and then his hand on the handle.

"Don't watch, okay? You shouldn't have to see it."

He pulled his arm in front of him and turned to face the wall. His other hand reached up on the wall. I held back the scream I wanted to unleash. He took a breath and rammed into the wall, forcing the blade into his stomach.

I ran, mad at myself for being paralyzed as he had stabbed himself. He was on one knee. I pressed against the blood flowing out, looking into his strained eyes until he squeezed them shut.

"Get to the elevator. I'll follow you."

I grabbed his hand, already bloody. He went to walk, to which I quickly protested. But he kept moving, grasping my hand until we were at the elevator shaft. I realized now my protest of heights would seem ridiculous and shallow considering he had just impaled himself, but my stomach still lurched at the chasm beneath me.

"I guess you need your knife back?" he choked out, and I realized he was holding the handle again.

"Keep it in. You'll bleed less. And like you said, it'll be proof."

Had he forgotten what he had said? I needed him to bleed less, to concentrate, to remember everything I said, to survive.

I needed a Sentry to survive.

I searched for an answer to another impossible statement in eyes that couldn't meet mine because they were closed with pain.

His hand grasped mine, shaking as I squeezed it.

"Well, at least I get a knife out of it." He said smiling, even as a tear formed in his eye and his breaths became ragged. His voice was strained and gravelly as he spoke into his radio, checking in.

All of his body that had been shaking froze, as he caught my gaze one more time. It felt caught by the sound of the footsteps echoing up the stairway. He wasn't screaming, he was giving me a few more seconds before that. His face contorted in agony. His mouth was open yet he was straining to breathe.

"Sometimes there is only one way," he managed to whisper as he held out the apparatus that would make my escape possible. We pushed open the door to see the lines. I grabbed the line-grip device. I saw the rope in the open elevator shaft that he was pointing to with a shaking hand. I put it on a rope, and clenched it shut. I leaned out to the edge of the shaft, squeezed the brake as the pieces of metal wrapped around the cable. I heard the hallway door burst open. We had one minute.

I attached the clip to my pack strap in the center of my chest. I moved out, released the trigger, before hitting the brake again only seconds later. I had dropped a few feet in the shaft with him only feet away, crunched in pain on the floor. I reached out for the floor, leaning on the edge so I was only inches from him.

"Brake every few floors," he winced every time he breathed. "Don't gain too much momentum. You can't drop…too fast."

He moved forward, nearly leaning over the ledge as he drew closer to me now. Then he spoke into his radio, "All men, upstairs. She's on the 14th floor. She's armed. Corner her and then come to me. That means everyone."

In a few more instants, I would be flying down a shaft. I thought I could hear voices, but couldn't hear anything past other than blood pumping in my ears and the sounds of him struggling. Even though I was secure, I didn't go. I couldn't go without knowing...

"Why, Alex? Why?"

"I told you why. My sister...this world....all of it." The words were fading, almost lost behind the deafening sounds and the struggling breaths. I still didn't believe the first answer he gave me.

"No, Alex. Why me?"

Footsteps were pounding. He leaned in closer to the edge, close enough for me to feel his breath as my hand grasped the floor and my other hand the clamp on the zip line brake.

"I think I told you that, too."

I blinked rapidly, feeling a denial should be coming from my lips. But it didn't. My lower lip was shaking, but I didn't bite it. I was unable to move from the shock of what he had done, and why he had done it. I didn't know what I was waiting for.

Except I did. There was only one reason to wait. If I didn't want it to happen, I should have just slid down.

But I didn't. I couldn't.

He reached in, grasped the back of my neck with his bloody hand, and pulled me closer. I went from out of breath to holding it as my lips met his.

It was electric, like a spark igniting as his lips moved against mine. It spread like a fire, fueled by a truth I could barely believe.

He was a Sentry. I was a Protector.

The dangerous miracle had just become more beautiful.

Then he spoke, as he pulled back.

"I love you, for what that's worth. It may be worthless soon enough."

My worst fear was confirmed.

He knew he might die.

I still was in shock. And he used that to let go of me swiftly.

He said, "Keep going."

And he pushed my hand off the ledge.

I dropped, almost instantly sick. I had grasped the handle with both hands for three floors before breaking. My grasp almost broke free, and I quickly realized what he was saying about momentum. I tried to look up, but he was gone.

Two more floors. Squeezed the brake. I heard footsteps.

Two more floors. Squeezed the brake. I heard him yell, raspy and guttural.

Two more floors. Squeezed the brake. Heard my own quiet sob and stifled it.

Two more floors. Squeezed the brake. Heard someone scream, "Call a medic! Now! 14-5C! Everyone on this floor and the ones directly above and below."

Two more floors. Squeezed the brake. Heard someone yell.

Two more floors. Squeezed the brake. Suppressed the urge to vomit.

Two more floors. Squeezed the brake. Hit the ground.

Two more buttons, and the device released the cable. I quickly pushed the doors open to find the lobby empty.

Realizing the only hiccup in the plan would be running into the medic team, I ran to the back of the building. There was not a soul in sight. I stopped only once as heard him yell in pain. It sounded horrid, and I almost couldn't bear to move the few more steps I needed to take to open the next door. I remembered his last words to me, perhaps his last ever, and I realized that unless I found a way for this to mean something, I would be failing him.

I kept moving, opened the door, and found myself in the service entrance. My thoughts were muddled, broken, and would kill me if I wasn't careful. I pushed them aside. The pull of gravity had pulled me down enough; I couldn't think about what had just happened.

The alley had no soldiers, no Sentries, and no one in sight.

A moment later I realized there was someone.

Just one.

Her green eyes weren't scared. They were wanting.

Pleading.

Hoping.

Dreaming.

I was almost incapable of processing it completely until I realized that she wasn't scared of me.

She wanted me. I could tell by the way she didn't hesitate to step out from behind the dumpster. But she had to know who I was, ragged and dirty, running from Sentries, with all the alarms and perimeters....

She held her stomach. She did know.

That could only mean one thing.

I was staring into the eyes of my first Vessel.

CHAPTER 16

I could hardly remember anything I was supposed to do.

She had to be a Vessel.

That was the only person desperate enough to be here.

I grabbed her hand and ran down the alley. She came with me without question and hesitation, another sign that I had been correct in assuming her identity. We made it down to the other side of the alley when an alarm went off.

They knew I wasn't in the building anymore.

"Well, they're persistent," she said.

I could hear the approaching vehicle's screeching tires.

As we ran down the other alley, I asked her the basic questions.

"How far along are you?"

She was panting now. I was running on adrenaline, and I realized I should probably slow down. She was pregnant, after all.

"I think four months. I can't feel it yet, though. Am I supposed to feel it kick?"

"No…not necessarily," noticing now that her abdomen was a bit enlarged. "Don't worry. Some don't feel it until five months."

She was about to ask something else when I cut her off.

"Look, we just need to get out of this first and then–"

She was only four months along. She could blend. One of the many rules came from the ashes of class to my panicked mind.

"If she can blend, blend."

I noticed her backpack.

"You got anything in there?"

"Some photos, money, and my phone."

Of course they never think of another pair of clothes.

"Look, we are barely going to make it out of here, but I need something to wear, a second to get them off my back, I don't–"

A police shuttle raced right past the mouth of the alley.

"Firstly, if they see us together, say I was asking you for directions. They can't tell yet," I said, nodding to her stomach.

She nodded and said a quick "okay" as my mind went into panicked scenarios. They had responded much faster than I thought and the main streets weren't going to be safe for even one minute.

"If you trust me…I have a plan," she said. Then she nodded, running, leading me back down the alley. We turned down another alley, and to my surprise, she said, "Our store is only two blocks down, and we can hide there and my boyfriend can get you some clothes."

"No," I said it so harshly I stumbled and made her stop in her tracks. "You don't involve anyone else but me. That's the rules."

"You don't understand….he's the father. He'll help us."

"You don't know that," I said. How could I tell her that so many women had made this mistake? How could I tell her that the person who just stabbed himself to save me was still regretting his mistakes so much that he occasionally drugged himself into a stupor?

I reiterated, "You may not be able to trust him."

"But I do. Listen, he was the one who woke me up when he heard the sirens. He wanted me to find you."

My options were disappearing. I laughed at the irony that I had wondered if I could ever trust anyone enough to save them again. To save her, there was more risk than ever.

I had limited choices, and I was probably going to have to make the wrong decision. But as I stared into her eyes, I trusted her sincerity. It fit the profile of someone who was a true Vessel. Collin's words burst into my head: "*You know they are desperate for their child to survive if they've already risked their life to get to you.*" In trusting his judgement, I felt close to him. Its familiarity gave me some strength: enough strength to go with her.

I pulled up the address on my phone as we continued to run. It was a clothing store: pricey, if the address was any indicator. I pulled up the architectural layout. There were lots of exits, including a line to the subways only 4 feet away from the basement, as well as three fire escapes. If this was a trap, a Sentry had picked an awful building.

She finally turned to go up some stairs, and I followed. We went to a side door that was near the delivery door.

"No deliveries today," she answered, putting her phone back in her backpack. "And I just messaged him to put a sign up that means there's a fitting for a high profile client."

I motioned to the door, taking a brief second to commend her competency. She opened it quickly. The backroom was well lit, and there was no one in sight. Rods of fabric leaned against the wall. The rods weren't that thick, not leaving a lot of room for someone to hide to entrap us.

I heard her call out to someone who called back in a questioning tone, "Sonja?"

So her name was Sonja. She looked like a Sonja. It seemed silly that her name would be a deciding factor in me trusting her. But there was something else in his voice. I had heard it in my own voice, when I had yelled Olivia's name in the woods or when I had said Alex's name moments earlier: the fear of losing someone.

Someone loved her.

And that meant she was telling the truth.

And neither of us would die.

I let my foot leave the propped open door, putting myself at the mercy of Sonja and my judgment. I now understood everything that Brie had said. Vessels make this harder. Unlike a child who held my hand and was ready to obey every word, I wasn't sure if she would follow me when and if she needed to.

"I'm sorry you didn't find anything. I thought for sure that all of that crazy noise" –only "crazy noise" was actually 3 curse words– "meant there was a Protector over there."

His eyes caught me and his voice froze.

"Nope, no Protector over there." I came out from behind the back room, watching as she beamed at him. "Well, not anymore."

"Wow," he said, staring in awe. His wonderment made me feel epic. Every moment like this was bliss, but I felt a pang of regret. I had let myself be flattered into a trap just hours ago. So as he spoke, I found my urgency interrupting him.

"Hello, ummm, my name is Neil, you must be…"

"In a hurry. Sorry."

"Yeah, well you should…go…wait, what are you doing here?"

"The random bullets and explosions weren't for fun. I'm in trouble. I need a change of clothes and to lay low for a few minutes, and then we need to get going as fast as we can."

I looked around the store, and took in the size and style. It wasn't crammed. That meant that each item had to be worth the space on this street. These people weren't poor. That meant we had an option I usually could never afford.

"I know it's pricey, but can you call a taxi?" I asked.

"Yeah, well here, he'll get you something to wear…and…" she looked at me strangely.

"What?" I asked impatiently.

"You're in need of more than just an outfit. I'll get my kit."

Sonja ran off to the back room, almost talking to herself. I turned to look pensively at his store. Then Neil bolted right to the front window.

"What are you doing? You can't give me a front window outfit!" I almost yelled while still struggling to keep it down. Did these people not comprehend blending?

"You don't understand fashion, do you?" he said, as he looked at each outfit, and then at me.

"Yes…well, no," I said quickly. "I know more than most."

"Fashion isn't personal, we just sell it like it is so it makes us more money," he said, pulling up one of the dresses next to me. "People wear something so that others look at the outfit, not them. The outfit tells them everything; they are rich, privileged, classic, hip, modern, somehow creative– even though they didn't create any of it. Do you want the dress or the ensemble with the scarf?"

I stared at him, not even knowing how to answer. I shrugged.

"You see, Protector, you are going to be wearing $10,000. You are going to be disguised by that fact." He took the ensemble off of the mannequin and came towards me. "No one is going to be looking at your face or your eyes, not even a Sentry. This is flashy and conspicuous by your standards, but it will make you invisible. No one will see you, because all anyone will see is this."

He came towards me with the outfit. I stared at it sadly, thinking of how many souls who were desperate to be noticed were never seen. He reached for my shirt, as if to pull it off.

"What are you doing?" I almost screamed and had to restrain myself from punching him before I remembered where I was. "I mean, I'm sorry, Neil, that it's…we usually dress in private."

"Oh, really? Okay…um… " he looked embarrassed, but also confused. "Bathroom?"

"Thanks," I said quickly, smiling and remembering he was just trying to help. "And…sorry."

I threw off my shoes just outside the bathroom, staring down at them. I realized that they would ruin the outfit. I turned around to open the curtain. He was already standing there with a pair of yellow shoes that probably cost as much as a month's worth of food back in the Territory. He gave me a wink. I turned around again to go into the bathroom, when I heard the sound of a Medic Transport shoot by the window.

The uncertainty weighed down the moment to a screeching halt. I know I should have been focusing on my escape, but the significance of his actions, his sacrifice, and his words were too much to ignore. I found myself hyper aware of the colors around me, of the cold metal on my feet, and the breaths I was taking. I felt weary from my hopelessness, but out of it, I prayed the most desperate prayer of my life. It probably wasn't enough to save him. It was only three words.

"Let Alex live."

I turned to the man, who was silent in my contemplation, but at meeting my gaze, his face was worried and compassionate.

"Friend?" he asked.

My doubt pushed away the simple answer. So I told the truth, however he might interpret it.

"I think so," I said, staring at his eyes, "But I'm not sure."

He seemed puzzled. But his perplexed look wasn't caused by my statement. He reacted as if he had an epiphany.

"You need a bag! Something soft and floral, to complete the look." He ran off in the direction of the windows again. I stood wide eyed. I scoffed low enough for him not to hear my disbelief.

"A bag. Yeah, that's what I need," I murmured to myself.

A small sigh escaped, blowing into the sterile air of the strange plastic world I was surrounded by. I headed into the bathroom.

One look in the mirror told me that they weren't exaggerating about me needing more than new clothes. My hair was matted with sweat and my face was covered with dust. I could tell where tears had streaked across the dirt. Had I cried that much? I didn't remember.

I was more clumsy than I wanted to be, but I moved as fast as I could. I wiped off my face within seconds and put on the fan to dry it. I pulled off my clothes and crammed them in my bag. It didn't need to be organized, I just needed to be able to find the ultrasound.

The ultrasound. I had already forgotten.

And in a locked room.

I was panic weary, almost too worn out to have a natural reaction to another threat. I finished getting on my pants, pulled out the ultrasound tool, and shoved everything in the pack. My hair had been braided, so I unraveled it, hoping it would dry it out as well. It didn't look that bad, but Sonja or Neil would probably have something for that, too! I opened the door quickly, hoping that if this whole thing had been a trap, I wouldn't be breathing my last breath.

But the only two people there to attack me held makeup and a curling iron.

And attack they did. She was spraying something in my hair and put something on my eyes. I tried on three different pairs of shoes while she was working. I chose to be numb in those three minutes, to let myself get lost in Neil's description of the latest trends in shoes. The pair of shoes felt so smooth, like a pillow…like nothing I'd ever felt in my life. I loved them. I thought about my pillow in my bed, soft, inviting me to sleep, dream.

"No, not yet." I realized I had spoken out loud.

"You know, you're right. Let's let that dry first," Sonja said, maybe thinking I was talking to her as she put down a product.

"You're done," the man said. "You'll knock them dead, well, relatively speaking. Or practically speaking? A little of both."

I smiled at him. I turned around to look in the mirror. They were right; the spray had made my hair appear to be auburn with highlights instead of just plain brown. The makeup was perfect. The jewelry was perfect. My outfit was the green we all joked about hating, but it didn't look bad with the black skirt.

Neil was right. No one who wore this ever had to show anyone who they truly were. That was why they seemed shallow all the time. But if someone weren't shallow, they would have to hide it.

Until a moment like this.

"You're ready to go then." Instead of the perky nature he had generally been speaking in, Neil's voice sounded strained, like he was holding back tears.

"He can't go with me, can he?"

I looked at him, almost wanted to break the rules again, but he shook his head.

"Sonja, no. And it's best if the store stays open, right? To avoid suspicion?" he looked at me for an answer.

"Yes," I said, but as I clutched the ultrasound in my hand. "I can do one thing for you, though. I just hope it's enough."

I placed the ultrasound tool on my MCU. They had a larger screen on their counter with an attachment for visual. I pulled the screen out, and faced it towards them, attaching the Ultrasound chord to the screen instead of to my MCU. As my first time doing this in the field, I hoped that I remembered how to use everything. I got the image within seconds, pointing to the screen. She was about five months as opposed to the four months she had claimed. That made me nervous about the baby's lack of mobility. I quickly ran through the stats.

"Okay, did you feel that?"

"Wait," she said, "that's the movement? I thought it was just–"

"No, it's subtle at first, like a stirring. No crazy kicking yet."

"Wow! So, all those times, all those moments, I didn't know it was the baby."

We looked for about ten minutes. I was about to be finished checking when I noticed something.

The moment. The look in their eyes was unmistakably one of the most beautiful things I had ever seen in my life.

Something so beautiful it hurt to end it. At least I could tell them…

"He's perfect. It's a beautiful baby."

"He?" she asked expectedly.

"He. Definitely a boy," I stated confidently

She smiled at Neil as he moved his forehead against the side of her head as she closed her eyes. He was still clutching to her, whispering something in her ear when I saw the taxi come up.

I didn't want to tell him, but he must have heard it.

"Sonja, take the bag. I'll tell people you went shopping for new fabrics and will be gone for weeks and at other parties, you know."

"Yeah," she said, but it was cut short by a sound in her throat.

I'm sure they had already done goodbyes, but repeating them probably made it worse: elongating the wreck and grief. I looked away as they embraced each other. I was starting to count the shoes on the shelf, hoping she knew she couldn't have too long, so I wouldn't have to pull her away.

I didn't know if I could pull her away.

I stared out the window at our taxi, which felt overwhelmingly large for just two people. I was just about to remind her we could all die if at any moment we were discovered in this store when they finally broke their embrace. He bent down to kiss her belly.

I heard her say, "I'm so glad it's a boy. He'll look just like you. He'll remind me of you."

I was transfixed on them, feeling like I was silly that I ever imagined to understand love.

He finally pulled her towards the door. I held her arm. We stepped out onto the street. Within the five steps, I saw two police officers still combing the area for me, as well as crowds of Elites and Citizens. Everyone glanced. Everyone noticed. Everyone looked at me. Sonja waved ever so slightly at someone. I just smiled and nodded on my way to the car, relieved as the shuttle door sealed shut, with the sirens on the other side.

We passed through every checkpoint, past every blockade, without any I.D. I was waved past: Protector, traitor, and sworn enemy of the state. Everyone had seen me, but no one saw me.

And so I became invisible. Just like them.

The rest of the escape was as uneventful as I needed it to be. We saved a whole day just with the car alone. We were dropped off far north: the closest to the border as we could be.

That night, we were out in the woods awaiting an EE and settling down for a little sleep. Michael said that with the issues surrounding the transports, we were to be picked up as soon as possible. I had told her everything else she had needed to know. Sonja told me everything from the moment she and Neil met to the time they had decided they were actually in love.

I realized with a pang of regret that I wished I had more time to talk with her, wander through the woods letting the beauty of nature work it's therapy on our souls. I wanted to hear every detail of how two people had found each other and fallen in love in the mess of the world they lived in, and had the audacity to feel something deeper than a love for themselves.

Even as she said that, about to fall asleep, she asked, "Sorry. You probably think I'm crazy don't you?"

I turned to face her, even as she was fading into sleep. I saw her eyes barely open as I spoke to her, solemnly and unwaveringly.

"I think you're brave. Bravery will make you do crazy things. It will make you risk something. If you have a broken heart, it means you were brave enough to have loved and risked everything for it. I'd never want to love any less than you have."

She seemed to ponder that for a moment, closing her eyes again. "You're brave, too. I could never do what you do."

I stared at her, falling into the bliss of sleep, clutching her stomach and humming to her unborn child, gazing at fireflies.

I blinked away tears. She had already done everything I had done. I wanted to tell her that, but she spoke first.

"I'm sorry about your neck, by the way. We should've got it while we were in the store. Does it hurt?" she said trailing off into sleep, so I was wondering if she was delusional.

I reached behind me to touch my neck. I had forgotten to wash it. I felt flakes. I pulled my hand back to stare at the dried blood on my fingers.

Finally, I choked out, "It's not my blood."

She spoke as her eyes closed, smiling.

"Oh, okay. That's…good."

Except it wasn't okay. It wasn't good.

She fell asleep, just in time for me to cry. The leaves were soon strewn with tears, but some fell into my hands with the dried blood on them.

Her steady breathing stopped me from falling down the chasm of grief, from thinking that it was never going to be okay again. So eventually I joined her in her soft, deep breaths, and sleep overtook the sorrow.

I would have risked anything– given anything– for it to be my blood.

CHAPTER 17

The few hours in between sending the last message to Michael and the shuttle's arrival were tense, but I tried to be calm for Sonja. I told her what my brothers were like when they were born, the moment Olivia took her first step, and other memories that made my heart ache. It made me smile to see her reactions, though. Her hope was almost contagious, and she laughed at every story. She was holding her belly, in contemplation, when a shuttle appeared.

Then, to my surprise, another shuttle appeared behind it.

I was a little confused, and fear was threatening to rise, but Will looked too calm.

"Aislyn! Glad to see you're back. The second shuttle is going to take Sonja back like usual, okay?"

He had a little extra emphasis on the "like usual," and I was about to argue. But then I quickly caught on and answered.

"Of course," I responded, thankful that I hadn't told her we were riding back in the same shuttle. "Sonja, this is Will. He's a friend of mine, and very experienced. He's going to attach a monitor like I did, even though there are no complications, and then they'll escort you to medical." I noticed the quick actions that everyone had even while acting composed. I all but ran to get in the other transport. Right before I jumped in, I heard two other transports further in the woods. And I understood.

Emily took my pack as I asked, "Tell me we aren't hiding beans under cups and shuffling them around the table?"

"Only the cups are shuttles, and we're the beans," George said.

"Did Patterson or you have the idea?" I asked, impressed.

"Me, actually. Thanks for playing it cool, by the way."

"Yeah, well, I wasn't going to tell the anxious pregnant woman that there were really shuttles to confuse drones who might be targeting us. It's brilliant, though. Four targets. It would work better if there were more, you know. Like eight."

Emily smirked.

"Here you thought you were smart, George."

As his smile became skewed, I almost coughed on a single laugh right as I asked, "There are eight shuttles, aren't there?"

"Nine. The Republic wouldn't have enough firepower to get all of them down all the time. We also made the two cloaked that are in fact holding Vessels or Unnecessary."

"So, we're cloaked?"

"No…a small error…" He jammed a button. "It's off and on. So hopefully it'll be okay. I'm just….I just would've…"

"George, it's fine," Emily whispered.

"I should've just grabbed an assistant. I didn't think…"

"You asked me to come. I said yes. Don't complicate it."

All of a sudden I realized why he was anxious. He had taken her instead of anyone else. His heart was probably racing. Even though I knew my life was also in danger, I found myself distracted by Emily looking at George as he stared down at the floor. Her hands were on the side of her legs, and soon he moved his hands from his head to his knees. They twitched, but then he forced them to remain still.

He was still only inches, and yet a world apart from Emily.

"Do you trust me?"

She finally spoke into the tense silence. George didn't answer, but his face was unmistakably answering her.

"Then trust me to know what I'm doing. There was a reason I came along. Trust me," Emily said warningly.

I realized there could be a camera, or a listening device. Emily still might not know how she felt, or not be willing to admit it.

Emily sighed, closing her eyes. George remained still. Emily reached out one finger, extending slightly until it reached the back of his hand.

I watched silently. All I could think of, despite my safe return, was how much I wanted to feel like I was home when I got back to Central.

Instead, I was left alone in my debrief to dread what I would see: Zander smiling at the thought of me stabbing a Sentry.

Thankfully, that was not who I saw first. The door handle jolted, and then the door sprung open.

"Collin?" I whispered in disbelief.

As he rushed up to meet me, his brow creased with a strange combination of relief and weariness. He pulled me into his arms so quickly I barely had time to tell him I was okay.

"I know, Aislyn. I only have a second. But I told you…every chance, any chance, I'm taking it. I promised you…"

I almost was afraid I was hurting him as I gripped him tightly to me. He didn't seem to mind. He was rubbing my back. Then my neck. He found the dried blood. But before he could ask a question, I did.

"Do we know if Alex is okay?"

I explained that John betrayed me, if that had really been his name. "And then, Alex found me. It was only a matter of time before the officers checked the floor. He thought that if they were focused on getting him a med team it might slow them down. So he…He took my knife, Collin."

Collin looked shocked, and pulled me back as if to see if I was alright, even though he knew I was cleared by medical.

"Did he threaten you? Did he hurt you?"

I felt my jaw shake before I pushed it shut, and even then, a small "no" just as a tear escaped my wide open eyes.

His eyes darted around, but then focused on me in horror.

"No, he didn't…to himself? He wouldn't."

I continued, trying not to shake as I said it. "He asked me to do it. I couldn't, so he stabbed himself. I went down the elevator shaft. I left him…would they kill him, Collin? Would they–"

"I don't know, Aislyn. I don't know. They honestly might have just tried to make it look worse than it was."

There was a part of me that was relieved by that, but another part that was terrified.

"We can't…." There was an odd sound from his watch.

He squeezed me before turning to leave. He quickly and silently slid through the door. I took the time to wipe away my tears as I guessed what the beeping must have meant. Within 5 seconds, just as composed myself, the door opened.

Patterson came in first, followed by Zander.

"Well, time for your debrief, Miss Williams. Or would you prefer the enlightened title of 27th, so we all remember how special you are?"

I didn't feel like discussing this with her now. I just took my seat and started at the beginning. I discussed how the Unnecessary had tricked me. I didn't talk a lot about evading five squadrons of Police, although I went through enough detail for Patterson and Zander's assistant to look genuinely impressed. But I didn't want to give her the pleasure of knowing the extra combat lessons had helped.

"Is John okay?"

"Why would you care?" she said, as if she was offended.

"I think the fear overwhelmed him. And I think..."

"What you think is correct. But anyone who is driven by fear is often destroyed by the very thing they fear. And they choose what they choose, even if it leads to death," she said sternly.

My eyes wandered to Patterson as her assistant took some notes. His eyes were sympathetic, but his eyebrows were stern, as if to say "not now."

I went through the details of the escape until she said, "That was the attack. On the 14th floor? We overheard the chatter, but there weren't many details."

"It was a Sentry."

She perked up, her eyes sickeningly happy. "Did he see you?"

"Yes." I felt the weight of my words as I said them, knowing their meaning like no one else could. "He saw me."

Patterson looked at me. He knew who I was talking about, but I could see the confusion in his eyes churning into panic.

"We did hear from the report that there was a Sentry injured at the scene. They said it was a foreign knife in the abdomen. We had no clue that was you."

Even as she said that, the assistant started writing furiously. She turned back to talk to him, cupping her face with her paper so I couldn't see her. I risked silently mouthing to Patterson, "He did it….so I could get out."

Patterson didn't look shocked, but instead closed his eyes slowly. He stared at me warningly, as he looked at Zander.

"After I stabbed him, he got confused. So he told the leaders I went upstairs," I continued. "I took his tool, for going down wires; it's like a cable-runner, only with a break. I hit the ground floor, and then…she was waiting for me. My Vessel's name is Sonja. She took me back to her place to clean up, we saw the baby….the father was very sweet. They–"

"I need pertinent details only, 27," Zander said.

I swallowed my anger at her disgust at such beauty, and finished the rest of the story, including getting my cover at the store and exiting the Republic without incident.

"Well, it seems you like a bit of action, after all," she grinned. "It's good to see you getting over your reservations to see the new vision we are pursuing here. We won't be able to see if he is dead or not, of course, because without the normal techs, no one can do that kind of hack. But…in the meantime, we can always hope."

I looked up from the floor, staring at Patterson's sympathetic gaze. I said the same words she did, only with a very different meaning.

"Yes. We can always hope."

Minutes later, I came out of the room, turning to see Zander with two assistants trailing after her. Patterson gave me a quick nod, which felt like it was intentioned to send me back to the Circle, not to secondary Central. He saw my look of protest, but nodded again. I grimaced, but obeyed and went to my Circle.

Where I found Collin's arms again. My tears were spent. I wanted answers I didn't know if I could get. I dreaded the answer so much that I just stood clinging to him.

He sighed. "I know you may not see this as the best time, but…I have some other news."

"I can't imagine there being any news that could distract me from this, Collin. Nothing could be that…"

But then I realized something could. I pulled away from him. He was smiling mischievously. Almost like she did.

"Eva?"

"Came back a few minutes after you," he said. I jumped into his arms. He continued to explain that she had lost her pack. "She traversed almost the entire 100 miles, about 7 miles a day. She even heard the explosions when the shuttles got hit. One of the shuttles they sent out for you in the last hour finally spotted her and her Unnecessaries."

"How…did she…Unnecessaries? As in more than one?"

"Both were siblings. Sub-Terra Vessel with a two-year-old. She was all but a slave, but hid the baby with the help of friends and a fake I.D. She was pregnant with her second child. She could hardly leave the two year old there."

"Did she give birth in the woods?"

He nodded. "Emergency C-Section. Eva handled it like a pro. She had her debrief before yours, which is why I knew I had time to see you. I wasn't expecting you to tell me–"

"Collin, I need to know if Alex is okay."

"We can't pull Michael away, Aislyn. He's coordinating all the shuttles, looking out for you, and running interference for three things right now. Not until Friday, and Michael is still on call."

"Collin–"

"I know you need to know, which is why I was so eager to share some news with you." He looked at me knowingly, looking for a reaction. "Find another way. There is one now."

Even as Collin said it, I turned on my heel and ran to Eva's Circle. Eric, her trainer, was outside pacing, rubbing his head at his temples. He was smiling, but still looked bewildered.

Despite my desire to know what happened with Alex, no anxiety or fear stood between me and unapologetic joy. Even as I was asking permission to come in her circle, and she ran into me, hugging me hard.

"You're back," I said, trying to keep my voice steady.

"Most people are saying, 'you're alive' as if I was a goner, or 'they're alive' as if I would fail. But the people that say 'you're back' should get bonus points, because you actually thought I was alive. You just all thought I was lost in the woods, hiding in a sewer, or in deep cover in the Republic. Wait, where did you think I was? I should take a poll before everyone knows for sure."

"I knew it would be a good story. That's all. They always take a little more time, but…they're worth it."

She looked at me, and winked. "Definitely."

I stared at her, just so happy that she was there to stare at, before realizing what I came to ask her. I motioned to Eric.

"Eric, can I steal her for a few?"

"Oh, go ahead," he nodded sarcastically. "It's not like I want to know what happened or anything, or maybe want to tell her…"

"You're awesome, Eric, and I missed you, too," Eva said, even as she left giving him a wave. He rolled his eyes in response and murmured something. But his smile was unmistakable; it was the reaction of someone who had been holding their breath and had finally exhaled.

"What do you need?" Eva sighed.

"What?" I tried to sound innocent, shocked that she had asked.

"Okay, while I know that you're glad I'm back, you've got that look that people get when they ask me for a favor. Usually, it's something small, but they think it's something only I can do 'cause I know everything around here. What is it? You want to know when Collin's birthday is? What Patterson's scar is from? What Zander's issue is, which I can't tell you anyway? Or is it a hack?"

I paused, not sure I didn't want to know the other things she listed off before answering her. "I need a hack."

"Ah! Easy."

"Into the…Republic Sentry mainframe."

It was like I was pulling the words out of me as I turned to see her begin to laugh, and then stifle it. She peered at me, as if to make sure I wasn't joking.

"Not so easy. And it will require a compelling reason why."

"Look, Michael can't get away from his desk. There's no one else to do it under Zander's nose! Besides, don't you want to do it? Do you want a reason when I've just given you an excuse?"

Her eyes lit up. And that was all I needed to convince her.

Five minutes later, we were in a level beneath Central that I'd never been in before.

"Alex André Anderson." She paused on his middle name, but kept typing. She must have recognized his middle name, as I had named one of my Unnecessaries after him. There was one secret already uncovered, but I was convinced to hide the rest.

"Okay," she started to read, "Sentry, scum of the earth, blah blah blah…he's the one who shot you. And 14 from a few years ago…not a kill shot on either. Citizen, has enough for Elite, but…" She trailed off. "This guy is weird."

"Why do you say that?" I said, trying my best to sound surprised.

She didn't answer right away, but my guess was that she was looking at all the pieces that didn't match.

"Well, he's rich, he's powerful, he's a Sentry, he should be an Elite. He's probably a…let's not use that word… but that's not what you want to know. The answer to your question: he's alive. Looks like the good doctors treated Alex for a wound from a dagger of 'foreign make,' no doubt yours. Puncture. There was a complication," she said, scanning the screens as I held my breath again. "Too much blood loss…it says that the dagger was removed on the way to the hospital against the Medic's advice by another Sentry. Hydech. But it looks like that note was deleted or buried; I had to dig it up in the deleted medic's notes."

"Wait," I said, "Isn't that against basic field medicine protocol? The rule is to keep the blade in. Don't they know that?"

"I'm sure they do," she said. Her voice became deadpan like it did when she was disgusted, or when she is problem-solving.

"I don't think Hydech did it out of ignorance, Aislyn. It hurt. It was probably meant to hurt. From the pictures and internal damage, it looks like the blade was turned while still inside of him, and then Hydech pulled it out."

Something sick was curling up my throat. They tortured him for just letting me escape; what would ever happen if they found out he actually had me in his arms and then freed me? The thought of that moment fueled an angry fire rushing through me. The thought of me "in his arms" made my heart ache to be somewhere else than a basement tech lab. For the first time, I allowed myself to remember the few moments before falling down the elevator shaft. They came back in flashes, and I felt my lips burn.

"So he's alright?" I sounded dazed, trying to pull myself out of my flashbacks.

"Yep, he's fine now. They gave him the good stuff: that tissue regenerator. Looks like they are releasing him in five days and will resume work in a week, on the 13th."

"He's going to be okay?" I asked again, filled with a tension that flooded, remembering we were supposed to be going to the ball on August 19th. Would he make that? Would I?

"Yep…he's going to be fine."

There was something different in her tone. I had been staring at the wall, and I quickly realized my daydream had lasted too long to avoid suspicion. Her eyebrows raised and I had the horrible apprehension that I might not have kept my secret after all.

"What?" I said, but my voice cracked as I said it, making me wince after I spoke.

"Nothing," she said calmly as she typed. "Logging out."

There was silence. Pure silence. She nodded as she shut down the screen. We quickly and wordlessly left the console. I cracked open the door. We both checked for anyone leaving, and then began to walk.

She still hadn't spoken a word. We got to the gardens.

Still nothing.

"You're not saying anything?" I asked.

Eva shrugged. "Well, I suppose I should say congratulations for stabbing a Sentry in the gut…but I'm getting this strange feeling there's no point in that. So I'm letting awkward silence force you to talk."

I had to tell her, if only because I didn't want her guessing.

"I didn't stab him."

"Yeah, I kind of put that together."

There was more silence. Eva was right. It made me want to spill.

"He stabbed himself, Eva."

She stopped, and looked at me. I sat on the nearest bench, hoping for a chance to explain.

"So I could get away."

She sat down on the bench, close to me. She opened her mouth a few times, only to close it without saying a word. Finally, I just wanted to know what she was thinking.

"Initial thoughts?" I said, waiting for her reaction impatiently.

"For someone who thought you were going to be a boring 27th Protector, you sure proved worry is useless. I don't think I'm ever going to worry about anything ever again."

I laughed at that, but at the same time, I wanted her to know how serious this was. I spoke in a foreboding tone.

"I don't have time to tell you everything. I'm sorry. I will."

Eva shook her head, and then asked, "Do me a favor?"

"Anything. What is it?" I said, expecting her to tell me to be careful. She did tell me, but not the way I expected.

"Don't fall in love with another person you're not supposed to, okay?"

"What? I…"

"Ugh! Just don't. It's harder for me to keep a secret for you when you deny the truth. If I'm keeping a secret, it should be the truth, not a lie. It just makes it more complicated."

"But I don't. I just care about him, and …no one can love him."

Even as I said that, the words choked in my throat.

That shouldn't be right. Someone should love him. She looked at me knowingly as I shook my head. She looked mischievous again.

"See? It's bad when people try to deny the truth. They can't. And then it gets super awkward. At least, before you denied it, you were just keeping the secret from yourself."

Then she said the phrase that struck me the hardest.

"There's nothing more dangerous than the truth you don't know."

She hugged me, winked, and then ran away.

An hour later, in my Circle, I was still trying to convince myself that she was wrong, arguing with an imaginary version of her in my head. I told myself I didn't feel anything I shouldn't.

"How's Eva?"

The voice made me jump, before I realized it was Collin.

I started to open my mouth, going to say something I couldn't say as I nodded. He reached out his hand.

"Did Eva find…anything else? Everyone okay?"

"I was just thinking the whole reason this happened is because we're fighting back now. The penalties for letting one of us go must be harsher. If I had slipped by, had escaped without injury…he might have been under suspicion. But I'm not sure if Hydech did it because of that, or just because he's a sadist."

"What did Hydech do?" He looked genuinely concerned.

When I told Collin what Eva had found out, his expression changed to disgust. He reached out for me, but I refused. I didn't feel like being comforted.

"It's all my fault," I whispered.

"No, it's not your fault. It's their fault– whoever was going to kill you and thought it would be fun to torture him instead. Hydech is a monster, we all know it."

The next words described those people in curses I recognized from Common Phrases 7. It was strange for Collin to curse, and it felt odd for him to be so angry all of a sudden.

"I thought you didn't like Alex," I remarked.

"At this point, I would certainly say he's proven himself. Shooting you in the arm to maintain his cover wasn't his best move. Stabbing himself to save you makes more of a statement."

I breathed a sigh of relief that I could be a little less defensive. "So, no one knew what happened there?"

"Nope. No one except Michael. He was on duty…I could tell he was freaking out, but he couldn't leave his station, and when he messaged us, all he said was, 'You are never going to guess what happened.' Then he could leave his station, but Patterson and I were on shuttles, since we are sending eight out at a time right now. It's been hard to coordinate time in secondary Central."

There was silence, then he looked at me. "There's so many things I want to talk about. I want to hear everything about the mission. I want to–" He cut himself off, suddenly exclaiming, "The 19th! Vinalia? Were we right?"

"Yes, we were. I'm supposed to help save a Vessel, and—" It was my turn to have a slight panic attack. "What's the date?"

I didn't even wait for his response. I pulled out my MCU as he sighed in defeat.

It was July 25th already. Eighteen days.

"I know. You're going to have to get back to the Republic and just stay there. There's not time for you to rescue someone, bring them back, then go back out for Vinalia. You'd never make it."

"Well, Zander won't mind me being out longer. She's finally happy with me for stabbing a Sentry."

"Oh trust me. I know. And I'm going to have to deal with it."

There was a harshness in his tone. I was about to ask what was wrong when he sighed, "I'm sorry. Obviously it's not your fault, but…I have to stop her. The next order that she implied she's going to hand out…it will ruin us. It will ruin you."

It was scary how laser-focused he was, but even more frightening was the tone in his last words.

"Oh, and there was a broadcast that aired while you were with Eva, about twenty minutes ago. That Unnecessary, John?"

"Yes?" I asked warningly. "Is he alive?"

Collin sighed, "Yes, but since you let him live, he's the one spouting out warnings on the broadcasts. You can tell when he's lying, so they have him telling the truth, for the most part. He'll say 'she begged me to go with her.' With the right bias and prejudice—"

"The truth sounds worse than if he were lying. What did Palmer follow up with?"

"Something like last time. 'It's our right to manage our own' and about their dominion over their own people. He said, 'they are ours, and it's our choice what happens to them.' And then he said he would act, but I don't know when…"

It was almost on cue. The alarm filled the compound.

"Here we go," Collin said, grabbing my hands. His reflexes to pull me to safety were already activated. "They might even hit us directly this time, so if you want to grab your journal…."

But I didn't move, even as he pulled me. My heart had fallen too fast to move. My feet felt like lead. I could hear my blood pumping in my ears, like an echo, but the pounding was too loud to hear Collin yell. His hand slipped away as he saw the terror on my face, but the confusion overwhelmed it more.

Then the urgency hit.

I ran, with Collin behind me, asking, "What was that all about?"

"They aren't going to attack us, Collin!" I said, not able to put into words what I thought might happen right now. "If Palmer was serious, this isn't about us! It's about the Unnecessaries. They are still breathing when their Society declared they shouldn't be."

I didn't know if he knew what I meant.

Until he cursed, and started sprinting faster. He was a few steps ahead of me, opening the door down to Central.

He was yelling. I could hear him yelling Patterson's name, even as he ran down the stairs. I heard the door open, heard the buzz of conversation echo up to me from the Hand in the lower level.

The buzz of a hundred people who were all busy protecting the wrong location.

By the time I got to the bottom of the stairs, Patterson was yelling for everyone to freeze. I ran into the silent room with people who stood frozen facing the security agent pulling Collin.

"Aislyn, go! You have five seconds," Patterson snapped.

"They aren't going to attack us!" I said, choking on the words because I was out of breath. But I pushed them out. "Not us."

Colling continued for me, shrugging off the security guard. "Don't...you see? The latest broadcasts. He keeps saying that it's up to them if the Unnecessaries live or die. They're taking back their power. They're going to kill them, one way or another."

Patterson turned in an instant. "Handlers, 1 through 3, you stay on defense here! Handlers 4 and 5, and..." he trailed off, looking furiously around the room. "Eva! I want you three on the Shelter defense. Support, security level 5 and up, you're on defense here. Lower than 5, you're on Shelter defense systems. Go!"

In a few seconds, the main on-screen display split in two. Eva jumped from the lower level through the steel railings and sat at a station, put on a headset. "Get me their director on the MCU; they've probably already evacuated downstairs."

Michael was waving furiously to get Patterson's attention.

"Sir, they've already moved down to the lower level, but not to the bomb shelter. They've confirmed everyone is there except those in transit. Do you want me to close–"

"The doors? Yes, it's protocol! And tell them to get to the lowest level. Now!"

"I don't have the code. Sam and Liam had it memorized."

Collin had now caught his breath, even as I was still gasping for mine.

"It's 96GZ5991. What about the transport with Maggie?"

I barely had time to panic before someone yelled, "They are fine. They've cut power, put on cloaking, and are waiting it out."

It was another minute of shouting orders when someone finally yelled, "Confirmed, the drones aren't heading for us. They were on target but just veered north. ETA to Shelter in one minute."

"Alright, Michael, close the dome. I want the group on security here, stay on it. We don't know if it will circle back."

"What dome?" I asked Collin.

"You don't think we protect them after you do? After the price you've paid? We give everything we have to make sure no one touches them again. Which is why their security…" He trailed off, looking at the screen as half the room stared at the gigantic metal walls closing in around the complex and sliding upwards to form a huge dome. It must have been a hundred feet tall.

I still had my mouth gaped open as Collin finished, "Is better than ours."

Patterson was yelling again.

"George, Avery, I need you ready to go upstairs as soon as possible. You're first response. Michael, how're we doing?"

"It's almost closed, sir." He was staring at what looked like animated blueprints as we saw the picture on the main screen. "Activating the electromagnetic shield now, but it won't do any good against missiles. Do you want the flares now, or wait?"

"Wait. They might not fire if they see it's secure, and I don't want to be accused of starting a war. They can make a flare look like we fired first. We cannot fire first, do you understand?"

Michael yelled that he understood, just as Eva yelled, "They are going to fire! I hacked into comms. I just heard someone acknowledge the shield, they are firing anyway!"

"When?" Patterson roared.

"At will," she said quietly, turning to Michael as she spoke.

"Michael, set flares! Be ready, but wait for Eva." Patterson then turned, and called for silence.

But it was already silent.

"Eva?" Michael asked, quietly. "You with me?"

"Yeah. I'm listening." She sounded focused, but her last words were shaky.

Michael answered back, calmly, "I have about four seconds."

"I know," she repeated, although more confidently than before.

She looked nervously at the screen, the screen we could all see. "There's going to be a delay. Sam would know what–"

"You know what to do," Michael said definitively. "And you're going to do it. That's all that matters now. Are you listening?"

"I'm listening, Michael. I got it," she said, her one hand clinging to the earphones.

No one moved. We just waited, watching them, with their hands hovering over their keypads. Eva's was shivering. The drone got closer. It made me want to run or hide somewhere, as if that would help keep them safe. There was continued silence that fell like a blanket, making it hard to breathe underneath of it. Eva continued to type something while looking at the screen. "Okay, so I can see the control board and the drone. They are still locked on…"

She trailed off.

"They fired! They fired!"

Michael hit three buttons at once, and then the button on the panel to his left lit up as he slammed on it. Within seconds, we saw the live feed light up. The flares rose up, shooting through the air pulling the missiles upward. It seemed to take forever, and then…

They exploded right above the shelter. It was a much larger explosion than I was expecting. It was 50 feet over the dome, which was blocking the flames. It must have been 200 feet wide. The one camera burned out immediately. The drone flew over.

There were two more missiles suddenly, but Eva shouted again and more flares went up, drawing them away.

"Get me Maria. Now!" Patterson yelled.

"Sir, I still have her on line 3, but it's breaking up. They just messaged me. They felt it, but they've all survived."

"Everyone listen up!" Patterson had lost the room in the flurry of panic, so he was louder than I'd ever heard him. "If you are a trainer on inactive duty, you are to follow Will's instructions. I need you to organize the evacuation."

"To where?" I whispered to Collin.

"To the only place that makes sense. Maybe it's not as safe, but it does hold all the people who saved them…at least once."

I looked curiously at him. Even as I realized, I asked, "Here?"

Patterson started, "Will, separate them by age and gender, and then assign to Circles. I need the nutritionist and cooks as well as the field med ops to be informed now. Megan?"

"Yes, sir?" She stepped out from a crowd.

"You're the only one who spent a lot of time there last summer. I want you to stay here. You're not going back out today as planned. You're staying with Will and help in any way you can. You will be the representative for all the evacuees. You're in charge when Will is off duty."

"Got it." She reached out to me when walking past, briefly to hold my hand as she whispered, "Good call."

There were several orders, even as Patterson nodded to George and Avery, and said loudly that Emily was in charge of operations until they returned.

"Where are they going?" I asked Collin.

"Protocol. Head trainer and two senior trainers go–"

"Aislyn, now!" Patterson yelled as he was heading up the stairs. I pointed to Collin, who shook his head, and waved me to follow. I wasn't sure what Patterson wanted from me. As I opened the door, a shuttle raced up. George and Avery were already packing up the shuttle when Patterson turned. He looked accusing. I was confused, but even more confused as he started.

"Did you lie to me?" he said, more hurt than angry.

"Sir?"

"No intel? That was the deal. Not one scrap of intel to your little side project. Tell me you kept your promise, that you didn't say the word 'shelter' or didn't even breathe while thinking about it."

Something sank in my stomach. I could barely react. Avery and George were putting on some type of armor over their clothes.

"I just told him…there was a shelter. I said, 'They are raised in shelters.' That's it. There's no way that was enough–"

Patterson bit his lip, "Enough to kill them? It could've been."

And they left. I stood motionless, the wind from the shuttles whipping around me, making me feel insecure and ragged.

Days ago, I had been betrayed.

I had wondered how I would ever trust an Unnecessary again.

Now, I may have betrayed every Unnecessary that had ever been saved. And I wondered how I could ever trust myself again.

CHAPTER 18

Everyone kept congratulating me: for my quick thinking, for guessing the attack would be on the shelters, for stabbing a Sentry.

This only made the self-doubt that followed every compliment more unbearable. I couldn't think quickly past my fear; the Sentry who had stabbed himself to get me out alive might have been responsible for the attack I just warned everyone about. Even as I strained to understand how my one sentence was enough intel for them to attack us, the doubt and compliments mixing made me a bit of a riling, anxious mess.

Thankfully, no one noticed. Mainly because no one had time. Hosting hundreds of kids, pregnant women, and newborns within a few hours notice had caused a unique, organized chaos . My small emotional breakdown was under the radar, even as I was stacking up pillows, running up medicine and formula, and filling up air beds. I hid under the cloak of productivity. No one knew I was unraveling.

Except Collin. He wasn't convinced I, or even Alex, was guilty.

"It's not a lot to go on, Aislyn. I assure you, not enough to pull off what they did. It could mean they didn't just punish Alex, but tortured him if they knew he let you go. If they tortured him…"

He trailed off. After a long silence, he repeated, "It's still not your fault."

But the silence had rendered his assurance meaningless.

The Unnecessaries came. They poured out of the shuttles in dozens. Their faces were full of awe, some not remembering the last time they were at Central, some having never been there at all.

But there were only a few voices I truly wanted to hear. Even as I wished I could find them, they broke through the crowd.

"Aislyn!"

Gabriel was first, then Amanda. Katerina came while I still had the two already in my arms. Maggie ran over to me and asked, "Are all of these yours?"

They all laughed at her comment, especially when she jumped on top of the pile. They squeezed, they pulled, they pushed at me, until I was on my knees, looking at Katerina's mesmerizing eyes. They were with me, all together, encased in my arms. For some reason, nothing felt like a crisis.

It felt like heaven.

"Are you okay, Aislyn?"

"Katerina, this is why I love you. You were just bombed and evacuated, and you're asking me if I'm okay."

"But you're crying," she said, taking her finger and wiping a tear off my face.

I smiled as I choked out, "You know how when you're tickled and laugh so hard you could cry? Well, my soul is laughing so hard right now, it's so happy. There's tears. That's all."

Katerina looked a little sad, "I can't find Collin since the attack. They won't tell me where he's going to be."

"He's going to be with Emily, do you see her over there? She's tall, really tall, with the slightly curly hair?"

Katerina ran over to Emily. I turned to hug Maggie.

"Maggie, I just wanted to say–"

"I'm fine. I don't think I am ever going on a shuttle again."

I giggled, only half-heartedly. Will called out age groups. Amanda leaned on me as we listened, her curly hair blowing in the breeze. I allowed myself a moment to be entranced, knowing she was still very quiet and private. Standing beside her was all she needed. She ran after her group was called, leaving only Gabriel. When they finally did call his group, he hesitated.

Thinking he might be scared, I asked, "Hanging in there?"

"Guess so. Not really bored, even though…"

"What is it?" I said, slightly concerned about his demeanor.

He looked at me as if he was injured.

"Aislyn, they won't let me paint."

"Gabriel, things are kind of crazy now. Maybe in a week–"

"No. They said never again."

"What?" I responded out of shock more than anger. But the anger was growing.

"They said it's too traumatic, or something. They don't ever want to put me through it again. Aislyn, they don't get…me."

I kneeled down and reached out and cupped his chin and brought his eyes from the stone to me.

"Gabriel, do you remember the painting, with the red line, with the light in the middle?"

"Yeah. You said I'd finish it when I got here."

"You will. But I need you just to wait a few more days, and hold on…to that little light in the middle, okay?"

I got up, kissed him on the top of his head, and said, "Head to your Circle, okay. And tell them they can take the roof off, open-air, and sleep in the middle. You can see the stars. Every last one."

There was a slight glimmer in his eyes, even as he took a double take of the roof, and he hugged me once before running off.

I wanted to head after him, but it wouldn't help.

Instead, I went to Lynn's old Circle, which was being used for infant care.

"Megan, Will, I need a favor."

Will turned, holding two crying babies, and looked a little ragged as he said, "Great timing, Aislyn. Every time."

But he was smiling. He even said a quick, "Thank goodness you guessed it was the shelters," as I grabbed the empty bottles from the counter and started filling them with water.

"How much for yours, Will?"

"Four and six. The six ounce one needs soy. What's the favor?" he asked as I put the cubes in, closed the lid, and shook the bottle. I placed it on the table.

"It's about my Unnecessaries," I started cautiously.

Megan was holding a crying infant in one hand and an empty bottle in the other, trying to unscrew it with one hand. I grabbed it from her, and took the top off.

"Eight," she said with thankful eyes. "What about them?"

"Gabriel. I need you to get Gabriel some paint," I said, even as I filled the water up to the line.

"Aislyn, I love you," Megan said as she typed in a message on her MCU with her one free hand. "But seriously? Priorities!"

"Yes," I said, putting the cube in and shaking the bottle. "But they said they'd never let him paint again because some idiot who only got half a psych degree thinks it will traumatize him because he'll recall life in the Republic and it will cause stress. They have no clue that it was what helped him hold on. And what better way to fight Zander than by proving how amazing these kids are? And not just Gabriel. Get Maggie schematics and, 3 MCUs, and access to a mainframe. Prove that they're worth saving."

I gave the bottle to her. "We don't even need to prove it. We just need to let them prove it."

She stared at me, nodding, like she understood.

"Consider it done," she said resolutely.

I turned to look at Will still holding the two infants; he began to sing, the same song I had the night we were in the Q station.

"Does he…need some help?" I whispered.

"He's already refused. He's probably going to hold them until they fall asleep," she said, looking back at him in contemplation.

"They were Lynn's?"

"Yeah," she said. "This one, too."

I held her shoulder briefly before I said, "I gotta go."

"Why? I thought of all people, you would want to stay. They are letting some of us stay. This matters so much to you. I can tell. Why are you leaving?"

I felt torn again, but the shreds were being stretched. And I didn't want to cry. I didn't want to sleep. I didn't want to see Patterson. I just wanted to run away.

There was only one place I could run. The place I already needed to go.

"Because I'm looking for a different miracle. I'll tell you later. Someday. When I find it."

She nodded, looking like a part of her understood it wasn't just to save a Vessel or Unnecessary.

Then Will said, "You fight for someday, okay? Come back."

I stared at him, unable to respond with nothing but a reassuring smile. I gave her a hug and left before she asked more questions.

I was moving across the yard when Collin saw me.

"Hey, um…so…"

"Oh, my Circle," I said. "Do I have to give them permission?"

"Aislyn that's not it. Well, they're using it already, but just as a nursing station for any kid who is ill or needs a bandage or something. Patterson's back. We need to, um…head to our spot."

It wasn't until then that I realized that Eva was right behind me.

"Hey, you going to talk to Patterson?" she asked.

"Yeah, why?"

"Tell Patterson that I need to talk to him. I'm going back out, under the radar, right now."

"Why?"

There was a strange anxiety I wasn't used to seeing in her as she explained.

"Tessa called in to make sure everyone was okay while I was still in the Hand. She talked to Zander…and I might have overheard the conversation."

We both looked at her, both sure she overheard it and anxious to hear what it was.

"It's the order some of us have been dreading. And she already has a two-day head start. Michael will drive us out as far as he can, to try to make up for the distance. But…I need to go in three hours, with or without you, Aislyn. We need to get there before Tessa."

I was trying to think of what could be happening, but I saw fear in Collin's eyes as he asked, "Which lab did she say to take out?"

Eva said, "Zander didn't say," but then Eva took out her MCU and put the screen up so we could see it. It was a message from Tessa.

"I know you were on comm detail, so I know you heard us. I am going for the lab on 20th Street. If you want to save them, save them. Just do it before I hit it on the 4th. I'm sorry."

"Tell Patterson," she said, her arm almost shaking as she pulled the device back. "I'm going, no matter what. But tell him."

"You aren't going alone. Tell Brie, and I'm coming with you."

She nodded, and walked away. Instantly, Collin walked the other direction. I waited a few more seconds, and then peeled away to the left. By the time I got down to secondary Central, Collin had already told Patterson what Eva had said.

"You!" Patterson glared at me. For the first time in my life, I was genuinely afraid of him.

"Sir, I'm sorry–"

"Sorry doesn't cut it! You are going to tell me everything you told him, assuming you disobeyed the direct order that you were never to tell him anything! Do you have any idea what the last few hours have been like? Do you not see how this has emboldened Zander to make bad decisions? Do you know how close I am to telling you to kill him?"

"I didn't tell him enough to even put this together!"

"Look," Collin said, cautiously. "Hear her out. But she didn't. Really. It was one sentence, just mentioning that there was a shelter. I assumed they already knew that, even if Alex didn't."

Patterson paused, and not seeing me break under his attack might have convinced him to calm down enough.

"I'm sorry, Aislyn. I'm not actually mad at you. You...you were broken and tired, and I just need you to go through it all, again. I called Michael down, too. I need to know every word that was said in every moment. I need to know."

Almost automatically, I wanted to protest. Patterson didn't need to know every word, especially not Alex's last ones. But instead, I started to recollect everything out loud.

I begged him to stop using drugs.

I told him about Maggie.

I was right about Vinalia.

He said that I saw him differently, and asked if I was raised with a lot of Unnecessaries and that was why I didn't kill him outright.

"And all I said was that they were raised apart from me, in a shelter. That's it, I swear."

They were both silent, as was Michael who had come in as I was talking. He was looking at me warily, though he did say, "Sir, no words between them were very long. According to the footage, it was all very short. Of course, I had to delete it…"

"It's fine," Patterson sighed. "It certainly doesn't seem enough to attack a random building in the woods, but I want you to ask Alex if he told anyone anything, even under duress."

I breathed out relief, even as Patterson asked, "Did he say anything else after he stabbed himself?"

I looked at him, shaking my head. I said, "No" as if I was lost in thought.

But he didn't buy it. He knew I was hiding something, and even as I could tell, his eyes weren't accusing. "I know there's something else, if only by the way Michael is acting. What is it?"

"It doesn't matter. I mean it does, but…"

I trailed off. The air felt thick. I was staring at Patterson, but had stopped looking at Collin, who was still beside me.

"Collin," I said, thinking of the only solution that wouldn't ruin us, "I need you to leave the room."

"What?" he said defensively, possibly out of concern for me, considering Patterson's temper. "I'm not leaving. Why would I?"

"Oh no," Patterson said as he let out a sigh of comprehension before continuing. "That's why he saved you."

I cringed in the realization that he had guessed when he turned to Collin, "It's because she doesn't want to tell you."

"Tell me what?" he said, staring at me as I stared at Patterson.

There was a pause: I was trying to use the right words when Patterson leaned against the rail, rubbing his temples as he spoke.

"The missing motive. And quite a motive."

I gazed up in horror. Patterson had guessed.

"Did Alex say anything ….or did he just…kiss you?"

Collin's reaction was instant denial, as if Patterson was crazy, but then he looked at me as the word was about to escape my lips.

"Both."

Collin's eyes grew wide in shock. Patterson mouthed a "wow," but then looked at Michael briefly.

"So other than Michael, who must have known, because he's acting way too calm in an uncomfortable situation…"

Michael looked at Patterson. "Hey, I guessed same as you. About a month ago. I kind of figured it would be enough of a motive. I'm sorry, I don't do awkward, so when I saw…," he was still stumbling as he turned to Collin, "it was– like I didn't see– Patterson, can I go?"

Patterson held up his hand at Michael, and turned back to me.

"What exactly did he say?"

"He said…he saw me. He said I was the first to see him." I tried to ignore Collin as he turned to face the wall and moved behind me. "I asked why he was doing this, why now. And then he kissed me, before pushing me down the elevator, saving me from everyone else scouring the building after he…"

I didn't have to continue, but I did.

"I know what you might be thinking, Patterson. But I believe him. That doesn't mean I feel the same way. I don't. But when he said he loved me, I believed him."

There was silence, except for Michael typing and staring at the screen. I had no clue what Collin's face looked like, but I noticed that Patterson was looking at him instead of me. Despite feeling secure in being honest now, I suddenly felt the guilt of every minute I hadn't told Collin weighing down on me, even as Patterson asked the question I was dreading most.

"And you didn't want to tell us because?"

But to my surprise, Michael answered.

"It's embarrassing, awkward, and will strain her relationship, however undefined at this point, with Collin, which…." He pushed two more buttons very emphatically. "Is why…I would love to leave this room as quickly as possible? I'm driving Eva and Brie and you out in a few hours; can I please just–"

"Go!" Patterson said as Michael hit a few more keys before his station powered down, and he quickly walked away, pulled himself up to the second level, and ran up the stairs.

"Well," Patterson sighed, "I don't have any advice or any cute anecdotes. I'm not going to tell you two how to figure it out; just figure it out. I need both of you with your heads on straight in a few hours, so no crying, no drama, no jealousy, and no fighting."

He stared at me with the eyes that had frightened me minutes earlier as he said, "And it's not your decision to decide what doesn't matter! I'm the filter that decides what matters. I don't care what Collin feels. This is an example of how your relationship could get in the way. I trusted both of you that it wouldn't."

I looked down, not wanting to look at him just to be scolded again. But his tone was gentler and sincere as he said, "And you remember what I said, Aislyn. If you think he's lying, you run. Be suspicious, if it keeps you alive. And if it matters, I still trust you."

I nodded. He looked at Collin, and then jumped up the stairs.

Leaving me alone with the man who loved me, who was being pulled away with every chance that we had promised each other we'd make count.

"When were you going to tell me?" he asked, pained but calm.

"It's not like we've had a ton of time, Collin. And it isn't like that. It's not like…It's not that I–"

"Say it, Aislyn! Because it's what we're waiting for. For you to say, 'It doesn't matter because it's not like I care about him.' And if you just say it, I'd believe you, and this wouldn't come between us at all."

I finally turned to face him. His hands were on the railing, his back hunched over. He looked calm, but his knuckles were white.

"But you're not going to say it, are you? Not because you love him, but you think he should be loved?" he said, his voice calmer.

I stood shocked, even as my answer escaped me.

"I can't hate him. I'm sorry. I can't push him away."

"And I can't be angry," Collin said resolutely. "I sent you out to love broken people. He's broken, he's lost in so many ways, yet he's sacrificed so much for you. Of course you love him. I even love you more, for loving him."

I felt the guilt pile on me. I wanted to speak, but couldn't.

"It's okay to be confused, Aislyn. It is. It's hard…" he swallowed, as he said, "Because I never thought you'd be confused. But maybe you can offer me just a little hope. So I'll ask the question I'm afraid to say." He paused, turning to face me, setting his jaw, his eyes pained for the response that might follow.

"This question isn't the one you're expecting from me. I'm not going to ask you if you're sure of anything. All I want to know…is if you're still confused. Are you confused?"

I looked at him, and then without saying anything, not even knowing if he would push me away, I ran into him. I wrapped my arms around him, my one hand running through his hair, wanting to feel close to him as I said, "Yes, I'm confused."

"Then there's hope." He put his head into my shoulder, deflating and yet clinging strongly to me at the same time.

"I can't believe you still love me," I said, my shame and anxiety seeping through, and then flooding. "I can't believe no one loves him. I can't believe I have to go try to evacuate a lab before it's bombed. I can't believe there are kids upstairs who have become refugees twice. I don't know how I'll remember the steps or find a dress for Vinalia. I want to love you, but why is this so hard?"

He sighed. "You just said it. I think we both are realizing that with everything going on, every crisis crashing around us, that we're less important. I always feared this, Aislyn. I lived my whole life rejected and forgotten for the sake of this mission. There are too many people to care about for you to love just one soul. You love them more. You can't allow yourself to love me, too. And I think that might start to hurt."

He grasped my hand, kissing the top of my head. I grasped him, tighter, as I choked out the next words.

"No. It's definitely starting to hurt."

CHAPTER 19

"We aren't going to have to talk about you and Collin the rest of the time, are we?" Eva's voice broke through the quiet night.

Brie and I turned and said, "No," simultaneously, although Brie had more of a warning tone to her voice.

I shook my head. "No, really Eva, we need to make a plan."

"Alright, we have four days. We need to let Tessa take down the building so she doesn't get in trouble…" Eva said.

"Because who would want that?" Brie asked dryly.

"She did warn us, Brie, and you didn't hear Zander," Eva said.

"You never told me," I started, "what did she say? Did she threaten Tessa with additional probation?"

"No. Zander she told Tessa that if she failed, the probation would be escalated to treason. She has to do this, or her family would be in prison for raising her to be a traitorous wretch. I'm Tessa's biggest fan, but that's harsh."

I considered what I would do in her shoes, but Brie interrupted my thoughts.

"So right now, we're going in the morning of the 2nd. We'll have uniforms, which…" she trailed off. "Aislyn is somehow going to get a hold of. And we…"

"We pull the fire alarm. We evacuate. We assume they'll leave the less valuable 'merchandise' behind, and we'll have a chance to save some of them–"

"What if they leave all of them behind?" Eva said nervously.

"They shouldn't. Too much money and research and development into making each child unique. They aren't clones. There's value in each one of them because their ability to create diversity keeps them in power. They like power and money too much to leave all of the babies die. They'll secure them somehow, or find a way to get them out."

"So, all we have to do is get in, blend, pull an alarm after I infiltrate tech, save any kids they leave behind as dead, and hope the media doesn't report that we stole them."

"Yeah, because them dying is somehow better than a Protector stealing them," Brie said, leaning back on the grass.

We had found a spot near a meadow to talk. The sun was starting to set, and we were still one day away from the border. The problem was we were about a day and a half away. I looked at my phone, wondering if I could make it to see Alex by the time he would go to cafés in the morning. Unless we made good time tomorrow, I would be waiting until a day before the attack to see him. I was counting on his help to obtain our uniforms and I.D.'s. I looked up from my MCU to see Brie glaring at me accusingly.

"What's up? That's the third time you looked at your MCU?"

I instantly decided that lying was pointless.

"Timing. I just wish we had another day."

"Why do you need another day to get the uniforms?" Brie asked.

Even though both of them knew about Alex, I wasn't sure if I wanted tell each of them every detail. I was pondering the choice I had ahead of me; would I reveal more about Alex than I wanted to, would that put him or me more at risk?

But then I didn't have that choice anymore.

Eva's face lit up in comprehension.

Eva said, "Oh! Is that how we are getting our uniforms? The Sentry who would-be-Elite who would-be-traitor is going to swipe them? That makes this more fun."

"What? How–" Brie asked, "The Sentry?"

And then, in a moment almost too comical for me not to smile, they both looked at each other and then at me, simultaneously saying, "She knows?"

"C'mon! Why does Brie get to know?" Eva whined.

Almost annoyed, I spoke in a very even tone.

"Eva, Brie knows about Alex because the night Brie killed the spy and we had to run for the border was the same night Alex had given me a baby that he was supposed to kill. We had to keep moving, because if they had found the baby, they would have killed Alex, the baby, and me. Brie, Eva knows about Alex because he stabbed himself in the stomach to divert the attention of the police chasing me. She hacked into secure files to discover Alex survived, but was tortured because I slipped through the perimeter."

Brie sounded scared when she said, "He stabbed himself?"

"He figured it would buy me time. And it did. It worked."

Eva said, "He gave you a baby? What the…"

"It wasn't a girl. The mother wanted a girl, so they gave it to him so he could dispose of it."

Eva cursed. Brie muttered, "That is messed up."

"And I needed to tell you both about it, so I don't know why I hesitated. I can't leave when we're done with the mission."

"Why not?" Brie asked. "We're going to need you, we have no idea how much help will be there, even with Eva's plan."

"Are you dissing my skills?" Eva said.

I ignored her to continue.

"I have to go to this party on the 19th, to help a friend of his. She's a Vessel. I'm guessing she's high-profile, because the party—"

"Wait, are you talking about Vinalia? The biggest party of the year?" Eva asked, impressed, yet terrified.

"Yes," I said hesitantly as Brie's eyes widened.

"More big fun. I'm…jealous. It's like a—" Eva said nonchalantly, but then shook her head. Her tone changed.

"No, I can't even fake joking about this. Please don't do this, Aislyn. This is a trap."

"No, it's not," Brie said. "That's not how they work. The last thing the Society would want at a huge party like Vinalia is a Protector showing up, even if it was to be arrested. It wouldn't be an example; it would be an embarrassment."

"That being said," Eva started, "I'm guessing you are hoping for the uniforms from him—" she paused as I nodded, "which is good to know. Do we need to hurry? We can run if we need to."

I nodded, satisfied that they were trying to comprehend the situation. "Yes. I know where he'll be in 24 hours in the morning. If we could shave off 6 hours to get there in a day, that would help."

"We could even move tonight. We can get another 3 miles."

I paused, looking for a bit of nerve or courage.

"Not until story time is over. And it's not." They look confused, even as I continued, "Now it's your turn. Zander. Go."

Eva started to groan. She put her head in her hands and rubbed her forehead, and kept groaning until Brie rolled her eyes.

"Okay, so...the thing is, I hate people who think that a person's backstory is everything. We make choices every day. For better or for worse. And if anyone knew the truth about Zander, it would destroy their credibility and any ability they ever had to help us."

"Whose credibility?"

Eva's jaw shook. "The Unnecessaries."

"But Zander isn't an Unnecessary. She was never registered. She can't be–"

My argument faded in looking at her eyes. There was a fear; the fear anyone had when they were about to share the truth for the first time.

"Aislyn, you weren't the first Protector to break the rules."

And with that one fact, a possibility I had never thought of was forming in my mind, even as Eva continued.

"I'm sure my mom wasn't the first either. What matters is that one day, my mom broke one rule. Matilda was 8 years old, but back then, the cut-off age to rescue Unnecessaries was age 6. What's stupid is that the Council would've probably let Matilda stay. She was near death from starvation and was about to get caught and trafficked. They have that list for girls, for Elites and Citizens. I'd rather die than have that fate."

Eva paused, now staring at the stick she was twirling. "The thing is, my mom didn't want the reputation of 'rule-breaker.' She wasn't as brave as you. So she brought her home, but instead of registering her, she took her to an older grandmother figure in town, a Katherine Zander, who had several children who lived in the woods. Hoping no one would check– and they didn't– the older woman told people that 'Margaret' was an orphan of one of her late daughters. The hope was that she would never know who she was. She would forget. There were a few downfalls."

Even as she said it, I thought of one.

"She didn't get the Shield Vaccine."

"Right, because the kids in the shelter always get special water and doses of the vaccine specially made. But with her age and the cover story, there was no reason she would have to get it. It was the first price paid for a highly costly mistake. The other was not so obvious right away. My mom picked the wrong grandmother."

"Was she cruel?"

"No. She was nice. Really nice. But I think she felt guilty. She died about five years ago, and after that…Zander kind of snapped. She switched gears. And nothing's ever been the same."

"You think she told Zander? Like a deathbed confessional?"

"Well, it makes sense, doesn't it? Zander's been out to get the Society ever since, so hell-bent on hurting them, not just saving Unnecessaries," Brie said, pausing. "I think that's why she has such a disdain for them. She wants to separate herself from them, somehow. This is why there has always been the 45th Mandate that an Unnecessary can't be a Protector or take office. It was meant to prevent this: an atrocious mess of insecurity and revenge."

I paused, taking all the information in before I said, "Eva, I know why you would know. But if there's no record, not even in sealed files, and this is a secret, how does Brie know?"

"Oh, that's easy," Eva said nonchalantly. "You see, Brie is the daughter my mom always wanted. She adores her. So my mom just told her randomly one summer day while they were bonding."

Brie looked at me and raised an eyebrow to confirm that was the truth. I expected her to deny it, but Brie just looked at Eva, almost protectively, as she continued to explain.

"It was my mom's secret to tell. But I'm letting you know, not so you can reveal it, but because…I thought maybe if you knew how the story started, you could try to find a way to end it. I don't want it to end with everyone discovering her dark past, and then judging Unnecessaries as heartless, crazed people who only want revenge. It can't end that way. How do we end this story, Aislyn?"

My mind was lost in the haze of the events that had just been revealed, making me feel both naïve and older at the same time. The warm breeze swayed the trees. My attention was diverted to them. They felt old. These trees had already heard these whispers before. Had Hannah passed through this meadow with her? Had Zander chased the moths thinking they were butterflies? Had she hugged her grandmother? Had she cried about never having children? Had she smiled in triumph the day she entered Central, her rise to power enabling her to make a difference? Had she cried the night she discovered her life she was a lie?

"Well," I started, "It's a tragedy. It only ends one way."

Eva sighed, "I was afraid of that."

Silence fell as we mourned our failure to find hope. Eventually Eva said, "Brie, can we just stay here? I'm feel…tired."

"Why don't we wake pre-dawn? It will be cooler then. We can make more miles on a good night's sleep," Brie suggested.

Eva and I agreed, even as we groaned a bit from being sore, and we laid out the sleeping bags. Eva set up the camo tent, setting the temperature match a little lower just to make sure a drone didn't see us. They laid down on either side of me. I was thankful, because sharing my secret and hearing Eva's had left me feeling vulnerable.

Eva said, "I miss seeing the stars. They are there. I know it. But they keep evading me. I'm in a sewer, or under a canopy, or I'm just too tired to look up."

I smiled at her, even as Brie, on the right side of me, shifted and said, "I miss them, too, Eva, but if you don't go to sleep after complaining about being tired, I'll hit you."

Eva turned the other way then, leaving me to turn to Brie and beg her to be more compassionate. Even before I did, she smiled.

"Love you, little sister."

Eva sighed. "Love you, too, big sister."

Even though Eva couldn't see my confused expression, she answered my silent question, "It's how we cope with that problem I alluded to earlier. Our strange little family dynamic."

"Yeah. George is like the older brother who always challenges us. Avery's the annoying older brother who picks on us, but will save us in a pinch. And Collin is like our quirky little brother…"

Eva interrupted Brie, "Which is why you will never, ever talk about kissing him around us. Never."

I laughed before saying, "Noted."

I rolled back over in my sleeping sack, letting the foam expand and shift and adjust underneath me. Brie was staring at her MCU. I couldn't see her screen, but I didn't have to. I could see her.

I regretted my conclusion that tragedies only have one end.

"You got to see Caleigh, then, before you left?"

"Yeah. She's so big. I hadn't seen her since Christmas. The…suspension on my application is still there. This mission probably won't help, but I do have one thing on my side."

"Zander's big secret," I said as she nodded. "I suppose that's leverage. Will you still try to adopt Caleigh then?"

"I can't tell her. Not yet. I couldn't stand to see her so excited, and then imagine what would happen if I…We still have about 6 active months, Aislyn. I don't want to orphan her in the middle of an adoption. She'll have to deal with enough, one day: the facts surrounding the death of a mother betrayed by her family. The fact that I couldn't save her mother. It feels so wrong that I failed…and I get to have her. Why? Why do I get to have her?"

A silence followed that I wish I could have filled with something profound and comforting as Brie continued.

"She said no one understood that she was already in love with the child in her. But I did. So she trusted me, and I…"

She was about to spiral. I said the only thing I could think of.

"She did trust you, Brie. Once, when it mattered most. I think she would trust you with her child forever."

The stillness returned, each moment more painful because I was worried about all the lies Brie might have believed as she dragged her finger along the MCU, tracing Caleigh's face with her finger. Maybe her courage was growing in that silence. But the calm was shattered by an annoyed voice.

"Why does 27 get to talk, and I can't?"

Brie smiled and rolled her eyes. "Because we're older and we get to stay up later." Eva cursed at that as Brie continued, "And because she says the right thing once in a while."

Brie smiled, blinking rapidly despite her usual cool exterior.

Eva said, her tone much different, "Does that mean you'll listen to her? Because Collin and I have been saying this for years, and you never believe us. Not that I'm jealous, or anything. I just hope it's just all adding up and that you're finally listening. To all of us."

Brie put away her MCU, her eyes glistening in the last light, looking at me knowingly, but she didn't respond. But as I was about to fall off into the void of sleep, I heard a faint whisper.

"I'm listening."

It echoed in my mind for the whole next day.

That was what we were meant to do: Listen.

Listen for a lost voice.

Listen for a person mention they were sick in the mornings.

Listen for rumors about Vinalia fashion.

Listen to Palmer's insufferable lies while you wait for one of his Sentries to show up for coffee and commit an act of treason.

I was trying to listen, but my legs hurt. They hurt when I stood, when I sat, when I breathed. We had run fifteen miles in the morning, and hiked the remaining five miles later in the day. I got a cab. Considering all the energy we had spent to get into the Republic on time, it seemed foolish to waste the effort and risk missing Alex by minutes.

But as I tried to listen to the broadcaster show glimpses of the crazed Protector with the rag over her face, I used every effort to withstand not viewing it, looking disinterested. I felt exposed, as if by watching the broadcast in any way, I would be under suspicion of being the person on the screen.

So I thought of my legs hurting, or stared at the table, creating a shape on the condensation on the outside of the cup. My phone was out, providing me the perfect cover: a million other things people could assume were distracting me, but I was more focused on my finger gliding on my cup. I swiped my finger from side to side, each time trying to decide how I would tell him what I needed and why I needed it.

Should I just be honest? I imagined having to tell him that Tessa was ordered to take it out. What if I wasn't honest? What would it be like if he gave me the uniforms only to watch a broadcast like this in two days? What if Tessa took it out violently? Would he ever trust me when I said that we were trying to defend the lives inside?

After all the days and hours waiting to see him, I didn't know what to say. And in that instant, he came through the door.

I continued to stare at the cup, although my movements were probably still too unnatural. I went back to swiping my phone. I risked a glance at the menu, thinking maybe that was appropriate because I had been there a while. I was trying to count in my mind as I controlled my breathing. It was then I noticed him staring at the window behind me, but with no direct focus on my eyes.

At first I had wondered if maybe I was supposed to play the part of an old friend and greet him, but I was thinking that it would be easier to follow him somewhere, or give him my number.

But then as he turned from the counter, his eyes fell right on me. Intense, as if they were asking for something. His smirk grew, and mine began to mirror it, feeling a little dangerous, annoyed, and breathless that he had chosen to flirt with me as our cover.

He had started the game, but now I had to play it.

He turned to take his order when his name was called, and then came to my table and sat down across from me.

"Well, haven't seen you around for a while."

"No, I wasn't sure…"

I trailed off, even as he leaned in across the table.

"That's enough for the crowd, and the man over there is about to leave. He was at the dance a few months ago, so I couldn't pretend I didn't know you, just in case he happened to remember seeing us both. Just look like I just told you something…flattering about the last time he saw us both together."

I instantly shifted, as if Alex had said something that intrigued me, and I forced a giggle. The man in the café who I now recognized from the dance left after a few more whispers between Alex and I. I could then take the focus off of my peripherals, and finally look at Alex. His eyes struck me, like always, but his other features were overtaking my thoughts as he still pretended to talk about the latest parties. I had never quite seen him in daylight, without shadows, fear, and blood. The green of his eyes looked clearer than before, a sharp contrast to the light skin and his dark, curled hair. He looked as perfect as everyone else in the Republic, but with a strange sense of nobleness that was rare. His smile was hypnotic. But his first words, his true first words to me struck like iron, almost stopping my breath.

"Aislyn…I can't believe you came."

I stared at him, knowing I couldn't look how I felt. This was the first time I had gotten the chance to thank him, and I didn't take it. Two other words escaped, instead.

"You're alive."

His breath shuddered for a second, but he hid it with a deep breath and smirk.

"That depends on your definition of life, I suppose, but yes, it would appear I'm alive."

"Thank you," I whispered, as I reached out to touch his hand. He opened up the palm of his hand and let mine slide into it.

"It's okay. It wasn't that bad," he said smiling.

"You're lying," I said, and this time I barely said it without my lip trembling. I couldn't hide the fact that I had hated what they had done with him, no more than he could hide his shock.

"You hacked the med report. Impressive. Why'd you bother?"

"I needed to know…if you were…are you okay, Alex?"

He moved to wrap his fingers around mine, his jaw trembling only once before he said, "I am now. You're here early, not that I mind if–"

"Alex?"

He looked up at me, confused, before reaching for my hand with his other one and now saying comfortingly, "You're going to be fine. If you want to, we can talk about everything. I have seven escape routes planned. If you're nervous, we can practice dance…"

"No, Alex–" I felt more guilty now, having to ask for the favor that I needed, while he was trying to be protective and reassuring. "I need a favor. Quick stop. Before the party. To help a friend."

With each part of my broken sentence, his confusion disappeared. He nodded, understanding. He looked as if he was about to ask me to be safe, careful, or give me more details when I had to interrupt. Deciding that I didn't want to risk confusion or broken trust later, I made the decision to tell him everything. But I started with what I needed.

"I need uniforms and badges to get into the lab on 20th."

If he was confused, he didn't show it. "How many?"

"Three, maybe four if it's not that much of a problem. And I need them by tomorrow or the next morning at the latest."

His eyes opened a bit, and his voice was strained. "A little less okay, but I should be able to do it. Why the rush?"

"Alex, you know that there's been changes. You've had to have known that after the drone attack…"

Something suddenly changed in his hand. It was rigid, no longer squeezing mine. I suppose that verbalizing it wasn't going to be necessary. He had already guessed, but his first guess was wrong.

"Are you…you wouldn't take it out? Not you."

"No." This time I squeezed his hand, reaching out with both of mine. "No, Alex, not me. Most of us would refuse. But one of us has been ordered to take it out. Her family is in danger if she doesn't carry out the order, and there was a specific reason why that lab was chosen. Tessa warned us which location she chose, so we could get as many people out as possible. I don't anticipate a huge attack, but…I need your help."

I said the last part in desperation, seeing something like disgust cross his face. He looked down.

And then, without question, I knew he was not reacting to me.

He looked up at the screen in the center of the wall in the café, and he pulled his MCU to the center. He yelled across the room to summon the Sub-Terra, who was holding seven cups.

"What's wrong?" I whispered.

"I am a Sentry, and the law, however menial it may seem, is law," he said, still leaving me confused as the screens changed, and what looked like the manager came out to our table, out of breath.

"We just missed the first minute, sir. I'm so sorry. I didn't realize there was a live broadcast this morning."

"You're supposed to have a schedule, and have it play exclusively on all screens when there is a live feed. You know that," Alex said harshly.

"I do apologize, sir. You know how much we support the Party."

"I'll write in the report that it was the Sub-Terra's error and was fixed by you within the minute. I'll also write that you were so apologetic that you gave over your day's profits to the Party."

The man nodded. "Generous, as always, sir. Thank you."

The man went back and turned up the volume. Alex had spoken in the tone I hated most: the arrogant voice dripped in disdain for others. He looked at me with one eyebrow raised.

"Gotta work at something if I'm not meeting my quota on Unnecessaries and Protectors. Getting money for the Party is the one excellent quality they see in me," he said, in response to my stare. I realized that any conversation between us was on hold. He would be expected to watch the broadcast intently. I would have to listen to the rumors as well. The word rumor echoed in my brain until I realized Palmer was saying it.

"There's a rumor going around, I'm sure you know. It's been a while, of course, but it's time to clear up how this all started."

"So we are about to hear the truth?" The reporter faked shock.

"Yes. There was no need for us to share it before. While we have been gracious to the Territory, as many are aware, only removing those who enter our state instead of retaliating against the Territory as a whole. I know we are all aware that most of them live in peace– while not quite living to the fullest of their potential. Some of our intel shows they have adorable little customs that are not all as ridiculous as their religion or concept of parenting. We know that leaps in technology and enlightenment abound, giving us hope for their future, which would otherwise be primitive. But with these attacks becoming more severe, we are afraid that we must now burden all of you with the truth."

I almost scoffed at the idea that the truth was a burden, but then remembered where I was as Alex squeezed my hand, and looked slightly more interested.

"There were traitors over two centuries ago that would become the Territory's first members. We allowed them to leave. No one debates this. We didn't follow through with military force. But something else…happened that night. Something was stolen from the labs at Goirson Tech. It was a nanobot-inspired serum–"

"Wait," asked the reporter. "You are saying there actually is a Serum?"

"Yes," Palmer admitted, almost acting as if it hurt him to allow that information to leave his mouth, and as if he wasn't aware he was giving this information to thousands of people. "This has been a rumor, and I apologize, because we called it a rumor. We've heard it for years. The Serum that hinders life. But we don't hinder life: we improve it. But in their history, they are taught that we ruined their lives by leaving their women infertile with this Serum. This idea has helped fuel nearly 200 years of Protectors."

Palmer paused, taking a breath as if he was about to reveal a tragic statement. "Our involvement with these people ended the night they escaped. You see, the truth I must burden you with is this: they vilify you, me, all of us. I never wanted you to know that. And if we had truly administered a Serum that made all of them infertile, we would have realized our barbaric mistake in seeking revenge after a few weeks. We would have offered them the technology to eradicate it, or permitted them to use our labs as a way to maybe bridge a gap for a few decades. It's so horrible that they reject babies created in labs, it really is. But that's not the issue, although some of the blame is ours."

I instantly thought of Brie, hoping she was still in an alley, not listening to this. Alex squeezed my hand again, and I thought maybe there was more concern on my face then there should be. I instantly readjusted my expression as the man asked Palmer, "I'm sorry, what blame is ours?"

He sighed, as if pondering a great injustice, but I had a feeling that he was about to reveal something that wasn't any injustice at all. I was only partially correct.

Palmer answered, "We shouldn't have made it. The Serum. We originally designed it to ensure that no woman had to worry about pregnancy, but eventually we used reason and influence, showing people the benefits of lab-created children. We chose to let you choose. You all rose to the occasion and chose correctly. We didn't need the Serum anymore. We should've destroyed it."

His fake grief was concerning me now. Even if he was going to say that killing us was no great tragedy, I didn't like his tone. And I had a horrible feeling as the interviewer asked Palmer the most obvious question.

"So, sir, when you said it was stolen..."

"You see, the traitors wanted to slander us as careless, heartless individuals. But we're not. We love. We create. We are free. The leaders of the Territory, in their exodus, took something with them to ensure that the Republic would remain the enemy they needed us to be. They took a weapon, not to attack us, but to attack their own people so that they would have what they needed to solidify their nation. The Territory would need to hate us to have the solidarity the traitors dreamed of. The Serum gave them to power to hate us forever."

Alex didn't move to remind me to take a breath; he was breathless, too. I scolded myself for my shock, and gave myself orders: Act bored, look at the screen, take a sip of coffee, breathe.

"And what was their initial response, Minister, when the Serum was first administered?"

"It was devastating, of course. Mostly because, again, they cling to their irrational beliefs of what gives life value. But I can imagine the pain they felt, along with the fear. Without labs, natural birth is their only option of their legacy. And we have to understand that fear. These Protectors have always been trained at a very young age in the shadow of resentment and hatred. Our leaders have known this for many years, which is why we only attack the girls who enter our nation, and do not retaliate against the innocents in the Territory."

"Now, Minister, I'm trying to keep up. If the Serum is meant to make them infertile, how are they alive at all? Or–"

"Ah, yes, with you knowing one rumor to be true, other truths must come out. We lost some good scientists to their self-destroying devotion to the idea of a God, or to the more sentimental ideas of childbirth. These scientists were able to filter a great deal of the Serum out, and they created an inoculation. The Territory has mostly recovered as a culture, but this terror hovers. It seeps into their minds when they see filters on all of their rivers. Then, a few years ago, we overheard chatter that the inoculation doesn't even work on all the girls. It can have fatal side effects. These girls who cannot have the vaccine are a reminder of why their culture should all hate the Republic. These infertile young ladies are a walking symbol of everything they think that we stole from them. Only we didn't steal it; their ancestors did."

Alex began to look at me for reactions instead of the screen, as if he was willing me to stay calm. Luckily, shock seemed to be a popular emotion in the room, so I wasn't that out of character or in danger of breaking our cover. But there was a horrible dread growing in me in swells, like a wave. And when it crested, I would lose my breath. Alex would squeeze my hand, gazing at me with confused eyes. But I saw a hint of something I decided I hated more than any emotion he had ever directed at me: suspicion.

"Sir, one more question. Do you think this recent push by their leaders to attack us, with two Sentries killed in the last month and one injured, is them making a move to actually bring on a real war?"

"No. No, not really. And I wanted to put peoples' minds at ease about that. I think what we may have here are a few– how should I say this? A few fierce hearts. It's why I hope they hear this message. I think they are brave, smart women, but they need the truth to channel their bravery differently. I hope that these Protectors can see this and respond to this positively, even independently from the Territory, and stop attacking us."

"Well, thank you for everything you have revealed today, sir, and for just being so honest…"

The rest faded out into the static of protests in my mind. I felt the distance between the Territory and me in a way I never had before. The people in Central were watching this message. I could imagine what must be happening. Collin whispering to George or Michael. Zander yelling at someone, or everyone. Patterson closing his stress-filled eyes. Eldridge lost in thought. Filters flowing with water. Unnecessaries laughing near the Circles, in the garden where Naomi put the rock from her garden…

Naomi.

I clung to her identity and her Legacy. Despite the paranoia that threatened to overtake me, I remembered that the Council refused to let anyone enter the Republic. The first Protector had never been inspired by the Council or revenge. Her cause was pure. Her words, the words written in ink in my journal, and her stone in the garden and the stones that made up my Circle stood as a wall, a barrier against the lies.

I realized as I saw the look in Alex's eyes that I would need that barrier to withstand all the questions he had, and I wasn't confident I could answer them all.

We faked a casual exit. I was a few seconds away from asking him what was going on when he grabbed my arm, and we headed down an alley.

We were ten steps down before I answered the first question I knew must be on his mind. But the answer came in curse words.

"So you're saying it's not true?" he asked.

I was almost stifled by my promise from Patterson not to tell Alex any intelligence, but decided to say, "Firstly, we would never do that. Ever. Secondly, the first Protector, Naomi, was rejected by the first Council in the Territory. They wanted nothing to do with the Republic. At all. She was the first Protector, and she went in for years, undercover, before they validated the program. Without permission or their support. This was never about revenge. I promise you."

He looked at me, that knowledge shaking him. It was only then that I noticed that he was shaking.

"One of you killed two Sentries. She wasn't defending herself."

"That's a lie. She came home with a Vessel," I shot back.

"But not the second one. Why the change in policy? Why do you need my help? Because one of you has been ordered to take down a lab. Since when?"

My anger was rising, maybe more because we were having this conversation when I felt betrayed by him. So I attacked.

"Since you shot down two shuttles and attacked a shelter full of children, something I was supposed to question you about."

"What are you talking about?" he shot back defensively.

"They think you're lying, Alex. Or they're not sure. They think that you're a spy and this is a long game to draw me in to get intel. We can't find proof of your sister. There's no account of a Vessel and child dying during childbirth that month. I told you about the shelters the last time we talked, and they were bombed a week later. There were attacks on shuttles. We're under new leadership, and yes, she's acting aggressively. Policy has changed."

I felt out of control. All the anger turned to fear, mutating with a horrible wrench in my stomach as Alex took a step forward I wasn't expecting, putting his hands off to the side, raising them slightly in surrender.

"If any of you were this close to a Sentry, what would they do?"

I swallowed, scraping the doubts away as they were forming on my mind, even as I remembered how much I hated this policy, hated Zander, how much I still wanted to be on his side, how much I still believed him. The truth might break me if I said it out loud.

A month ago, he would have only been labeled a threat if he was interfering with a mission. Now...

He asked again, as he moved right in front of me.

"Aislyn, if any Protector was as close to me as you are right now, what would they do?"

He stared, his eyes piercing my soul. I told myself to stand still, just in case he mistook any movement as a threat. But the only weapon I had was the truth, and it stung more with each moment I didn't say it.

"Kill you. They would kill you." I faltered on the last word.

He nodded, looked down at the ground, and said, "Well, then, how do I know you aren't following orders? What if you have a long game to get intel from me? Or how do I know that any moment, you won't do what they would do? Would you kill me?"

He stopped, maybe expecting a long silence to follow the challenging stare he was forming. But it didn't last. Because I spoke into it, breathlessly, but with more conviction than he was expecting.

"Never."

I saw him tense up, his brow squeezed with confusion even as I tried to explain.

"Alex, I can't ask you to trust the people I take orders from. I can't trust them. I don't know what to think about your sister. I don't want this to be complicated. It's simple, really. I just want one more person to be breathing instead of dead."

And as I stared at him, through the haze between us, I felt the tension diffuse into a strange sympathy before he spoke.

"I know exactly how that feels," he choked out.

I played back the words in my head, feeling a strain on my heart that I didn't expect. I walked a few steps forward, closing the gap between us. I'm not sure why I reached for him— maybe because we had a common goal now, maybe to tell him I still trusted him, or that he could still trust me. But he pulled me in, familiar with the fear I now felt. He leaned his forehead to mine, where his lips had first touched me. I tried not to think about that moment, but it was impossible.

Almost not able to keep my voice steady, I repeated the first words I had said to him that day.

"You're alive. And I won't be the one to kill you."

I pulled back from his grasp, my hand still on the back of his neck. I could feel the sweat from his anger or worry. He lifted his eyes to gaze into mine. I leaned in, pulling him slightly towards me. I kissed his forehead, feeling him shake beneath me, and then I lowered my forehead against his. I stayed there, just far enough away to feel his breath on my lips as he began to speak.

"I believe you. Or I want to. I know Palmer lies, and I know the lab will get attacked with or without my help getting the uniforms. It's...there's these voices screaming that I shouldn't trust you. That I can't. That I'm crazy, only because I..."

He paused, as his eyes met me critically, and said, "You have the voices, too. You don't need me to tell you what they're saying."

I nodded, even as I was backing up.

"Just promise me one thing, Alex."

"What?" he said, nervous that he wouldn't be able to it.

"I will keep all the voices screaming. I will let the doubt and faith rage on until I discover the truth. I'll keep the voices that tell me to trust you, and hope they're louder than the ones that tell me not to. Even if it makes my head and heart hurt more, I'll keep them shouting. For you."

He lowered his head as he nodded, even as I felt it was odd that it was so close to the request Collin had made: to sustain turmoil to keep hope alive. He looked vulnerable as he made his next request.

"Keep going, Aislyn. I'll see you here tomorrow at 7. If you aren't here, I'll put the things behind that box or in the dumpster."

He reached into his pocket and pulled out a roll of cash.

"Here's some money for the dress. Also, we need a cover story, some way we could've flirt, the kind of flirting that happens before the ball. If you are having doubts, you don't—"

"I'll see you tomorrow. I'll think of something. I promise."

I kept my response short, to show there was no doubt left. With that, he pulled me in, kissing my forehead once more. Then he left me without looking back, standing in the alley with my heart pounding so loudly that I was surprised that every Sentry couldn't hear it and descend on me. Every self-accusation and worry condemned me.

I didn't know if this was love, but it was strong.

And I couldn't ignore it anymore.

I now felt the pressure of it flood me, making me promise something to myself I couldn't dare speak out loud. Even to him.

I would trust him, or I would die trying.

CHAPTER 20

I forced a casual smile as I walked into the art gallery on 32nd, wondering if it was too forced to fool Eva and Brie. But I quickly found relief that neither of them might notice, feeling the tension as I saw both of them staring at pieces on opposite sides of the room. I moved to Eva first. I was about to ask if they had seen the broadcast, but then I noticed that while Brie looked calm, even tranquil, her fist was closed, and her knuckles were white.

Except for the fresh scrapes that looked bloody.

"That good, huh?" I said as I walked up to the piece, next to Eva.

"Oh, yeah. It's been a blast. First, she almost cried. Then she walked for twenty minutes without saying anything, and then she stopped behind a dumpster and phased for a while, like I wasn't even there. I knew that she snapped out of that when she took the box she was sitting on and mercilessly pounded it into the ground."

"Eva, there's no way Palmer's right, is there?"

"Above my pay grade there, 27. I might know everything now, but I wasn't around back then to sneak around corners and hide in air ducts. We do know something, which I think is what snapped Brie back into place."

"Which is?"

"This was presented to the people of the Republic as an explanation for why our recent attacks, which have been more violent. But the three of us know who is causing this."

I sighed and smiled, seemingly admiring painting. "Zander, a revengeful Unnecessary. It has nothing to do with the Serum."

"Exactly. That being said, there's a huge complication. Even if they're lying, which they probably are..."

"We are about to play right into that lie. If Tessa takes out that lab, it's going to look like our response. And right after Palmer said we don't respect the lives made in labs."

"I think Brie is phasing because she just figured that out."

"I figured it out the first time I phased," Brie's voice said from behind us. "Now we're here to fix it."

"Oh, is that why we are here? I thought it was to look at this blob of red and call it art," Eva said, shifting her weight slightly to pretend to stare at it from another angle.

"No, we're here because of the Amelia principle."

"Oh, is that this gallery?" Eva said in awe, which I for some reason found annoying, perhaps because of my ignorance of a legacy that still seemed too massive to learn. If she caught my irritation, she ignored it to continue, "so what makes you think she'll be here now? I mean she is a...."

Eva cursed, but just at that moment, someone echoed that curse, almost at the exact time that she said it.

"I suppose I am, but it's not a great way to start negotiations."

"Tessa," Brie said, tensely and almost between gritted teeth.

"What's the Amelia principle?" I asked Eva, hoping I had one second to ask before Tessa would roll her eyes.

Tessa sighed, "45th generation, there was a situation where Amelia, 18th Protector, needed some help. Another Protector ran into her, 12 blocks away, in an art gallery. It was just by chance. Amelia said she felt it was fate or destiny or God, and she went back to that gallery, only to find that another Protector needed her help. It's an old school rule, under duress. If any of us knows we may need to talk, we meet at a gallery."

Brie turned to Tessa, "History lesson is over. What's the plan?"

"I was going bomb it. Can't do that now unless I want to start a war. I'd rather see Zander kill me than give Palmer an excuse to pull a trigger and kill everyone back home."

"So…" Brie prodded.

She took a tense sigh. "I'm taking out the intel."

"How?" Eva said.

"EMP bomb, like Lynn set off, with a small bomb to blow up some equipment. That's all. Enough to cover your tracks."

"Except we're going to be accused of killing who we claim we want to save," Eva said. "Palmer could use that against us."

Tessa took a breath. "I thought of that. Which is why I came. I knew Brie and Eva would try to convince me that there's nothing Zander could do to me, even though I'm sure you've both been equally threatened. I'm guessing Brie's in danger of not adopting Caleigh. Eva is regularly reminded that the entire Hand is still being tortured. Megan didn't get pain meds a month ago. I don't know what they will threaten Aislyn with. And if you knew the intel that Avery sent me about this lab before I left, you would want me to take the place out brick by brick. You have no idea what they do there. I'm going to stop it. Don't try to change my mind."

Brie sighed, then pretended to look at her phone and take a picture of the piece.

"So why did you come here, then?"

"I can't believe I'm saying this, but I needed Aislyn. I wanted someone who might be able to think of a way to minimize the risk of a backlash from Palmer. I knew she'd be with you."

While unexpectedly flattered, her words didn't make me feel that way. I felt trapped, because I didn't have any solution.

"There's nothing, Tessa. I've thought of a few things. But Palmer is going to spin this as a tragedy, as long as he doesn't..."

I stopped. My head burst with a flood of thoughts that surrounded the event I had been preparing for: Vinalia.

And I knew the answer to at least one problem.

"Time," I said almost to myself before turning to her. "Wait."

"What?"

"Wait another four days. Vinalia prep and chatter will be in full swing. Palmer wants to prove a point, but not at the risk of losing the focus on the biggest social event of the summer, especially if there's rumors or doubts that it's just an accident. Even with him lying about the Vaccine–"

"Is he lying?" Tessa interrupted sharply with the uncertainty that had haunted us for the past hour. Brie shifted her weight onto her other leg, maybe feeling the weight of worry that we had all had been part of a scheme that was orchestrated long ago.

I surprised myself by starting to speak, not even sure what I was going to say when I started. It was a blurry thought that I hoped I could find the words to convey.

"We've all seen the reasons why we can't trust the Council. But we know Patterson. We know our trainers. We know the fear in the eyes of the people we rescue. We know the look of hope in those faces when they see us."

I paused. "Maybe it doesn't matter how the story started. It matters more that we write our chapter well."

No one spoke for a second. Eva turned to me slowly, softly smiling, but no witty remark came. Finally, Tessa backed away and exited the room. Not sure what Tessa was thinking, it left me wondering if I had said the right thing. But I looked over at Brie. She looked like she had the first time I had ever met her, a stare from icy blue eyes that only intensified, as if drawing in the vibrant red from the painting and lighting her soul on fire.

I had said the right thing to her. That was all that mattered.

"Ladies, were you interested in purchasing the piece?"

The lady's voice startled Eva. She didn't react physically, except her eyes grew wider. Brie also turned to me in a panic, and then was confused when I smiled confidently and winked.

"Yes, I am! I just wanted their opinion first, so I asked them to come look at it. I need…a hint."

"A hint?" she said, looking intrigued at her potential customer.

"He's invited to the ball, in the secretaries house. He doesn't have a date. I could go alone, but…" I looked at the piece of art longingly. "I'd rather not."

She smiled, sounding impressed.

"Well, it certainly is a statement. It is also twenty thousand, you are aware."

"Not a problem," I said, pulling out my wallet. It was almost all I had, but as Alex had said we needed a cover story with us publically flirting, I hoped he would understand I needed more.

"And the recipient? We will deliver it, of course, free of charge."

"Alex André Anderson. His address is…"

"Oh, we've delivered to the Andersons, before, dear. He will indeed love this piece. He has a red floral to match it that would coordinate, yet set it off. And it's in the bedroom. And for an extra two hundred, I can get it there in a few hours."

"That would be perfect, thank you." I moved back to the piece, briefly appearing far more confident than I felt.

I whispered urgently, "I need to borrow two hundred."

Eva stifled a laugh as Brie shook her head and smirked.

"I gotta hand it to you, though–" Eva said, about to say something else when I interrupted.

"Just hand me some money, then compliment my quick thinking later. I probably need to put in a good tip, for delivery."

"I still don't like him knowing about the lab. You do realize that if he's been playing a longer game, to trap you, this is what he's been waiting for. Something exactly like this."

"I know," I said, staring at the painting instead of Eva.

I glanced down again at the signature in the lower right-hand corner. My hand reached out and grazed the pieces of gold lined with aqua, only a small dot in the midst of the red.

One glimmer of hope in war.

"But maybe he's just trying to write a good chapter in a horrible story, filled with tragedy that no one calls tragic. And neither of us thought that we'd be characters in each other's chapters, but we are."

I turned to face them, captivated by the odd mixture of emotions in both their faces.

"And if I was reading the story, and she didn't trust him when she should have, I would hate her."

Brie didn't react, looking like she was suppressing sharing her opinion. Eva started to smile her lopsided grin.

"Still, trusting him is one thing. Buying a twenty thousand dollar piece of art? There were cheaper pieces in here."

"I didn't buy it for him. I bought it so that when I went back home, I could tell a little boy I knew exactly who bought his last piece of art."

"What? No, seriously?"

Just then, the woman came out to take my money, saying, "Well, this will be worth more in years to come. This is one of Kalahan's last pieces. It was supposed to be part of a series he never will finish. He's retired now. Lost his muse, I guess."

Brie didn't even try to hide her smile. After I paid, the woman snapped her fingers and a man brought out three champagnes on a tray. We each took a glass, and to my surprise, Brie raised it, pausing to toast.

"To lost muses. May we forever find you."

It was the next morning before I felt sure about the words I had spoken to Brie. I was nervous in the café, only because Alex was late. I remembered what he had said about leaving the needed items in a box out in the alley, but I still felt as if I would be disappointed if I didn't see him.

The thought that followed wasn't comforting, but confusing. *"Why would you be disappointed if you didn't see him?"*

The voice in my head had the tone that Eva's voice did when she was fishing for an answer. For some reason, I could always silence it. But then the silence always lingered. I had a horrible feeling I was losing the fight with my mind the more I kept arguing. And with a pang of guilt, I pushed aside all feelings except the fear that had previously occupied me. I clung to fear; it felt better than coping with the more complicated issues that surrounded Alex.

It was at the moment I just pushed him out of my mind that he came in. This time was different. He looked directly at me. There was a warmth I had only seen rarely from him.

"I got your present. It was subtle, and by subtle, I mean screaming. Is that your way of asking me to a certain event?"

He was talking plainly, loudly even, so I realized the game and played along.

"Maybe. I mean, it depends," I was keeping it light, seductive even. "Did it work?"

"A Kalahan? Yes, that got my attention," he continued smoothly, with a wink that I was sure was for the few people in the room staring. I rolled my eyes as he took the chair across from me, leaning in to talk to me, our conversation was drowned out by the chatter: their guesses in whispers to each other that was now masking what we were discussing.

"The uniforms are in the box outside of the bakery next to us," he said quietly. "The badges are in there, too."

"Alright, what about…"

"Here."

He slid something under the table, and even as I grabbed it, I felt the weight and thickness of the envelope with surprise.

"It's fifty thousand. It should be enough to get you through the ball and any other issues in the next few days. But don't go buying me any more art I don't need."

"Thanks. We are going to wait a few days. Until closer to the ball," I said, hesitating.

It felt awkward to take his money this time. He misunderstood my anxious movements as hesitance that I didn't want him to feel.

"If you don't want to go, Aislyn…"

I reached across the table, sliding my hand back into his.

"I'll be at the hotel. The one on the corner of 11th."

He nodded, "Good choice. Be careful. You got this."

I nodded, winked, and he pulled his hand away. He must have sensed I was nervous. I saw sympathy in his eyes, even as he looked back, challenging me to live long enough to see him again.

"I'll see you then."

I gazed back, smirking as he was forcing me to be at least a little confident, in a promise I answered back, "I'll see you then."

A few days later, I was staring at the lanyard around my neck. It almost felt like it was choking me.

"Are you in position?"

For the third time, I whispered, "Yes."

We had entered the building, but we were about to scan into the secured area. We needed to appear incredibly competent when we had no idea what we were doing or where we were going.

We had a crude layout of the lab. With Eva outside to coordinate, I thought I would feel more assured. I ran through the blueprints in my head again. It didn't help calm me. Remembering the blueprints now was easy. I knew that remembering them when the lab was under attack would be much harder.

"Brie, how are you doing?" I whispered.

"I think...I might just be sick. I'm in the bathroom."

Eva sighed. "We don't want to know, do we?"

Brie's hollow voice answered, "No."

"Aislyn, you've got some people coming your way..."

I spoke to the nearest worker among many in the hall, since he was the only one making eye contact with me.

"Hi there," I said. He took a small double-take, smirked as he raised his eyebrows, and then turned a little as he walked past.

"So, Brie just threw up, Aislyn is flirting with evil scientists..."

There was a part of me that regretted having Eva in my ear, but no matter how we tried her hair and make-up, she looked way too young to be in the lab, even as an assistant. We decided to make her look younger, not older, to avoid suspicion. She was set up in a café in a corner with a CU, looking like she was working on homework. She was able to figure out the tech enough to work with the ear pieces that Alex had placed in the bag for us. I wasn't happy that we didn't have a third person in the building, but then an answer to my half-desperate cry of a prayer came gliding through the café the previous morning.

"Cassidy, where are you?" Eva's sing-song voice rang through my earpiece.

"I'm on the third floor, where I'm supposed to be. I'm currently at a station pretending to type…something."

"Tell me you're hacking in," Eva said, with some urgency.

"Cassidy," I said between my teeth in a warning tone.

"It's just a baby hack, Aislyn, don't freak out. Besides, all I've found so far is food orders from N dash…copia?"

"Yeah, that's their food supplier, for anything grown in the Republic. It's the company that owns the farming machines."

"Drug orders, birth records…the usual. No sign of Tessa. Are we sure this is the room she'll hit?" Cassidy asked warily.

I was holding my breath without meaning to. I forced breath in my lungs, scolding myself again.

It was Brie who said, "Yes, just stay up there. And for the love of God, don't come down here. Tessa was right. I'm this close to tearing down the whole building with my bare hands."

I had chosen the positions we would be in, but it was Brie that volunteered to take the basement. I had no clue what she had seen that would rattle her so much. She had seen much worse. And as usual, anything that upset her made me sick with dread.

"Do we still know that Tessa is coming?" Cassidy asked.

It was Eva that answered. "Well, I just got off the intel grid, and last night a lab tech reported a break-in. They reported several pieces of jewelry stolen. Not a uniform, but...."

"They probably didn't check for it," I said. I was finally alone in a long sterile white hallway. I saw the camera at the end.

"I see you, Aislyn," Eva said. "The whole second floor is on a loop, so no worries. You might just want to keep pacing."

Each room had large windows. I saw doctors monitoring the tubes that held the fetus that was developing in each one. It wasn't until I walked by the third room that I heard a cry.

A perfect strong cry that struck me in a way I couldn't explain.

There was a baby on a table, but it was off to the side and neither of the doctors was facing the newborn.

The nonverbal cues from the doctors gave me the horrible feeling that something was wrong. Whether it was because of the raw instinct to want to cradle the soul that had just discovered their first breath or because I worried as I saw one of the doctor's check their watch, I swiped my badge. I entered the room. Eva was cursing, protesting in my earpiece.

I didn't hear her.

The doctor turned, looking more aggravated than shocked, which was what I was hoping for.

"It's about time! We called twice," he said, rolling his eyes. "Well, it was almost perfect. Brilliant, too, from the results of the mind test. But it has heterochromia. It's usually an indication of other issues, lately. Tag is on the bracelet. Take it down."

I was waiting for a second, almost afraid I would blow my cover if I asked the obvious question. So instead, I faked an ignorance that might be acceptable.

"I think that's why they sent me up, they were confused about where exactly it was going. Well, not confused, but–" the last word was used in a horrible attempt to try to mask what my confusion was, but also my disgust. "The usual assistant had a break in–"

"Oh, yes. I heard about her apartment. That's unsettling. Let me just give you the order," he said, signing what looked like a small screen on a card. "No, no need for Basement 1 on this one. Send it to B2. They'll harvest what they can out of it. No need to sedate, either. It'll be better for the trials if it's awake."

I struggled to keep what was wrenching in my stomach from bubbling up as I took steps toward the baby. I took the card, forcing a smile. They turned from me, barely giving me or the life I now placed in my hands a second thought. I realized if they were paying attention more, I would probably have to hold the baby differently, but as they weren't, I cradled and soothed him, rubbing his back as I took him from the room and re-entered the hallway.

It was like I was being shot; my body and mind unraveling in the revolting thoughts screaming out protests and grief. I heard Eva's voice in the earpiece despite a ringing in my ears, echoing of silent cries of every lost soul in this place.

"Aislyn, are you okay?" Eva asked urgently.

"I think I figured out why Brie was throwing up in B2," I whispered, trying to force myself to breathe. The sterile white walls seemed to be sucking the oxygen right out of the air. The baby softly sighed, every one of his contented breaths pressing a weight against my chest. "I think I figured out why we were meant to take out this lab."

She didn't reply for a few seconds. "Aislyn, I know…this is horrible. But we're in the middle of a mission. You have to do what a person in the uniform you are wearing would do right now, or it compromises that mission. You have to know what I'm going to say…and I don't even want to say it," Eva said.

I knew. I swallowed the knowledge down along with vomit. The baby in my arms wasn't the mission. He wasn't the reason I was here.

But if I didn't claim him, if no one claimed him, every beautiful piece of him would leave this world uncherished, discarded and forgotten. Brie answered my silence.

"Aislyn, you risk exposure carrying him around more. If Tessa doesn't come in five minutes, you have to let him go. You have to—"

"It's too late," I said, surrendering more of myself than I thought I could risk. "I can't let him die. Not to fight the greater war or see the bigger picture. Not to finish our plan. Not even to save my life."

I looked at the baby, stirring in my arms.

"I can't let him go."

CHAPTER 21

I stepped into the elevator, and pushed the button labeled "Main Floor." I didn't have a plan. I was honestly hoping just to buy time. I wondered how much longer we had before Tessa arrived.

"Tessa doesn't happen to be walking in the door, is she?" Brie asked. I realized she must have been thinking the same thing, and I could hear the frustration in her voice.

"Actually..." Eva started.

"You're kidding?" I asked.

"Nope," Cassidy said. "She just walked in. And for the first time, I'm thrilled to see her."

"Brie, are there any down there?"

"Yes, I'm supposed to be delivering the three I have to the operations room and..." Brie trailed off, shuddering a bit. "They're operating on one. It's too late. She stopped crying a minute ago..."

"Hang on, Brie," I said. "Cassidy, what's she doing?" My thoughts drifted to all the children in the tubes upstairs.

"She's moving across the floor to the servers, and she's pulling out the console..."

"If she sets off an EMP like Lynn did, all of those babies in the tubes will die," I said in an urgent whisper. "I don't know why I didn't think of that before."

"Well she must have thought of it. She's at a server that is only backup info," Cassidy said. "She has... a small cylinder."

"Smoke bomb," Brie said. "Everyone will evacuate. The babies in the tubes will be fine. The doctors will be fine–"

"Can we let Tessa set fire to B2?" I said, shaking with fury. Except I remembered there was a baby in my hands, so I forced my arms to release the tension building in them.

"Keep it together," Eva warned. "I know it's gotta be–"

Cassidy interrupted, "She just signaled me. She put up one finger on her hip, but she's waiting by the door–"

"Signal back a small circular motion, if you can manage it," Brie said, "That means it's a go now. I think they're coming, or someone else is–"

Brie cut off. I was slightly confused, and then I realized it must be someone else dropping off. There was a cry, but it didn't seem to be getting further away.

"I've got four now. They're going to die if we don't hurry. Where is the–"

There was a sound. It was similar to the one I had heard hitting the shuttle, but was muted, like something had sucked the energy out of it.

I had reached B2.

"Cassidy?" I asked, even as I was beginning to hear the alarm. I had just gotten off the elevator when the doors locked into a barely open position. I squeezed through just in time to see someone running up the stairs.

"Leave it, just get out!" he yelled as he ran up the first stairs.

I got my first glance at B2. The room was like a warehouse in that there were no walls, but there were individual stations covered like a tent with an opaque wall.

"Brie, where are you?"

But before I knew it, she was walking quickly up the center. She had three babies on the cart, but then she nodded behind her.

"One's in my pack with the oxygen. Where are we going?" she said as I picked up a baby. She quickly put one in her arms. They weren't crying, like mine was.

She rolled her eyes. "You really have to get over this. It's safe."

She put a cloth over my boy's mouth. He was instantly asleep.

"Elevator is a no-go. That means everyone's using the stairs, but police will be coming any moment—"

"The moment's here. First response just arrived on site." Eva spoke matter-of-factly, but there was a tinge of panic in her voice.

We were supposed to take the stairs, but the EMP would have caused an evacuation with no immediate police response.

"Make it to Level 1."

"Eva, we can't—"

"The police have all gone up to the fire," she interrupted. "They'll send more to canvas the building later, but you have a window to get out. Once you are on Level 1, there's a back way."

Eva was beginning to whisper, which means everyone in the café must have been watching the chaos erupt across the street.

It was another reminder that we were running out of time.

"Tubes?" I asked quickly.

"The tubes are fine, thankfully," Cassidy answered. "So far, no lives lost, but there are technicians reporting slight burns from the sparks from the initial explosion. They were near the server," Cassidy said, louder than I was expecting. I heard her say, "You wouldn't believe it, Rachel, it is absolute chaos. The fire came out of nowhere! You'd think it was an attack, but it wasn't! The server just blew! You saw that too, right?"

She was pretending to be on the phone while speaking the rumors that we needed her to spread.

"Cassidy," I said. "When you hear Eva give us our way out, make your way to the exit. Eva, we're almost on level 1…"

Eva cursed.

"What?" Brie asked, trying to open the door with two babies.

"Run. Go left, there will be a hall to the dining room. Go through, go back, and then leave out the service entrance."

"Eva, why did you–"

"Sentries are here. I can't loop the video more than a few more minutes. I've gotta pull out and so do you."

"Footage?" I asked, slightly rocking the one baby as it stirred.

"Burned the logs and footage. Get out of there; it's Hydech."

A new urgency burned in my veins. We ran as fast as we could. Brie was as quiet and fast as a cat, climbing every other step with an insane amount of balance and control. She opened the door silently with her back. I was starting to show signs of weariness, but her every movement was intentional, and she was silent and graceful as she jumped out the back and into the alley.

I wasn't sure where Cassidy was going to meet us now. I knew we only had seconds before Eva pulled our video.

Palmer would have footage of two Protectors stealing babies from a lab. The rumors that the fire was an accident would never spread. Someone could recognize me as Alex's date.

I heard Cassidy say, "I'll meet you a few buildings down."

I sighed a bit of relief. We had our meeting spot. The only problem was that we had no cover. We were holding two babies each. There was no quick exit. There were cameras. They would have been taken out with the EMP. One look from Brie after the first block, and I could tell she was thinking the same thing.

"Hydech's not dumb. He'll have them checking out alleys in no time; we've got to move quickly, and we've got to get over the perimeter with no suspicion."

"We can't," I said. We probably only had one minute.

"Video's down," Eva said. "There's no more surveillance in the alley for another hundred yards in either direction. That's your window. A hundred yards and one minute."

Brie leaned her head back in desperation, even as I prayed for a way out. I looked at a plastic container marked "sense-tech" amongst the trash in the alley. It was a crate they would use for transporting tech for creating the babies. Brie noticed me staring at it and calculating.

"We can't...we can't put them in there," Brie said.

But there push at my heart as my head flashed through a story I heard as a little girl.

A story about babies being drowned, killed without sense or reason. Every baby boy. Except one.

One was drawn out of a river of hate and madness, so that he would have a chance to fight it.

"This is our basket, Brie. We're in the reeds. We'll have to hope there's enough air. There's no way out. Please."

She scoffed, but then looked calm and nodded. I already had the lid off and was placing them inside. There was just enough room for the four of them. I asked if I should check on the baby in her pack.

"We don't have time. They won't last long," she said.

"They won't need to," I said, sealing the lid on the box and moving up from the alley. Even as she was asking me what I was doing, moving toward the street, I was placing the plastic crate down, and sat on the lid.

Looking as if I was waiting. She followed suit, beginning to look at the movement at the lab as if it was a nuisance. There was a police officer who noticed us and began to approach. I answered the question he would ask quickly.

"We weren't in the building. We were outside waiting."

"We had a delivery to make. Test material," Brie said.

"Understood," he nodded as he looked at the crate and peered at its contents.

"We need to get them back in our lab to freeze if we really can't get in here," Brie said matter-of-factly.

"I understand. Um…was there someone in the building who could verify that you were supposed to make the delivery?"

Right on cue, Cassidy came up from behind.

"Sorry, I got stuck back there," Cassidy said, extinguishing the panic that had begun to rise in me. She looked at him more directly than I would have thought, "You're brave to come out and save us, you know. It's kind of a turn-on."

She looked at him in a way that would have made me blush, Brie rolled her eyes, even as she said, "We're working."

"Yeah, we're not working later though…" Cassidy said, maneuvering closer to him.

I noticed a shuttle pulling up, and it took me a second to realize that Eva was driving. The back of the shuttle popped open and we moved quickly to put the box in. Cassidy was still flirting with him as Brie grabbed her. Both Brie and Cassidy played their part very well. She gave him a wink, and the officer, both distracted and flattered, let four Protectors leave the site unscathed.

I breathed out. The thought of breathing in air made me sick.

"Open the box!"

Brie quickly said, "Cassidy, check my pack."

I leaped to the back. Cassidy turned to open Brie's pack. I pulled the lid off quickly. My boy jolted at the sound and movement, and began to cry. I regretted being so cruel, especially as his arms shook in fear. But that cry was the most reassuring sound I had ever heard. The rest remained still, almost eerily so, but when I checked them, they were all breathing peacefully, the one wincing at the sound of the other one crying.

"Brie, the newborn in the pack is fine, but I'm adjusting the oxygen tubes," Cassidy said. "Eva, why are you slowing down?"

"We gotta pick someone else up for our awesome party," she said loudly out her open window, stopping completely. Brie gave a shout out the window. I felt the rush as the door opened. I heard a few forced reactions of joy from Brie and Eva as Tessa entered.

"Nice cover," Tessa said, rolling her eyes as the door closed. "So, what's the plan?"

"Didn't Eva tell you? It's a party. We have five babies. I have our packs back there," Eva said.

"So then we'll all take one baby back!" Cassidy exclaimed.

I held my boy's hand, wishing it was that easy.

Eva shifted in her seat, and as Brie turned to stare at me, the mood shifted. I knew what she was silently asking me. She was asking for the status quo– that I stay with the soul I just risked my life for and with the people I just risked my life with.

But I returned the stare that was usually hers: stubborn, strong, and pained.

Tessa was the first to ask.

"Do we get to know what's going on?"

"No," I said, resolutely.

Brie looked at me, still intense but sad. "No, you don't."

"Eva?" Tessa said, almost warningly.

"Oh no! I wish I didn't know what she's planning. I wish it so much, I don't even want to tell anyone else."

It was my turn to ask the silent question. Brie nodded.

"Brie is going to be taking mine back," I said, swallowing the choke in my voice as his cry calmed. "I'm staying."

"What? Why?" Cassidy said, looking betrayed.

Tessa sighed. "I'm guessing that's what we can't know, genius."

But even as I turned back to the baby in the box, watching him grasp my finger as Eva said, "we have about ten minutes," and knowing it may be the last time I saw him, or them, again, my choice began to crush me. This was the reason Sam and Liam had sacrificed themselves, and this was the reason Collin told me to go.

"Are you sure?" Cassidy said, still leaning over the seat with me as we both looked at the tiny sleeping souls. But I didn't look at Cassidy. I stared at the lanyard she had just ripped off and placed in her bag.

That small piece of plastic was the one that Alex stole.

He had paid dearly for it.

He had held his breath while stealing it.

He had stolen it to give me a chance to save the souls in front of us. A shimmer shot off the glossy plastic, a light that pushed every fear out, as if it were the greatest gift of courage in the world.

I wasn't going to waste his courage.

"Yes, Cassidy. I'm sure."

Days later, I was sweating in a dress that was barely covering anything. I had determined that it had nothing to do with the dress. But it still struck me as ironic.

From the minute I handed baby Mason off to Brie, I had felt like I was chilled or sweating. Brie had asked why that name and I had told her it was my father's. I could tell that made her nervous. She didn't like the symbolism she saw forming in my mind. But I knew this could be my last mission, and it was the unofficial rule to name your last Unnecessary after your father or mother. I made her promise to send Michael a message about the mission details I had. Leaving baby Mason had been hard, but not being with Brie, Eva and Cassidy was much harder. Eva had hugged me as they had all started walking into the forest.

She had started to cry, which only made it worse.

"Tell Collin…I'm fighting for us. He'll know what it means."

"Yeah, Aislyn," Eva said, back to a slightly arrogant tone, "I may be fifteen, but even I know what that means. But he's a guy, so just in case, I'll explain that you're madly in love with him even though you're risking your life for someone else who has feelings for you, because you trust him, and he just helped us by risking his life. And all that it means is that you're insanely alive and full of courage and love. And he'll get it. That's the best part about you."

She was nonchalant right up until the last sentence, when she looked weak again, before saying, "The best part."

She hugged me again, and then turned to leave, not looking back. It made me feel cold even as the heat was making me sweat.

For the next two days, I cloaked myself under some leaves in the forest, sleeping under the stars. I needed to feel everything I felt, without covering it up: the desperation, the anger, the desolation. I needed to cry without judgment: without thinking it made me weak, because it didn't. I woke up stronger than I ever was before.

I checked into a hotel, cleaned up, and then laid in the room, running through media to soak in all new cultural trends and reading the "who's who" would be at Vinalia posts on my phone.

When I emerged, I had gone to several stores and hadn't seen anything that stood out. I was losing my confidence merely because I hated the fifth dress I had tried on. The store associate was very accommodating and patient, most likely because I had mentioned my budget.

At least I was playing the part: picky, snobbish and indecisive.

The associate sensed my dissatisfaction again. "Well, I think it looks excellent on you, but perhaps you are unsure?"

"A little," I said.

"Well, we just got another piece in. It's very different, very elegant, yet subtle, and not so streamlined. It's $35,000, but…"

"I have that, I told you."

I was able to shift my insecurity into disgust that he didn't remember my budget, even as I tried to remember what locker had my shoes in it so I could save money on them. I only had $35,000 left after the money I had to save for miscellaneous expenses.

"However, the designer insisted on approving who purchased it if they were going to wear it to the ball tonight. It's a signature Linden Croswell, you see, and he wants whoever is wearing it to represent the piece well."

They brought out the piece. It was a shade of pink that looked like a sunset on a cloud in summer. The dress had lace covering an underskirt that was alternating strips of satin and tulle, making it look like a lacy pink wave. Occasional gems rested in just the right places as the skirt flowed out beneath the waistline.

I could hear Neil's voice in my head say, "You'd be invisible."

No one would doubt who I was in that dress.

"It's perfect." For the first time, I meant it. It would also be much easier to carry my knife in my thigh holster under the dress.

The associate echoed my praises about the piece and its fit. I was still standing in front of five mirrors when another the associate said, "Linden just saw your picture, and approved you."

While I was sure that more than one person in the Republic was named Linden, I had to wonder if there was any chance that the person who had flirted with me at the first dance and cornered me in a café could be the same person who created the piece I was now wearing.

"When you sent Linden the picture, did he say anything else?" I asked, hoping there would be a case for my curiosity.

"That he did. I believe the line was, 'Tell her she'd look better with it off,' and that you'd know what he meant, and then he said to give it to you for $30,000 so you could get the matching shoes."

I pretended to smirk, laughing off the comment. I slipped out of the dress, paid the associates, including a hefty tip, and left.

Then the flurry to prepare began. I slipped into the shoes, out of the shoes, into the spa, out of the taxi, into my room, into the shoes, and finally, back into the dress.

This time, I was wearing my dress facing five screens. My phone, playing names and faces on repeat. My MCU, showing dance moves. One of the three hotel screens was a report that the lab fire had been a technical error. The other screen had an exclusive interview with Palmer on repeat. The last screen was throwback footage of Brie and I the night the undercover Sentry had attacked us and baby Hope was born.

They might as well have been mirrors. The images echoed and blurred together behind the reflection of myself I could barely make out, wondering if I could make it out of this night alive.

I felt myself getting feverish. The only part of me that felt cold was right under the holster of my knife, even though it was in a rubber case. It was that it could give me away. There was so much that could give me away.

My cover wasn't in place until Alex was here.

I was walking down the stairs into the lobby of the hotel when I saw him. There was the briefest moments when my eyes met his before he closed them, in thankfulness or disbelief that I was there. I saw his shoulders fall, his tension probably releasing to reveal a slight smile.

But as his eyes reopened, there was an awe and wonder.

I stared at him, descending the stairway. My fear fell away, step by step. I drove every anxiety into the ground on my way towards him until I was only inches away. His smile faded, only to have the hope that was there move into his eyes.

"I was afraid you wouldn't be here," he said, wrapping his fingers tightly around each of mine, slowly and intensely looking to my hand, and back into my eyes. "And that even if you were alright, you wouldn't…"

"Come with you? I wouldn't miss it for the world."

He looked at me, almost pained by my loyalty.

But my fear had transformed into a nervous excitement that made me smile.

The transformation was my carriage, sweeping me towards the ball to be surrounded by fake beauty that would last only until midnight.

That grandeur and my trust in him would need to overcome every fear, because if that fear caught up before midnight, I would lose more than a shoe.

CHAPTER 22

I rolled my eyes at the size of the shuttle, but then looked impressed, like I should have. He helped me get in. The driver was far away from us, so I was happy we could whisper.

"Alex, I heard there were cameras taking pictures of who came, on the carpet in front…"

"We're avoiding all of that. I know the back way in."

"So, kind of like a service entrance?"

"Your favorite!" He said it sarcastically and I had to smile. "I'm sorry you're going to miss the lobby, though. We'll have to backtrack to see it. It is stunning."

We were nearing the chateaux before I had the courage to whisper, "So, this is the Undersecretary's house, right?"

"If, by house, you mean mansion, then yes," he whispered close to my ear, so I could feel his breath. "His name is Yates. He's Palmer's right-hand man, along with his own staff, who make sure they all get what Palmer wants. Palmer plans the party, though. By the way, I need you to giggle once in a while if we're whispering."

I almost didn't understand what he meant, and then I began to laugh. He followed suit. His lips met my ear again.

"On Yates' staff, there's a girl in charge of taking care of some people in Palmer's family. Her name is Kaitlyn. She's the Vessel."

"She's an Elite?" I said, turning more to whisper in his ear.

"No, an Elite could never turn." He leaned back in to whisper, placing his hand on my leg. "She's a Citizen, but she just became a Citizen recently. She said she was desperate. I believed her."

"Why?"

"I know her, or I did," he said. Something in his posture shifted, and was uncomfortable. "That is to say…"

"Alex, you live here, in this world. You don't need to explain that you have had…" I trailed off, not truly wanting to process how many girls he had been with. "Were you and her a thing?"

"No. I was a 'thing' with her boss. It was a long time ago, but it was…it wasn't as meaningless as people like it to be. Kaitlyn didn't approve of me. Her boss and I broke it off over a year ago. I told Kaitlyn I wasn't sure if you'd come, after the lab…"

He trailed off, as if in thought, but also anticipation.

"How many? How many did you save?"

"Five," I said. I felt breathless at seeing his smile widen. I felt as if I was touching those five souls again. His eyes were closed, he met my forehead, leaning in to hug me.

"I'm sorry I didn't thank you," I said, sensing the tension it had made that I hadn't said these words. "I should have. I think…"

He leaned in and held my cheek as the shuttle slowed. There were cameras flashing outside. I turned to face him as he spoke.

"We're here. Remember: keep your feet low, hold on to me, and I'll keep an eye out for Yates. Just look amazing and look amazed by all you see. Oh, and I'm going to have to kiss you."

"What?" just before I couldn't speak anymore as his lips drew nearer and then crashed into mine. That feeling returned, making each second more dangerous, pulling every breath away. I realized what he was doing when a valet opened the shuttle door. Alex continued to kiss me, placing up his hand to ignore the valet.

We were playing our parts already. It had gotten us past every camera, and to the service entrance without any notice.

"Sir, this is not the appropriate entrance for guests…"

Alex shifted, moving his arm back to show the man his badge, pulling me in as he continued to kiss me.

"Sorry, Mr. Sanderson," the man said, with forced happiness. "Sir, if you want to avoid attention, you should most likely hurry."

He pulled away, and whispered, "Hear that? We should hurry."

Beauty was a word, an elusive concept.

The ball was beauty manifested in a way I could have never imagined. My dreams could have never done it any justice.

There were lights gleaming in the air, seemingly floating down to the floor. I wasn't sure how the illusion was created, but I found myself in childlike awe as it glistened against the crystals, reflecting from where they hung on invisible wires. I scorned myself for loving everything around me, from bunches of white roses adorned with diamonds to the ice sculptures to the floor, which looked like it was covered in blue ice. The chandelier in the center shone with blue and white crystals, and was at least fifty feet tall.

Some things took me by surprise and held my mind captive for minutes in a way that both fascinated and frightened me. Alex seemed to sense that, because he grazed my cheek with his finger once in a while, as if to bring me back down to reality.

He was pulled aside to have conversations several times over the course of the hour. I was relieved that people were content to talk to him exclusively, whether it was to bully him about when he'd buy his commission to be an Elite or encourage him in his continued quest to fight the Territory.

It became easier each time, almost like a game. I continued to smile and weave my way in and out of conversations. With each one, there was a silent triumph, making my smile more genuine.

Eventually, we had gathered in a group of Sentries, enduring their gossip. Alex held my arm, sometimes steadying it, as the conversation shifted to the lab attack.

"Palmer says there's just not enough evidence, and the truth is, it's just a server. It blew. It happens. And it was a weak attempt to attack us, if it was the Protectors."

"Well, I suppose it just shows how weak they are," someone commented, even as Alex smirked and the rest of them chuckled at the remark.

But a Sentry in the group looked serious suddenly, as if he saw something behind us, even as someone in the group said, "But in the end, you should never underestimate a Protector, right, Sir?"

Then a voice boomed behind me. I almost cringed.

"You can underestimate them, but not their resolve."

Alex squeezed my hand, almost until it hurt, but I couldn't feel the pain over the fear that coursed through me like fire.

Pain would have been preferable to the terror that overtook me. Alex smiled, as if prompting me to do the same.

I smiled. And then I turned to face Terrance Palmer.

"Sir!" Alex said, smoothly. "I must congratulate you, not only in dealing with the escalated problems, but on the party this year."

"Thank you, Alex, we do try harder on Jubilee years. I am glad that it was enough for you to make it out. We missed you last year. And you're here with…" he trailed off, looking at me.

"Elysian," I said, hoping he would not ask for a last name.

He looked at me, intrigued. Then he turned to Alex.

"Does you bringing someone to Vinalia mean—"

"Possibly," Alex said, arrogantly. "You must know you haven't been the only one to ask tonight if I'm going to be an Elite soon, but I do like my job. I don't know where I would be placed as an Elite. And yes, I'd rather chase down Protectors than go to parties and sit in meetings. To be honest, sir, I'd get bored."

"Well, that's what you have beautiful women and millions of dollars for, Alex. Besides, it's about time. You've been able to help so much. I just wish you'd reconsider the offer to have you share more about the story of the attack on you."

"Pride, sir. I still feel like such a…"

In a humorous way, each of the nine men put in a curse word when Alex hesitated. Alex laughed harder with each one.

Palmer smirked and shook his head. Finally, as they were on their third run, he asked, "Well, miss, what do you think? Should he share his intrepid tale of getting stabbed by a Protector?"

"Personally, sir, what makes the recent broadcasts so interesting is…mystery. If people solve it on their own, coming to the conclusion that you desire, that will make your position stronger. A Sentry surviving a wound from a mysterious Protector might be more powerful, more fearful, than an attack that's perfectly described to them. A person's worst fear is always more powerful than the truth. It will always paint the darker picture."

He eyed me curiously. I pressed a smile against my lips, threatening to quiver and give me away. He then smirked and winked at Alex.

"If you decide to purchase your commission, keep her. She knows what she's doing. To the night," Palmer said, raising the glass of champagne in his hand.

We all raised ours. Alex said jokingly, "To knowing what you're doing."

I only had a sip, thinking I needed to stay focused. Within a few seconds, there was a chance to mingle elsewhere.

After some more chatter, Alex led us away to dance one of the few movements I had told him I knew well. I was settling into a strange small sanctuary. We could finally speak honestly.

I wasn't expecting his first phrase to be an accusation.

"What were you thinking?"

"Um…I wasn't," I answered, feeling strained by trying to remember the steps.

"Listen, *you* can't comment on Protectors. You can't."

"Why not? You're afraid of a spontaneous confession?"

"Honestly...yes, a little."

"Sorry, I couldn't help myself," I said. I felt torn away from him each time he had to spin me.

"Well, as long as we're doling out apologies..." He hesitated, and then said, "I'm sorry. I feel awkward telling you this, but I still feel bad for...doing that to you, unexpectedly."

"Shooting me?"

"No," he said as he shook his head as his eyes lost focus. "I mean, I do feel...bad about that, so yes, sorry. But I'm sorry about the other thing more."

I was genuinely confused.

"What's worse than nearly killing me?"

"Kissing you."

He said it as if it were obvious, looking at me with deep repentance before answering my bewildered gaze.

"Aislyn, I...I think I might have made a horrible mistake. It happened the second time we ever met. I knew then that every part of me loved you."

I stared at him, wondering if I should interrupt his declaration. I was wondering why a part of me wanted to hear it.

"Alex, I should tell you..." I was going to tell him about Collin, about how I wasn't sure if I loved him, about the moments I felt ashamed for being confused. But it all stopped at seeing his eyes, dark and wounded against the backdrop of jewels and lights. I was more curious than determined that I told him of my confusion.

"Alex, what was your mistake?"

"I should have never let you know. I should have never admitted it to you."

The song ended, or was on its last chord. But he didn't flash a smile. He remained intense, his eyes stared, under a creased brow. I couldn't fake a smile either, so I just looked at him, as bewildered as I felt. He pulled back in after I spun out.

I felt like I was being pulled in...

"Okay, it's time," he said as he caught me.

"What?"

"My phone just buzzed five times. I'll look at the message on the way, but that's the signal. Just move towards that staircase."

He took quick strides, pulling me along. We flew by people, I saying "hello" as we rushed be. I was pretending to drink from a glass. This was different than the other party, if only because it was harder to not think about his words, especially when he looked at me like he was convincing everyone else that he was in love with me. Even as he led me up the final stair, he looked at his phone. He saw the message, and then looked at me. "749. It's down this hall. There's an adjacent room, 750, that connects through a door. Great escape route, or it's a–"

"Room full of police," I said, feeling my pulse quicken.

"If anything goes wrong, just go down the dumbwaiter. There's $4,000 under the dumpster outside of the kitchen. It's for you, just in case. Promise me you'll run, and you won't come back for any reason."

I stared at him, knowing I couldn't promise that.

"Alex, why don't you come in? Then if it's a trap—"

"She's just expecting you, and a quick exit," he said firmly.

"Look, I don't care that you both don't get along. We need to both be able to get out. Just give me a minute to meet her. You can see if there's movement out here to trap us. We'll both know by then. And then it'll be more…you know, realistic?"

He looked off the side of my dress, holding my arm, tracing my scar with his fingers.

"Okay," he said finally. "But if it's a trap, you leave me here."

I nodded, but didn't answer him. I moved down the hall. I quickly entered the room. I turned to close the door, my hands resting on the carved wood with embedded diamonds placed there.

I turned to see the room.

She stirred, and then stood.

She was, without a doubt, the most beautiful woman I had ever seen. She was so stunning I was almost mad at Alex for leaving that detail out. There were only a few women in the world whom I could ever use that word to describe. She had the deepest aqua eyes I'd ever seen. Her skin glowed, her face was perfectly shaped, and her figure moved with the grace of a dancer. She was at least thirty weeks, but someone could still mistake her rounded torso as some weight gain if she had hidden it under the right clothing.

"Kaitlyn?" I asked.

"Yes, that's me. You're a Protector," she looked down at me, and she continued, "in a pricey dress. I expected–"

I looked down at my dress as she mentioned it, and whether it was out of the need to impress her or to use the tools, I pulled up my dress, pulled the knife from my sheath, and then pulled the MCU from my purse and threw it on the bed.

"That," she said comically. "That's what I was expecting."

"I need you to lift up your shirt," I said, grabbing the MCU.

I noticed she looked at the door. Her one hand shook as she put down her phone even though all her other movements were fluid.

"I'm pregnant. I'm not entrapping you. I just want to get out of here as soon as possible. I'm more exposed than I wanted to be."

I was reading her expression carefully, even as I could now see her torso and her stretch marks forming.

She wasn't lying.

But her arm jolted again.

"So said the last pregnant woman who tried to kill me. Look, Kaitlyn, you seem nervous. That's all."

"If you knew what my position was, you would never doubt my fear. You'd probably be in awe that I could even do this."

She seemed honest, and her determined look pushed out any doubt that her apprehension wasn't genuine, which was both comforting and disconcerting.

"Okay." I said, somewhat resolved. "I'll start the ultrasound. Look, Alex is going to come in…"

"What?" she almost yelled, and something like a lie crept up like a shadow behind her eyes. She was about to be caught. Her panic made that clear. But it wasn't just the lie. It was the fear as she clutched her child, encased in her flesh.

"Kaitlyn? Alex is not going to try to stop you. I promise."

The door opened to interrupt me. I turned to see Alex closing the door. I hoped that maybe he held the answer to calming her.

"Alex, I–"

He didn't wait for me to finish. Quicker than I thought possible, his weapon was in his shaking hands, facing her.

"Aislyn, go! Now! She's here to kill you." His voice trembled.

"No, Alex, I'm not going to leave her here!" I almost shouted.

"It's a trap!" He shot back at me. "She can't be a Vessel. She can't be preg–"

She pulled up her shirt as if she was answering his statement. He stared in disbelief, his mouth gaped open. I stood between her and the weapon now aimed at her, trying to convince him to lower it more.

"Alex, please lower the weapon. Please...you ...you were the one who wanted me to save her."

Alex slowly lowered his weapon, his eyes still locked with the woman behind me. "Kaitlyn needed out. That's what you said."

As I said her name, I heard a shift behind me.

"You can't take her, Aislyn," he said determinedly.

"Alex, please," she begged.

I turned to her, clinging to her torso that was now exposed. Every sympathy exploded from me as I moved to protest.

"It was you all along?" Alex was talking to her again, ignoring me, which at this point was infuriating. "So, Kaitlyn was a—"

"Decoy. A way to contact you. I couldn't tell you…it was me."

Alex scoffed, pulling his hair as he squatted down, and then stood back up with disgust, but before he could speak, I did.

"What is going on?" My tone had changed dramatically, and I moved to Alex just so he could know how frustrated I was.

"You can't. You take her back to the Territory, this whole thing blows up in your face."

"Who is she?" I asked. "Is she not Kaitlyn?"

He turned toward her, and I turned around to face her.

"My name is Becca," she said, but it sounded like she stopped short. I didn't have a chance to ask even as Alex stepped forward to confront her.

"And you would risk your life, her life, and the lives of every soul in their nation to escape? What do you think? That your father would let any of them live if he found out?" he growled.

"Who's her father?" I asked, wondering how that could affect anything. But even as I did, I stared at her eyes. I realized I had seen her features before.

Those perfect eyes on a screen, either calm or furious.

But always calling for my death.

"What's your name?" I asked, my voice faltering at the end.

"Rebecca. Rebecca Palmer."

My breath caught in the back of my throat. I almost coughed.

"How does your father not know about this?" Alex said, frustrated, putting his weapon in the back of his shirt. He moved closer to her, in a familiar way. I'd remembered what he had said about Kaitlyn's boss, but pushed that away.

"He doesn't know, does he?" Alex said.

"No," Becca stated, as if insulted that she would be that ridiculous to let him know. "It's a Jubilee year, Alex. He's been in the studio or at the office all year. And you'd be crazy if you think he has time to care about me when there's politics at stake."

"You're calling me crazy? You dragged me into this, and now her, too. If you really are trying to save your baby and yourself, I'm sorry, but you have to find another way that doesn't include risking him retaliating on the Territory in devastating ways!"

My voice was still trying to interject into the conversation as my shock was fading, but I was processing what Alex was thinking; Palmer would accuse a Protector of kidnapping his daughter.

"My child is dead if I do nothing. I did this to make a statement. Let me make it. I'm not risking my life or my child's any more than I would if I were to do nothing. I'm just—"

"Risking hers! And I will die before I let you risk her life!"

She blinked, looking at him curiously.

Within an instant, he was shutting his eyes, breathing heavily as if to control his anger.

She looked around him to gaze at me. Not gaze; evaluate.

"Wow. Out of all the reasons I imagined that Alex would have allied himself with a Protector, I didn't see that one coming."

I felt the tension in the air grow thicker. I squirmed a little as she continued to stare. Alex finally continued.

"You can't do this. They will track you, and they will kill her."

I wrote the story in my mind. The cost of taking her could be devastating. But the cost faded in the light of the life at stake.

I would pay it.

"Alex?" I finally spoke. I was hoping my voice stayed just as steady as I said the next sentence.

"What?" He looked back at me, probably frustrated that I was interrupting him while he was trying to defend my life.

"I need to do this. I need to save the baby."

Her eyes closed, in relief, and then opened with a rush of gratitude I didn't think possible.

Alex's voice shook as he said, "Aislyn, this is dangerous—"

"I know. But it's not your choice who I protect. It's mine, and only mine. And I've made it."

"You can't take Becca, Aislyn. You risk more than your life. They could bomb the Territory. Stealing her is an act of war."

"I know that, too. But that's not going to happen. Because..."

My voice finally dropped out from under me, feeling guilty for giving Becca a false hope. I had to tell her.

Why couldn't I tell her?

Why did the words refuse to leave my mouth?

So I asked her instead.

"Do you want your child to live?" I glared at her. "If this is just revenge, I won't save you. No one can save you. But I can save…"

Becca moved her eyes down, caressing the bump, feeling the life move in her. I think she might have known what I was asking; that the moment she met the life growing in her, she would have to say goodbye.

She looked back up, and nodded.

"Then you have a choice, Becca. I've made mine. I will do everything I can to save your child, despite the increased risk. But you have to promise the same thing."

She stared at the floor, deep in thought. Her heart must have been shattering in pieces, as if strewn on that floor, every moment she would never have with the baby she was now clutching.

"You need to take the baby and not me, don't you?"

I nodded. Alex went from looking infuriated to confused to then stunned.

Becca choked out, "Would that work? Would it be less risky?" She was still looking at the floor, but I had a feeling she was talking to Alex, not me. "I mean, my father will never know."

Alex said, quietly, "Yeah. That shouldn't be a problem. We'd just have to keep it a secret. I mean, there's no way anyone would know. You understand that Becca? No one could know."

Becca still looked dazed. There was too much despair for her to run through, like a maze building around her. But somehow in that maze of her grief and worry, she had found a way out.

"We'll know. That changes something, right?" she choked out.

I stepped in front of her and said what I needed to say, no matter how cliché it sounded. Because it was the truth.

"No," I said, smiling. "That changes everything."

CHAPTER 23

A few minutes later, we were staring at a screen with every small feature of her unborn child on display.

"You see? That's her arm…"

As I moved the monitor, she followed every part I pointed out, knowing and feeling that what I was showing her was just under the skin she was touching.

"Is that her hand?"

I nodded, holding hers a little tighter as it started to shake.

We went through the entire checklist while Alex walked by the door again. I was trying to give her a moment of peace, which was only possible because he was standing guard. She was beaming despite the danger we faced. Alex kept looking over, both fascinated when he experienced a little of her excitement, but then tortured when he ripped his eyes away to continue to pace in worry. He kept the bubble of joy intact, guarded by his anxiety and dread. Whenever he would hear a noise, his hand would reach for his weapon and his other hand for the door.

"And her feet…look fine," I finally said. "All ten toes, and all the bones seemed to be structured just fine." I was stalling, awkwardly, and I could hear it in my voice.

She echoed it softly.

"All ten fingers and toes. I suppose that was all you needed for a perfect baby, back before any of us could remember."

I nodded, not sure what to say in response.

"Do you have family?" she asked, absentmindedly.

I didn't answer, although I wanted to. I was almost about to risk it when she said, "No, don't answer that. What was I thinking? Don't tell me anything personal, just in case I get caught."

I could sense Alex's stare getting a little more intense as we heard yet another person walk past the door. He once again braced for an impact that didn't come. He let the silence hang for a second, but then whispered urgently, "We need to go!"

I turned to her, but she was already shaking her head and pulling her shirt down.

"You've done enough. I'll get out of here," she said decidedly.

I didn't want to be too insensitive, but I realized she was probably used to having her orders or wishes carried out quickly, so I packed up. But as I was placing the last thing in my purse, I was reminded of the one thing that Collin had said as I packed my backpack back in the med room: *"Remember: they can be suspicious if you give them something for nothing. They never think it's for free."*

I could ask her for something. And she was in the unique position to know the most coveted piece of intel.

"What is happening on Jubilee Day?"

She stared at me, as if she had half expected me to ask. She answered sympathetically, "I don't know, officially."

"You have a guess, though…and your guess is probably better than ours."

Becca sighed. "It has something to do with you. With the Protectors, specifically. But it's changed three times so far."

"What do you mean?" Alex asked, confused.

"A few months ago, they were talking about the border. They were discussing land mines and other things. Then they were talking about the shelter, but then they bombed it..." She paused.

I nodded and quickly said, "Everyone is fine, Becca."

"I'm glad. I heard they hit a few shuttles, too. But the last I heard, they were discussing the border to the south, and someone said, 'Just in case'...and then the conversation ended. It was strange. We control everything to the south. You've haven't wandered down there? Our food supply might be a target–"

"No, and we wouldn't starve everyone to make a point," I said, feeling a little guilty at the thought that Zander might think it was a good idea. I realized I was getting lost in my thoughts when I noticed her looking at me.

"Anything else you want to know?"

I pondered, biting my lip, almost not wanting to know for sure.

"The Basement? Is it real?"

She nodded, "It's real. It holds everything you would ever want to know about us. It's currently the base on 11th Street. The Basement moves every three months. It'll be on 11th for two more weeks."

I nodded, then she asked, "So, anything I need to know?"

I rattled off the list of things she should avoid, things she should limit, and things that were safe. I had to explain to her that she shouldn't drink any alcohol. I told her to take certain supplements. I was remembering what my mother had done rather than what we were taught in classes. Usually, the nurses at the Territory handled all of these details when we got the Vessel back. Alex was all but shaking when she finally got her bag.

She turned to Alex and hugged him.

"Thank you. I know it's still a risk for you, too," she said. Then she whispered something else I didn't hear.

"Just in case, okay? Say it. And then deny everything."

He nodded and said, "Message me when you're home, okay? Use the word 'gift' when we're talking about the baby."

She then turned to me, looking oddly reverent. Almost fascinated. She opened her mouth, as if to say something. But she didn't. She turned to leave, headed out the door to the adjacent room next to us.

Alex breathed out loudly, then he slid against the wall, his hand reaching upward on the desk to slow his descent to the ground. I had reached him before he hit the ground, only to fall with him, clutching to his jacket.

"I just need a minute," he said.

"I know," I said. My hand grabbed his shoulder. He was sweating. He looked embarrassed as I reached out to touch his forehead.

"Trust me, Alex, I was faking bravery, too. You have nothing to be ashamed of."

"Well, at least it's over for now. We just have to–"

He was cut off by a knock at the door. I could feel his pulse begin to race under my fingertips.

"What do we do?"

Instead of answering me, he placed his finger over my lips.

"I'll handle it," he whispered in a panicked tone as he stood up. I had a moment where I almost wanted to refuse, but then I heard a voice from the other side of the door right before Alex opened it.

"Alex, it's not polite, you know…to not share."

"Linden?" Alex asked, almost surprised. I cursed in my head.

"Hey, I wanted to see how the dress looked on her. Heard she's been up here for a while."

Alex opened the door just a few inches, but Linden still couldn't see me.

"Then you should know the dress hasn't been on much," Alex said with a teasing tone to his voice.

There was an exasperated sigh, but even as Linden started making remarks that I wish I hadn't heard, I bit my tongue. I hated the words I was about to say and how I would have to say them, feeling a blush hit my cheeks as I unzipped the back of my dress and stood up, holding it in place across my front.

"Alex, be nice," I forced out in a playful tone.

Alex turned around, still leaning on the door, looking at me in sheer panic as I motioned for him to open the door and moved towards it. He mouthed "no" three times before I reached it, and then forced a look of curiosity on his face.

"After all, I could use a little help." I looked at Linden, glad whatever I was doing to capture his attention was working.

"If you want to see the dress on me, Linden," I turned, "then zip me up."

He looked intrigued, smiling as he took a few steps to me.

I caught Alex's gaze for a second; he looked calm, but there was a fear underlying it, and then he was glaring past me at Linden.

I hoped Linden was misinterpreting the shudder that escaped me as he grazed my lower back for something other than the disgust I felt. I was glad he couldn't see my face, but Alex could. His eyes were tortured, thinking of the risk I was taking. Linden took a long time just grasping the zipper, he leaned forward as I stared at Alex, and began to pull the zipper closed as he stared at me. He did it slowly, even as he leaned in more as he got to the top. I thought for one horrible moment that I was going to have to kiss him, which I was sure I couldn't do, when he gazed at Alex.

"He's jealous, you know," Linden whispered in my ear. "Look. Look at him. Wanting something he doesn't deserve, something he knows he isn't good enough to have. His eyes are burning, Elysian, because he knows this is going to happen one day. That you'll belong to someone else, and he'll be alone."

I turned then, as he finished the zipper.

I found my words quickly. I didn't have to think of a lie.

"But today, I'm his."

Linden smirked, shook off a bit of disappointment in his overacting, and as I mirrored his smile, trying to remain seductive, he said, "And the dress is so perfect."

"I'll be sure to keep it on for the rest of the night. I promise."

With his laugh and sigh, I closed the door, quickly turning to lean against it. I was staring at Alex, who was cautiously trying to gauge my reaction. I smiled, thinking that would convince him I was okay. But I couldn't read his response.

He whispered, "Good job. I was a little unsure for a second."

He was getting his coat back on, when I noticed his collar was popped. I reached up instinctively, but he backed away quickly.

"No, Aislyn, just…" He covered his mouth slightly. "I got it. We aren't out there, pretending. You don't have to touch me."

Something had changed. I wondered if Linden's words had affected him.

I realized they only would if Alex thought they were true. I now felt guilty for prompting Linden to speak any words at all.

"I was trying to get us out of here with a good cover. That's all," I said. "I didn't know he'd say anything to you–"

"You were perfect, Aislyn. Don't worry about it. Let's go."

He had disheveled his hair and pulled out his shirt, which was almost too cliché.

He left the room first, with me following a few steps behind, pulling up beside him, holding onto his arm. As we passed, a few heads turned. It took getting down the stairs until I breathed. The further we distanced ourselves from that room, the safer I felt. I did feel horribly scared for Rebecca, though even as we moved down the final stair.

"Do you know how to dance to the next movement? It's not that hard, and a few more dances will make sure people notice that we didn't slip out too early."

I didn't want to dance.

I didn't want to play the game anymore.

My resolve had left me when we'd left the room.

The ordeal had left me exhausted with worry. For her. For him. I think he sensed it. I thought I'd be headed home by now.

He took my hand, not just to pull us forward, but to physically help my posture.

"I know you're tired. One more step. Then another."

I could feel my motions, almost sluggish. He found a corner, out of the way while still visible. My adrenaline drop had left me nearly paralyzed, and I was embarrassed. There was nothing that could keep me going.

"I'm okay, I just need a second to…"

I stopped talking. He didn't ask why. When he could tell no one was looking, he rubbed the lower part of my back. I found myself calming down, but almost too much.

I was losing my defensive edge and focus. I was imagining I was in the woods. I was in my house. I was in my Circle.

I was safe.

For some reason, that one thought being a lie made my blood surge again. I opened my eyes from the dream, awakening to find myself where I was when I fell into my trance, reminding myself I was in the middle of a lion's den dancing with a lion. And I found myself suddenly alert, aware of the fact that I had been leaning on him the whole time. His expression was glowing, as if infatuated with me. But underneath was worry.

"You okay?"

"Yes. Thank you. I just got lost in my thoughts for a moment, and remembered who I was. I could just be me, for a moment." I smiled. "So, this is how it feels to be protected?" I said sarcastically.

"Yes. This is how it feels," he said, more meaningful than my little joke. "You make everyone feel this way. It's why I think I lo–"

He stopped short. I couldn't avoid the intensity of his eyes, flooded with the emotions behind the word he didn't say. His gaze only broke when he looked down at the floor.

"Sorry. I can't believe I almost said that."

"Alex, I–"

"No, let me explain," he begged. "Between us being so mad at each other or in mortal danger, I never got to tell you..."

Whatever stupor I had been in, it had faded completely by now. His touch on my back was now electric, holding me like a magnet keeping me from falling off a cliff.

"Alex, I should probably tell you something first..." I was trying to get it out, but hesitated.

What was I going to tell him? That I had Collin? Did I have Collin? We were being torn apart, and he might still choose his position over me. But then, as I was about to continue, Alex surprised me by saying the one thing I didn't expect him to say.

"You can't love me, Aislyn. Ever."

"What?"

I almost missed a step, but my eyes didn't leave his.

"I made the mistake of telling you that I had feelings for you, but I never thought that would lead you to feel anything for me. Because you can't. You have seen me. The real me. And while you have seen some good, you've seen the bad. You know I am broken. I'm shattered, Aislyn. I'm in a million pieces. And some of them are good. But some of them are worthless. Some of them are revolting. Some of them are so black with sin, they'll doom me. You, Aislyn, are whole. You're not perfect, I'm sure, but I can tell: you're whole. You'd feel ruined by your regret if you loved me."

I looked at him, almost bewildered as he was speaking. I felt compelled to argue, except I didn't know what to say.

"Alex, I don't…" I stopped, staring at his eyes even as he held me in a sympathetic stare. "The dark, shattered pieces, Alex…they don't matter. If you love me, that's what matters. And if you won't let me say that I…"

He paused, then reached out and put his finger over my lips, almost afraid I might say it, as if it scared him more than anything we had ever experienced together. But I reached for his hand, pulling it down, feeling it pull down on my lip as I finished my sentence.

"I'm actually not sure of how I feel, Alex. But I wouldn't have you think that your love is being wasted on anyone ungrateful or arrogant, who would ignore it, use it to manipulate you, or thoughtlessly push it away. I couldn't do that. Instead, let me just say…that it matters to me. It matters that you love me."

He looked at me, examining me to see if I was telling the truth. And then he breathed, as if the air had been cleared of some poison.

"Well, in that case..."

He was talking. But as he continued, his voice became muted. In fact everything did. Because I saw her, standing by the side of the dance floor. She was beautiful, with long hair that cascaded down her back, the jet black that I remembered from...

I stopped. Mid-step.

Every other thought went fast, as if by the speed of light.

I remembered her. I recognized her.

"Aislyn?"

He looked at me in panic, as if he was remembering how vulnerable we were for the first time since we had started dancing. I realized with a pang of regret that I should've been listening.

I should've been listening to him.

I should've let Rebecca come with me.

I should've told Alex about Collin.

But I shouldn't have recognized her.

She was dead.

Alex must have felt my back tense. He misinterpreted it, quickly leaning in to whisper, "What's wrong?"

His voice was so steady despite the fear I knew he felt.

But I couldn't tell him what was wrong. I wasn't sure. It was just a glance.

"The girl. Your one o'clock. She's not watching us," I said, eager to calm his nerves, but knowing that if I was correct, he would feel just as much anxiety as I did. I had to ask…

"Who is she? Pink dress, silky black hair. You should see her as I spin." After I had continued to spin, I could tell he must have caught her in his peripheral vision.

"Valerie. Came to Elite about six years ago. She makes too much money to associate with me, which is saying something. She came from…I don't know where she's from, actually."

"I do," I said, my hand grasping on a little more tightly as I risked a glance at her one more time, but there was no denying the features I saw in her. "And her name isn't Valerie. It's Vanessa."

"How do you know her name?" he said, confusion infusing his words, the terror building behind them.

My words mirrored his tone, but were full of an inescapable disbelief.

"Because Vanessa is, and always was, the 5th Protector of the 182rd generation. And she's been dead for three years."

He stared at me, his curiosity transforming into terror.

Then he looked at me, realizing what had just happened.

"You're sure? You're absolutely sure?"

I nodded, seeing her figure in the corner of my eye.

"Will she recognize you?" his whispered voice shuddered.

"No, I was after her generation, and I didn't train at the Academy. I mean…" I cursed under my breath at sharing intel.

The truth was that she would have recognized any of the other Protectors of our generation, because they would have trained at the Academy at the same time. I was the only one who could recognize her without getting caught.

Just as I thought that I was meant to be there, and unlock the mystery of who rebelled, I was filled with the urgency to leave.

"Alex, I need to get home. Now."

He stared at me, and with a new intensity, nodded.

"Follow me."

Ten minutes later, I found myself driving a shuttle down 17th Street.

"Whose shuttle is this again?" I said, speaking on the phone.

"It was an Unnecessary's. The vehicle was impounded after we caught them. Because it's an Unnecessary's property, we usually destroy it or burn it. But I saved it, just in case."

"Good call," I said. "Where are you meeting me?"

There was a silence. It made my forehead burn. That was where he had kissed me before I had left him.

"Alex, you promised," I pleaded in the silence on the comm.

"I can't. I need to get back, play my part. I'm sorry I lied."

I panicked, not wanting to leave things with him where I had, but unsure of what else I could say. I almost turned around. But I was far enough away to see the scope of the intel I now carried. I felt emboldened by everything we had pulled off.

"Do you think anyone will miss me?" I asked.

"Well, I'm going to have to go back. I'll say you went home. Aislyn, about the Protector: you said she was from an earlier year?"

"Yes. Five Protectors fell that night. But I think there might have been one defector who betrayed us this year– in Spring– the night you shot me, the night that eight of us died."

"Wait, eight of you?"

"Yes, well…seven, if there was a defector."

"Aislyn?" He said it as if bracing me for something. "We only killed six. There were only six that night, not eight."

I swerved to miss something, even as I headed straight for the fence by the border. I realized with a pang of regret Palmer never said how many Protector's died.

"Aislyn, if you're near the fence, just plow through it."

I thought it would be hard, but the urgency and paranoia overwhelmed me. I found myself speeding up as I neared it.

I burst through, feeling the jolt of the shuttle on the fence.

"Alex?" I called, but the signal was fading fast.

"Aislyn, you're about to be out of range. Come back in a few weeks. I'll try to find answers. Have your people watch me, okay? I'll do everything I can."

"I will. And Alex?"

"Yeah?" he said, his concerned voice patient as I searched for words I couldn't find. But then I realized I had already said them.

"It matters. It all matters. You matter. Please…"

"I'll keep going if you do," he said, and then before I could say anything more, the signal broke. The buzz of the comm was deafening, because all that was left was the echo of his words.

And I scolded myself for thinking that no force could ever push us together.

I found myself having to use all of my strength to leave him.

A few more hours of thoughts and tears and words spoken out loud to myself, I arrived at the front gate of Central in the shuttle. Michael had messaged me several times, tracking me and assuring me there was nothing in the air. They had moved some extra shuttles out to provide cover. The last message was that Brie had just arrived with Eva, Tessa, and Cassidy. I got out of the shuttle, almost tripping on my dress. But my next step was intentional. I felt emboldened by everything I finally could say.

"You have all the fun," Cassidy said, even as Eva got done hugging me and staring at my dress as I reached for baby Mason.

"Yeah, that's what we're calling it. Fun," I said, urgent to get in front of Patterson. Even as I thought it, he appeared, motioning for me to come. George, Emily, and a few other trainers were coming out of the shuttles, viewing me in near shock.

"Leave the baby with George, they'll get him checked out," he said, even as George opened up his arms to take him.

I followed Patterson, not able to tell them what I wished I could through my intense gaze. But I did need to tell him one thing.

"Patterson, the shuttle. Alex said…"

Patterson nodded. "It's probably clean, but just to be safe, he said you should burn it?"

I nodded. I jolted a bit as Patterson yelled, "You heard her."

Only a few seconds later, the night lit up with the flames from the shuttle that had gotten me home. The flames overtook the darkness, like the truth they had brought me here to share. I turned, the brightness creating shadows on the floor of the hall, the intensity of the blaze fueling my resolve.

Because now, all the broken pieces fit into the story.

I had been chosen to write this chapter.

And I was going write Zander's epic ending.

CHAPTER 24

She was in the room when I entered. I had hoped for that. I glided in, taking a few bold steps before standing in the center of the room, my aching feet staying as graceful as they could in heels.

"Well, this is different," Zander sneered. "Coming home without anyone this time?"

"I came home with someone, just in case you didn't notice. Someone you ordered Tessa to kill."

"Yes, and I see that I'll have to be a little clearer when I say 'attack the lab' next time. Your point?"

"There's not going to be a next time," I said, my voice almost shaking, but I sounded surer of myself when I said, "Brie is holding my Unnecessary. And I have a Vessel."

"I don't see a Vessel."

"Exactly," I said, as accusingly as I could manage. "You wouldn't see her. Because you've convinced everyone that they are careless, heartless, and can never be changed. But I have the one thing that will tear all of that down: the truth. In the many nights you couldn't see, and in one brief hour of a ball, your entire case against them fell apart. It fell apart with artists, with coffee cups, and with one Vessel who is nothing short of the most dangerous miracle of all."

"And what, 27th, makes you Vessel so special?"

"She's an Elite," I said, getting some satisfaction from her shocked reaction.

She was still in disbelief, not capable of any disdain as she asked, "And what Elite would that be?"

"Rebecca Palmer," I said, making Patterson shoot up, looking at me with a mouth now slowly gaping open.

And after that, I laid out the facts of everything that had ever happened that she had never known: twenty minutes of the most rapt, amazing story I had ever told. And in that story, there were words that resounded. Alex. The dance. The shot. The elevator. The lab. The ball. Rebecca. Vanessa.

And then there was her silence. And in her silence, I declared the truth I had won by living through the story.

"You were wrong. They aren't all monsters. They are heartless, but some are feeling their hearts beat for the first time. They are waking up. I have returned, safe, because of a Sentry. I am hiding a Vessel who is Palmer's daughter. I saw a Protector posing as an Elite, proving a Protector betrayed them and it probably wasn't the Hand who betrayed us. Every lie you have spun, every story you have woven is unraveling, and you are clinging to no more than a thread of your power."

She breathed in, slowly taking in my words. But what she did next both surprised and terrified me.

She smiled.

"But the story that you have told me will never be uttered again, so it will never unravel me. The ball ended at midnight, darling, and all you've brought back is a glass slipper for proof."

Knowing my proof was scattered but sufficient, I said, "But the glass slipper is enough to prove everything."

"But you won't share it. You'll hide it, 27. You will not debrief the Council on these circumstances," she said, the arrogant tone having returned.

"You can't stop me. There is nothing, nothing you could ever do to me, to stop me from telling this story to the Council."

"Oh my dear," she said, in the fake kind tone that made me want to lunge at her in anger, "What would make you think I would do anything to you?"

Patterson froze, and I could tell he was holding his breath. His eyes met mine in dread, even as my mind began to spin.

"Let's see, we have Patterson, with a horrible first year as Head Trainer, sending people who are untrained out in the most horrible death toll of all time. There's a career-ender in that, if not treason for allowing you on a mission."

I looked at him in desperation; he shook his head as if I should ignore that, but what worried me most was that he braced himself.

"And if you tell the Council, I could suggest that Patterson will be able to keep Sam and his friends company for a while. And I could make sure it was a while. I could, ever so gently, suggest to a Protector that a certain Sentry is causing particular problems, and needs to be…taken out."

I stopped breathing then, scrambling to think a way to warn Alex. She took a breath, to continue. My breath shuddered.

Because there was only one person left to attack.

"And do you know it is within my power to report that Collin has gone to the secondary Central without permission? That Collin knew about Alex and didn't report him? Or maybe there could be a new law that would make him responsible for his lapse in training, becoming too entrenched in all the secrets you have kept, that would enable me to punish him to the harshest extent of the law? Of course, it wouldn't need to be that bad."

I backed away as she made steps towards me, my determination failing in the wake of her last words.

"In fact, there's only one law I will change: should a trainer fall in love with a Protector, he will be sentenced for endangering her safety. He will be banished from the Territory, or tried for treason."

She stared at me, her hazel eyes burning the light out of mine.

"Your move. I guess we'll see what the truth is worth after all."

Her tongue stayed in between her teeth as she glared at me. She was perfectly still for a few seconds, reminding me of an animal hunting their prey. She turned to leave the room, not even looking at Patterson as he sat, defeated, next to the door.

The second she left, I felt one knee give way, and then the other. To my surprise, Patterson lunged from where he was sitting and caught me before I hit the floor.

"I...I can't...not just because of Collin, but all of you. I can't—" I was near tears and it had only been seconds.

A second later, the door opened. I already knew who it was.

"No, Collin. It'll make it worse," I said, shaking. "Just go!"

His eyes hurt as I pushed him away. He looked at Patterson.

"Nothing, at this point, could make it worse," Patterson sighed. I hadn't turned to look at Collin, even as I gave up and could feel his arms wrap around me. Collin pulled me up, putting his arm under my legs and cradling my head against his chest.

"What did she say last?" Collin asked.

"You were listening?" Patterson said.

"Yes. But I left when I heard her start to threaten Patterson, Sam, and Alex…and…?"

He looked at me, his eyes torn by fear. I was wrapped in his arms, but further away than ever. She had made sure of that.

"Aislyn," Patterson started, "you need to convince the Council of your story before the general session begins tomorrow. Zander can't make any new law before then. You have to convince them."

"What if I can't?"

"Then you will never see Collin again."

An hour later, I was still huddled in a ball, watching Michael throw something against the wall. Again.

I wasn't paying attention. I pulled in my knees more. I didn't care how weak I looked; I didn't feel like proving my strength to anyone. I was wrecked.

It only made it more ironic that I was wearing more money than most of us had ever seen in a lifetime.

I felt as if they were rags.

I sat on the metal table in the med room, feeling a chill run through me. Collin reached out to hold my hand. I needed him near me almost as much as I needed to push him away.

His proximity to me was why he was now in danger.

"She just did it to intimidate you. I'm sure of it," Patterson said, pacing as he continued, "There's no way she'll stay in office if you convince the Council that Alex is defecting, Rebecca Palmer is a Vessel, and Vanessa is a traitor. But if you don't convince the Council, and she starts the general session…her threat can become a reality. Any of her threats."

Michael closed his eyes, bringing my attention to the blue circles underneath them.

With a desire to change the subject, I asked a question, knowing I cared more about its answer than my despair.

"Okay, quick recap. Michael, did you…"

"I tracked you the entire time. No other handler saw you. I erased any footage that Alex missed, but he deleted most of it."

"Thank you," I said, not even knowing if Michael could really process my gratitude amidst all the stress he was feeling. "Really. Thank you. I was wondering…did you watch the ball after I left?"

Some of his frustration actually mellowed away as he continued. "Alex is fine. He slept for a few hours and then hit one of his cafés by 9, like clockwork. And…you're welcome," he said, genuinely, but then something in his voice shifted. "So we survived the night, and found everything we had ever wanted to know, only to have it be worth nothing. If you don't tell the Council everything…"

I looked down at my feet as my knees pulled a little more under my chin. Michael had trailed off, maybe realizing how anxious he was making me feel. They must have all known. I was ignoring my breakfast, stacked by the side tray. Even though I was starving, I couldn't eat. I stared at the lace that was dirty along the edge of my dress. Collin moved his other hand on top of mine. I felt his watch scrape my arm…

Time. We only had twenty-four hours to think of what I was going to say and to ensure that she couldn't threaten us. I cursed my need for sleep. But my mixture of nervous energy and rage had made it impossible to calm down. My tired eyes would close, but my heart kept racing.

My regrets echoed, in time with my racing heart.

I should have let Tessa burn the lab down, because I couldn't burn the images out of my mind.

I should have never infuriated Zander, because she was always going to have her revenge.

I should have never left Rebecca, because she was now alone with terror and hope now weighing on her equally.

I should have never tried to tell Alex…

I stopped.

Because I could never regret what I told him. What I told Rebecca. What I did in the lab that day.

Regret was losing the battle this time.

The one thing that was breaking me from my haze was sheer curiosity. What emerged was the need to know what information was unlocked once I shared my intel.

"Okay, so what do we know about Vanessa?" I asked.

"Not much," Michael said as he turned in the chair, pulling up his MCU. I turned at the larger screen in Medical to see the few blurry pictures he had probably hacked in the few hours he had.

"Looks like her. And at a lot of pricey parties," Patterson said.

"So, she betrayed them? The night the five of them died?"

"Yep. Her death must have been staged. She must have given them the locations through the phone numbers that she had. That's how they were tracked down. And then, there's this…"

A report on the screen was highlighted, featuring the face of a Protector that had died two years ago.

"She identified her, we think. I looked at the last feed we have of her alive. I checked. Vanessa is across the street…"

He zoomed in, and Vanessa was on her phone, watching the Protector after she walked by.

"She could have leveraged that and had been recognizing Protectors for The Society for years. She couldn't know that this year…."

"There's a 27th that she would never have seen in passing at the Academy," I sighed. "The sooner we warn everyone the better. Especially Brie and Tessa. They might've been in the same classes."

"And Eva," Patterson said. "They are the most at risk. She would have seen them for years, she…"

Patterson stopped, rubbing his eyes. "She used to braid Eva's hair, back when it was longer. I remember now."

I felt the weight of the air in the room change, as if soaking in his grief. I found it hard to breathe. I had thought the worst moment was seeing Vanessa in the flesh, alive and smiling. But seeing those she rejected and betrayed, who had thought they knew her, was so much worse. I changed the subject again.

"Sir, I suppose the real question isn't how it happened three years ago, it's—"

"How it happened this year. We know," Patterson said.

"The timed messages. With the time...there's no way Vanessa would have known, right?" Collin asked.

"No, they are far too random, and the schedule is completely different than it was three years ago, you know that. And you are only given the schedule for the next month. It was someone from this generation who told them." Patterson was squeezing his joined hands behind his neck. "Alex said they only killed six?"

"Yes," Michael said, "But that's not all that I found. So I looked up the actual report on the EMP site..."

All three of them were silent and still.

"They didn't find Lynn, Patterson. I triple checked. They took a shot at a Sub-Terra instead. The media and other sources reported there were shots fired, but they did that just to ensure that the media didn't report that the Protector that set off the EMP escaped."

"But...what..." Patterson stopped mid-thought. "Lynn's the one who spilled the intel? Then why would she set off the EMP?"

"I can't believe that for a second," I said, trying to keep my voice down. I wanted to scream it out of disbelief, but there was no way I wanted Will to hear this, even if it was unfounded.

"We don't know it was Lynn. Besides, there are two missing. Eight were reported dead. One escaped, and one is a traitor."

"Speaking of traitors, what about Rebecca Palmer? Is she okay?" I asked, hoping to change the subject.

"She seems fine." Michael nodded towards Collin.

"She hasn't left her house since she arrived home. Nothing to report," Collin said, adding with more compassion, "I'm sure she has to be terrified."

"What…umm…" I stopped, silently running through the list of everything I was worried about. "The lab? What about the lab?"

"Executed perfectly," Patterson jumped in, with a smile I hadn't seen since I had returned. "And Zander can't argue that her order wasn't followed. Tessa did bomb it. You got some kids out. Because it was so close to Vinalia, it was labeled as 'an accident.' They didn't even report anyone dead or missing."

"Do they know it was us?" I said.

"I don't think so. You see Tessa, as much as you might not like her, is smart. She probably didn't tell you this, but she hacked into everyone's MCUs and started a gossip trail that the servers were overheating the day before. She used the ID she had stolen to file an official report. Everyone had heard rumors about the problem, so when it blew…"

"They all assumed it was just an accident! That's brilliant."

"She has her moments," Collin sighed. "But the issue is still that she might be ordered to do it again. Or worse. I didn't like what Zander implied about Alex. And we've checked; we have no way to warn him without putting him in further danger."

The awkward silence grew. It was the person who couldn't stand it the most that asked the uncomfortable question.

"So, what do you say to convince the Council to sack Zander so she doesn't have a chance to order them to imprison Patterson or me, kill Alex, or banish Collin?" Michael asked. "Or all three?"

Patterson sighed. "That's what we're going to figure out, but not now. Aislyn, you need to sleep for just a few hours."

I was about to argue, but I couldn't even think of words to put together that would convince him. Then I thought of being in front of the Council as sleep deprived as I was now. I'd be incapable of convincing anyone of anything.

"We're heading out. If anything happens that you should know about, we'll wake you up," Patterson said, in a tone that made me believe he understood how much this meant to me.

Michael left behind him, saying, "I'll see what I can find out about Lynn."

"Just keep it–" I started to warn him.

"I know; on the down-low. Because everything I've done so far has been so transparent," he said sarcastically as he turned to leave.

I know I needed a shower, I needed sleep, I needed the hours of oblivious thought that I missed in the woods on my return trip. All I felt was an anxiety that nothing had the power to take away.

Well, almost nothing.

"Here." He held out his hand, helping me down off the table. As I slid down, he didn't take a step back. He stood there, his eyes locked on mine as I stood only inches away.

"Shame we didn't get to dance," he said, all the things I didn't know he was thinking creating a fog of fear and regret around us.

I leaned into him. Even as he caught me, he began to sway slightly, until I could hear a song that might be playing in some memory, when this was easier.

It had never been easy, but now I knew what horrible sacrifice we were going to be asked to make.

And I dreaded his willingness to make it.

"I don't know what's going through your head right now. I can guess. You're thinking that you can't let her win. But they don't need my testimony. We can find another way," I said, reassuring, but unconvincingly.

"Aislyn, you are bound by law to tell the truth, no matter the circumstances of what happens to us. I'm not worth a lie. We both know that. But I have thought of another option."

"What?" I said, straining my mind.

"I know that if I fill out my self-evaluation form, my 42-A, and report that I'm going to continue to serve, she won't have my feelings to use as leverage. By filling that out, I publicly say that I'm staying here, that I wouldn't retire when your year of service is done. If I say I'm returning next year, she can't know I love you…"

"She'll still have other things she can threaten me with," I argued. But it was a powerless argument.

She would never have anything that mattered more than him.

He reached out, and pulled up my chin.

"I did make you a promise," he said, pulling away from me before pulling me in to meet his forehead with mine. "That we'd take every chance we had. But if you have to choose between me and the truth, I can't let you choose me. Everything in me forbids it. And I won't be the pawn that stops you from bringing her down."

He pulled me into him until my cheek was resting on his shoulder. After a few moments, he began humming a song, the notes ringing through my ears, both exhilarating and calming. He talked to me, asking me obscure questions that were somehow the ones that mattered most. How I felt when I heard about the Shield Vaccine lie, how I felt when I discovered they were harvesting the body parts of newly born infants, how I felt when I entered the ball, how I felt when Rebecca revealed her name. He only asked about Alex once, listening quietly with a controlled emotional reaction.

And even as I finally hit the bed in the med room once more, I felt a horrible sinking feeling as I fell into my pillow. It seemed like everyone I loved was pushing me away, making genuine love a sin. It felt like I was back in the Republic instead of home.

"Fight for us, Collin; no one else will." I begged him.

But he leaned on the doorway, shaking his head. "But you said it, the first time I ever told you. There can't be an us, can there?"

CHAPTER 25

I awoke a few hours later.

Collin wasn't there.

However, the three people who were standing in my doorway made me jolt awake and smile, even though I didn't think I could.

"You know, I'd agree with Cassidy that you get to have all the fun...except...." Eva took a deep breath even as I began to smile, "I'd probably rather do anything to get out of wearing that dress, and...I couldn't dance, and I'd scream if Linden Cromwell ever talked to me ...and yeah, that's about it. Never mind. Not fun."

Brie smiled slightly at me, but otherwise remained still.

Cassidy looked at me, smiling as she held...

"Is that Mason?" I asked, sliding off the bed.

"Yeah. The volunteers here are still a little overrun, so I was keeping him for a few hours. I thought you might like to see him."

I touched my forehead, feeling a few aches that I didn't even know I had. While I knew I was thinking more clearly, I could just tell my body would have rather kept sleeping.

"Where are the others?"

"The babies are a little scattered because the moms are staying with them in each of our five rooms in our Circles. We had some babies in your rooms, but those moms have already left to go to their houses in the community. Your Circle is the only quiet one."

Eva said, "Yeah, I have ten babies in my Circle right now. I love babies, but…"

"You're not even sleeping in there, are you?" I asked.

"Nope. We crashed here last night after you fell asleep. I was on your sofa in HistCulture. Cassidy and Brie crashed in Med. So, any horrible secrets you found out at Vinalia? Because none of your debrief was recorded for us to hack it. We double-checked."

I stared at them, trying to hide the fact that I couldn't tell them about Lynn. It would crush Eva and Cassidy if they knew she was alive, or worse, that she might be suspected of treason.

"A few," I said, deciding to at least tell them what was at stake. "Enough for Zander to threaten something…to someone."

"Yeah, we…figured."

"What do you mean you– Where's Collin?"

"He's out in the woods, Aislyn," Brie said. "We found him to ask if we could…you know, crash here. He…um…"

"Was a mess?" I asked, staring at the floor.

"Like when you were missing. As if you were missing."

I turned away and closed my eyes. I couldn't take the time to think about it now, with them there. I went behind my privacy screen to peel off my dress. I found the most comfortable clothes I could find. I held Mason, finding a moment of peace feeling him in my arms. Brie volunteered to take my dress down for someone to try to clean it and repair some snags. It would have to be handled with the care that hardly any one handled garments in the Territory if I was going to re-sell it.

I was walking with Mason out of my Circle with Eva alongside me when I noticed the black curtain in Lynn's Circle was gone. Even as I poked my head in, I began to hear a small voice I recognized. I saw Maggie with three MCUs in front of a huge blackboard pad, on which Will was writing furiously.

"Maggie?"

"But that makes less sense, because the heat from that would…" She turned around as if she had heard her name on a three-second delay.

"Aislyn!"

She ran up to me, giving me a hug. I reached out with my one free hand to hold her head, kissing the top of it.

"What are you doing?" I asked, looking at the boards briefly before quickly giving up trying to understand the numbers on them.

"Having fun! This is amazing, I never knew what I could do with all this… and look, do you see?" she distractedly said, looking back at the MCU, which had a blueprint on its screen.

"What's this?"

"If she's right," George started as he walked around from the other side of the board, "it's the successful blueprints for the kind of machines the Republic uses for farming."

"Actually, it's the blueprints for four different machines, most of which are very efficient on their own, as well as a frost barrier that you can spray on plants late in the season so they don't get ruined. It biodegrades within a day when heated to fifty degrees."

"What? Are you serious?" I said, looking at George for confirmation. He smiled uncharacteristically and shook his head.

"Yes. It's just placed on one side of the field by this, and is rolled out with a small aircraft. And once the sun hits, it all but evaporates. It'll be pricey to make, but it works great, and…"

She stopped talking instantly. She looked off into the distance. I was about to ask what was wrong when Will said George's name. George said, "Give her a second," in a way that told me that this happened a lot.

"I'm sorry," she said, as she met my eyes again. "Hi, Eva. Who's that?"

Eva gave a quick "Hi" as I said, "This is Mason."

"Oh." After an awkward silence, she finally spoke again. "He's a baby. I don't know what to say to him. There are a lot of babies around here. Did you like saving him?"

I laughed a single laugh. "Yes. Did you like creating tech that will potentially change all of our lives?"

"Yes!" She was so excited, but suddenly her face fell. "But I still can't figure out the problem."

"What problem?" I asked, but I saw Will's smile disappear as he leaned on the chalkboard.

"Lynn's problem. It doesn't work, Aislyn. The Republic's farm machine; it doesn't work. Lynn knew it. Will told me when we were in the shuttle that it was Lynn's problem that she wanted to solve. I told Megan I wanted to solve it. Megan is amazing. She got me all this stuff. She got Gabriel paint, too.

Everyone says his work is beautiful. Except me. I only think 43.5% of it is beautiful."

I laughed at the disconnect they shared, as brilliant as they both were. But then, even as she was smiling, it faded again, looking at the board where Will and George were still drawing formulas and things I could never understand. I leaned down to try to draw in her eyes to encourage her.

"You created something amazing. So what if we can't copy the Republic's machine?"

Eventually, she turned to face me, slowly, making everything around her seem to slow down.

She sounded eerie when she spoke.

"Aislyn, if it doesn't work, how does it work? It doesn't feel right. I think Lynn knew that. It feels like something's wrong."

I thought of souls murdered who had never breathed, traveling up to heaven. I thought of Rebecca and Alex, trapped like puppets on strings made to dance to a song they despise. I thought of the baby I held who was perfectly healthy, sentenced to a gruesome death because of one defect. These atrocities mocked the simplicity of her statement that something felt wrong.

Everything felt wrong.

"You'll find it. The answers. A friend of mine…he always tells me to keep going. It's good advice." I swallowed, hoping I had made a mistake in trusting Lynn, hoping we would be her rescuer, and there was no reason to be suspicious of her.

Brie entered a moment later, waving at Maggie with one hand. Her other hand held Caleigh. Brie placed her down just as George said, "Brie, you're late. And you're supposed to be on a run."

"George?" I said, almost accusingly.

He popped his head out from behind the board. "Oh, never mind. Hi, Caleigh. How are you today? It's good to see you."

He gave Brie a knowing look.

Shortly after that, Gabriel and Amanda came rushing in, at which Caleigh darted out, dragging Eva out to dance with her.

We followed them out into the courtyard. I was holding Mason again, but he had all of a sudden squirmed, fussy and beginning to cry.

"Hold him on his side," Brie said, "like this." She took him, and held him a little sideways, faced him front, and held his torso with her forearm and with his back leaned on her hip. She proceeded to rub his back. Almost instantly, he calmed down.

There was silence in the wake of the question I wanted to ask. I turned to her, gathering what courage I had to confront her again.

She was already saying, "If you're going to lecture me again, you can let it go. I'm going back out after your debrief tomorrow."

I bit my lip in disgust, even anger. "You once said you couldn't have anything. But she's there. She's here now."

She looked at me, frustrated with me– or even herself– that she had told me her secrets in a few rare moments of vulnerability.

"She deserves someone better." Brie said it resolutely, as if she had just recently come to that conclusion. "And besides…"

Her voice broke for a second. She hated what she was saying, but said it like a soldier would, forcefully, as if it pulsed through her. "You said it yourself. We need to make it right. There are far more souls out there that need to be saved."

Amanda joined in with Eva in whatever silly game they were playing. She laughed an almost infectious laugh that even made Brie smile. I looked out past them, wondering why Gabriel had just stopped and stared at the stones. I spoke through my own doubts to say the revelation I discovered bringing Gabriel home.

"They do need to be saved. But in more ways than one. It's not my job to save them once, Brie. It's my job to keep saving them. That's why I told Megan to get Maggie three MCU's and begged her to get Gabriel paint. And I think if you keep saving her, it might just be enough of a reason to live, after all. Don't you?"

She stared at Caleigh playing, giggling, her black hair catching rays of reflection of the sun. I knew she was in deep thought, so I expected silence. She surprised me as she spoke.

"I suppose saving her every day wouldn't be so bad."

I knew she probably hadn't changed her mind about going out the next day, but I could tell there was something under her icy stare that I had rarely seen.

Gabriel, who had started putting chalk on each stone, said something about dinner. The kids all ran up to Brie, who was holding a very alert baby Mason. They all made faces at him, even Gabriel. I headed toward Eva to ask her if she knew where Collin was. I breathed in one perfect moment of innocence, smelling summer and feeling like the sun could burn every despair away. Eva was holding Caleigh at almost eye level to me for the first time.

"This...is Aislyn. She's the 27th, and one of Brie's friends."

I must have confused Caleigh in that instant.

My smile fell suddenly.

The warm summer breeze felt frigid.

Because although I had seen Caleigh many times that day, there was one part of her I had never been close enough to see.

Her eyes.

Her blue-green eyes with a circle of brown around the edge, making them seem like the sea below a cliff, under the shadow of her black curls flowing in the breeze.

Then the facts flooded in, fighting with the truth of Brie's story, trying to decipher the lies in Alex's story.

The mother had been betrayed. Alex's sister had been betrayed.

The mother had died. Alex's sister was dead.

Caleigh was almost three years old. Alex's sister went missing almost three years.

The baby had died. Alex had–

No. The Republic said the baby had died.

And all of a sudden, the last piece of the unsolvable puzzle was solved. Alex had always told the truth.

But the only truth he had ever known was the lie.

The Republic told that lie to keep Alex in desperation and shame, fighting to gain status again, seduced by what relief they could offer in return.

"Aislyn, what's wrong?" Eva asked warily.

Caleigh's eyes glittered as I smiled finally, and she mirrored it.

Alex never lied to me. This would be the tipping point for him to trust us. Her eyes sparkles as I said, "Nothing's wrong."

Her eyes would be the proof that would finalize his rebellion.

She had no clue what power they held.

Before I knew it, before I could even say a word, they heard the word dinner and were running. Brie approached me. Maybe she noticed I had gone rigid.

"What is it?"

It was Eva who asked, but Eva asked while shaking. I spoke quietly. "Brie, I think I know why we can't find any record of Alex's sister and her baby dying."

"Why?"

"The baby didn't die."

It took her a moment to digest what I said before shaking her head.

"No," she said, not in denial as much as rage.

Eva shook her head, squeezing it. "Brie, it's almost a match on timing. I've only seen pictures of him, but if Aislyn—"

"We're not doing a test because Aislyn has a feeling. We're…"

She trailed off. She knew it wasn't just a feeling. I realized the truth lied in what Brie had never shared.

"What did the Vessel say? Before she died?" Eva prodded.

"She said that he wouldn't help her. That 'He's in a position where he could help, but he won't. I'm alone for the first time.'"

Brie looked up, almost defensive. "It never made sense to me. That she said, 'for the first time.' But it's because…"

She didn't finish. She didn't have to. We stood there, locked in a quiet debate in our minds, uncharacteristically silent.

"Knowing the answer isn't that complicated," Eva said finally. "I need a safe place to hack Caleigh's initial med report, which is attached to Brie's debrief. That's assuming you two actually want to know the truth, and aren't both totally afraid of it."

We both stared at the stone in front of us. I thought of Palmer's words. The truth felt like a burden now. But only because of the lies that were told before us.

"I'll get the files," Brie said stoically. "But Zander's got eyes all over Central. There is only one place for Eva to do the hack."

We were back in secondary Central, only it felt more crowded with Eva and Brie there. At least, this development had gotten Collin's attention. He was watching from the second level up, his legs dangling off the edge of the walkway near Brie's shoulders.

"Caleigh's DNA is on the file. It's just disorganized. Can we hire better techs at the Shelter?" Michael asked.

Patterson sighed, "Not unless you're volunteering. Move it to center screen, then to the display board."

Michael pulled down the image and overlaid it with the one that Patterson had pulled off of the database. Collin was not looking at me. His avoidance and red eyes didn't comfort me.

He had kissed me when I found him in the woods moments earlier. It had been intense, but pained, as if I was leaving on a mission. But I wasn't leaving. It scared me, especially when he wouldn't look in my eyes afterward.

"How'd you...you didn't hack the police database that fast, did you?" Michael asked, looking over at Eva's screen.

"No," Eva said, with slight satisfaction. "No need. He was a patient a month ago. That's how I got the record he had survived. Okay, I have it. We just need to compare. Brie?"

We were staring at the screen, but I had no clue what I was seeing. There were two separate lines with blobs on them. Patterson, Michael, and Eva turned to both Brie and Collin.

"I think it's a match. You're running a genetic simulation test just to make sure?" Brie asked. She looked expressionless, but her one hand was tightening into a fist.

"It's running," Michael started, but looked down. "But I can already tell it'll be at about 95% or higher for a match. There's obviously so many markers, not to mention..."

He put up a picture of Alex and Caleigh.

The shape of their face was very similar, as well as the bone structure. And then Michael placed one more picture up.

"I couldn't find a picture of her, before now. The Republic would have deleted everything. But when you said Alex and Rebecca Palmer knew each other, I went digging in her old phone. Found this. Brie?"

Brie's face was unmistakable. She closed her eyes.

"That's her. That's Emmy. Only...Emerson?"

"You guessed her name was Emily, which is what you reported. It seems she was using some pricey drugs, just like her brother," Michael explained. "That's the reason for her stats being off the charts, but her neurotransmitter levels suggest a spike in depression at least a week before she died. She died due to low blood pressure and a...okay, is broken heart a medical term, Brie?"

"Yes," I said, maybe too quickly. I knew how sentimental it sounded, but emotions shouldn't devalue what is actually happening. She was betrayed. That was a fact that killed her.

The screen lit up with the flashing words: initial possibility of inquired family match 95%.

"Well, that's it then, isn't it?" Collin said, almost sounding like he was choking. Patterson buried his head in his hands.

"What is it?" I asked.

Collin shook a little as he said, "Aislyn, we don't have long. We can't think of any way around Zander. We know Alex is telling the truth now. About everything. It was the only uncertainty..."

"I wanted you to think about this carefully. Unless the law changes, you can't change this decision," Patterson said firmly.

"Can we have some space?"

Patterson nodded to the stairs. I was thankful that none of them said anything sarcastic, but it almost made me feel doomed that they didn't look at us as they left. Even Eva stared at the ground the entire way up the staircase.

"Okay, now that the room is clear...what would you like to—"

Collin sighed, "Send me the 42-A. We're not going to get around this, Patterson, and you know it."

Something dropped out from under me. The room was silent, and I stared at him, confused and terrified I was going to scream before he turned to me.

"I love you, I do, but the truth is that even if I acknowledge it, and say I'll go with you, there will never be an end to this. They will destroy your reputation and mine the second they find out. I'll still talk to you. I'll still train you. I just can't be with you."

"You aren't serious?" I asked, probably sounding more desperate than I felt, if that was possible. Then I turned to Patterson.

"Is he right?" I asked.

Even as I felt betrayed and even abandoned, I was curious to know if Collin was right from Patterson's perspective, so I knew how mad I should be.

Patterson sighed. "Yes. I could foresee that happening. You lose an Unnecessary, you miss a target, you can't throw a knife as well…it will all undoubtedly be blamed on your relationship. Even if you win the day tomorrow and Zander retires, if Zander gets a chance to accuse Collin, this one doubt will linger. It will echo."

That was always Collin's fear: that if he was kind, caring, even loving, it would lead to my death.

And that fear made a silence that encased us.

Patterson shifted under its pressure. "I'm heading out. I will tell you that if Zander can't hold Collin over your head, you will most likely succeed in bringing her down tomorrow. And the only way for Collin to be safe…" Patterson swallowed, and then, with almost a hurried tone, said, "I'm sorry."

He hadn't gone up the first set of stairs before Collin spoke.

"He couldn't say it. What we both know, and always knew. The only way for us to be safe is to be apart."

I almost laughed despite all the painful thoughts attacking me. Collin was still, perhaps awaiting my fury. But I remembered the last time I was furious at him. I almost left on a mission without saying good-bye. I had left a moment before he was trying to say that he loved me. I didn't know what to say. I wasn't walking away this time.

He was.

"Aislyn?" He said my name and I felt my stomach tighten.

"Collin, don't…"

He trailed off as he lunged towards me, reaching for me, pulling me into him. I could feel his heartbeat racing, his body shaking. I was pleading, but he shook his head.

"Aislyn, I can't let you risk all of this for me. Not the truth. Not those you've rescued. Not for the sake of everyone you have yet to rescue. And not the chance to tell Alex his niece is alive. That's what we're risking. And Zander needs to know that her threat is empty before you get to the Council."

I wanted to protest, but it just came out in sobs. He held my head, his thumb wiping away tears, even as he looked not panicked, but calm and resolute. He was holding my shoulders, now shaking. He opened his mouth a few times just to close it, unsure of what to say or how to say something he knew would break me. He pulled me in, maybe not being able to look at me as he continued.

"Don't you see, Aislyn? I can't be with you, or you'll do something you would never do. You'd hide the truth. You'd let her win. You'd let people die. That's not who you are. I won't risk you loving you if it means…you wouldn't be you. I need you too much."

I nodded in pain, the tears were forming despite my resolution for them not to. He let me go too early, before I could think of something to say.

He ran up the stairs: running to everything that mattered more than me. I backed up several steps to finally run into a desk littered with dust covered papers. I slid down it, onto the floor. The regrets came, not in a list, but in a swarm. And even if I fought them off with hope or ideals I knew to be true, they defeated me with one horrible, paralyzing truth: He would never love me enough to be with me.

Minutes went by until I broke from my trance. Then I couldn't leave the room fast enough. I pushed to open the door. The strength left my arms. I slammed my body against it before it opened. I didn't want to see anyone, so I resolved not to return to my Circle. Tessa luckily avoided my gaze, not acknowledging me stumbling by, but ignoring me in the way that still silently infuriated me. Michael looked worried, but I couldn't look at him either. I needed to hide in Central, but the last thing I wanted was a lecture from Patterson. I cursed as I saw him at the top of the stairs with Eldridge. He was holding his MCU, staring at the screen that was probably displaying the form with the signature on it that I wished I could burn.

But it was going to save us all.

I tried to turn to go to the garden, but he must have seen me. I heard footsteps rushing behind me before hearing Patterson's voice.

"Aislyn? Aislyn, stop."

A part of me wanted to keep going, but I heard something in his voice that didn't make sense. I couldn't miss the chance to know what it was, so I turned around.

"I'm having my full debrief with the Council, okay? You can go back and tell Eldridge that I'll tell everyone everything. You can be happy. Because he said he doesn't..."

I couldn't finish. Because Eldridge looked at me as if I were wounded. The words caught in my mouth, and even though I knew they weren't entirely true, "Collin filled out his 42-A, I'm guessing. It'll hopefully clarify things for me, so I don't make any more stupid, emotional decisions ever again."

I felt past the point where my reactions could be diffused. I was mad at Eldridge for some reason; maybe envious that he had remained calm for the solution he patiently waited for. That solution had caused nothing but pain.

"Aislyn?" Patterson said, with a strange mixture of pity and strength. It infuriated me.

"What? You should be happy, right? You have your trainer back, he doesn't love me anymore, and –"

I wasn't even sure where I was going, but he cut me off.

"Aislyn, I'm sorry, but...you couldn't make me believe that he doesn't love you. Not in a lifetime. And it's horribly immature that someone is using it against you, but please....Don't tell yourself this is anything more than what it is.

Okay? Work with me, and push through some of the lies that your teenage girl freak-out is telling you. See this for what it is."

"And what is this?"

"Fear. This is the desperation it brings. It makes you lie. But lying to the world and lying to yourself are two different things. Don't lie to yourself."

I closed my eyes, taking a breath that felt hollow. I tried to take another one that was deeper. I glanced at his MCU.

"The law? About the 42-A. Can it never be changed?"

"Not without Hannah's permission. The chance of that…"

Patterson took a breath and then said, "Listen, maybe when this is all done, we can save it. But… for now…"

"You need to coach me through what to say tomorrow."

Eldridge had finally caught up. "Seems a waste to throw away all the sacrifice that Collin made– that you both made– and not do our best."

"Why is this so hard?" I asked, maybe out of habit.

"Oh, but you answered that question already," he said, with eyes that mirrored my pain in a way that made me wonder if he had ever felt like this once.

"Love is real. And anyone who dares for love to be real, and not just a fairy tale, will have their heart broken."

No more sympathy came after that.

None was needed.

Patterson and Eldridge coached me for the rest of the day. I memorized specific phrases and words for what happened. Michael came by hours later. He found footage of Vanessa at parties, Alex leaving coffee cups, and Rebecca hiding. Even as he talked about my conclusion, I was distracted by the dandelions in one of the flower beds, almost all of their fuzz having been blown off in the breeze.

All except one.

I was going to be giving the speech of a lifetime. I was going to depose Zander. But I would have traded all the wisdom Eldridge was giving me if I could claim the freedom to walk away, to run over to the dandelion, and let the last pieces go.

But I didn't. One seed remained stuck on the weed, forced to blow in the breeze without freedom, yearning for something it could never have.

I finally knew how much I loved Collin.

But only in the aftermath of his decision to push me away.

CHAPTER 26

Reading my name had never been more meaningful.

It was painted on the bottom of a canvas outside of my Circle, in a unique aqua shade that reminded me of the Alex's eyes.

I had almost cried seeing the paintings I had promised Gabriel he would finish; the red became a sunset of colors under the ocean. It felt like my biography, but not in any obvious way. It reminded me of the waves of emotion I felt all the time: their dissonance and disparity crashing together to make something beautiful.

That's how the debrief to the Council had felt.

It was finally over. The aftermath was now unsettling me.

Memories and thoughts from an hour ago came rushing back. I had been about to vomit when I first arrived. Then I saw Zander's face as she was informed of the 42-A by Patterson. I glared at her shocked face. It gave me the last jolt of confidence I needed to tell my story.

I was nervous, almost all the way through the debrief. I found myself having long awkward silences after mentioning that the babies were being harvested for parts. I found myself at a loss for words when someone asked how I could trust Rebecca Palmer, before answering the council person by saying, "you can't fake real fear." Then the revelation that Vanessa was alive threw the room into turmoil. I hardly spoke at all after that. I turned it over to Michael, happy to leave the room and the politics to him.

I had been out of the shower for a few minutes when I found myself staring at the plethora of canvases surrounding Lynn's Circle. It wasn't until I found the canvas that was named for me that Megan found me, staring at the art that captured my turmoil.

"Thank you. For Gabriel and Maggie," I told her, hoping she knew how much it meant.

"Well, it's been an exciting month around here."

"I've heard." If anything, I was feeling almost jealous of her. I wished I could have stayed behind and helped, fought for them, helped others see the beauty in what they could do.

"I wish I could stay," I said, knowing I couldn't.

"Maybe you should stay for a few weeks."

Megan's offer was tempting. Being with the children had given me a new energy, but I saw Michael approaching from a distance, like a looming smoke.

"I can't stay, Megan," I said, seeing the worry on his face.

"I figured. You gonna let me know what's going on next time?"

Michael walked up to stand beside us, only to stare at the picture. He didn't speak. He hardly moved. Finally, Megan spoke.

"I can't know what Michael is going to say, can I?"

"Not yet." Michael was short, and Megan rolled on her heel and left us alone. This is the first time I had any hint of what had happened after my debrief. I didn't even need to ask.

He shrugged. "Everyone was screaming at her when I left. A motion to release Sam and the others has already been passed. You did great, by the way."

"So…" I asked, prodding.

"There's no way she's going to stay in power if Patterson can help it. They called for her resignation. I had to leave the room."

"But that's not why you're here." I knew it. There was something nervous about his energy, not confident. "Michael?"

"It's a match," he said. "For sure. Test results just came in; we did a full panel. It was 100% match for maternal uncle."

"I have to tell Brie," I said, almost instantly and determinedly, wondering how I would even start that conversation.

"Oh, Brie knows. I'm sorry." He looked at me, scared. "She was around…and she asked. She looked at me kind of like you are now…with that stare thing she does. I have no spine when it comes to her."

"No spine?" Brie started, "is that what we're going with?"

I shook my head, enjoying a smile at Michael's expense even as I said, "Michael, thank you. Really. And for the debrief…"

I trailed off, not knowing if I should or could share what happened, even as Eva came up from behind her with a sly smile.

"So, 27th. That's a big deal. Almost as big as the 27th going to the Vinalia ball where she dances with a Sentry, meets Palmer's daughter, and finds a fallen Protector. By the way, next time," Eva said, switching from her very severe tone, "don't mention that we all hung out in cafés waiting for days. It doesn't help our budgets for the upcoming year. We all need more petty cash, not less."

I was about to ask how they possibly knew about the debrief. Then I noticed a comm in her hand with wires hanging out of it.

With that moment of clarity, I realized I didn't have to explain. All of them had heard– and possibly seen– the entire debrief.

In response to my groan, she said, "we lost visual a lot. You seemed pretty heroic though. What was that last line?"

I didn't even answer her question. "Wait, if you're out here, that means the meeting is…" I started, but stopped to ask, "Is she done?"

Eva nodded. "Immediately. There's a talk about restructuring, and objective 141, declaring that our main goal is to injure enemy soldiers, has been suspended until further notice. It's over."

I thought I should feel differently, victorious even. But then I thought that Collin wasn't even around to know about it. I didn't even know where he was. Megan was still caring for orphaned Unnecessaries, and almost everyone else was on extra shuttles to try to protect us from drone attacks.

In the moment of our victory, I felt as if we hadn't won.

"It feels like it was all a waste."

"Nothing is a waste." Eva said it with a tone that made anyone want to ask what was behind the skewed smile. And as emotionally spent as I was, nothing could hold back my curiosity.

"What did you find?" I whispered, as Brie looked at Michael.

"We found a way to confirm what Rebecca said about the base on 11th street. I had already heard rumors. It's confirmed."

"And…we might have a way in," Brie said.

"You mean…it's the Basement?" I said, adrenaline kicking back into my system.

Eva nodded, "This is only the third time in history we have known where the Basement is. And we have more than one reason to hurry."

"Zander, upon her resignation, admitted something to Patterson. Abigail was ordered to take out the base on 11th Street," Brie explained.

"What?" I was shocked at the coincidence.

"Patterson asked us to try to stop Abby. We're supposed to get cleared, and then…"

We could go back out. I saw the fear, the urgency in her eyes, but it turned to worry when we saw Collin bolt out of Central.

"Don't tell him!" Brie said with urgency. "Aislyn, you can't. He made us promise to never attack the Basement."

I realized she was right. All he knew was that Abigail was about to bomb a base. He didn't need to know what was there.

I needed to go, once again, and there wasn't time. He must have seen that I was torn.

He just misinterpreted it. He probably thought it was about his broken promise to me. Not the one I was about to break by going into the most secure facility in the Republic.

"Okay, you're all cleared. George is going to take you out…" he looked at me, "Megan got cleared as well. She's a little stir-crazy."

I nodded. I knew that meant telling her everything, which I owed her at this point, but it still made me queasy.

"Eva, get their packs. Abigail was sent out a week ago. Brie, get the MCUs. They're all still updating."

They split off, leaving only Michael staring at his MCU. It wasn't until he looked up that he cursed and dashed away in panic.

"Smooth," I said, almost being able to smile. But then it faded.

The few inches between us seemed insurmountable. I wished I could say that I loved him. I wish I had the courage to tell him. But I was too afraid that it didn't matter anymore. That fear crushed any chance I had to hold him again. Confusion was drowning out the nerve I was trying to build to tell him. But he interrupted those thoughts.

"Go, Aislyn. Just go. Tell Alex his niece is alive. Watch him smile, and then cry. Deliver Rebecca's baby. Watch her smile, and then cry. Save them. It's what you were always meant to do."

I shook my head. "But not without you."

His head dropped. "You were never supposed to choose me." His voice broke a little as he said, "This is more important than anything I could ever imagine, or be. Aislyn, even my own mother didn't choose me over this. She chose this."

His insecurity shook me. His fear was now clarified, I wanted to scream in protest.

"Collin, you can't say that. I know you're scared. You can't believe that just because—"

"Isn't it true?" he said, his eyes watering. "She did, Aislyn. She left, because this matters more than me. It's the truth."

Maybe it was, but it wasn't the only the truth. My desire to know made me brave enough to ask.

"Do you still love me?"

He sighed. His blue eyes containing a calm despite the hurt he was hiding. "Before I met you, I strived to save lives without knowing what it was like to be alive myself. But I will always push you away for the thing that matters more. That's what I was raised to do. So even if I did love you, I couldn't say I did."

He paused. He sighed, resigned to a fate I couldn't fight. "You shouldn't have to choose between them or us. You should always choose them. Choose them, Aislyn. Choose him."

He reached out his hand, like the first time we had met. I reached out, mine shaking until I held his. I wanted to cry, to pull him in, but the fear stopped me again.

But he would push me away.

My hand slipped from his as he backed up, eventually turning and heading back to our Circle.

Every one of his footsteps made it feel more real, beating the truth into me: he was always going to push me away now.

"So…Zander's gone?"

For some reason, Abigail was wary to believe us, even after she saw the order from Patterson and a signed form for her to cancel the order from Zander. I was beginning to wonder what it would take to convince her.

And then I thought of what it would take.

"Abigail, say we all wanted to stop you from attacking the base," I said, as if it was only a hypothetical.

"Which you shouldn't. They killed us, you know. They lied about the Serum. They would kill you now if they–"

"Abigail, think!" I said. "If we just wanted to stop you, we could. There's five of us, and one of you!"

She closed her mouth to ponder that. Brie gave her best glare. Eva and Cassidy smirked. Megan rose her eyebrows playfully.

Abby shifted slightly, and then said, "So, what was the plan? All five of you were supposed to scatter to find me?"

"Yes. We'd have no clue you'd be so close, or that one of us would find you so fast," Brie said, having been the one to find her.

"But then…You said it was the Basement, and Zander didn't even know. So, are we just going to do nothing?" Abby asked.

I sighed, and then said, "Not exactly."

At that, Megan and Cassidy turned to face me.

"We were ordered to stop you from bombing it. Not from breaking in," I said defensively.

"Aislyn?" Megan sounded confused, even betrayed.

"C'mon. Look at us. We actually know where the Basement is. We don't need to take it out, but we need the intel that's in it."

"Aislyn, I don't need to remind you who has already died–"

"Let's do it." Eva looked right at Brie, "And don't you dare lecture me on being too emotionally compromised."

"We're not going to lecture you, but you aren't deciding, Eva." Brie said, very evenly. "I'm calling it. Reports. Now."

I wasn't sure what Brie meant, until she said, "Cassidy, tech."

Cassidy was hazily looking at a tree, but clearly seeing something in her mind.

"The probability of success is higher with all of us together than on a solo mission. The chance of them catching us goes way down with multiple players. The chance of gaining viable intel also goes up 45%. Abby has grids and blueprints. We are prepped."

"Megan. Thoughts?" Brie glanced at me with an odd expression. Maybe Brie was suspicious she would take my side, just because we were related.

"I'm half and half. I see the value of it, and it's such a rare chance, but…it doesn't seem to fit with the objective we have. All we've wanted is just to rescue people. That's been taken away from us the last few months. I feel like I just want it back. I want saving them to be easy again."

"Saving them was never easy," Eva said. "Nothing about this is easy."

"Eva, you're not talking. Abigail?" Brie asked.

Abigail said, "I'm in. I'm a go. This is the only thing better than bombing it. I want them to pay."

Brie closed her eyes, and breathed. I was starting to wonder what was happening when she said, "Aislyn, we need our cover."

I wasn't expecting that, but within a few minutes, I was coming up with one, step by step as Brie closed her eyes.

"Option one: we do something to remotely access security, and then send in two people at the least guarded entrance point. We could probably use the lab uniforms to help with that, as our general appearance may be able to get us in a back door, or close enough to a guard to take them out without them shooting first. Those two people find a way to get us in. We hack the system for the information, and try to get out as quickly as possible, hopefully undetected. The other option is a three person team: everyone else as support, the back-up plan featuring Abby and you doing what you two do best if things go bad. We'll use information about voltage and infrared to try to target the intel."

Brie snapped her eyes open.

"Okay, I like the three person team idea better. We're putting Eva, Megan, and Aislyn in."

She turned to Eva. "Eva, if at any point you are not objective, I'm pulling you out of field-tech and put Cassidy in. I love you. Deal with it. Abby," she turned to Abigail, who looked like she was about to protest, "you are too gun-happy, girl. I'm putting you on the part of the mission where if it goes south, I'll want you to be as ruthless as you can be. If this goes badly, at all, I won't be holding you back. Megan, you'll go in with Eva and Aislyn. Are we clear?"

Everyone nodded, even Megan. Brie was looking at her, even as we turned away from the center of the circle.

"Where are we going to prep?" Eva asked.

"Here," I said, even as I pulled out the money. "We'll each hit a hotel for two days. Three sets of two. Brie and Abby, you can talk logistics and tactical stuff, especially in the event of it getting violent. Megan and me can talk up cover stories and what to do while inside. Cassidy and Eva, talk tech. We'll meet at the nearest gallery. Amelia Principle. 7:00 PM each evening."

Brie nodded. I threw each of them a ream of cash for the hotel, and we headed out.

We all scattered. It took Megan and I three hours to reach up north far enough to cross the border. By the time we reached the fence, we had caught our breath enough to talk.

"Sorry, by the way, for not supporting you more. I didn't mean to be the voice of dissension," she said.

"Megan, you told the truth. I almost wanted to say it, to argue with myself. But I can't miss the chance, not when everything is lined up."

"I know. It's almost like it was meant to be, as if God had it planned. That's what strikes me. Does it feel that way to you?"

It did, but for some reason, it was hard to admit it. "I'm always scared, somehow, that if He has a plan, I'll mess it up somehow."

"Well, you're not alone," Megan said, smiling at that.

"I know." I said it, feeling sure for the first time in a long time.

I put away my MCU, but the A-42 Form hovered over the other forms. I stared at his signature. It felt like a dagger that I let sink into me; that I couldn't pull out or I would bleed too much.

"Is that a form?" Megan asked. "What does it say?"

Despite her clarity, I gave her a vague answer.

Because it was true.

"That I'm alone."

We were wearing the lab clothes again. It was the best cover we had. Having Cassidy in our ears was better than having Eva chat in the earpiece the whole time. But for some reason, I missed her voice, even as she was right beside me.

As we approached the door to one of the service entrances, holding a medical bag, I kept a close eye on the guard as we approached. H barely moved. Then, he finally gave a head-nod.

"What do you have?" he asked.

"Biological evidence for a case. We thought it might be more discreet to bring it around here. We need to make an accusation for breaking law 3-78, but it's…complicated."

I was specific where I thought it mattered. 3-78 was made on the 3rd Jubilee year and was the 78th law passed. He would interpret this as a case being made against someone who was pregnant and didn't terminate their condition fast enough. The fetus would be the proof, I theorized.

My theory passed. He checked our lanyards, letting us through and barely looking at our faces. Eva, who still looked almost too young, was just appearing to be an assistant typing away as she walked. Megan barked an order at her as we entered, at which Eva looked nervous, and started messaging faster on her phone.

We were seven steps in the mission goals. We had gotten past the first phase. I breathed shallowly. We began walking down the hall. We were supposed to go all the way around, past the elevator, and take one of four stairwells to get up to the next floor.

But just as we were about to pass the elevator and I was trying to look interested in my phone, Megan stopped. I heard a whispered curse under her breath. Out of the corner of my eye, I saw Eva that had stopped walking.

And one of the last great mysteries of the last week was answered by the person now walking toward us. Except I still didn't know if she was a friend or an enemy.

"Well," Lynn said with her usual confidence, "took you long enough."

CHAPTER 27

Lynn moved her hand towards the elevator. My heart was racing. I was searching for my peripherals for any movement that would indicate this was a trap.

But then I saw the look in her eyes. It didn't feel like she was trying to hide something. It was a look my brothers sometimes had when they were proud that they had just succeeded in fooling everyone around them.

And I had a distinct feeling we weren't the ones being fooled.

She swiped her card to get on the elevator, we all entered, and she closed it, leaving behind twenty people and a few police oblivious to our presence.

"Video is on a loop for every floor you need to access. I can't guarantee your safety in this area. What I can guarantee is your safety when you leave, which has always been the problem." She reached out and gave Eva a large storage card.

"We have one," I said. Even though Megan was wary, she seemed to be taking it better than Eva, who was staring at Lynn as if she was betrayed.

"Not like this," Lynn continued. "See, that's the thing with the intel. Once it's copied, it has a source code embedded in it that's almost like a radar blip. In fact, they have satellites which interface with this code, anytime it's written. It tracks the files when they are downloaded and wherever they go. That's why…"

"Everyone's always gotten caught," Megan finished.

"This cars is the key. This will jam that signal. It has its own internal server, extremely small, and I've created it to…"

We walked out of the elevator onto the floor we were supposed to be on, but then we went to a small room. As we entered, I realized the hallway camera was faced away and the room camera was off.

"It emits its own signal. But with both signals running…"

"The satellite doesn't catch it, because it's slightly different."

"That's brilliant," Eva said. She looked vulnerable, like she had said it to Lynn too many times for Lynn not to respond.

Lynn looked at Eva sympathetically, but continued. "Once you retrieve the intel, you should get out without the files being a blazing signal leading right to you. I can show you which station is best to retrieve them. Still no word on Jubilee Day. Eva?"

She had said what she needed to for the mission. I knew that she didn't have much time, but the shock of her being alive had rendered Eva almost useless. Even then, there was a voice in my ear which was Cassidy. "Seriously, is that Lynn?"

"Eva, there was no time. I got in, set the EMP, and then I had an idea that might keep me alive. I had knocked out a guard and got their I.D. It was crazy that the next person I came across was someone from Southern control who didn't recognize me. It was just my plan to follow him."

"Why?" Eva said, almost in tears.

"My problem!" Lynn said, as if it was obvious. "I need to know how they hide their information, what is happening on Jubilee Day, and even how the farming machines work. I was dead already. I figured it was worth the risk. Once I was undercover, I thought I'd send you the info, but that's when I found out about the satellite that reads the code. I didn't have any of your numbers, and I could only contact Central once. I don't think it went through. Then this became the Basement. What in the world has been going on back home? Did the Council take crazy pills or–"

"Zander," Megan said plainly, with less anger than I would have.

Lynn moaned. "Well, that explains a lot. Take the intel, and run, as fast as you can. Eva, stay safe. And it shouldn't be you who gets it. If they get you, I'll never forgive myself. It can't be you. It'll have to be Aislyn or Megan."

Lynn hugged Eva, who was either still in shock or felt too betrayed to move her arms up to return the hug. I stared at Megan, even as Brie asked, "Aislyn, it's your call, but I think Megan's the obvious choice."

I stared at Megan, who was already accepting her fate of being in the most vulnerable spot of this mission. I began to shake my head at her when Megan reached out and touched my arm.

She stared at me, more confident than I ever could be.

"Remember, this is meant to be. Even Lynn is here."

Eva must have thought it was a good time to ask.

"Lynn, can you..."

"I'm staying, Eva. I'm sorry. I have to leave this building now so I'm not suspected." Lynn's voice faltered for the first time. "If I get word of Jubilee Day, I'll get it to Central somehow. I promise."

"Hang on." I grabbed her MCU and wrote down a number on the pad off the side. "Send it there. It's a secondary cell. It's safer. And don't send Jubilee Day intel if you think it could…" I stopped short of saying it, but she continued.

"Kill me? Haven't you heard, Aislyn? I'm already dead."

She left. She didn't look back. She had left us ten minutes and 50 yards away from the most dangerous intel of our lives.

"Aislyn, go to the left, Eva to the right, and keep it together," Brie said in our ears. We walked down the hallway. I sped up. Megan remained at the same pace, and Eva walked toward out exit. Anyone walking down the hall would see Eva veer away without suspicion. Then Megan veered off. I turned to loop around the hall again, to see or stall anyone that could approach the station.

By the time I reached then end of the long hallway, Cassidy Megan said she was plugging in. She said the storage card was emitting the signal, the light was on, and we were good to transfer. Eva commented that she had gotten the one code, and sent it to Cassidy already. There were three codes needed, so it wouldn't trigger an alarm that someone was accessing it. Eva quickly hacked in, double checking the codes.

I heard it all happening, but it felt as if it were in slow motion, hundreds of miles away. I was pretending to look busy, but each time I felt someone pass me, I doubted every reason we came here, feeling like I was choking in a room full of air.

"Get upstairs, Eva," Brie said to Megan. "Status, Megan."

"It's loading," Megan said. "It's encoding it automatically…"

She trailed off, and in another instant said, "There's a file open. Not encrypted. It isn't on the server, but it's…it's here."

"What? That makes no sense." Brie's voice sounded wary.

"It's like…it's on the workstation, but not on the server. As if it's here to be accessed, but left over from a portable drive…"

There was silence. I pretended to laugh at a joke someone said as they passed. They looked at me, satisfied that I had just kept my cover intact. But I felt panicked by having to speak to another person. It had been three minutes. "Leave it. It's not important."

"Yes, it is. I can tell by…" she said something to Cassidy that I barely understood as tech speak. She said she needed help to hack in. I cursed in my head.

"Megan, please," I whispered.

"Almost there. Okay, I'm in. It's….an inventory."

"An inventory? For what?"

But she didn't answer. She started a sentence she didn't finish, only to have a single phrase leave her mouth in the most haunted, futile tone I had ever heard.

"We're going to die."

"What?" I whispered urgently, almost forgetting my cover.

"They'll never let us live. They'll bomb us all. Oh my…"

Eva was the first to tell her to get out of there. Brie echoed it.

"You have to put in the next code," Cassidy said. "You need three codes to log off so the alarm doesn't sound."

"What's the download at?" Brie was frantic.

"90%," Megan said, as Cassidy said, "490RG."

"That's one," Eva said, in a warning tone. "I got two; it's 750HQ."

"97%," Megan said, and I could hear her voice whispering, trembling now. "Three?"

Static. Nothing. No sequence. No code. More nothing.

"Cassidy?" I said warningly into the phone I was pretending to talk into, clutching it so hard I wondered how someone hadn't noticed. I was surprised I wasn't breaking it.

"I don't…I can't…it's loading…" her panicked voice yelled.

"Grab the card and run," Brie said, in a way that made me know how fast her heart was beating.

"Then the alarm will definitely sound," Eva said. I heard a door open, which had to mean she was heading to find her way to Megan.

Brie was yelling. "I'm sending Abigail out in front, just in case. Megan you need to hurry. Eva, just head up, you're too far…"

Eva began to argue even as Megan whispered, "Moving."

I breathed in relief. "We have about one minute before the alarm sounds, and…"

Megan cursed.

"Someone just checked the station…they just screamed to–"

The alarm hit.

"Abigail, plan B! Now!" Brie yelled.

I was in the lobby, looking at the glass windows to the left and right of me. The security doors were dropping in front of the glass on the peripherals. We'd all be locked in the building within a few seconds. Nothing could open them.

Except one thing.

I didn't see Abby. But then I realized I would never see Abby.

I just saw the cylinder in the air, about to hit the window.

It instantly shattered. I was already taking cover when the shattered pieces of glass began to fall to the ground. They were thrown out, blasting away from the small explosion. No shrapnel. It was a small device. It caused one flame and a large smoke cloud.

The alarms would detect a confirmed fire.

The steel gates that were closing opened up instantly, leaving room for people running and screaming under them.

"Megan?" I called, now that I could yell, even as I dashed for the back of the building.

She didn't answer, and even as I heard the last of the steel gates clink open, there was a loud metallic noise that didn't sound anything like the gates.

"Brie?"

"That was gunfire. Abby is covering the entrance still; I'm heading for the exit now. Just head down…"

I didn't care where she was directing me. I was running even though I couldn't feel my legs. I couldn't hear myself screaming Megan's name, even though it hurt my throat as I yelled it. I got to the back entrance.

The first thing I heard was another gunshot.

But I couldn't see what was happening.

Because a fist hit my temple, and everything was blurred.

I barely had time to yell.

I thought I should yell if I was going to die.

I moved to swing, but he was far too fast. I could already tell by his movements that I was unmatched.

His hand caught my wrist.

I twisted and wrenched away, rolling towards him, pushing him down with the same motion.

It almost worked. He released my wrist and regained his balance, only to grab the other wrist with both hands and turn my arm to pin it on my back.

The pain was so intense that I could hardly breathe. I lost a breath with one single cry before he stifled me with his hand across my mouth.

"Don't move, scum. The second I–"

Then there was a thud. A sickening thud. I turned around to see the police officer hitting the ground. Eva had a long metal bar in her hand. I didn't stop. She was going to ask something, but I thought I already knew the heart-sinking answer.

She hadn't found Megan either. We ran a few yards, searching.

Only to find her.

Her blood.

Her squirming body was gasping for air.

And the guard standing over her, turning his weapon to us.

But it never fired. I threw my knife at his weapon, and another knife came flying from Brie. He was on the ground.

Brie shouted, "Clear."

I slid down to the ground, the gravel tore the fabric and flesh from my knees. I lifted Megan's head gently up off the ground.

I wanted my heart to stop beating. It was doing nothing but beating in my mind, like a drum I couldn't bear to hear. I wanted her heart to keep beating instead of mine.

But that choice was ripped from me now. It would never be my choice again.

Brie was pulling out a pack. I kept saying her name, over and over, but her blue eyes were unfocused, not even squeezing in pain. I kept pushing on the wound, willing the blood to flow inside of her instead of gushing out; to keep pumping life and love into her.

"Aislyn?" Brie said ominously. "We can't move her. There's—"

"Work!" I was yelling. I think I was crying when I yelled it.

I turned to Megan. I could see her eyes now. She should know.

"I'm sorry. I'm so sorry," I said amidst sobs.

"It's not your…"

"It is," I said, leaning down nearer. "Why did I do this?"

She swallowed. I tried not to think it was blood, but her voice was becoming muted and choked.

"You don't. When you see it…you'll know why. You'll know."

"Know what?"

"We were…supposed…to be here."

In that instant, Eva ran up. Brie stopped working and reached up to Megan.

"I love you like a sister. Please know that, Megan. But I need to know. Where is it?"

She pointed her shaking hand to her back pocket, and Brie reached under Megan, who groaned. Brie threw it to Eva.

"Run, Eva. You don't look back until you get to the rendezvous point, you kill anyone in your way who wants to stop you, and you don't dare care if any of us die. Is that clear?"

In that instant, a guard came from behind Brie to charge us, but Brie grabbed the knife on the ground and took him out in a second.

"Is that clear, Eva?" she yelled again. Eva nodded, looking almost as frightened by Brie as she had been by the guards.

And she ran.

It took a second, but I pulled myself back to Megan, reaching down.

Her hair. Her hair felt like mine. That one fact wrenched me.

But I didn't talk first. She kept choking...

"You'll save them."

"Save who? Who, Megan? Stay with me."

She smiled, even as the tear fell to unite with the blood pooling on the gravel, all the life and emotion leaving her in a flood that was pushing against the concrete, cold world around her. She was pulling away, yet the weight of her life, of everything she was and ever felt, crushed me with each breath.

And if the look on Brie's face was definitive, these breaths were her last.

"Aislyn, when you see..."

Choking.

Tears.

Coughing.

I held my breath, as if that would push it in her lungs, forcing them to breathe it in.

"You'll...know..."

I don't know how I spoke, or even if the word escaped me.

"What?"

Her eyes weren't hollow. They became clear.

"The dead aren't dead."

And then her voice was ethereal.

"We never die."

And her eyes, so clear and sure, still loving me, went blank.

And soul left body in a moment that felt unnaturally real.

I was blind. There was a light. I screamed her name.

Abby yelled Brie's name. "Brie! You promised!"

And then there was a sharp pain.

And then dark.

CHAPTER 28

My head throbbed as I opened my eyes to see the light.

The light felt old.

Dirty. They were…

Territory. Was I in the Territory?

No. I couldn't be.

I could never go back to the Territory again.

I bolted awake, starting to scream. It was Cassidy who got to me first. She was pinning me down, but I was thrashing, and I knew it. I wanted answers. I wanted to hit her. I wanted Megan.

Megan.

It was strange to say her name. To think her name, as if I was still screaming it.

Because Megan was dead.

And in the instant I remembered, that all the flashes came back to me, I sat up slowly. Brie was staring at the wall. Abigail was at the sink, washing off blood. She looked pale. Eva was at the console. She was covered in dirt, except for the streaks on her face.

But now that I wasn't yelling myself awake, I couldn't speak. It was Eva that was throwing something and screaming next, only to be silent a second later.

Brie turned to her. "Eva, it doesn't mean–"

"I don't know what she saw! The images are corrupted. I just have the list. It's just a list, and I can't read it."

"It's encoded. She said that," someone said.

I was closing my eyes. Megan had said that. But they didn't want to use her name either.

Because Megan was dead.

"It doesn't seem to have a..." she threw something. "There's something here about shipments and this is...this is so strange, but I don't know how..."

"Brie?" I finally spoke. I felt like I would never talk again, so it felt strange to hear my voice vibrate in my throat. "How did I..."

"Abigail drugged you; I hit you. We dragged you out. You can hate me. You can be alive long enough to hate me. But there was no way I was going to lose you, too."

I almost wanted to charge her. They must have had it as a contingency plan if Megan or I died for getting the other out if we were reacting too emotionally. That infuriated me more than anything: that anyone could have imagined a plan going wrong enough that Megan would die.

There should have been no reality where she was dead.

Even as Brie spoke, I could tell her voice cracked. She stopped short. Eva began to curse. Cassidy was the only one that was calm, but perhaps that was just shock.

It felt like believing the truth and wanting to breathe were opposing forces. I had barely known her, yet I had loved her more than I thought possible. The possibility of me loving her more was always there. But now everything she could have meant to me was lost, along with everything she was. I would never know.

"It's um…" Eva looked at it, closing her eyes. "I can't even…"

"Put it up," Brie said. It came up on the screen.

"See, it's jibberish. It's just a paragraph of…"

"Elite language," I said, without even realizing it. I hated myself for talking or thinking, using my voice or even the air around me when Megan couldn't breathe anymore. Because Megan was dead.

"Brie?" Cassidy said.

"Aislyn's right, I think. It looks like the sub-standard version of Latin the Elites use. But, we don't know where to begin to translate it. We don't know–"

"I do," I said, almost too calm that I criticized myself.

"Aislyn, we need to get Abby back," Brie said, and even as I asked why, I noticed her lower leg had dried blood, and there was a black mark above it wrapped in gauze. She was starting to shake.

"Where are we?"

"Q station, abandoned two decades ago," Brie said. "We are going to get Abby back, and then we're coming back together to find out what this is…"

"This is a waste." Cassidy, who I mistook for being composed was now talking into the floor. She was beginning to shake, "One code. All my life all that mattered was one code, and…"

"They were headed down anyway," Abigail said as she shook.

"We're not doing this, Cassidy." Brie said. "We're–"

There was a noise above the station. It sounded like a person jumping, and then there were steps.

"No one move." Brie pulled out a grenade, her weakness disappearing with adrenaline. She moved toward the ladder.

But then we heard the voices.

"Those aren't police," Eva whispered. "They sound like…"

It was almost impossible for me not to attack. A child had already betrayed me once. I found myself unconvinced right up until the latch opened. I looked on the floor for answers.

Barefoot footprints.

Trash.

Leaves.

A sharpened stick.

I said as quickly as I could, even as Brie reached for her knife, "No, Brie! They must live here."

She nodded. "I thought so. I need to make sure they're alone."

Something instantly happened to Brie. Her hard exterior and pained expressions melted into a gentle smile. She moved with the grace of a dancer. The door opened. She didn't jump like we did.

"Hi there," she said in a gentle, sing-song voice. I could hear the quick movements in the dried leaves of the forest floor. "It's okay, we don't want to hurt you. In fact…you probably know how we know this station is here."

She backed up from the ladder, and to our surprise, two kids no older than seven came down the ladder. The girl had a knife. She held the knife in the correct position, but her hand shook.

"Are you Protectors? How do we know?" the little voice asked.

"Don't you see? That's how we knew this station was here. It's old. We abandoned it a long time ago, but someone wrote about it in a journal we all keep, so I remembered," she continued to talk, but her voice was weakening. "My name is Brie. This is Abigail. Over on the bed is Aislyn. They aren't feeling well. They are lying down. This is Cassidy. And that's Eva at the device."

Even as I wondered why she was bothering to say all of our names, I noticed the boy take off his hood and lower his weapon. He must have trusted her.

Almost.

"Prove it," he said, the doubt still on his face and in his voice.

Brie confidently pulled out a meal bar and threw one.

"You've seen these. They were probably in here. You know they are from us," Brie said, as Eva opened up her pack and pulled a few out. The children either measured the risk and decided to take it, or completely believed Abby and Brie, because within two minutes, they had each devoured three meal bars and were starting to tell us their backstory.

"What are your names then?"

"Erin and...Aaron. Keeps it simple," he said. "We were in the Sub-Terra program. I was in for intelligence, but I was super awkward. Kept messing up. I was never going to make it. She was in it as well, and her parents had her as a natural birth."

"They tried to hide it," she said. "They loved me, at first, I think. The debt was too much, the police started coming, and then I started in school as a Sub-Terra. But...I'd felt love. In a way they didn't. I think they knew that. I escaped with Aaron. I wanted to cry, but I couldn't. Like the girl over there on the table."

She stared at me, even as I stared back in shock. Anyone with that extent of emotional intelligence would be a threat to them.

"You've lived her for a while?" Abby asked, even as Brie took a step forward to force more pain meds in Abby's foot.

"Six months," Aaron said.

"Prove it," Brie stated.

They reached for their I.D.s when Brie shook her head. "No. Prove it. You're sunburned, but it's not enough proof."

Aaron started to take off his shoe, and I noticed the one toe was blackened, as if frostbitten. Erin pulled up her sleeve to show scars from poison ivy and a scratch by a cat she said attacked her when she tried to catch it. It was most likely a large lynx.

When they had finally passed the test and were talking to Abby, Eva headed over to me. She gave me a quick hug, and then nodded at Brie. Brie looked wary at first, and then walked over to join us.

"Okay, here's the deal," Eva started. "We need to put it back in a station that can read it, or get a second opinion. We need to get Abby home, we need to get these two kids home, and the disc..."

"To Alex." I could tell they were both wary of him. I was about to explain when I was interrupted. Something buzzed.

"Oh, Aislyn, it's your phone again. It's like the fifteenth time someone called.

"What do you mean? Wait, my green phone?"

"You have two phones? Why do you…"

I was running over to my bag, even though I almost fell trying to stand. The blood was pooled in my legs, but I could hear it pounding in my ears.

"Who is it?"

"My…Vessel," I said, hoping the long pause was enough for both of them to understand. Eva took one second longer than Brie to realize that I meant Rebecca, and gave me the phone. The messages were all the same, begging for help, scared to death.

Megan was dead.

"Early contractions," I said, stoically. "Probably just upper, not real. And with no real consistency."

"You can't message her from here," Brie said, giving me a warning I should have known, but I didn't remember.

Because Megan was dead.

Over and over again, this fact repeated because I yelled it as I reacted in terror every time. It seemed like the world didn't know: Megan was dead. The world should have stopped turning, no one should be talking. No birds should be singing.

"I'm going back," I said, "You and Cassidy will take the kids…"

"Perfect, and I'll stay with you," Eva said warningly.

"Eva, you have an Unnecessary. It's a card someone died to get. The least you could do…" I stopped, something was pulsating in my lower ribs, something hurt and burning, "is make sure it's safe and it gets back there."

Brie looked down to the floor. "If you think…for one minute that you are the only one who loved–"

"I don't." I said it honestly this time, my voice cracking a little and a tear escaping. "I saw your face. You all knew her, maybe even better than I did. But it was my idea. It was my call. I sent her down when Lynn said Eva couldn't go…" I shuddered then. Would Eva have died? "Look, it doesn't matter. Staying and figuring this out is how I put this right."

And then I reached out my hand expectantly to Eva. Eva surprised me by saying, "I'm staying with the data. You're right. I have my Unnecessary. And I'm staying with it, until I can read it."

Brie sighed, "I don't like this. I don't want to leave you like this. The only way I leave you is with Eva."

"I'm going to be back inside the border in a few hours. Eva can stay with me." Then, realizing the birds were getting louder, I asked, "What time is it?"

It wasn't dusk. It was dawn.

Eva said, "I think you have a date for coffee?"

I nodded without thinking.

"Coffee. We have two hours to get there. It's…Thursday."

I struggled to remember his routine.

"You're a mess," Eva said.

"I'll clean up then," I said mechanically. I pushed through them to get to the tiny shower off to the side, thanking the person who lived a century ago for making something so well that it would still work. I thought I would lose it once I was inside, but I didn't. I had to keep it together. My desire to make this worth something was fighting my basic need to feel anything deeply, to go back home, to be comforted. If I allowed myself to feel any emotion with perfect clarity, I wouldn't recover for days.

I barely knew what I was doing. But I did it.

Cassidy wasn't looking at me. I wanted to tell her not to feel guilty either, because it was my fault and not hers. I couldn't. If I said her name I might lose it. I tried to hug Brie, like I normally would, but it felt perfunctory. She whispered something to Eva.

I walked.

I took a cab.

I waited.

Eva kept reminding me to look at my phone, which was good.

I could look at it and feel everything, or nothing. I was staring at the screen. I could call anyone in the Republic right now.

Could I call Linden and ask for a dress to sneak into a party Palmer was at so I could kill him?

Could I call someone and ask if they could make a cure for death?

Could I surrender if there was a way she could be alive again?

Would putting a knife in anyone in an act of revenge make me feel better? I think I remembered the answer was no, but felt like it would make me feel better. The caffeine made my heart rate jump faster, even as I focused on staying still.

Look happy, keep your feet down, look happy, look at your phone, look happy…

Door opened. No Alex.

"Stop looking at the door every time it opens," Eva whispered.

"Sorry," I said again, but as I had jumped, the waitress came up and said, "Looking for him, huh? How was Vinalia?"

I hoped that she would believe my bad acting.

"Oh it was amazing, and magical, and…divine!" I said. "And I feel like I'm still recovering. We were supposed to meet this morning, but…life of a Sentry. So instead I'm just hoping he shows up, even though he's messaging he can't."

"That's the most deep, romantic thing I've ever heard," she said, genuinely impressed and totally fooled by my performance.

It was almost time for the window to be up. Where was he? I was trying to fake conversation with Eva, but at 9:00, I got up. I left a hefty tip at the counter for the waitress who spoke to me, and we headed out.

"Something's wrong, Eva," I said the moment we were outside.

"What do you mean?" she said. "You sure it's this café today?"

"Yes," I said, recalling the schedule in my head. I remembered the one café where the boy was taken already…

The boy.

And in the sudden alertness I felt, I realized we weren't the only ones who were waiting for Alex.

As I moved to the alley, I prayed if there was an Unnecessary waiting for a cup, he was still there. Maybe prayed was the wrong word. I pushed any thought that God would care out of my head.

But it wasn't true, I scolded myself. God probably cared. I just messed it up. My chest started to tighten again. This wasn't the time for any spiritual introspection. I needed to look for…

I saw something move. Eva whispered, "Freeze."

I began talking, hoping the Unnecessary would understand me. "He's not here today. But we are. And if you haven't guessed already…" I looked over at Eva as I said, "We're here for him."

The words felt jumbled coming out, but there was a sound around the corner, even as I wondered how he had gotten that far without me noticing.

His amber eyes pierced me. He was like an angel, with a glowing face, the slightest blond curls coming out from under the hood of his jacket. He was most likely seven years old; no older than eight.

But my first wariness kicked in. Why was this boy an Unnecessary? But his question came first.

"Are you…Protectors?"

I wanted to say no. I didn't feel like one. I felt like a mistake, a blemish, a convict not yet accused, a horrible nothing.

But in the end, I just wanted him to live. I still felt like I was lying when I said, "Yes, we're Protectors."

Eva introduced us and asked his name.

"Warren. They named me...I'm Warren."

"Warren, how are you...why are you out here?"

"Yeah, Alex wondered at first, too. I know I look okay. But I'm not. I have seizures. They're pretty bad."

"Were your parents–"

But he cut her off. "My parents were...they were arrested. Treason. I'm a ward of the Society. They saw a lot of promise in me. They saw my intelligence, mostly, but...my nurse saw that my serotonin levels were too low. She didn't tell them. She wanted to help. I try to drink a lot of milk, eat a lot of turkey, all that, to try to get it up, but it only does so much...I can fake it, in school."

"Wait...you're in school, still?"

"Yes. Alex brings me my medicine. I can still blend in. Do you have it? I can't last long without it."

He needed meds. I looked at Eva for an answer.

"Um..." She was looking in her bag as I kneeled to talk to him.

"Do you still want the medicine? Or do you want to go?"

He looked torn. This wasn't what he was expecting, but even as I asked, I felt him tremble as he thought out loud.

"I kind of want to stay. I just need meds."

I stared at him, not sure what my eyes were asking.

But he answered. "I remember this one day, in class. The meds didn't work. I felt one coming on. I spent the whole minute in terror until I could go somewhere and hide. I spent an hour in a closet. I need meds, but I'm always worried it will happen again."

He sighed, looking away at the empty space behind me.

"I don't know what your world is like, Aislyn, but if you save the people you do, I wouldn't have to be afraid, would I?"

I nodded. "It will be different, Warren. Not perfect. Not without fear. But the next time you have seizure, someone could hold you, instead of being alone. You wouldn't be alone."

He breathed out, even as his lower jaw shook slightly. "They said I'll fit in one day. But I feel like it's all for nothing. The one moment when I accidentally reveal who I am...it will be my last. That would be my last moment. If I go..."

He trailed off, but I took his chin and lifted it, staring at him with a challenge.

"That moment, when the world sees who you are and doesn't shy away? That moment will be your first."

His eyes held on to mine like he understood me. But then he cringed as he suppressed a scream.

Eva was behind him, a syringe in her hand, injecting his neck.

"Eva?" I accused.

"What?" she said, withdrawing the needle. "It's better he didn't see it coming."

"What? Was that..."

"Serotonin injection. Better than pills. It will work quicker."

He tried to look at his neck, still feeling the cool of the needle or the sting, and he said, "I still want to go with you, but there's just one thing."

I waited, wondering if he would ask a specific question about the Territory that I would have to either shortly or exhaustedly answer. Instead, he asked the one question I couldn't answer at all.

"Where's the Sentry?"

I smiled, which for some reason hurt, and kept my composure.

"He tipped us off. He wants to help you. That being said, I'm going to be honest: I don't know where he is, Warren. And I need to find out. You are going with Eva."

"Aislyn?" Eva looked at me, betrayed. She must have known I was about to break my promise and leave her.

I gave her a warning look, and then told him, "Eva's here to take you back. She's going to leave me. I'll find out what happened to the Sentry. Eva will take you where you'll be safe."

I gave Eva a look at that moment, even as I saw her eyes forming tears. I knew her anger and worry for me were crashing together, and maybe she was mad I had now put her in a position where she had to leave me or take Warren; it was a horrible choice.

She blinked rapidly, but didn't reveal any emotion in her tone.

"We'll head back now, Warren. I have about three more vials of serotonin, and it should last us a little bit."

She turned to me, reaching out her arm. "You'll need this."

It was a square pouch. She didn't have to tell me what was in it. I hated having to take it. It was like holding the bullet that killed Megan in my hands, except it was the only thing that was going to make her death mean anything.

"You be careful," she said. She hugged me, much harder than anyone ever had in my entire life. "And I mean it. Take care of yourself."

I squeezed back as much as I could. They left. He smiled. I said I would wait to see if Alex would come.

I wished I hadn't lied.

But I already knew that I couldn't stay.

The worst possible outcome had already broken into my mind, stealing away any hope I had left.

Despite all of our efforts, they must have caught me on camera attacking the Basement.

Someone recognized that I was with him at Vinalia.

Alex might be dead.

This one sentence shook my core. Every muscle felt weak, pulled apart at the seams, physically ripping through the shreds of my life that were left. I only had one option.

I needed to disappear, until I had enough hope to look for him.

CHAPTER 29

There are moments in life when breathing feels like a sin. I felt the void of my breaths as I inhaled slowly. I watched the sunrise, looked for Alex, and then watched the sun fall. There was a weight on my chest at night, making it entirely hard to breathe.

I kept blowing on the dandelion, giving all the pieces new life. Some always stuck. Not leaving. Not living.

They were the most beautiful summer days. I thought of Olivia singing, dancing in a field somewhere, not knowing I was in this wretched state. I thought of Megan's father chopping wood in the hope his daughter would be home late winter, maybe even imagining long talks in early March snows with the firewood he was chopping...

Then I would curl in a ball.

Tears fell to the grass. Shame burned in my heart.

Everything I should have done and should not have done played in my mind. But it all faded eventually, becoming a series of whispers.

I should've had a better plan.

I should've stayed closer to her.

I should've never let her come.

I should've died instead of her.

I should've died.

I kept staring at the grass, blowing in the breeze under trees that remained untouched by any sadness I felt. They had outlived so many others, and would probably outlive so many generations. I thought of the subtle suggestion in the breeze: that life kept living.

But I didn't hear it.

I kept catching one thought, a mind-crushing thought that echoed, shattering all the black that filled my mind.

The dead aren't dead.

I thought of that often, even as I had to admit it didn't make any difference. My faith felt weaker the longer I didn't see Alex in any of his usual places. The hours passed until they became long days of tears and anxiety. I kept thinking about everyone and their reaction to our failed mission. It was a horrible thing to be writing this story, seeing how it would play out today, and possibly in the weeks, months, years to come.

My mother would cry. That one fact made me cry the hardest. My father would be ashamed of me. Collin, knowing someone else died for this intel, would feel even more despondent. Now I knew what it was like to lose someone in pursuit of this intel. Now I knew why he had signed the 42-A.

He was never going to pick me.

He was never going to love me.

No one could love with this need for revenge in their soul.

I now knew this need for vengeance. It was consuming.

When I wasn't careful, I slipped into planning a revenge plot that I was sure I could never execute. I would stop, and calm my mind. Palmer would pay; they all would pay. But it wasn't my job to kill him. It was someone else's. I struggled to remember the hurt that Zander's search for revenge had caused.

And on the morning of the fourth day, I realized there was only one way I could get revenge that was meaningful enough to crush the Republic. I could save one more soul.

I needed to see Rebecca. If Alex was no longer alive to be our liaison, I was unsure how to proceed.

All I knew was that I needed her to be safe. She became the first hope I had felt in my despair: the Vessel of the first traitor would need me to be the Protector I wasn't sure I was anymore.

But even as I received the message back from her on my phone that she was fine after she had followed the advice I had given her, I messaged her back that I wanted to see her. And I found that even this one task made me feel a desperate need for coffee and food.

I looked at the time. Maybe it was out of desperation to hope that Alex was still alive, but I chose the same café where he normally would have been.

I shouldn't have gone. With each minute past 9:30, a little more of me slipped away. I would tell myself that Rebecca needed me, but then I felt like that was just like crudely placing tape on a part of me that had slipped away.

But my fear became more urgent when I realized something.

I was being followed.

I didn't know why, or who it was, but I could sense it.

I went down several blocks. But my tail didn't divert. I could always see her in my peripherals when looking at storefronts.

I quickly dashed behind a storefront that was closed, still looking like I was on my phone. I was going to head quickly in the other direction to try to see if my suspicions were true.

I turned quickly again, just to be face-to-face with her. She stared at me, not flinching under the flurry of her perfect golden hair flying in the wind.

"Who are you?" I asked.

Her voice was heavenly. "Most would say I'm nobody. I suppose I am. But I am someone's nobody. I believe you've met."

I looked at her curiously, and then with a little understanding, I said, "What does Becca need?"

She smiled as I recognized her. "She said she'd love to see you tonight at the party. On 14th. She gave you an invitation, and something else that should help as well. Bring a friend."

Then she was gone.

I opened up the envelope she had handed me and found enough money to get me a dress. I tried to remember the date and realized it was the beginning of the athletic games they held the last two weeks of summer. There would be a lot of parties tonight, mostly centered around gambling. A perfect cover.

So the hours slipped by, almost like they had in the forest.

I fell into a pattern, so I didn't think about anything too complicated: Feet down, look at phone, wink at guy, feet down, get dress, let people pull at my hair to make it pretty, pay an extra tip for them not to ask questions of how leaves had gotten knotted in it, watch them smile, feet down, look at phone.

The only thing that broke my pattern was wondering who she was referring to when she said, "bring a friend." I wanted to scream at her, that she would be so insensitive and self-absorbed to not notice that he was dead. I rubbed the satin of the green dress I was wearing, even as the man in the taxi told me we had arrived.

My distracted thoughts focused in reaction to the initial danger. I received several compliments. I was initially worried that I would be quickly targeted because I didn't have a date, but I noticed that everyone had their eyes on their phones, were joking with each other, or were looking at the massive screens surrounding the room, despite the party being elaborately decorated and ornately designed.

There were flashes of games on each screen, and several teams listed for each event. Everyone seemed to mirror the formal attire I was wearing, but was too preoccupied to notice tonight. Someone mentioned that I might be more comfortable in one of the dining rooms if I was just waiting for someone who was placing bets. I was a little confused, but I followed their advice.

I wondered where I should look for Rebecca, or who to even ask. I began to ask the questions in my head I couldn't ask anyone but her.

How could she not know what had happened?

How could she not know that I wasn't up for this tonight?

How could she not care that Alex was dead?

And then as I took a step inside the room, looking immediately to my right, I froze as the breath felt like it was pulled out of me.

Maybe Rebecca would know, or care, if Alex was gone.

But he wasn't.

And as I looked into his eyes, even from a few yards away, I could tell I wasn't the only one struck with the terror of looking at a ghost.

The hallway was dark, nearly abandoned. I wondered why he had motioned that we come down here. I barely had any time at all to react as he stepped out of the shadows, putting a hand up before I could run to him.

"I'm sorry." He sounded fearful. He reached behind his back.

"For what?" I barely breathed out.

"For this."

Then he pulled out his gun and aimed at me, his arm shaking.

"What….Alex?"

"Aislyn's dead. Who are you?" He sounded like he might cry, even as he was accusing me.

"Alex, it's me. Just…" I was staring at the weapon, trying to control my emotions and think of a way to prove it to him.

I turned my hand over, to reveal the remaining lines of the scar.

"This is the only proof I have that you loved me. You love me. You saved me. I'm me!"

He looked in disbelief, but I had just revealed two things that no imposter would even know. But his breath was still quickening.

"They gave us all the descriptions of the attackers. I even did a match on the DNA in the parking lot. You can't be alive."

I started crying, pleading now for my life, because he had misunderstood the one thing I wanted everyone to understand.

"I didn't die, Alex. That was Megan. She died. I should've died instead...I should've...."

I felt weak. Everything I had been able to fight alone in the woods came rushing back to me. He was still holding his weapon at me. It shook in his hand.

"What did I say to you the very first time we met?" he asked.

I strained to remember. I didn't want to say what I needed to say for his final test. I would have rather said a hundred other phrases that would hurt less and make me feel more.

"You asked me...who I was. You said you saw me. So see me."

He closed his eyes, sighing as he pushed his hand on his head, pressing against his jet black hair. He looked warily at me.

"I'm sorry. You're okay. You're...you're alive."

And I could tell he couldn't handle the fact that I was alive.

And neither could I.

If he had asked me who I was now, I don't know if I could've answered it. I had no clue who I was. So I focused on him.

"And what about you?" I said, my voice quivering. "You didn't show up for coffee, you didn't show up in any of your usual places. Alex, I thought someone had caught me on camera, recognized me, and they'd killed you. I thought you were d—"

I couldn't finish, but I didn't need to. He reached out for me, pulling me in. He buried his head in my shoulder. His whole body shook underneath me. I slowly wrapped my arms around him.

"I'm sorry. After the DNA match…I couldn't move for a day. It was your DNA, it was your description, it was…"

I sighed, answering the question even as I was about to ask.

"How did you–? My knife. They found a partial?"

"They assumed it was a match based on the fact that the sample from the knife was so small. But…how?"

Even as he began the question, I started to answer it, but I found myself unable to choke out the words. They came out broken and strained. I still couldn't believe they were true.

"She is my cousin…was my cousin, Alex. She was…"

And I felt myself unable to speak. But I had said enough for him to understand, and he grabbed me again.

"Don't. Not here. I need you to stay together 'til we can get out of here. Crying for her won't help right now," he said.

I realized he was probably talking more from experience than anything else, and the thought of that struck me. He got out his phone, and urgently looked around him.

"I'm going to message Becca. There's no way you can–"

"No, I can. I can. You're alive," I said, as I took one calm breath. "I thought you were dead. You didn't show up–"

"I'll never forgive myself for that now. I think the boy I was taking care of is dead. I tried to find him, and he didn't show up for school…"

Alex trailed off, his words lost in the shadow of regret.

"Alex, we found him. He's with another Protector."

"Really?" he said, and then without hesitating, he spun me, almost laughing in joy. He was still holding me when he asked innocently, "Why didn't you just go with him?"

"You didn't show up. I know you love me. And I told you…it matters, Alex. It matters. And when I thought I'd never see you again, I realized how much it mattered."

I reached out to touch his chest.

His heart was still beating.

It started to beat faster.

And faster.

And then I realized why.

I now heard the footsteps moving closer, even as I heard him whisper a curse. Quickly, he lifted my head with gentle fingers and said, "Aislyn, I'm so sorry."

"For what?" I said through quivering lips.

I pulled back from him, scared of what had happened after he had used those words a few minutes ago. He was staring intensely at me. I was waiting for him to move, to run for it. But he didn't.

Until he grabbed the back of my neck, and drew me in.

"For this…"

Before I knew what he was doing, his hand had curled around my back. I barely had time to breathe. I think I almost said his name before his lips silenced mine.

The kiss deepened just as I heard the voices. I opened my eyes briefly to see two staff members from the ball, along with what looked like a special guest. While there would have been suspicion if we were down here talking or even trying to mask our escape, in this state no one would question our intentions, nor would they suspect us of anything. He kept moving his lips gently against mine, separating only to whisper every few seconds: "I'm sorry."

He had promised not to kiss me. Not to love me. He wasn't trying to confuse me or make me fall in love with him, or make me want to kiss him back. He was just keeping us alive.

He pulled back for an instant to whisper again, "I'm sorry."

I could feel the apologies hit me. They burned more than the kiss.

Because as I came to know more about him, the more I wondered: how could this person believe he was so unlovable? This person who risked everything to save strangers? Maybe when you look at a wall of guilt that high, it makes your sins seem like a fortress instead of a wall– you seal yourself in, making new definitions of everything.

You're not just heartbroken, you're broken.

You're not just uncertain, you're misguided.

You're not just human, you're a mess of emotions to be avoided.

Those were the lies that he believed. They were a fortress he built around his heart.

And it was about time someone broke through it.

The group of people had turned to go down the next hall. The next moment, I heard the door shut. Alex broke free, giving me a chance to breathe. He looked down the hall, in both directions.

"Clear. It's over. They're gone. You don't have to–"

We both knew what he was about to say. The cover story had worked, our players had been convinced. But I hadn't moved.

I didn't have to kiss him again.

But I knew I was going to.

He was about to say something, but all that came out was a whisper.

"Don't. Aislyn, don't–"

And then my lips found his again. His breath staggered. He had enough time to get a breath in and whisper "But you don't have to." Then I lunged forward, my lips meeting his again, hoping to rip down every wall he had barricaded himself around. I pulled back, hoping I could penetrate his doubt with my stare. But then my phone beeped, reminding me I wasn't here to save him.

"We need to go see Becca," I said, out of breath. He breathed in sharply, and we headed up the stairs.

It was a tense few minutes heading upstairs. Alex explained that he had come to tell Rebecca that I was dead and to try to come up with a back-up plan.

Luckily, Rebecca must have speculated that our tension was due to the fact that her father had made an appearance at the party, which was the reason for her nervousness. She was lying on the couch with the monitor over her growing stomach.

"Okay, you're…" I paused to watch the monitor closely as I said, "That's normal. That's not a real contraction."

"I know. I mean that's what you said." Her voice sounded sure and calm, and as I stared at the monitor, I wondered what she had overreacted about.

Until the real contraction came.

I heard her sharp intake of breath, and then I saw it. The graph spiked. It could only have been moderately painful, but...

"How long in between?" I asked quickly. We didn't have long enough to monitor her in this location for me to get a reading.

"Sporadic. An hour can go by. Sometimes only 20 minutes."

My mind was racing. There was very little chance of her making it to term in the four weeks remaining.

"Becca, I'm going to give you some meds. I need you to stay calm the next few weeks."

She nodded. I realized just how pointless that advice was if she stayed in this room, as being close to her father was making her more nervous than anything.

Her voice was shaking. "Aislyn, what if..."

"I'm not going anywhere, Rebecca. I was going to go back...but...I can't leave you now. Not with you contracting like this. I'll be with Alex. You can find me through him. Okay?"

I reached out to touch her arm, feeling it stop shaking under my hand. I was trying to transfer any feeling of hope I could.

It must have been failing. She looked at me sympathetically.

"I'm sorry. One of you died in the Basement attack."

I knew she might even know more than I did, but then I realized that she wasn't talking to her father much.

"We didn't even get the intel–"

"What do you mean? You got it," she interrupted. "At least, they think you did. They're just happy it's encrypted."

"But…it doesn't make any sense. None of it does." My heart raced with anger at the cost of the contents of the nonsensical intel.

"Whatever it is, you have it," she challenged, and I wondered if this wasn't another act of her exacting revenge upon her father.

She touched my shoulder as she left, nodding at Alex and then exiting out the back door. I echoed my last words to her, even though she had left.

"It doesn't make any sense. It doesn't make any sense."

After the third time I said it, Alex ran over to me. But the confusion was blinding, making it impossible for me to look at him. I was falling apart, and I risked everything, including his life, by staying there. The anxiety of it crushed me, like I was being sucked dry and shrunk into a tiny ball.

"I barely knew her, but she was the only family I'll ever have again. The rest of my family will hate me. Olivia. She'll ask questions one day. She'll ask why I let her die, and I can't–"

I think he caught me. I caught glimpses as he carried me.

Through the lobby, through a hallway, to his shuttle.

I think I spoke enough Elite language to fool someone in the lobby who saw me shaking and assumed I overdosed, and a Sentry was taking me home.

I couldn't remember how I got to his shuttle, to his place.

"Do you need—"

"No," I said, feeling the need to be independent, or at least, more alert, since I was about to go into his….house. I hesitated every time I thought 'house,' considering its scope and opulence.

I found myself overwhelmed by curiosity, almost forgetting why there was a reason to be cautious. My shoes clicked against the hard, marble floor. The other parts of the floor outside of the small circle were hardwood. It was the size of the rooms that struck me, and they made me feel smaller than ever before.

I should've kept it together, making sure Alex knew I was okay.

I should've checked Rebecca for each complication.

I should've smiled more in the lobby, diverting suspicion.

I should've…

The last one faded.

My anxiety and lack of sleep were all catching up with me. I thought back to the last time I slept: it was over a day ago.

I think I complained about having to be carried again, but he was holding me too close for me to breathe out the answer.

He was saying something.

He thought I was dead.

The dead weren't dead.

"Alex?" I said, with a clarity and purpose that must have scared him. I only wished I could have had this energy burst in the hallway an hour earlier.

He looked at me, almost scared. It was only then that I realized that he had several glasses of water and tea, and a blue liquid I eyed curiously.

"It's to calm you down. You put it in water. It's some kind of herb, not a drug—"

I smelled the water. Chamomile. And while it was calming, it was one of the worst things for me right now.

Because it reminded me of home.

"Sorry, are you okay?" He looked nervous. I realized where I was in the room. I was on the couch. I'd been laying down. He had pulled up some the ottoman and was sitting a few feet away.

"I'm fine," I said, but I did grab his hand.

"Are you okay?" I asked.

"I…you're alive. And I'm having trouble believing it."

"Yeah, well. I'm still having trouble believing that I should be."

His head fell as he reached his other hand out to mine.

"Don't say that. Aislyn, don't."

I looked away from him. I saw the vials on the counter as I looked around the room. They were emptied. I closed my eyes. A part of my head screamed not to say anything, not to accuse him.

He knew what I was thinking as I looked at the vials.

"I kind of lost it, Aislyn. The DNA match came back. I barely could make it out of the office. I took it all. For days. Until I remembered…I promised you that I wouldn't. I dumped the rest."

He knew. He had a grasp of every feeling that was now pulsing through me: shame, guilt, and overwhelming regret. Even as I thought it, he said, "Aislyn, please don't do this to yourself. I know what you're going through…"

"Of course you do!" I yelled, choking back tears so it made it sound angrier.

I felt the cold vacuum of my words spoken in hurt and fury, as if his sharp intake of breath at my unexpected outburst had sucked all the heat out of the room.

I was stumbling to apologize. "I'm sorry, Alex, I'm so sorry, I don't know why I said that—"

"I do," he said, looking at the floor now, instead of me. "Because it's true. Because I killed Emmy, and her baby, and—"

"No, Alex…you didn't." I pushed everything else from my mind for a second. Out of desperation to atone for my words, I decided to take the chance to tell him. I hated how needy I was being, but it was mostly because I felt a complete lack of purpose.

This. This was now my purpose.

Just to tell him.

"Alex, do you know how I said that…the Society lies?"

"Well, not specifically, but it's an understood quality of egotistical tyrants. Cheat, steal, manipulate, lie."

"Alex, I can't prove they lied about the Serum. I can't prove they lied about what intel we were gathering in the Basement. But if you believe me when I tell you this, I will never ask you to trust me again. They did lie."

"About what? The intel? Palmer? The Serum?"

"No," I said, wondering how an intense moment could arise that wasn't about the power and war and politics. It was one single fact that would shatter his reality and change everything.

"Alex, I...we looked for a record, for your sister. For a Vessel who didn't make it, along with an Unnecessary left in the womb."

"You didn't find one. You said that," he sounded nervous.

I grasped his hand tighter.

"I was stupid, Alex. I trusted the lies too much. It left me blind to the half-truth I almost missed."

He looked at me, bewildered, as I breathed in deeply again.

"They only told you half the truth, Alex."

And suddenly my grief was miles off, and all that I could see were the eyes that gave Caleigh away. His breath shuddered for a moment before he steadied it, maybe about to ask a question as I continued.

"That lie died the second I saw her eyes." I was looking at his, which were starting to look calculating, and then widened.

"They looked just like yours," I whispered.

He was shaking his head in disbelief. "How did you—"

"The shelter was bombed. They came to live in the Circles until it is safe for them to return. I saw Emmy's baby, Alex. Brie told me.... Your sister died in her arms, but the baby was fine."

"You can't...how do you know?" His breath became more uneven, his voice uncertain, accusing, and then frail.

"Do you know? For sure?"

"Alex, your DNA was on file due to your injury. The statistical probability of a genetic match was over ninety-nine percent."

It was a fact, and yet it was the most emotionally charged news I had ever given anyone.

"She's alive, Alex, she's…" I couldn't continue, because his hands were pressed against his forehead, and he looked like he was going to cry or break something. "Just don't overthink it right now. Don't blame or hate or feel anything, but relief."

"I know. I get to feel a lot of that tonight," he said, fighting back something in his throat. "Is she okay? Is she…happy?"

I reached into my pocket and pulled out my phone. I had saved just one picture of her on it. He looked at her, covering his mouth with one hand, pulling it back only to speak.

"She looks just like her. She's…"

He leaned into me. I held his head, temporarily jealous, wishing that he could confirm Megan was alive in an interrogation room.

"You know," I said, faking hope in my tone, "if there's ever a perfect set of circumstances, maybe you can see her one day."

"No, Aislyn," he lifted his head up, looking pained as he looked at the picture again. "I could never see her."

"Why not?" I asked, almost betrayed. Maybe it was jealousy that made me incapable of understanding him. He could see her. I could never see Megan again.

"She would never want to see a monster like me," he said.

I pulled his head up, lifting under his chin.

"What makes you so horrible? One mistake? A million?"

He shook his head. "It's not what I did; it's who I am. It's the same thing, and I can't separate them."

"Yes you can, don't you see? That's the whole point! That's what makes your soul...yours. That's why you're able to fight the fear and leave cups for kids, and risk your life for me."

I trailed off, not realizing why my conviction had vanished until he said, "Except you have the same guilt. You can't escape it either. And I still don't know why."

The silence seeped in the moments that followed. I finally found the nerve to tell the story I swore I would never want to repeat. I walked through every horrible moment in the Basement.

When I got to the part where we approached her, as she lay on the ground bleeding, I think the words I needed had finally sunk in. I stared at the storage card on the table. The blinking of the lights giving out the interference signal irritated me.

"She had the intel. It's in Elite language, but she didn't know. But she saw something else she understood. When she told us, she didn't make any sense."

"Why not?"

"Because she was shot...through the heart. And her blood was pouring out. She was confused because her head....because..."

I was overwhelmed with a need to explain.

"It's all my fault, Alex. We had a status quo. I broke it. And she died. Just to find out something that didn't matter."

"What do you mean? What did she say?" Alex said.

"The dead aren't dead." I swallowed. I kept talking, figuring it might stop the rush of tears that would only make him worry more. "She said it would change everything, and that the dead aren't dead. And then looked at me with a hope no other person taking her last breaths could have. I don't know— I guess the fact that she didn't want me to feel guilty for getting her killed hasn't quite settled in, or ever will. I don't deserve to be let off the hook by the fact that she'll live forever."

He looked poignant, but I could see curiosity flare in his eye.

"It's what we believe, you know. That you don't really die."

"Yeah, I've heard. I...we had a servant who was a SubTerra who still had an old roll of paper where they tried to copy the words of the Bible when they were first banned. When most of you left for the Territory, the rolls were all that was left. They were on toilet paper, mostly. And to be honest, despite the ban on anything religious, we all understand sin. The rest of it, we dismiss. I sometimes hope there's nothing else after this life. I figured I'm going to the other place. Not...where Megan went."

I looked at him, and without thinking, I said, "That's not how it works. That stuff doesn't matter. If anyone, if God's son, ever loved you enough to die for you, why wouldn't you want to believe him? People can complicate it, Alex, but if anything divine or cosmic can touch you, at all, it's God dying. Jesus bleeding. Because it is spiritual, but it's real. And how, Alex, how can you risk everything for an idea, for the light, and not believe it?"

He looked at me, now through tears, even as he shook his head.

"But you…you don't believe it either. Or you wouldn't hate yourself. You wouldn't have just said you wished it was you who died. And you wouldn't be running."

Every voice that had been in my head that had been screaming fell silent.

And then a voice in my head, louder than any of the doubt, called my name as Alex said it out loud.

"Aislyn, I don't know if I could believe it if you don't."

All terror and shame flooded me. And then gushed out in tears and tremors, wrapped in his arms again. I realized my whole life, this was an idea. A thought. A theory. I needed it to be real.

In the instant I needed forgiveness to be more than a fairy tale, it became the truth I needed to save me.

A chained-up soul couldn't protect Vessels, Unnecessaries, or Alex. I had to risk faith. I had to be free.

I cried some more, spilling out the regret on the floor. I wasn't even sure what I said, because I wasn't talking to Alex anymore.

I spoke every sin, hoping it would leave me.

And in the second I was free, now believing everything I had ever uttered in my soul, my eyes snapped open.

The world might as well have stopped. I felt clarity, as if shame made everything a shade darker. But the filter was gone.

Everything was brighter. I had sunk onto the floor. Alex was beside me.

"Hey, how long was I out?"

"You weren't out. You were just mumbling. It was actually…" He didn't look worried for me, but I was temporarily embarrassed as I told him I couldn't stay awake.

I caught more flashes: the marble floor, the gold railing, the door. I jolted when he opened the bedroom door and rolled back the blankets.

"I'm sleeping on the sofa downstairs. I promise. Don't worry."

And so I didn't worry, and fell into dreams that were hauntingly beautiful blurs of everything and everyone I had ever loved.

I should feel dead inside.

I should feel self-loathing.

I should feel unimaginable guilt.

I didn't feel any of those things anymore. It was the only proof I had that the voice in my head was real.

It was all the proof I'd ever need.

CHAPTER 30

Proof.

The word hung in the air as I woke, stirring in the bed, staring at the red painting I had sent him.

More proof. But of what, I was uncertain.

It felt strange to be alone in a huge room. I quickly rushed downstairs. I wasn't sure what I would find, or where he would be, but hunched over the counter in concentration was not on the list.

"Alex, is everything okay?" I was about to say his name again when I noticed the packages on the counter. There were several boxes, but the most noticeable was the tiny box with the cylindrical shapes along the outside.

"Alex?" I eyed the package, looking back at him, taking caution and making sure I was looking at his eyes.

"I told myself I could dump it…I did. Well, the first one, and then…I was trying too hard, and I felt too angry, and it broke. There's some… glass over here…"

"Okay, I'll clean it up." I moved forward, trying to act as naturally as I could; nonchalant even. "Can I do anything else?"

He hesitated, and then lowered his head. The counter shone, almost too bright for the dark thoughts looming over it.

"I want to think I'm strong enough to do it by myself, but…"

"I'll dump the rest, Alex. If you want me to," I said.

I would have been glad to smash them into a million pieces. I hated that the Society could get away with so much because they encouraged people to veil pain, not allowing any emotion to break through. I waited patiently, making myself stay still.

He started talking to himself, whispering, "No, you don't need it…you saw her…you don't need it…."

I spoke some of the words I had said last night. Then I waited. After a minute of silence, he turned to me, focused and alert.

"Aislyn, dump it."

I took the package, opened up all the vials but one, and dumped them all within a few seconds. He exhaled as if in pain. When it was over, he got up, free from whatever demon had attacked.

But I wasn't that naïve. I had field med training, so when he saw that the last vial wasn't drained and I was holding it out to him…

"No," he said. "I just want to…"

"What? Have a horrible headache? Throw up all day? Get chills? Go through more horrible symptoms of major withdrawal? By all means, that sounds like it will be very helpful."

He sighed, took a gulp, leaving about half, and then said, "Dump the rest. That should be enough to help me concentrate."

"On what?" I asked as he moved over to the side of the counter with his MCU. There were images on the wall, with an image sewn in seamlessly, almost as if it wasn't screen.

There were names. Numbers. I recognized them.

The facts that came with no answers.

Alex held the card in his hand. I stared at it. I hated it. It might as well have burned my hand as I got it back.

"Do you recognize any of the names?" I asked.

"Only one, but…I think there may be more questions answered than we could have imagined, because…he disappeared. His name was Neil. He was a designer. His wife Sonja…"

I felt the familiar nausea of guilt. "She was my Vessel. Did–"

"Two weeks ago we arrested him. They were going to question him, but…" He trailed off, leaving me to follow the trail he had started earlier. I found myself sitting down on the chair beside him, and reaching for the carrots on the counter.

"So, his name is on the list. Do you think…"

"This is the disappeared list. I think that's what you found."

"Great, I found a list of dead people."

But even as I said it, there was something disconcerting haunting the words I had just spoken. And one look in his eyes showed me it had already haunted him for hours.

"But…why is this intel so vital? Why keep it hidden?"

"Well, there's one reason," he said. "You see this note, and this marking," he said, as he showed me some crude 'v' shapes with lines and dashes. "They are dates, from…"

"Roman numerals," I said, looking at them while speaking to myself more than him. "Wait, these are all from just one month?"

"A lot more than even I would expect. Maybe they include all the lab babies as well. But maybe if someone knew this many people were dying, it might activate some kind of rebellion."

"People know they die. Their names would make them care?"

"Look, Aislyn, you gave me a picture of my cousin, and I can't get it out of my mind. It's changing everything. And it's going to matter...whenever you feel...like you can tell me her name."

He paused, waiting. Maybe afraid I wouldn't say it.

"Caleigh," I said, smiling. "Her name is Caleigh."

He smiled, though there was a hint of embarrassment in his eyes. "It's beautiful."

I nodded, still not quite believing what we had discovered. I was feeling more satisfied that we hadn't risked our lives, losing Megan, for nothing. Collin's mother had died to get this information to us.

"Speaking of people who have died for this intel, your trainer: You think it'll matter that he knows what his mom died for?"

Alex talking about him brought my heart to a dizzying rate almost immediately.

"Yes, I know it will," I said, imagining Collin's reaction.

"Do you think he'll want revenge? You don't think–"

"No, he's too calm for that. He's...good. He's really..."

I trailed off, remembering the calm of his eyes. For the first time, I was struck by how much I missed everyone. But as I lost myself in that desperation, I realized I hadn't spoken. Maybe Collin was back at Central, moving on. Even if he loved me, in the end, he thought the mission was more important. We were done. But I wasn't sure why that fact wasn't stopping me from wanting to see him again.

As I turned to Alex, he was already typing, ignoring my silent one-minute trance. "I'm sorry...I..."

"You don't have to explain, Aislyn. I get it. He sounds..."

I almost asked him to clarify, wondering if what he thought of my sudden absence of conscious thought, but then he asked, "There was no copy of the images at all, right?"

"No, but she said they were there. It seems like a waste to take pictures if they're just killing them."

He looked contemplative before shrugging. "You're right. That doesn't make sense. Well, I'll think about it on the way."

"Where?" I asked, worried that my reaction had set him off.

He downed a green vial next. I recognized it: Recharge.

"Work. You can wash up and change– I got about a dozen outfits for you on the counter. I guessed your size, but then ordered a few more items, including," he paused to pull a box out, "these black market contact lenses for a certain Unnecessary. They'll be going in a coffee cup within the hour."

I scoffed a laugh. "You wonder how I could care about you? You basically go around saving lives all day. You know...last night? Did you hear what I said?"

He threw me a warning, but playful smile as he left. "I did. I thought about it. A lot. And we can talk some more later, but I just need to get there on time. She can barely see without them."

I leaned in on the counter.

"Please be careful."

He smirked and said, "Always."

The house was different alone. I found it hard to relax, even after sleeping, showering, eating. I did go exploring, at one point. I touched every fabric, looked at each piece of art. It was one way I could know him better. If it really was a way to know him better.

But I had a feeling it wasn't.

So I did what I always did when I felt restless.

I wrote.

It was hard at first, but I found the way to turn the fireplace on. It helped to be in familiar surroundings, something like home.

I messaged Rebecca a few times, reminding her to drink water. I had just finished a huge journal entry on my MCU when he came back in. I was reviewing the names of the deceased on his huge pristine wall, hoping he would bring more hope than what I was seeing projected right now.

But then I noticed the contacts lens box was still in his hand.

If it was still in his hand, she wasn't there.

He looked deflated, pale, and troubled. With all his power, all his money, and all his effort, he had lost the life he was trying to save. I didn't know what to say. I just reached out for him.

He threw the contacts in the fire, and then after that took a seat on the table across from it. Then he pulled something out of his pocket. It took me a second to realize it was a weather-beaten coffee cup. He pulled money out of it, pocketed it, and held the cup in his hands silhouetted against the fireplace. I wished he would throw it on the fire, because I had the sense that it was terrorizing him. He spoke as I moved closer to him.

"How I silently rebel. I think you've noticed by now. Sometimes it's more subtle. I try to convince myself it matters…"

He stopped. His breathing was uneven as he continued.

"Last year, there were two. The bottom alley at the 9th Street Café Dornon, and the girl on Beech Street, with the most beautiful eyes you've ever seen. One was half green, half aqua. The year before that, the boy you saved. Almost twenty have died, Aislyn. And then …there was another boy with seizures a year ago, like the one you saved, only…" He trailed off before looking at the cup.

"This cup's two weeks old. I hoped it was a fluke. But if they aren't there to pick them up, it means they're…"

The Unnecessary hadn't collected it. Because they were gone.

"She's dead," he choked out. "I tried so hard. What for?"

I held his arm, moving close to him, but knowing what I was about to say made me keep a little distance between us so I could concentrate.

"Alex, did it matter to you…when I kissed you in the hallway?"

He stared at me, curious about how that kiss was relevant.

"Did it matter that I wanted to show you that you could be loved?" I said, asking him in a way that I hoped would induce him to be honest.

"Yes. I didn't even want you to, but yes...it was like..."

I didn't wait for him to continue.

"Don't you think they felt that, Alex? Loved for? Cared for? Part of an outrageous, almost insane effort to keep them alive?"

I reached out to take the cup from him.

"Loved. I get it. I still wish they weren't dead," he said.

Maybe it was because he used the phrase when Megan did, but the phrase echoed again.

The dead aren't dead.

"Not to be morbid," I said, hoping it wouldn't set him on edge again, "but couldn't you check and see if the girl was picked up?"

"No. There's a different database. It's not a part of a Sentry's protocol to record anything. This list that you have? That's the record. But if I tried to check it back at base, I would get blocked by protocol Sem-141."

"What?" I asked quickly.

"Semsiol is the term for all protocols for the disappeared. They are a special branch of police, even politicians. It's even in the–"

"No...I mean, I know." I stopped, just to ask him a horrible question I hated myself for asking. "I know you just implied you don't know, but ...where do the Unnecessaries go?"

"What do you mean?"

"Alex, they don't shoot people in the streets. They don't kill them in cars. They don't burn them in incinerators. The smell of human remains–"

"I smell the labs, Aislyn. It's wretched. What're you saying?"

"Where do they go before they die?" I said intensely.

"We drop them off at the station. Then they are taken by the police in the Semsiol division. They deal with it. They drug them. They take them out on stretchers."

"Where?"

"Why is it important? They die. Everyone knows they die!"

I stared at the wall, but I imagined the stars that I had seen months ago. Their massive energy and light burning through space to reach our eyes only to be blocked– mocked by a wisp of air and water. It made me thing of all truths that were lost.

"You know, I think we all stop asking questions. Either because we feel like it's unfair to ask, or we just live with the reality. But I think, for the first time, I know why I'm here."

"Why?"

"To ask. And Alex, this question should have an answer. If we find that answer, it may give us a chance we've never had before."

He looked confused, and then I watched as his eyes slowly widened, pried open by the dread that was seeping into me.

"I wonder…if that's what Megan saw. Maybe she meant…the dead aren't dead yet," he said, looking ominous. "Alex, do you think we could still save them? If we could find them?"

He opened his mouth, but a reply didn't come out. He pulled my hand in as he reached out to cradle my head and pull it into his shoulder. He pulled me in, and was still for nearly five minutes. I wanted to urge him to say something. Then I realized I already knew what to say: the phrase I should have never forgotten.

"It's the part of the story you can't see that will give you hope."

I was two bites into my sandwich, trying to ignore how good it taste, when I had to put down the report Alex had given me and find a way to argue with him. Again.

"I still think this is a horrible idea."

"Well, I haven't heard that before," he sighed sarcastically.

"No, I mean...look what happened to Megan. Anyone who gets this information is automatically targeted, and..."

I trailed off. He closed his eyes in response to the possible end of the chapter we were now writing. But before I could choke on my silence, he spoke.

"It was your idea to find out where they go. This is how we find out. How do I download to this storage card? Is there a special way to encode it?"

I sighed. "No. It takes the data, copies it, and starts repeating it a few seconds back. It masks the satellites looking for it."

He cursed and said that was amazing. I rolled my eyes, and turned away to watch my screen again. I was reviewing dance moves, almost cringing. For the first time, I wished that he was an Elite. An Elite Spectre Day party was simple, with little dancing.

"We have the device; we have the party...I have the codes to access Ramien's computer, assuming he has what we're looking for as an Elite council member. We copy it, and we get out."

He reached his arm out. I closed the screen, but the music continued to play. He led me over to the area between the kitchen and the living room. Watching was over, and it was time to practice. But even as he reached out and spun me playfully he asked, "So, tell me something I don't know about you."

I laughed, hoping he wasn't serious. But he continued, "You don't have to tell me about training. The Academy and all that."

"Alex, I should've told you this a long time ago."

"Oh, here we go..." he said, still playful. "You have six toes? You like to sing in the shower? You have a boyfriend? You like scrambled eggs but hate fried? You hate mornings?"

I laughed again, despite my nervousness.

"Really?" he said after a few moments. "Tell me."

He was too close to avoid, and even as he corrected one of my steps, I said, "Well, I think you know one thing. They don't normally teach Protectors this fluently in dance."

"So what? Did you start at the Academy early or something?"

Here it was. The thing that might break any credibility I had.

"I never went to the Academy, Alex. Ever."

He stopped, even after slowing at my words.

"Wait? You're...you're a 27th?"

"You know about the 27th?" I asked, somewhat defensively.

"Yeah, but I didn't know there was one this year. I mean, we missed the memo. I'm not sure where the intel comes from. All

503

we know about them, really, is that they tend to be specially trained in one area, are randomly picked, and they tend to die–"

He stopped short. I shook my head. "You should know your chances for getting through this. Everyone should get a pep talk before they risk their life."

I was trying to look away, but his eyes drew mine back to his, provoking a hope I had not felt in a long time.

"I'd rather it be you. You're more…alive than they are. More than me."

I laughed then, only because I remembered Eldridge's words. And then, wanting to explain to answer his puzzled look, I said, "It's just something our leader said, before we all left a few months ago."

"What did he say?" Alex looked intrigued.

I was temporarily mad I couldn't remember the entire speech, but I remembered the meaning behind it.

"You don't have to be a hero. You just need to be alive enough to discover what matters. And once you know, you'll fight for it."

I paused. "And while I think he meant it for me, I was thinking of every way you think you're not good enough. And it infuriates me, Alex, because you're alive enough to see what matters. And you do fight for it."

"But they still die…they still…"

"That doesn't change who you are," I said, almost too close to say something so personal. "You're not who they say you are."

He leaned in, still moving me with the music, but pulling me into his chest, holding my head as he kissed me where he first did, on the top of my forehead.

He whispered, "Don't say it, Aislyn. Please."

How did he know? I was falling in love with who he was.

He took a breath. "I'm trying not to hate who I am. But who I pretend to be is the only hope I have of escaping them. Being someone else, in plain sight. Saving you."

"What are you scared of then? I mean...other than the usual—"

"I swore I would never, ever buy my commission. I'd rather die. But the pressure is getting too intense. The questions are coming more frequently. And I'm in more danger of losing myself than ever before."

I was searching for something to say, but I never got a chance.

There was a knock at the door. I turned and froze. The marble suddenly felt colder beneath my feet.

"Alex?" I whispered, trying to sound calmer than I was. But it didn't. Because it was like that gravity I felt in the warehouse and in the elevator shaft.

His hands squeezed my shoulders reassuringly. I felt them shake as whoever it was knocked again. After the knock, there was a light that went on over the door. It read, "Food Service."

"I didn't order anything," he said, his eyes full of fear.

He took a determined breath. Then he moved so quickly I could barely keep up. He was holding on to my shoulders, taking one arm off of me to open the door, to swing it open, and to push me inside a dark room that I assumed was a closet.

"Alex, just don't answer. Please!"

"It might look suspicious if I don't. It might be nothing."

"Alex, you can't do this just to–"

"I'm locking the door. Stay quiet, stay down. No matter what."

He hesitated, and then leaned in to kiss me quickly. Then he let go, pushing me away from him.

I heard the door close and lock, but my eyes were still closed.

In the darkness, I tried to concentrate on keeping my breathing even and quiet, so I could hear every noise outside of the door.

An instant later, the door opened.

I heard a voice.

"Where is she?" It was muffled, accusing, angry, determined.

And yet...it was almost familiar.

"Who?" I could hear his voice more clearly. It was still very calm, nonchalant, innocent.

"The Protector. Where is she?"

I froze. I recognized the voice. But that couldn't be her....

"I don't know what you're talking about." He sounded perfectly clueless and detached.

"Tell me where she is. Now!"

That time, I heard it clear.

It was Brie.

I knocked on the door, pounding on it.

And in an instant, I realized that was a bad idea.

I heard a shot, heard a knife clatter on the ground. A second later, he grunted and I heard her strained voice and a thud.

She thought I was being held against my will.

He thought she was here to kill me.

I began to scream, not sure if they could hear me as I raced towards the door, trying to open it. There was a scream.

The third time I ran for the door, something began to crack.

There was more scuffling, and thuds. There was gasping.

Someone I loved me could die protecting me. That one truth burned in my head as I charged the door one last time, feeling it finally give way. I yelled the moment I was out, even as I was still falling and hit the floor.

Brie was in the middle of a kick that Alex blocked, only to be blindsided by Brie's quick turn and elbow to his ribs. His breath was knocked out of him as he reached for his knife.

Brie called my name.

And then he froze.

"How do you know her name?" he said, heaving breaths.

He glanced at me as I yelled her name. He must have realized who she was. He put out his hands, trying to gesture for her to stop, but without hesitation she kicked the knife out of his hand, pulled out hers, and slashed his chest. Deep enough to draw blood.

"No!"

He was already talking to her as she approached, his hands were up, walking backward to the wall. "I didn't know who you were. I thought you were here to kill us. I hid her. Please!"

"Brie, put your weapon down. He's not a threat."

"Aislyn, I don't know what happened–" Brie started.

"He didn't do anything to me, and he's not keeping me against my will. We were trying to– wait, how did you know I was here?"

She was still walking forward, forcing Alex back to the wall as he stared at the knife approaching him.

"Michael's been watching the location. You've been missing for two weeks!"

She was speaking to me as she stared at Alex when his back hit the wall. She reached out the knife to below his throat, making it impossible for him to move. My heart was pounding in my ears.

"I thought you were sent to kill her. I'd never hurt you if I knew who you were," he said, struggling to swallow. Then he added, "Especially you."

She looked curiously at him when he said that, but there was still doubt in her mind. His hands were still over his shoulders. His breath was shallow so the blade didn't pierce him.

I asked, "When you called my name, what did he do?" I decided I would have to lean on her powers of deduction. "What did he do?"

She sighed, and lowered her knife as she turned to me.

"He put his hands up…and he surrendered."

He breathed easily, letting out a cough from holding his breath. Brie sank to the floor, her adrenaline draining.

She turned to stare at me accusingly.

"See what happens when you don't check in?"

CHAPTER 31

I was on my fifth apology by the time Brie had finished her second glass of water.

"What were you thinking?" she yelled, pounding the cup on the counter. I watched as what little contents that were left almost exploded out of the cup, concentrating on that as I spoke. I couldn't look at her eyes. They looked like they were on fire.

"I didn't think anyone would miss me for a while...since..."

"Since what?"

"I killed Megan."

"First of all, you didn't kill Megan. Second of all, even if everyone had declared you MIA, did you really think that Collin would just let it go? Or Sam? Liam? Michael? Patterson?"

"I promised Collin that I would never pursue this! He's probably mad at me, and– Eva! Abby! Is everyone else okay?"

"Ugh...yes. I feel like you almost don't deserve to know that for being so masochistic and locking yourself up here with...him." She eyed him up with disgust. "And then you almost made me almost kill him, just because he was trying to keep you safe."

Alex was listening, but wasn't hiding his confusion as she continued. He started to ask something, but she put her hand up and said, "Not yet."

He looked at her, grimacing as he sat down. She continued.

"When we all got back and Eva called in, Michael and Patterson went crazy searching for you, Will was a mess because of Lynn being alive this whole time, and Collin was...well, it was like last time. Then, Michael started watching Alex. He noticed the clothes order. Third of all..."

She paused. Alex had been trying to take off his shirt to clean his wound, but now that he had it off, it looked much worse. There were lines of blood running down his chest. I was trying not to look at the huge scar on his stomach. I was about to interrupt when Brie suspended her accusations to ask Alex, "Are you okay?"

He was cringing as he replied, "Yeah, just...second shelf. White cream and a towel. And a few questions?"

She opened the drawer, found the cream and the towel, and threw them at Alex. She sighed, "Bleeding get's you a few. Go."

"When was Aislyn supposed to check in? Is Warren okay? He needed a high dosage. Why don't you have a copy of the information you stole? Who's Michael? Patterson? Collin?"

She looked annoyed, but began to answer him.

"She was supposed to check in. When we check in is none of your business. It's what keeps us alive. Yes," she softened a little, "We realized how bad the seizures could get on the way back. Eva handled it, and he is fine now. We upped his dosage," her edge returned. "And no, we do not have a copy of the intel. Michael is the tech geek who always monitors you. Patterson is who you probably think he is from the way you said his name. And Collin is Aislyn's trainer, who also happens to be in love with her."

An awkward silence spread over the next few seconds, and I found myself wishing I had a few seconds before she burst in to explain who Collin was. But I was more distracted by my need to correct the lie she had just spoken.

"Brie, he doesn't love me. I know…what he said—"

"Whatever he said to you when you left was a lie. He hasn't slept or eaten in days. He's threatened to leave the compound to come find you, but I got him to promise to let me find you first."

"What? No! He doesn't love me anymore! No one can!"

I realized that I sounded like Alex, even as his eyes hit me with conviction. But I had to ask her, "Collin knows the mission specs? What we were searching for? The Basement? He knows…the promise I broke."

She looked at the counter, sighing as she said, "He does. I'm sure he was mad, but love usually sees right through that. It doesn't matter. We've already forgiven you. Even Patterson. Call it…your own personal scandal of grace. We just want you back."

I felt a rush of overwhelming guilt as Alex stared at the same spot on the countertop.

"Wait, how did you get here so fast?" I asked.

"They dropped me a lot closer to the border than normal and I ran the entire twenty miles over the course of the day."

I sighed, and in the silence that followed her accusing look, I decided something.

"Well, after all that, I suppose you deserve to know."

"Know what?"

"What we found: the truth with no answers."

I told her that the list was Unnecessaries on death row, shared our plan to get the next of the missing pieces of the intel, and reviewed our prep for the party on 5th Street on Spectre Day. In the middle of the conversation, Alex's package arrived for the day. He drank a swig and then began to dump the rest, with Brie watching curiously, but also threateningly.

"We have a plan. We were just working though it…"

Alex finally spoke. "But we may finally have the missing piece we need."

"What do you mean?" Brie asked suspiciously.

"Look, the problem with the intel is the same thing. Whoever hacks into this intel is a target. And it seems almost rudimentary to have the person who hacks in also hold the intel while trying to escape. But we can't transmit it far, either. Brie, if you stayed within 5 miles, we could transmit the location of the Unnecessaries who are still alive, and you could get it back to the Territory undetected."

"Yes, but then…there should be someone to run interference and tech for you on site. So we'll have to wait."

I was confused, but then asked, "Eva?"

"She should be here. She's late. She's not responding to any of my messages. I'm trying very hard not to worry right now."

"Well, assuming that it's just us three, it can still work," Alex said, but then made a point to stare at her until she met his gaze. "But you will have to trust me. I'm not sure you're capable of that."

Brie shook her head. "That would require a reason why. Come to think of it, why do you even trust me?"

"You tried to save her. You tried to save her. Emmy. And you saved the baby. That was you, right?"

She glared at him, which was probably the opposite of the response he might have been hoping for and said harshly, "Yes, I'm the one who helped your sister after you abandoned her and said you didn't care if she or her daughter died. That was you, right?"

Her tone was like the ice in her eyes: bitter, cold, and as unrelenting as the pain she felt. I knew it was only because she was angry that she had to trust him, but she asked in an accusing tone that made me want to hit her, "That was you, right?"

There was a pause. Maybe she thought he would react more defensively. She seemed surprised by his hesitancy to speak. Finally he said, "Yeah, that was me."

He pulled the towel off, staring at his blood on it. I could tell he was spiraling again. I wanted him to say confidently, *"That's not me anymore."* But he didn't.

"Alex, you're still bleeding." I didn't know if he noticed, or perhaps I wanted to make sure it wasn't a simple mistake that he had stopped applying pressure.

But he just stared at his counter.

"Yeah." He sounded defeated, but not dramatic. He asked, "Um…do you want to get my MCU? For the building layout? And I want to check, to see if anyone has picked up…Eva, is it?"

"Yeah, I'll grab it," I said. I shot a critical glance at Brie. She rolled her eyes before looking at Alex. He was blinking rapidly.

I was at his MCU in the other room when I finally heard movement. Brie cursed under her breath. I turned to see her pick up the towel and press it against his chest. He winced, looking confused at her moment of compassion.

"This is the only apology you're going to get from me, so…."

"This is an apology?" he said, wincing again.

"Yeah, well, considering I still have plenty of reasons to…"

There was a silence that followed, intense and brooding. I tried to ignore them as I pulled up the building specs.

"Do you…" He hesitated, maybe afraid of her reaction. "Aislyn only had one picture of her. Caleigh. Do you have any more?"

"Yes." She answered coldly, and I winced at the finality of the tone. He didn't ask again, leaving an awkward silence behind.

I continued to type, and then slid him his phone. It was far too awkward to know what to do or say. She had moved a few steps backward as she put the towel down. As I was putting the body glue Brie had gotten me on his wound, he was staring at his phone.

"What are you checking for?" I asked.

"Anything out of the ordinary, any unusual activity…what does she look like?"

"She's younger than any of us. Only 15. You sometimes can't tell, because she's really confident. She's short, brown eyes, shoulder-length brown hair. It flips a little…"

Brie pulled out her MCU and showed him a picture of Eva.

He continued to concentrate, looking more worried, as Brie made her way over to me, looking at the list again. I wanted fresh eyes to make sure I hadn't missed anything.

"Okay, I'm going out. I'll see if a patrol saw her," Alex said, looking at his phone as it beeped. "I'll leave the other phone…"

"Where are you going?" Brie demanded.

"Work? I'm not scheduled, but I'll make an excuse. It's the best way to find her. I have a few runs to do. Not that it matters. They will all probably end up dead, anyway."

Brie hesitated, sighing loudly as if she didn't want to reveal something.

"Alex, did you have one…who needed the contacts?"

"Yes? Do you mean…Did you–?"

"Erica got her. I saw them on my way back. She couldn't see well enough for them to walk in the forest. She mentioned the cup was supposed to come that morning but she had gone swimming at school. They fell out. She couldn't go home. Erica found her in the alley a mile away, crying because she couldn't make it. The shuttle that dropped me off picked them up."

"And she's okay?" He looked at me, full of suspicious hope.

"She's fine," Brie said, almost a little unsure of his reaction as he hugged me. I squeezed him, almost tearing up, knowing what it meant to him. In an instant, he said, "Thank you," as he turned to hug Brie.

It was about two seconds before he realized that was a bad idea. He pulled away from her stiff body.

"Sorry."

"Never touch me again," she almost growled. "Ever."

"Got it," he said, sounding only a little nervous, but then smiling again. He mouthed "wow" as he turned around. I walked over as he headed for the door, and he turned to me and said, "You going to be okay here? Alone? Or…with her?"

"Yeah, why?" I said, realizing he was nervous because of the way Brie just acted. "She's not really that scary."

He gave me a playfully suspicious look. "Six hours."

I nodded, and then he left. Brie got every knife out and laid it on the counter. She claimed she was just cleaning, but she kept staring at the doors and windows.

"Brie?"

"Just being cautious," she said warily.

"Brie? At this point…"

"Fine. We'll trust the murderer. Anyway, if you're right, and I think you are, I'll take the chance you're taking. I don't like Alex. You probably could tell. But if we can find a way to save hundreds of Unnecessaries, I'm in. You don't need to convince me with any big speech or story. So, what do you want to know before I crash?"

"Just go to sleep, Brie. Everything else can wait," I said, but almost without meaning to, I blurted out, "but Collin."

I couldn't say anything more than his name. But in response, she said under her breath as she turned around, "And I knew it would be that."

She didn't say anything. She pulled out an envelope and slapped it against the counter.

"Is the couch okay?" She eyed the living room.

"Yeah. I'll let you know if I hear anything."

"Read it and have your cry or whatever before I wake up. We need to focus if we're going to pull this off." She jumped on the couch, leaving me staring at the white envelope on the counter.

I found myself waiting an hour to open it, pacing and afraid for what was in it, feeling like opening it would bring no relief, but only more torture. But in the end, I loved him too much not to open it, even if I risked every heartbreak imaginable.

Aislyn, I can't write everything I'm thinking. I'm copying this letter for the second time and giving it to Brie. I hope you get the first one I sent with Eva, but just in case....

There was a pause in the letter, reminding me to take a breath instead of holding it.

'Just in case' is why I'm writing this. Just in case you forgot, you have Unnecessaries praying for you. Just in case you didn't know, Sam and Liam are searching for you. Just in case you forgot, Megan was brave and she signed up for this. It breaks my heart that she's gone, and that your heart is hurting. I know, maybe even more than Patterson, why you need to make her sacrifice mean something. That is why I think you are staying, and I just hope it is that and not shame.
Just in case it's shame, fight it. And come home. You are not at fault. You are still you. Too many people have died for this. And please, don't. Eva and I don't care if there aren't answers for our parents. We'd both rather have you.

Michael and Sam found you– it was Liam's idea to follow Alex. I hope he's fine now that he knows you're alive. It was hard to watch his reaction when he thought you were dead. It was like looking in a mirror. For what it's worth, I trust him now. I trust his grief. And just in case you thought that because I made the decision to choose the mission over you that I would never regret it...you should know. You were wrong. I regret everything I said to you much more than I thought I could. I wanted to tell you...but your heart shouldn't be won by my regret. I'm not asking you to love me again. You may never be able to even trust me like you did before. But you should know... just in case. I am now convinced that I could never lie. I could never say I didn't love you again.

    I stared at the paper for about ten minutes. I did notice that on the bottom, there was something added at the last minute about telling Lynn to come home if we saw her again, but I almost laughed at that. She was even more committed to finding answers than I was. When I thought about her passion, I found mine paled in comparison. I went over all the dance moves, browsed over all the specs for the building, and read profiles on all the guests.

    I kept moving around to stay awake, but as I went in the other room and found Brie sleeping, I felt weary. I was struggling to stay awake until I lost the battle only a few minutes later, closing my eyes to keep from being paralyzed by the fear of running out of love for those who I needed to Protect.

I woke a few hours later. Brie was still out, and I was temporarily soothed back to sleep by the familiar sound of pans and plates somewhere behind me. It was familiar, so it soothed me back into a nap.

Until I remembered I had left the letter open on the counter.

I jumped up from the couch, running until I saw Alex standing over a pan of roasted chicken. There was something coming up from the service chute next to the counter. It looked like a vegetable, steamed in a strange case.

"Aislyn? Are you okay?"

"I'm fine. Bad dream," I lied, scanning for the open letter.

It was back in the envelope. I glanced at it, and then at him.

"I won't lie. It took a lot of resistance on my part to not read it. But I put it away. It's not for me to read. And it...it shouldn't be any of my business."

"Alex?" I said it, much weaker than I wanted to sound.

"We don't need to do this, Aislyn. When you talked about your trainer...I think I've always known it. I didn't have a chance."

"Alex, Collin and I...kind of had a rough time. I didn't think he cared about me anymore. And then, I broke a promise."

"What promise?" he said, sounding guilty. "About me—"

"No, it's not what you think. His mom died trying to infiltrate the Basement seventeen years ago. He was only a baby. He made me promise never to go after the intel, even though..."

I trailed off, but Alex knew. "He still wants to know what happened to his mom. Wow. That's intense."

He looked like he was digesting the information, even as I was trying to explain without sounding like I was making excuses.

"I thought we were done. If he pushed me away before I lied to him, there's no way we had a chance. I didn't think he still loved–"

Alex cut me off. "I trust you enough to know you aren't trying to hurt anyone, Aislyn. And not me. But I knew Linden was right. For all the wrong reasons, he was right. I'm going to lose you. You can't be mine. No one can be mine."

I started to shake my head, but he stopped me. "Aislyn, it's true. And you know what, I say I love you. But I don't even know what love is, really? And I can tell you're torn. Where does that leave me? Or you?

I took a breath, and even as I told myself there would be no lies spoken to him ever again.

"Torn. I do feel…torn. You deserve to be loved, Alex."

His voice quivered. "That's a reason to be my friend, Aislyn, but not to give up the person you love. Just choose him."

I scoffed a laugh, and he looked up. "You know, he said the same thing. Maybe this wouldn't be so difficult if you two weren't so masochistic and complicated."

He laughed once, but then his hand reached out. I collapsed into this arms. I shuddered as he spoke, whispering in my ear.

"I'll be torn with you, then."

He let go, kissing my forehead. I could have stared in his eyes for hours, but his eyes turned towards the couch.

"Speaking of complicated, is she always..."

"Brie? Complicated? Yes," I said matter-of-factly.

Then, in a panic, I asked, "Wait, how long has she been out?"

"About...seven hours? Should she be awake by now?"

I put the letter into my pocket, and watched her on the sofa.

"No," I grimaced. "She is awake right now."

"What?" He turned quickly, looking as self-conscious as I felt.

"She breathes a little slower when she's truly sleeping. And her shoulders freeze so it looks like—"

"Okay, fine," Brie said, and snapped her eyes open.

"Having fun catching up?" I asked her, feeling a little betrayed.

"Well, it wasn't as bad as I thought it was going to be," she said, standing up and taking long strides to me. She spoke a little lower, "He's not as bad as I thought he would be." I turned to see her get to the counter just in time to ask Alex for water. Alex reached down under the counter to get her a bottle and push it towards her.

"Anything on Eva?" she asked him, eyeing him warily.

"No, nothing out of the ordinary," he said, looking worried.

"Because the ordinary is so pleasant," Brie said harshly.

"Were your...kids...okay?" She asked out of genuine concern, in sharp contrast to her first sentence.

He shrugged. "Guess so. Cups from last time were picked up."

With the slight edge to her voice gone, we gave her more details about the Spectre ball. Brie was much better at the mechanical logistics than I was, and even though her conversation with Alex was very short, and snide comments crept in, they were much better at planning a cohesive mission. We went over several scenarios, which made me nervous, because with her there, it felt familiar, just like it was the last time– with Megan. And I wondered why I was doing this again. Why wasn't I just saving a Vessel and heading home? Why didn't I just grab one of Alex's Unnecessaries in an alley? Why was I about to risk Brie's and Alex's lives? After a moment, I realized they had both stopped talking. They were both staring at me, blankly, waiting to hear the thoughts in my mind.

"We just earned back the right for this to be simple. We should just go save an Unnecessary. We should just–"

Alex interrupted me. "These are Unnecessaries. I know what you're afraid of, but they shouldn't be left to die, not when we have a chance to save them. That chance was costly. Let's not waste it."

"He's right, Aislyn," Brie said, getting my attention just because that wasn't something I ever thought I'd ever hear her say.

"I just can't believe no one has ever figured this out," I said.

"Well you said it. The Republic lies. At least, that's what you wanted me to believe about what Palmer said."

"Are you referring to the claims about the Serum?" Brie asked. He was a little tense now, maybe a little annoyed by her constant jabs at him. I knew this was still a reason for him to doubt what had happened years ago. But I really didn't want him bringing up the Serum. I wasn't sure if it would be impolite for me to explain quickly to Alex that Brie was still a victim of it. I almost felt too exhausted, physically and emotionally, to intervene.

"Yes. I had my doubts," Alex said, but he must have sensed the mood change, because he added. "I'm sorry, the effects of the Serum must be horrible—"

"They're dehumanizing," she said, boiling with anger.

"Well, there's a vaccine. For the Serum. Doesn't that—"

"It doesn't solve every problem."

Her voice shook at the end. He looked up at me. I wondered if he had figured out why she had said that.

"Well, I'm sorry. But that's no excuse to call it dehumanizing."

She looked up at him, now either livid with rage or pain, maybe both. She spoke with fury instead of pain, though.

"They never get married, you know? They never live a normal life. They can't. They're worthless."

He stared at her, now shocked but also confrontational.

"You can't say that. You, of all people, who save those others push aside, should know that they are worth more, not less. I think they would be seen as braver and stronger."

"And why would I know that? Why would I see anyone who didn't have the vaccine as anything more than a hollow shell?"

Brie asked accusingly, maybe wondering if I had told him. But I shook my head. She caught the movement in the corner of her eye.

He stepped toward her, stopping until she was looking at him. The mask of rage was off, and her eyes were starting to glisten as she held back tears.

Alex shook his head, his eyes locked on hers as he continued.

"I don't think…anyone believes that. Or you wouldn't be crying. I think they all know something. There is no brighter light than the one that shines from a soul who has almost had their light stolen. I would count such a person better than me in every way. I think she would be the bravest person I knew."

She finally breathed out, after holding it in as he spoke. She blinked her tears back. "What if she wouldn't believe that?"

Alex looked at her with a kind of sympathetic reverence before saying, "I'd hope she would. Endlessly hope. And I'm sure…I wouldn't be the first."

Her voice evened and she swallowed back what was left of the choke in her voice. "I'll take that opinion under consideration."

Brie murmured something about needing the restroom, and left in huge strides. I got up off the stool and moved it closer to Alex. He turned to face the screen again.

"Alex, you caught…what was happening there, right?"

"Oh, yes. And you yell at me for being self-loathing. So she…she can't ever…"

"Have kids? No. She can't."

"Is it really that bad? Do people treat them…like outcasts?"

"No, not really. Sometimes I'm sure they feel left out. Sometimes it's awkward, when they have a friend who has children, at holidays, but they're never abandoned. Many of them do get married. Some adopt. Everyone copes differently. Brie just…she finally got to a good spot where she was going to adopt an Unnecessary, but she can't seem to stay there. Her own despair keeps dragging her under. It's an identity thing, like you wishing you could avoid being an Elite forever."

He looked from his MCU to the doorway she had left through.

The look in my face must have answered his question, and he continued, "Was she going to adopt Caleigh?"

"Yes. Which is why, with you, she's so…"

"Complicated," he said, swallowing while trying to smirk.

I sighed, and even as I reached over to put my hand on his shoulder, he sat up straight, suddenly rigid.

"It's not complicated."

"You just said it was," I said, confused.

"No." He was up at his keypad. "If Eva is fifteen, and were picked up, they wouldn't believe she was a Protector. They'd…"

He was still on the keypad when a new screen popped up on the display. He logged in as I resisted the urge to stop his concentration.

"Not report her." He paused for a second, but then looked back at the MCU, and yelled out for Brie, even as he held out his hand to me briefly, only grazing it. This didn't help, but made me instantly more fearful of her fate.

"What is it?" Brie asked, any hint of the previous conversation having melted away.

"I think….I found Eva."

With a click of a few buttons, the display was on the larger screen in front of me. And he cursed. Repeatedly.

"The list. I didn't check the list," he said in a disgusting tone. "Alex?" she threatened, but her voice sounded more fearful than intimidating.

"She's on the list. I'm almost certain that's her."

I instantly caught the emphasis he had placed on "the list," but was unsure of the context. For whatever reason, he seemed to think Brie and I would understand. I was about to demand an explanation when he continued, "Thirty minutes ago, three girls got added, one as a fifteen year old. Most are thirteen or younger. Two have been sold to clients, three to middle-men."

"What are you doing? Why don't you–"

Alex was picking up items, and went over to a drawer to push out a coded key. He punched in a few numbers. "I already missed any chance to intervene. The person who bought her is a middle-man. I have to try to get to him before she goes to a client, and hope I get to him before anyone realizes who she is."

I was starting to realize what the list was.

I felt more scared than I had ever been for her. I wanted to scream, but Brie was the one who spoke first.

"Alex, I need you to get to her before the first sale."

"I don't know if I can make that. I have a better chance–"

"You need to!"

Brie was shaking. I had heard Eva once speak of her worst fear, which wasn't dying, but what was about to happen to her right now: that her soul would die if her body were sold. She obviously had shared her fears more with Brie, who was continuing to yell at Alex.

"Alex," I added, "you need to fix this. It'll destroy her. She said once that she'd rather die." I felt as desperate as Brie looked.

He put his hands in his hair, moving them down to the back of his neck. He was rocking slightly, but Brie hadn't asked him to move. Finally, he looked at me, his eyes filled with more pain than I would have thought possible.

"Do you need me to do whatever it takes? Even if it messes up the mission? No matter what the cost? If you tell me to, I'll–"

"Yes," Brie interrupted. Her jaw continued to shake. "Why won't you do it?"

He covered his mouth with his fist, staring at me in a despair I couldn't understand.

"Because I'd have to believe I'm not who they say I am."

He cracked his neck, cursed, and went to his MCU. He pulled up a file I recognized immediately. It was his monetary account. I was relieved that this was the next move, but also wondering at the cost and how it could possibly mess up the mission. I think I imagined that he was going to have to make a huge sacrifice, wondering if I would see it empty by thousands. Even as he was typing something, there was a beeping sound. He put the phone on speaker, and asked to be transferred to Trakovic.

"Alex Sanderson? I didn't ever expect a call from you."

"Please hurry," Brie mouthed to Alex, who was starting to shake. He looked away from me, as if I knew something that was about to happen. I could tell he hated the words that he was about to say.

"Yeah, well, you usually don't a fifteen-year-old girl," he sounded playful, using the arrogant tone I hated so much.

"Alex, you don't have first bids. That's for Elites only."

I opened my eyes wide, wanting to scream "no" as his hand hovered over the computer.

But he had to save Eva.

I knew it would kill him inside. He never wanted to be this.

He looked at me, with the same surrender as I fell down the elevator shaft. I reached out my hands, wanted to prompt him not to hit the button. But they shook in fear.

His hand reached out to the button, and pressed it.

His monetary account plummeted. It was nearly empty.

"Yeah, well obviously you haven't heard. I just bought my commission."

A small jolt making him lean forward. He started to sink down on the counter.

"Wow! Okay, she's yours, Alex. You going to have something for me? Other than promises? I don't take credit, you know, not even for Elites."

"Fifty thousand. It'll be cash."

"That'll do the trick. She's a handful; hope you're ready."

"She's not been touched yet, right? That's what it says—"

"Yeah, if you want to ensure that, it'll be sixty thousand."

"Done," Alex said, heaving a breath as the phone died.

Alex moved extremely quickly. He pulled out a weapon and said, "Forgive me."

"For what?" I asked.

"For all the stuff I'm going to have to say, and be, to save her."

Waiting can be horrible, even if you have hope. Any hope we had was flowing away, as if down a drain. Alex had to make another call to the middle-man confirming the sale, and had to use incredibly vivid and crude language. I was terrified for her, knowing everything she must be fearing; being sold over and over again to any man with enough money to have her.

I swallowed, or tried to, but it kept getting caught because my throat was too tight. Brie was silent. Any conversation we had was about Alex's fear of becoming an Elite. I tried to help her understand. She looked more contemplative than accusing.

It was a long hour before his comm on the counter beeped. The display read "shuttle phone." Brie pressed it before I could even point to it. "Is she okay?" she asked quickly.

"I think. No one else touched her. I got there…you know, in time. But she looks like she's about to vomit."

"Eva, can you hear us?" I screamed into the speaker.

The only response were ragged breaths.

"Brie? I can…I can hear you. Can you…code in?"

"I just had that happen to me last Friday in the café," Brie said, matter-of-factly, and very clearly. "You're fine, Eva, we're –"

And then the sobbing came: acute, louder, and more pronounced. It sounded like she was probably struggling with her tied hands. I heard Alex say, "Do you want me to get it?"

"No, I got it!"

"Are you sure? I can…"

"Don't touch me! Ever!"

That was followed by a string of obscenities Eva shouted at Alex. I wish I could tell him what to say, to know she was safe.

"Eva, I know you don't trust me–"

"I trust you. I know you…I just…I don't want…"

The tears, screams, and cursing continued. Finally, he said, "I'm just going to let her cry it out. I'll call you if I need to."

Brie hung up the phone.

Even though we had silenced the phone, the last thing we had heard was her sobbing. The sounds echoed in me, shaking me.

I wanted so badly to kick them out of my brain.

The door opened minutes later, and my arms were around Eva instantly, even as she said to back off because she had been sick. She kept shaking and heaving out sobs until her voice was hoarse.

Alex went into the other room after a few moments. It was twenty minutes until we got her to move to the couch and got her to change. Alex had left water on the table, and we struggled to get her to drink. Her eyes finally opened, to reveal not a darkness, but a void. I was afraid she was trying to hide it until…

"I'm so sorry. I got caught. I was just…"

Brie held her until she stopped muttering. Eva touched her forehead, finally emotionally exhausted.

"I'm tired."

We helped her get up the stairs and onto a bed in one of the spare bedrooms. The room had two sofas, and Brie said she would sleep there and watch Eva. I told her I would sleep on the other.

"Is she okay?" Alex's voice sounded tired. He leaned on the doorframe with one arm. His bloodshot eyes were hardly open, and his arms were shaking slightly every few seconds before they would tense up as he tried to control them.

"For now," I answered honestly, but unsure of what else to say.

"I know what you meant now. She kept…she kept repeating…love is real. Over and over. You were right. She'd rather die than be sold, like a pawn. I know how she feels. Because I'm their pawn now. I'm…"

Alex was going to be an Elite.

Eva was in horrible shape.

Brie was still completely unable to trust Alex. I felt pulled inward, not wanting to worry about Unnecessaries. I just wanted to protect the people in this room from the heartbreak that was now ripping us open.

"We're not giving up. I got her out so we wouldn't give–"

He couldn't finish. He trailed off, leaving the last of the hope with him trailing behind us as he turned and leaned his forehead on the door frame. I moved towards him, stepping forward to hug him the moment before he broke. He was shaking, and I felt his temperature was high. I pulled away, feeling his forehead and looking back to Brie.

"It's not just emotional exhaustion. I mean, I'm sure it is, but…" he wasn't looking at me anymore. His eyes were dilated.

Brie was already taking his pulse and pulling his eyes open, surprising him a little, but he seemed too exhausted to care.

"Withdrawal. Do you feel nauseous? Is your throat tight?"

He nodded. He pressed his head against the wall.

Brie shook her head. "Pulse is threading, and then it's…" I said, even as he almost fell on me.

"Move him to the other couch," Brie said, moving to support his other side. By the time he was there, he was shaking.

"Alex, we can get you a little, just enough–"

"No, I promised. I'm done. I was going to be done with all of this after the ball. I was going to escape. I was going to…"

I touched his forehead with mine as he trailed off, once again willing him to find some kind of peace I couldn't bring him, praying he would find it. But there was one overwhelming thought I had to voice: the one thing I had felt like I had heard the morning I woke up free.

"You're not who they say you are."

The phrase shook him to his core. I could see it in the tears that formed and the way his face contorted, as if every doubt was a wall to be broken through. So I repeated it, for twenty minutes, until Eva was repeating it. Until the wall fell, the bricks of lies dispersed, and the shaking slowed with the rate of his breath.

Finally, he spoke. "You should get some sleep. We need to…"

"Alex, I'm okay. I–"

"Need sleep." Brie was the one who spoke. "I'll keep watch for a few hours, and then I'll wake you. I'll watch him, too. I promise. If he seizes again, I'll wake you. Until then, I know what to do."

I detached from where I had bent down beside him, moving up to the other couch. I saw Brie take an ottoman and move it over to Alex. The last thing I heard before sleep crashed into me was her echoing my words: the truth I hoped she could believe.

She reached out to touch his forehead.

"You're not who they say you are."

CHAPTER 32

The next morning hurt in every possible way.

Except one. The lonely-fear was gone.

We were finally all together.

I awoke, and for the first time, was certain that I didn't have to worry about Brie. Maybe it had been what Alex said before he'd left. Maybe had taken Brie repeating the sentence over and over again last night. But I had a feeling she was going to stop taking jabs at him every few minutes. They were both missing when I got up from the couch, so I went downstairs. Brie was eating breakfast.

"I woke up a few seconds ago," I said, moving across the cold kitchen floor. "Alex. He's not–"

"Bathroom. He got sick about an hour ago. I didn't want to wake you. He had to take some, but we lowered the dose again. He's not too happy with me about it. He probably felt a little…"

"Tricked?" he interrupted, emerging from the hallway, looking half-annoyed, but smiling.

"She was talking, saying something really deep, and spiritually profound. Then, she injected me when I least expected it."

"It was fun," Brie said sarcastically. "We almost had an all-out fight again. I got to hear some wonderfully diverse language before he calmed down."

I looked at him warily. "Are you okay now?"

He nodded, almost smiling. "Feels like it. Just drained. Not very fond of my doctor, and not quite up for forgiving her."

"Well that's good," Brie said, "because I'm not up for apologizing. Meanwhile, we've spent the last hour pushing all of that 'fun' to the side and...coming up with a new plan."

"What? There can't still be a plan."

"Well, here's the deal. He can't go to the party you were going to go to, because he's a qualifying Elite now. That party was for Citizens. It would be considered below his rank."

"But I'm a new Elite, and wouldn't usually be invited to a party thrown by someone on the Board, who would have more intel."

There was a sound in the delivery chute near the center of the counter. A few seconds later, a vase with flowers came up. It wasn't until then that I noticed there were several gifts all over the counter.

"I'm guessing...all morning?"

"Yep. It's to...congratulate me. But it is what put the idea in my head. Mavery is one of the people that sent gifts. I think he knew my father."

"Okay, what's the issue?"

"Well, the first issue isn't a problem; it's a gamble. He's an Elite. He's on the Board. But...he's the chief financial officer of the corporation that makes agricultural machines. He's more detached from the whole process and anything central to the Society Party, I would think. We'd have to hope that being on the Board would afford him a few key information points that would be present on his MCU. So that's a huge risk, because..."

"He may not even have the intel we want. I get it. Second?"

"I don't know him. So to get in, we'd have to hack into his system to get an invite. At the party, no one will kick a standing Elite out, probably. He did know my father, I sent a public thank you for his gift this morning, and he responded. No one will be overly suspicions, but that being said…"

"We can't draw attention to ourselves or his staff might remember that we aren't on the guest list. Got it. Anything else?"

"We've barely got enough money for me to be debuting as an Elite. I'm in withdrawal and having occasional seizures. Your friends barely trust me. Becca just messaged me. She's having contractions every two hours. And we don't have anyone who can hack in to get us invites, because Brie's been trying and has…"

There was a beep. Brie lowered her head on the desk.

"Has failed again. So, unless you know someone…"

"Eva?"

He thought at first I was suggesting her, but then I got up and moved to hug her. She felt warm, but not feverish.

"I'm fine. I felt better after I showered, that's for sure." She was quieter than normal, but the tone of her voice wasn't as low as it was when she was panicked. "I could use some more water."

"Yeah, I got it," Brie said, standing up quickly.

Eva looked calm, but wasn't looking at my eyes.

"You okay?"

"Yeah," she said. I pulled up her chin to meet my eyes. Her lips quivered for a second, but then I saw her take a breath. Maybe she thought I wouldn't look at her, see her the same way.

"Nothing happened, in the end. I'm not saying that to be defensive, but I don't want anyone to feel guilty. I just got so freaked out. I realized what was going to happen when they started talking about everything and I…" Her voice started to fail again. "They told me…you know what? Nevermind. It doesn't matter. Then, they told me a Sentry bought me. I thought maybe it was Alex. But I was terrified if it wasn't, or if you were wrong about him. Then they kept saying…"

"Eva, we never have to repeat it. What they said, what you said, any of it."

She sighed, a shudder running up her spine. "And that's the worst part."

"What?"

"I yelled and cursed at the person who saved me. I called him…" She paused, looking more sure of herself. "Where is he?"

Alex was headed back in the room and was already saying something about getting a recharge on a comm when he froze. He put the comm down.

"I'll head back up for that, then," he said, looking warily at her. "I wrote down the safest way back to the woods, Eva, so…"

"Thank you, Alex, but I'm staying."

"What?" Brie said, returning with the water.

"Look. I can tell an op when I see one. I've slept for 6 hours, I feel fine. I really do."

Alex protested, and I was about to, when Brie interrupted.

"Prove it."

Eva looked up at her, only to have Brie repeat, "Eva, prove it."

There was a challenge in her icy eyes. I thought this was odd therapy, but then I remembered how familiar this was to her.

"Alex, what's your least favorite piece of furniture?" Eva said, in a playful tone, as if nothing in the last 48 hours had happened.

"The green chair?" he said, still looking at her skeptically.

Brie took out a knife and threw it up in the air. Eva caught the handle and flung it at the chair, hitting it in the center of the back.

"I'm fine," she said confidently.

In the silence that followed, Brie smiled, I probably looked as uncertain as I felt, and Alex seemed shocked at either her abilities or her recovery time.

"Eva, are you sure you're ready?"

"What, you want to give me another knife and ask Alex which piece of art looks like the worst rip-off interpretation of the early French impressionistic revival from twenty years ago? It's the piece over the fireplace. I still like it, though."

Alex scoffed a laugh, Brie rolled her eyes, and I hugged her again. She pulled away, now turning to Alex. His eyes were filling with regret, but she put her hand up as he started to talk.

"Don't say you're sorry again. I heard you the twenty times in the shuttle ride here. You're sorry, I'm sorry, we all get it."

He nodded. "So, friends?" He reached out his hand, then quickly retracted it. "That was silly of me; I didn't–"

"Don't take anything I said about you never touching you again seriously. And you aren't…everything that I called you. I should have never said all those things to you, after you…"

She looked truly calm, herself again as she said it, swinging her arm out to him to shake it. He took in a breath and held it for a moment, letting it out as he shook her hand.

"And you owe me a chair." He smiled, making her laugh.

"So, is there a plan, or are we just winging it?"

A few hours later, we had gotten the specs on Mavery's second home. Eva had also replicated a storage card for Brie, so the data would be secure after it was transferred. But our fear was still transferring it securely. That was the biggest chance we were taking. Alex was going over the file again, listing the things that were unusual about the invoices that Megan had gotten.

"So, these are not matching?" I asked.

"No," Alex said. "It looks like it, and then…see, they become abbreviated here, but then they are all re-classified."

"Maybe it's—"

"Eva, don't get distracted by worrying about that. Worry about tickets."

"It's going to be fine. It'll work this time."

There was a noise from the red square that blinked behind her as she looked more irritated than ever.

Alex moved close enough to whisper to me.

"Did you practice the new moves? We shouldn't have to dance, we're in and out, but…"

"I think I got it," I said. "Besides…it won't matter if–"

Eva cursed again. Brie scolded her for her language, to which Eva replied, "Fine. How about instead of cursing, I just tell us all the truth. Nothing else can go wrong at this point."

Almost on cue, there was a knock at the door. Everyone froze except for Eva, who kept moving and said, "Stupid consequences, never missing an opportunity to prove me wrong."

"You weren't expecting anyone?" I asked, unpocketing my knife as Brie pulled out the one in my boot.

"No," Alex said, tense and looking at Brie, and then at Eva. "But it could just be a package. Hopefully."

But then there was another knock, followed by the voice that shocked me.

"Alex?"

Brie turned to whisper, "Who is that?"

I breathed in, opening my mouth in shock.

"It's Becca."

"Wait….Palmer?" Brie whispered.

"Yes." I said, heading for the door. But in the instant I started for the door, Brie cut me off.

"We have a mission in five hours. We don't have time."

"We at least have to let her in. Brie, she's dead if she gets caught, you know that!" I urgently whispered. Brie bit her lip.

"I just got– wait, who are we letting in now?" Eva asked. I noticed that she finally had a green light on her screen.

I paused, turned to look at Alex. He was grappling, probably with the risk and the timeframe.

"What do we do?" he asked me. I gestured to the closet. He nodded.

"In the closet," I whispered to Brie.

"Yeah, because that worked great last time," Brie whispered sarcastically.

I threw her pack at her and headed for the door, and by the time her angry glare hit me, I realized the one door was missing. But it was just as well. We just needed to be out of sight, but I wanted to hear what was happening.

There was a click at the door, it swung open, and within a few seconds, there were footsteps in the hall.

"Are you sure you weren't followed?" he asked. We could hear her entering. She sounded out of breath.

"Yeah, I made sure…Alex?"

Her voice was weak. Something was wrong.

I went to move when Brie grabbed my arm. She pulled me back.

"I know what it sounds like, but just wait," she whispered.

Alex said hurriedly, "Becca, this is really, really bad timing, and…"

There was a sharp cry of pain. I could tell she was breathless.

Brie turned to me, now more sympathetic. She looked as if she was trying to debate what to do.

We heard Becca gasp again just as Alex said, with a panicked tone, "Um…why is there water all over my floor?"

My breath deflated. Brie let go of my arm, which she was squeezing, to sigh as her head hit the closet wall. Eva said, "what are the chances she just spilled a gallon of water?"

Then I heard Becca nervously ask, "who's here?"

"Like he said," Brie said as we stepped out into the hall. "Bad timing."

"Which means?" Becca stared at me in fear.

Eva shrugged. "It means we're winging it."

CHAPTER 33

My hands were holding Becca's sweat-drenched arm, trying to lead her to the living room while telling her she needed to sit down. In a quick minute, Alex came back with a lot of blankets.

"I feel like I need to stand, like I need to push."

"No, you need to fight that." I said it quickly, knowing that if she pushed at the wrong time, it could be the end of a natural childbirth. I was frantically looking for my pack as I turned and found it flying towards me. I caught it, and without thinking, searched for the sanitation powder. Brie already had the MCU out. The sani-powder dispersed. Alex looked around, slightly lost.

I started giving her instructions, but realized she needed more than that.

"Lean back on the couch, Becca. This is Brie, and she's going to check on the baby. This is Eva, she's going to check your progress. I'm going to give you something for the pain. Wait, why aren't you in more pain?"

"I took something," she said, starting to breathe louder and harder. "What in the world are three of you doing here?"

"You know that thing we said about timing that you're completely ignoring– albeit to push a six-pound human out of your…um…Aislyn?" Eva had the blanket over Becca's knees and was checking her progress.

"Pain killers aren't working anymore, and I really need to push," Becca said, grabbing me.

"They should be working fine. Don't push! If you aren't 9 or 10 centimeters dilated, you will make it impossible to deliver the baby naturally. And if we do a surgery, it will be really obvious what happened. Brie?"

"Um…Aislyn?" Eva repeated.

But Brie answered, "The baby's heartbeat is a little…stressed, but it's stable. The baby's really low, probably…"

"Aislyn!"

"What is it, Eva?" I snapped.

"We might make the party after all," she said.

I reached down to check Becca. She was fully dilated. The baby was low.

She should be pushing.

I was still in shock. "She's at ten. She's at ten. What the–?"

Brie looked at me and shrugged.

"It's certainly not the first hour long labor, Aislyn, and it won't be the last. Besides, she's been having contractions for days. If she took too much pain-killer, she's probably been in labor for hours."

Becca shrieked.

"Can't you give her any more?" Alex said.

"It's hard to explain, but it's not pain- it's pressure. It's called back labor. It's just very uncomfortable."

"Yeah, almost as uncomfortable as you being next to me while I'm delivering a baby," Becca said.

He rolled his eyes. "It's not like you have anything to hi –"

"Wait, you aren't the father, are you?" Eva asked.

"No!" they both shouted. Alex added, "It's been years since we were...No, it's not me. I can't believe who the father is, that you ever were with—"

"Everyone shut up!" Brie shouted. We were all listening to the heart rate. But there was another sound.

It was coming from Eva's phone. It buzzed with the same rhythm as the heartbeat, competing for our attention.

Eva turned to me. "That's my cue to get in position and finish getting your tickets. I need to leave or...."

It was 3:45. I felt panic crawl over my skin, but I found myself saying, "Go. Get cleaned up and go."

Eva got up. I saw her washing her hands in the distance as I watched the monitor.

"How do we do this, Brie?"

"I don't know. We can't miss the next window. I'm supposed to be leaving in less than an hour to get a head start. You can't go to the Spectre Ball with a baby."

"What is going on?" Becca said through strained teeth.

"We don't want to distract you," I said, wincing under the grip of her hand.

"Yeah, that would be stupid. Distract the woman in mind-shattering pain." She got her sarcastic comment out before screaming again. Brie's eyes were glued on the monitor.

"We have a mission. We've been planning for a few days. We are going to a party on 7th tonight."

"Mavery's?" she asked.

"What is it?" I asked, sensing she knew something.

"Nothing, just..." She was gritting her teeth, trying to maintain sanity through the pressure. "It's always....felt so weird that he's really involved. He talks to my father a lot, always secretive. He knows way more than a man in his position normally would."

She screamed again.

"You have to try to make it, Aislyn," she said.

The pregnant women, in horrible pain, was asking me to leave her. The only answer I could give escaped me.

"Okay. We'll try," I promised, squeezing her hand.

Contraction. I counted down from thirty, watching Alex call for Eva and said that the car was almost here.

Becca's eyes strained to see me. She nodded.

I left her, running to Eva.

Alex said, "Be careful," just as Eva reached out to grip his hand.

"Eva?" I cried.

"Crowning. I see the head!" Brie screamed.

My attention felt strained. I wanted to give Eva some kind of encouragement. I looked at her expression, calm and tranquil. She smiled at my confusion and said her next words breathlessly.

"She's crowning, Aislyn. Don't you dare worry about me. An Elite is giving you her baby. I only regret that I'm going to miss it: the birth of the first traitor. It feels like royalty and rebellion mixed in the most beautiful story you've ever written. Go write it. Make it good."

She backed up as she spoke, slipping out the door.

So I turned back to Becca. By the time I looked at the monitor, Brie was nodding, "She's not going to last more than ten minutes."

"Um…the head?" Alex stopped short, but was trying not to panic. I couldn't tell if he was about to vomit, smile, or cry.

"You okay?" I asked.

"Yeah, is it…supposed to do…"

I never knew the question he wanted to ask. I was hoping he would be able to handle what was about to happen next.

Brie screamed to push, and in that instant, I knew the head was ready to be coaxed out. The most tedious moments began. The most beautiful pattern: push, cry, push, breathe, push, reposition, push, pray, dream, push.

"Okay, here we go. Becca? Rebecca! These are the last few…"

"I can't. I can't push anymore."

Her head was circling, swaying without control as she said, "I can't, it hurts too much, this is too much. I can't handle it."

"Sweetie, millions of women have done this before," Brie said.

"But they weren't me! They weren't here!"

"No! They weren't. But you are," I paused, hoping she would believe me. "But if you don't push, Becca, all of this is worth nothing. All the secrets you've kept, all the lies you've told, all you've pushed already for this child. This isn't just revenge anymore, and now you know it. So push…"

Brie stared at me. The words seemed to hang in the air, dripping with the significance of the moment.

"For the love you didn't know you felt, push."

Becca shrieked a few times. I yelled back until the head finally came out.

A beautiful head.

"Coloring's good! The head's out! You need to keep pushing."

She groaned again. Brie and Alex were on either side of her, repeating everything she needed to hear.

"Rebecca, this is the hard part; I need you to focus. You need to keep pushing. There is only one more, you need to push as hard as you can. Just tell me when you're going to give that next big push, and we'll work together," Brie spoke softly.

I thought I might cry, but I refused the impulse.

I wanted my eyes clear. I didn't want to miss a thing.

My hands were shaking until I remembered who I was holding. They steadied, catching the beauty born in the turmoil.

I briefly looked at Alex. He saw the baby. His voice trembled.

"She's beautiful. She's already, beautiful, Becca. Just…"

Becca shouted, "Now!"

So it happened.

Pushing. Breathing. Screaming. Crying.

Bloody. Messy. Panicked. Frightened.

Perfect.

Her life fell into my hands. And I caught her.

She was cherished in every way every soul should be in those first seconds. Brie helped me clean her. I handed her off to Alex, whose expression I still couldn't read.

It was the same look when he learned the Unnecessary didn't die. Everything was possible as long as this baby was alive.

Brie agreed to deal with after-birth and to make any sutures with the body glue. We both knew, without saying, the risk of anyone ever seeing any scarring. No one could know.

Alex was looking at the baby, still amazed, when I finally asked.

"Becca? Would you like to hold her?"

"Just for a moment. Not long. I know…"

She lost her thought, but we could all guess what it was.

"What do you want to name her?"

She looked at me, like it was odd that she would get to name her. I thought she was about to say a name when she asked, "Alex? I know we all called her Emmy. But what was her full name?"

Alex looked at Becca in disbelief before answering.

"Emerson. Her name was Emerson."

"That's a beautiful name. She'll have that name. She should be named after someone braver than me."

Emerson started crying. Brie closed her eyes for a second, finally losing to tears but blinking them away just as quickly.

Becca looked down at her, cradling her. "But then her expression changed. "I don't want…I don't…I can't hold her anymore." She winced in pain.

"Do you want me to take her?"

It was the wrong question. I shouldn't have asked it. But she smiled through her only tears so far and said, "Yes. I do."

Brie whispered, "Aislyn, I need your help."

I gave the baby to Alex. I reminded him to support the head. He nodded, looking intently at her.

"Sorry," Brie said quickly. "I need to do this perfectly. Afterbirth is out, bleeding is minimal. Just hand me what I need."

"Yeah, I got it." I unwrapped the second surgical tool roll as well, pulling out a very expensive tissue regenerator that I had only seen once in a Q station. I asked, and Brie said, "Yeah, that was from Patterson, for her. We know there can't be any proof."

"Um…baby?" Alex asked, but a bit nervous. He almost seemed to want to know what he should do with her next.

"The baby is exhausted," Brie said knowingly. "Once she feels secure, she'll fall asleep."

"What should I do with her next?" His voice almost faltered.

"Just sing," I said without thinking, like it was obvious.

"Sing what? I don't know many baby songs."

I looked at him, temporarily lost for how to describe a lullaby when Brie said, "Just think of something innocent and something about stars. It seems they're all about wishes, stars, puppies…"

She squinted in concentration when she trailed off. A few moments later, Alex began to sing.

"*Stars in the sky,* um….*lalalala.*"

I looked over at him. The tune wasn't horrible, but he was fumbling over words. He kept singing "*lalalala*" until a few more words later.

"Dadada something until night is nigh. Then something..."

Brie asked me for more glue. Becca's lip trembled.

"Something...lalala ending happens and all of it by and by."

His voice was hypnotic. He seemed less confident in his abilities.

"Try again."

He looked at me in desperation, then back to the baby. Even as little Emerson pulled an arm free from the blanket to reach out to him, he looked at her lovingly, but almost apologetically.

"I don't have a song."

His eyes met me, tortured and desolate. He was across the room, but I was afraid his fear and his grief were taking over and pushing him miles away. I didn't know what to say.

"Alex?" Brie paused until his eyes reached her. "Try again."

She looked far more determined, almost defiant at him. He took a breath as the baby cried.

"I see stars in the sky..."

Sutures. Brie was biting her lip, back to working. Alex stalled, searching for words.

"All wishes made were flying by..."

Brie breathed out through pursed lips, in concentration. Alex was staring at Eva's pack in the hallway.

"They will reach the star to try, to try...."

Becca winced as Brie rubbed her stomach and explained that she would have to do this daily. She nodded. A tear fell. I injected a painkiller that wouldn't stop the pain I knew she felt.

"Lalala....That comes true."

Silence.

The baby had stopped crying for a moment.

"Before the sun is nigh."

Brie whispered, "She's done." Her jaw was set as she moved her sweaty hair out of her way with her forearm. Her lip trembled.

"The wishes flying by…."

We took the gloves off and Brie started folding the blankets. Becca stood up slowly. She held on to me a moment longer than it took for her to stand up as I injected her with a few more meds.

"They will reach the stars to try, to try…"

Becca grabbed her bag and headed into the bathroom, looking determined, yet broken.

"To catch a star so it comes true."

Brie stopped cleaning up. She looked up to where Alex. Maybe she already knew it wasn't going to be me.

"Brie, you're going to have to…."

"To hope it doesn't just fly by, For out there it flew…"

Alex pulled the baby in closer. It was the only movement in the room. And somehow all of us felt it. The baby's arm flung, wildly catching the air and then curling up again.

"You want me to take the baby, don't you?" Brie whispered.

"And the wishes that were wished for you…"

He faltered. He must have realized what we were planning, because his focus was now on Brie, his eyes locked on hers, in silent grief. He nodded, mouthed, "It's okay." He took a breath.

"A star will catch them just in time…for the dawn is nigh."

He kept singing. We kept cleaning. She went to check on Becca, who was doing surprisingly well with the medication and the body glue. Compared to a normal birth, there was minimal bleeding. I also did a quick check, and told her some basic drugs to stay on and off of for the next few days.

She stopped me. "I didn't think it would be that hard."

"It's difficult, and your body…"

"No. Not that." Becca was staring at the sink. I stumbled to think of something to say. I wasn't sure how attached she was going to feel, in the end. But I could tell she didn't expect this.

"Now I know why can never have children. They would never want us to feel anything this strong. I thought I did this to prove him wrong, to save her life, but now I–"

"He's wrong. She'll live. And now you'll know. But…but you know what going with her means." It was just short of a threat.

She nodded at the words I hated myself for speaking. She bit her lip. "I wouldn't do that to you. I did want to ask you, are you going to Mavery's in a few hours?"

"We're…" I looked in the mirror, about to say, "running out of time." But I realized I was out of time. My face was a mess, my hair was worse, and my confidence had been sucked dry.

"Here, this should help."

She was sending a message to someone, and then shocked me by taking my picture. Before I could argue, I heard a phone ringing and someone answer.

"Paul, I'm going to be sending you a new client. She has money, and what she doesn't have, I'll cover you three times over. Be nice."

She then proceeded to throw money on the counter next to the sink. The voice on the phone said, "I'm processing her picture now," as my brain processed that she had given me three times what Alex ever did. They said something flattering to Becca, who didn't bother to listen to it before hanging up.

"You...you don't have to..." I started.

"Paul's on 2nd Street, then to the Marrioh for your dress on 3rd if Paul can't get it delivered from there, though he usually can."

I stared at the money again, feeling hesitant to take it when she said, "Wow, you people are weird. If I gave money to anyone else, they'd take in a second. Just in case you feel guilt– if, for some reason taking money for the service of risking your life to deliver and rescue my child wasn't enough, remember my other goal."

She looked at me, "And while it seems childish, I want to see you make him squirm. Because now, I know everything he's stolen from me. He's stolen this from all of us. He has to pay."

Whatever the last statement, calling Paul, or giving me the money had done, it brought her back to a place where she could return to her emotionally sterile world.

I walked with her as she headed to the door. But just as she grabbed her bag at the door, she half-turned to glance back, and then, as if she thought that would not be a good idea, she left.

By the time I came back out to Brie, the living room looked pristine. Like nothing had ever happened.

Alex would say life never happened in it.

I turned to Brie. "So you take the baby. We'll be able to relay the information out to you...just like we planned."

She nodded, still staring at baby Emerson as Alex sang softly in the background.

"Don't overthink this, Brie. Get Eva's pack, and leave us."

I was always frustrated by her ability to stuff her emotions in a box and keep moving, so I hated myself for wishing she would do it more effectively at this moment. She took a few steps forward, then stopped again. She stood like a statue, a silhouette in the late afternoon sun hitting the large windows. Alex and her seemed so timeless in that moment, like legends from a story I once read. We were taking the forbidden princess where she would be safe. I hoped that Collin would hold her, feeling every sacrifice made for her. Alex had gotten up, and held out the baby to Brie.

And I thought the reality had surpassed the fairy tale in beauty.

That moment when beauty overtook all despair, she began to sing his song.

"I see the stars in the sky..."

She put the back-pack around one shoulder. Alex held out the other strap and she pushed her arm through. She continued to sing the song, even as he murmured directions to go out the back door. Tiny Emerson was nearly asleep.

"We'll contact you," I whispered. "We'll get the intel to you, somehow. Just stay around the border. It'll be just in range. We'll hope for the best. If anything goes wrong...get her out."

Brie continued to sing. She continued to the door, her voice ringing through the now empty mansion as she pulled away from the aftermath. Even though I knew we didn't have the time, I was too desperate for the serenity in that moment to miss out on it.

"You know, anyone about to risk their life should probably get a pep talk," I said to Alex.

"I don't need one." He sounded as deflated as I was. But his voice was stronger when he said, "I don't think I'll ever need another reason to risk my life ever again."

We watched Brie walk backward through the doorway, allowing her words to echo through the foyer, shattering me with their overwhelming hope and fear.

"*All the wishes wished for you...*"

The last tear I allowed myself for Emerson fell from my wide open eyes.

"*A star caught them just in time, before the dawn was nigh.*"

CHAPTER 34

Reality pulled every other tear back.

"Time to work."

With only a little more than two hours to go, his words snapped my mind back to the three tasks at hand. Alex sent a message to Rebecca, confirming that she had gotten a taxi. I washed up quickly and called Eva. She told me that Vanessa was going to be there, so it was good Brie wasn't going to the party at all. I showed Alex the money.

"Oh, and she called Paul on 2nd Street for us," I showed him Rebecca's card and the money that she had left. His eyes widened.

"Oh, that's huge. I'm freaking out a little less now. A little."

Alex called for a shuttle, even though he had his. He held my hand in the car, more to comfort me than to convince the driver we were together. Only one minute passed by before he whispered, "take a few." His eyes closed, and he leaned his head against the seat. I closed mine and leaned against him, hoping the few minutes of oblivion would give me the alertness I would need in the next hours.

I had fallen asleep by the time the shuttle arrived. It took me a while to fully wake up, which was thankfully not an issue. Apparently, when someone went to see Paul, you didn't have to do anything. My measurements were taken, a dress was ordered while my hair was done. I got to close my eyes for a quick facial treatment before my makeup. I spent the time in concentration trying to remember the floor plan and dance moves. But I also allowed myself a few moments in the abyss of my mind, to think about Maggie's chalkboard, Gabriel's paintbrush jar, Katerina's pictures that she had placed in the sewer, and Emerson's small cry.

It wasn't until an associate was finishing my makeup while my dress was being laced that the person I assumed was Paul approached me and asked, "Are you satisfied, ma'am?"

"Yes," I said, and then thought of a more believable answer. "Maybe next time we could do something different with my hair."

"Yes, of course. Whatever you wish." He snapped at someone.

"Although," I said, staring at the lose strings of braids meeting in a bun, "this is one of those events when this classic look is best?"

"That is why we chose it, but I will make note of your preference for the latest looks for other events. Alexander is ready. It's been a pleasure to see him again. And going to an Elite event at last. You must both be very happy."

I remembered what Alex said about timing. And with the status of Citizens who are eligible to become Elite now public, I was wondering...

"Is it official, then?" I smiled, hoping that was the right reaction.

"As of an hour ago! I checked the status updates when I saw he was coming to see if that was why got the call."

He was still talking as Alex came in behind him. "Well, Paul, you certainly will never be accused of not being thorough."

"Not at all," Paul smiled.

I knew Alex was faking his excitement, but when his eyes met mine, he looked mesmerized. Paul waved, asking his masterpiece to spin. I obliged.

As Alex saw all of me, he repeated, "Not at all."

Paul smiled at that and escorted us both out, congratulating Alex over and over again. I knew he was strained, but he hid it so well.

We stepped in the shuttle. We finally had a chance to breathe. I used the term lightly because my dress was laced very tightly. He told the driver where to go, and at hearing the address officially, I felt my dress tighten even more.

"It's very convenient that everyone knows when you qualify to be an Elite. Then you can be treated accordingly." I was only half-sarcastic, thinking the driver would not pick up on it.

Alex looked at me, his green-eyes sparkling at my half-joke. He whispered, "It won't matter after tonight."

He put his arm around me and whispered in my ear where we were going. I had remembered, but his reminders helped me concentrate and not let my anxiety push me over the edge.

It was a grand edge: an elaborate, outlandish, and almost overwhelming edge, surpassing my imagination. Gold figures were accented by the shimmer in the frame of each piece of art.

I felt suddenly underdressed and under-prepared. Alex whispered suggestions for what I could say as some people would approach. I only had twenty Elite-language phrases memorized. For the most part, we whisked past people too full of self-importance to notice anything but themselves.

Except, one person tapped him on the shoulder. I saw her hand first, the wrist covered in bracelets. Before Alex had turned around, I had grasped his hand. Because I heard her voice, even before I turned around.

"Aislyn? I never expected to see you here."

I gripped Alex's hand harder, letting him see a glimpse of terror in my eyes as I said her name. Because the last time I said her name was at her funeral three months ago, mourning her along with the other Protectors. Now I knew who had betrayed them.

I know the Protector who had betrayed me.

"Sarah?"

I squeezed Alex's hand twice, paused, and then squeezed again. That was our code for "we're dead."

"And who is this, Aislyn? Fraternizing with the enemy?" Sarah asked casually.

I felt my lower lip quiver. I wished I could hide Alex; shield him from her, just in case she called me out in the middle of the room. I wondered if I could make Sarah believe that I was undercover, that my mission didn't involve him.

But then he answered her.

"I'm a Sentry. Alex Sanderson. And I'm guessing we have something in common." He said it as if he was flirting.

"What is that?" she said, in a mysterious tone, shaking his hand.

"We've both betrayed everything we've been taught since birth to become who we are. The only difference is that I did it to save lives. You did it to kill them."

Her eyes focused on him like darts. I shot a warning glance towards him. The last thing I wanted to do was antagonize her.

"I didn't do it to kill them. I did it because I wanted…this. And in our world, we can't just leave. This was the only way." She gestured to the room around her. "If you don't believe me, you should. For at least one reason that should be clear right now."

Even as Alex opened his mouth to speak again, I stepped on his toe. I ran through the story in my head, realizing something in what felt like a horrible miracle.

"We're still alive," I started. "You…you wouldn't want to lose what you have gained for a chance to reveal us. Not now," I started, even as images began to flash in my mind.

She was eleven years old. She was bored.

She was recruited. They showed her videos.

She wasn't passionate to fight them. She was passionate to be like them. And she had discovered the only way to get there.

So she acted disgusted. She trained. She learned. She got in.

But that would mean…

Alex caught on, and said, "You don't want us caught, do you? Your handler would wonder if your loyalty's been compromised."

"Not to mention the fact that it'll ruin a good party," she said, and then more seriously, "Look, I never wanted so many of them to die. I'd like to do one thing to make up for that." Her eyes glanced at my purse, and then she reached out to hug me.

My skin felt clammy and cold as she touched me. I wasn't sure if she was just nervous, or if it was my opinion of her that made her skin feel frozen.

"It's a transmitter, not just a storage card. You can safely transmit a cloaked message as far as the border, maybe beyond, so you don't get caught with the info on you here. I can't ensure your safety past that, but it means you'll get…whatever is here."

"We're in the right spot, aren't we?" I asked, as eerily as I felt.

"Let me put it this way. I just found out Palmer paid this guy an extra five million. Whatever he does…it's not farming."

She turned. Something in her body language told me that all loyalty and all connections would furthermore be lost. We moved past hundreds of guests and headed for the north hallway.

I was halfway down the hallway before I felt my shoulders fall a litte bit. I think I was scared at any moment she would change her mind and call us out. I had to try to find faith in her selfishness; that for her own good, she would remain consistent.

"Where are we going?" I whispered, holding my hand to my earpiece. I was hoping Eva could hear me. But I realized she could hear me the entire time.

"Um…I'm all for you going back and killing Sarah."

"Eva, that is not an option," I sighed.

Alex was looking around him nervously. "Eva, please."

She started giving directions. He grabbed my hand. Before I could ask him what he was doing, he spun in front of me, walking backward as he stared at me and behind me, ensuring no one was following us through the maze of hallways. But we looked playfully charming, if someone came out of nowhere.

And I could stare at his eyes, and forget where I was.

"Turn left?" Eva said, but sounded uncertain.

"Are you sure?"

"Yeah…I'm…sure." She kept leading us through turns, until we got to a hall with only one set of two mahogany doors. The art lining the walls was different than the other pieces.

"This is it," Alex said. A slight moment of hesitation took over both of us, but we both silently restrained it and stepped forward.

It wasn't until we closed the door behind us and turned on the MCU that the beads of sweat started to form on Alex's forehead.

"You okay?" I asked.

"Yeah," he nodded, and then said, "Eva, can you still hear us?"

The voice in my ear was muffled, but from the torn up sentence she repeated three times, she said she could hear us.

Alex sprayed something on his fingertips and the keypad.

"Is that…?"

"They won't track us that way. As long as Eva has video…"

There was a faint voice in my ear, but I then I heard a distinct phrase

"First phase through."

I forced my lungs to take a deep breath as Alex confirmed, "Okay, first attempt at the first password Brie hacked. It will last one minute. The second one that Eva got will also last one minute. We only have those two passwords, each lasting a minute."

I nodded, clicking on the clock on my phone. I knew all of this. We'd gone over it a thousand times, but I still felt shaky. I told myself the adrenaline would help.

"Okay, here we go," he said, as each finger weighed on the key pad, each touch lighting them up like a threatening beacon.

We both saw four files on the main screen. Alex instinctively went for the invoices, but I shook my head and pointed to the file I needed him to open.

"Security?" he whispered. "We need the transport file..."

"No, Alex. That's the file that's wrong. It's not supposed to be there. You said there are police that get them, that kill them. Why have security? Why have private guards?"

He looked from the screen to me, his eyes growing dark under his brow. "And why would anyone guard a grave?"

He opened it, and in an instant, the screen filled with a file of hundreds of names. Not a hundred. Hundreds.

"Way too many guards to guard a grave. Why didn't you–"

"They aren't police, Aislyn," he said, not sounding defensive, but haunted. "They're private security. He would be the only one to have the record, maybe, as chief financial officer and..."

"What?"

"Hang on..." he said, trailing off while typing.

He was searching the files for "incident report" while I imagined a horror story in my mind. I needed to imagine it to understand it, but it sickened me to my core.

"I just put the second password in...one more minute."

I looked up, even as I saw a report.

"Unnecessary left trailer, fought with guard…"

"Vessel moved to JW-903," he kept reading, "and she was given a sedative…Why sedate her?"

"Unnecessary moved to YOP-905. What do these numbers mean? Allergy to Typhlenerol. That's for motion sickness…"

"I have no idea." But then I got the sinking feeling that I was lying without knowing it.

"What?" he noticed my eyes, staring at the numbers.

"Alex, I've seen these numbers before. I've seen…"

Lynn's obsession.

Maggie's problem.

Lynn's blackboard.

I was mesmerized by the memory of Maggie's haunted eyes, her words echoing in my head.

"It doesn't work, Aislyn. It would never work."

"Something's wrong."

And at the moment that we only had twenty seconds, I shoved the storage card in the system.

"I just need the supply list for the trailers," I said, moving to copy just one file over. "The dosage for the motion sickness meds."

I saw the progress on the screen match the timer almost by the second. The pictures flashed. Faces. Trailers. Warehouses. I was leaning over Alex, seeing the sweat bead on his neck. I was holding his shoulder, right up until I pulled out the storage card.

Alex logged off and put the system on standby.

We both breathed out in relief. He was heaving, with his shoulders hunched as he held his head in his hands. He asked in-between his staggered breaths, "What….what are you…just for numbers? We have–"

"I know those numbers, Alex. I know why the chief financial officer of the company would have them. And I know why the Unnecessaries are assigned to those numbers."

"Yes, but that's after they're transported. We're supposed to try to save them before they die."

He was speaking as if he was worried about me missing the point. I shook my head, now seeing the incident reports and numbers that signified the worst secret the Republic had ever told.

"That's the point, Alex. They don't die."

"Then...what are the codes?"

"They're the parts…of the farming equipment, Alex. The codes are part numbers for the machines that supposedly produce every piece of food you eat."

"Are you saying…Are you saying there's no machines? That these people… make all of our food? The tranquilizer…"

His broken words were forming conclusions, just as my broken thoughts had. The most horrible images I could imagine were now paling in comparison to the reality I had just learned in this dark, cold room.

But in the dark room, one light now blinked.

"What's that?"

The screen had shut down after he had logged off, but now it was turning on. Eva was screaming something broken in my earpiece.

It was blinking red.

I held my breath as he sprayed the keypad again, and then touched one key.

I think he cursed. I didn't hear it. The blood rushed to my ears pounding through them, even as I strained to hear Eva.

"Eva, there's a log out code," he said. "It assumes the owner wouldn't put in a code to log out as well. And…Aislyn?"

I had already picked up his arm and began pulling him out the door. The timer on the side of the logout feature only had two minutes on it, and we weren't going to waste time guessing.

Once we stepped out of the office, Eva's voice become clearer. By the time we reached the end of the hallway, she had said she had already displaced. "If you can hear me, just get out of there."

"We got you, Eva. Where do we go?"

"Garbage chute. Closet to your right. I'm looping video still, but they'll find my hack in a few minutes, you've been in the system…"

"Stop. No, Alex, you aren't taking the garbage chute."

"What? Why not?" He looked worried that maybe I was losing my focus or resolve.

"I'm going down it alone," I said. "I'm going to send the transmission, before it's too late. You're going down to the dance, now. When there's a problem, you can respond. Like a Sentry."

"We have a minute people," Eva said in our ear.

"Okay," he said, but I could tell from his eyes he hated the plan, even as I climbed in the chute.

"I'll meet you at Rendezvous Four."

I was about to fall. He put his hand over mine, which was grasping the ledge to stay up. The situation was all too familiar to us.

He said, "I won't kiss you this time. I have more hope now."

He let go of my hand. In the same instant, I let go of the edge. I gave way to gravity, being shaken and jolted down the metal tube, causing bruises I knew I would see tomorrow.

I hoped I would see the bruises tomorrow.

It dumped me in the alley. I tore my dress on the side of the dumpster. I was careful to wrap up the pieces and wrap them around my hands. I didn't want to leave any evidence that could lead back to Alex. I ran two blocks before dumping my shoes.

That was when I heard the first siren. I didn't stop. I ran as fast as I could in bare feet. My feet were burning on the pavement, a familiar emotion of shame and hurt coming back to haunt me.

I tried Brie again.

"Brie, tell me you're at a station!"

"It's an old R station, but yes. Why?"

"This needs to get to Patterson. It needs to…Brie, the–"

"Wait, are you out?"

"Yes, and I'm sending you something."

"I got something a minute ago. What is this? It's just a chart!"

"Yes, for motion sickness medicine…" I said, while continuing to run. "Look at the amount per order. That's per person, Brie."

"That wouldn't kill them, Aislyn."

"I know, Brie," I said. "Each Unnecessary is assigned to a number. It looks like they are trailers, but the numbers match something. They match the parts on the farming equipment."

"But the farming equipment doesn't work!"

"Brie, think! Connect the pieces! The dead aren't dead."

I finally knew she understood when her tone changed.

"Aislyn, do you know what this means?"

I flashed back to Megan bleeding, thought of Eva's father choking, and Collin's mother dying alone. I knew what each of them saw moments before they died.

I now felt what each of them did.

"It means there are thousands of people who are working as slaves. It means we waited too long before asking questions. It means we never saved the people who needed us the most because we were too busy mourning them. It means…" I trailed off, taking a breath. I wasn't able to continue. It was Brie who spoke in the earpiece, through the growing static.

"There's nothing more dangerous than the truth you don't know."

CHAPTER 35

In the minutes that followed, I kept telling Brie everything Alex and I had seen.

"How do you know this line is secure?" Brie continued.

"Long story. It starts with Sarah and ends with her wanting me out of her hair."

I stared at my other phone. The other phone holding a message.

"*The place I found you the third time.*"

He sent it just in case I forgot where rendezvous four was.

"You're still moving, right?" Brie asked nervously.

"Yes. Did you send it?"

"Yes, but there's been no response."

"Brie? Just leave. Get this to Patterson. Get Emerson out."

"We're not leaving you alone again, Aislyn. You didn't go home the last time we did."

I stopped for only the third time since I had started running.

I began to walk down the alley behind the building, about to go into the abandoned section outside the city, when I heard a noise. I froze, slinking back instantly against the wall.

"Get to Alex. Then I know you'll try to get out." Brie was still talking in my ear, despite the fact that my silence was crucial.

I tried to remember exactly where I was. This was the building I had hidden in, where he had found me. I remembered the relief that washed over me when he had found me.

It felt the same way when I heard his voice this time.

"Aislyn?"

I took four strides to reach him. I reached up as he pulled me in his arms. But before I could even say his name, I was talking to Brie.

"Alex is here," I said. "Brie, you need to—"

There was a squeal in the ear pieces. Eva was on the other line.

She was yelling.

"I hacked into your feed. Sorry. Aislyn, there's chatter and a lot of police headed your way. Check the storage card."

I pulled it out.

The light was blinking off and on.

Then off.

It flickered once more, the light flickering and then softening, mocking any chance we had left.

"Lynn didn't mean for the battery to last that long. Ditch it."

"It's the only proof we have," I argued.

"Is Patterson going to need proof?" Eva asked.

I shook my head, even as Brie said something strange.

"Alex! The coat in the closet is colder than the air."

I was utterly confused by her statement. Until Alex grabbed the card from me and shattered it on the ground.

"What was that— Brie, stop making contingency plans!"

"Sorry, Aislyn, your self-preservation button is broken. Besides, I have the copy that you sent me. I confirmed it."

I didn't argue. I heard the sirens as Alex pulled me up of the ground where I had hovered over the shattered pieces.

We sprinted up several floors, including the one I had hidden on before. Alex was drenched in sweat. We finally reached the seventeenth floor. From the moment I opened the door, I was taken aback by the strange room before realizing what it was. It was a pool. It was at least two hundred yards. It was an empty void of tile, long abandoned. It must have been one of the public bath houses that were popular a century earlier. There were shower stalls that lined the wall. The curtains were all mostly open, but some were closed.

Alex cursed, grabbed my hand, and we ran for the stalls. Alex pulled as many curtains closed as he could. We raced to the end of the row. We were hoping for a Sentry who was too incompetent to look carefully. We pulled almost every curtain across every stall.

Until we heard the door slam downstairs.

Alex nodded. We ran into one of the stalls. Alex had drawn the curtain, but I wondered if our effort was in vain. Any good officer would check behind all of them.

I was trying to be quiet, but I risked a whisper.

"What happens now?"

"Their procedure is they sweep the top and bottom floors with the most agents, then send the rest onto the other floors. We can't attack the officer who comes in. They check in every 30 seconds, and if they don't check in, they send everyone up to their location."

His eyes were darting around, as if searching for answers in his own mind and not being able to see them.

"We're cornered. They haven't brought in thermal which is the only reason that they don't know exactly where we are. It's only a matter of an hour for that. This unit is made out of Semsiol recruits. They use them on the outskirts for a reason."

He began a checklist in his mind, shutting his eyes. He squeezed his eyes together, trying to think of something.

But it never came. A light came from the building across the way. They must have been searching both. His squeezed his jaw, but looked like it could tremble at any moment. His eyes shimmered. He couldn't say it, so I had to.

"We aren't getting out of this, are we?"

His eyes locked on mine. He took a breath to speak, but only shook his head, and in the smallest, slightest whisper, he released the answer.

"No."

My first thought was the despair everyone must feel before they learn they have only minutes to live, but the next was panic.

Especially when he pulled out a black pill from his belt buckle.

"Listen, Aislyn, you don't want to be captured by these guys. They are sick and twisted. They will torture you. Or worse."

I looked at the pill, shaking my head in disbelief he was giving me a choice I didn't want to make. But a part of me knew I was better off dead than captured. A part of me knew that he was, too.

"What will they do to you?"

He shook his head, but he didn't need to say it.

My voice was choking, and I think there was vomit– no, blood– at the back of my throat.

"I have a plan," he said carefully. "I can cause a diversion. I'll make a run for it. They'll find me. You can take this as a back-up."

He placed the pill in my hand.

"Alex, they will find you…"

"But you'll be gone. You'll be safe."

He was still forming plans and counting on his sacrifice to save me.

But from the moment the pill hit my hand, I knew there was a different sacrifice to be made.

Mine.

"Do they know you betrayed them yet? Do they have proof?"

"No, but us being together now is all the proof they need."

I took a step back. I grasped my fingers around the pill.

"I mean, there's no way you would be identified as a traitor if I was dead, since it would be your job to kill me…"

One more step. My left heel hit the wall.

It was too late. He was already looking up, and realizing in horror what I was suggesting.

"Aislyn?"

Take it.

I screamed at my arm, but it didn't move. I cursed the power of self-preservation that Brie just accused me of not having.

Move your arm to your mouth and take it. Every minute you stand there gives him a chance to be stupid enough to save you.

"Aislyn...give me back the pill."

"You never gave me back my knife," I said, faking a joke.

The door opened downstairs. We couldn't talk now.

"Please," he whispered through tears. "It's not the plan."

The tears fell. Didn't he know?

"This was always the plan."

"But you weren't meant to do this for me."

I stood my ground and hoped I looked intimidating. I saw him shake, his eyes desperate, he started to take steps forward. I grasped it the pill tighter.

"Look, it's simple. We both don't die. I die. You fire a shot in my chest after the pill works. It won't hurt. I'll already be dead."

His face was crumpling. He was begging, pleading with every glance. I could feel it. It was ruining my resolve. He began to shake his head, even as he lowered his hand, and instantly began to whisper, "Don't do this. Don't do this."

"It's kind of my job. I'm protecting you now. I choose who to save, remember? I decide."

"But I'm not good enough!"

"That's never what matters. I love you enough."

"Aislyn, I told you not to love me!"

I tried to muster up enough confidence for my last words.

"Well, you see, we aren't supposed to listen to enemy soldiers."

Alex kept his eyes open as I lifted my hand slowly.

Stop.

It wasn't Alex. It was the voice.

Stop.

It was screaming, coursing through my body. I paused.

And then it was too late.

Alex grabbed my hand first, and instead of pulling it towards him, he lifted my entire torso and reached out my hand as far away as possible. He was pulling, ripping my hand open.

The pill fell. He kicked it.

It was gone.

My chance to protect him was gone.

Hide.

I felt it.

That thing from when I was dreaming. The feeling that would overwhelm me sometimes when Collin prayed. The sense that someone was calling out, desperate to listen to their ridiculous directions. I could almost hear a whisper on the breeze as if God was screaming something, and I could just hear the reverberation.

"Hide." I said, echoing the words I heard.

The doors banged open. There was a click. I could tell it was an automatic weapon, because he put in a clip. We had no chance with that steady stream of bullets. Alex held my shoulders as I grasped his neck, leaning into each other. I felt claustrophobic. I looked up. There was nothing in the shower stall, except…

Our enemy's voice filled the room, echoing loudly. "You know what my favorite part of hide and seek is? This part."

There was one chance we had. I pointed to the soap-holds on either side of the stall.

The officer yelled again.

"That part in the beginning, when you're on edge…"

Alex looked confused, pointing down. He wanted us to duck.

I shook my head, and pointed to the holds, and then to my feet.

One look from him confirmed it was a crazy idea.

I reached out, holding his head in my hand. "Trust me."

Alex nodded. He leaned over, and whispered, "Make an arch."

The officer's booming voice continued. "When you get to say 'Ready or not'…" There was a click from the weapon. Alex grabbed some dirt. He rubbed it in his shaking hands.

"'Here I come!'"

And it came.

We moved the second the stream started, as the bullets hit the first shower stalls. I turned to face the wall, so did Alex. I jumped, pulling up on the soap-hold and risking putting my fingertips on the top of the rod for a moment. I was jumping while trying to duck because if he saw us above the shower curtains, we were done.

I turned to see Alex perched on the soap-hold, barely hanging on. I was losing balance by the second. Alex was waving, and then amidst the gunfire growing louder and louder, shattering tile, I knew what he wanted to do.

And he thought I was crazy.

I had one foot on the small ledge. I turned to face him instead of the wall. His hands began to reach out. I realized they weren't going to meet mine if I didn't move up a little more, which put our legs out of range. We had to make a perfect bridge, from soap-hold to soap-hold, if we were going to hold on.

He grabbed my hands, and we quickly interlaced, making an arch. Almost every vital body part was hovering over the stall. The bullets would hopefully flow right under us. He was still squatting, attempting to balance us on the small, one-foot perches. He was trying to match my height. His knees were still in the line of fire, and starting to shake already.

It seemed like forever. I was staring into his eyes, seeing the sweat drip next to them on his temple. I was blinking and wincing as the shots got closer. I lowered my head to try to block the sound. He had his eyes closed, but opened them the instant he heard the shaking in the stall next to ours.

His eyes pierced me, mouthing something as the first one hit.

I mouthed the same thing back.

I looked down only once, to see the bullets hit only five inches up from the floor. If we had hit the ground and ducked, we'd be dead. But then the stream of bullets traveled upwards. My eyes met his again, staring intensely.

"Hold on," he mouthed, or yelled. "We'll drop." I wasn't sure what he meant, but I realized the curtain was blowing away. It would still protect us after he was done.

With the sound of gunfire, he wouldn't hear us fall.

The bullets whizzed by my legs now, making me move my one leg to avoid it. Just enough to get off balance. Alex held on, trying to steady me. He pushed his knee out to balance himself.

The tile was shattering, grazing my legs.

But they were moving to the left to Alex, who was still trying to keep me steady, his one knee dropping slightly.

I think I screamed when I saw it, but stopped short.

A bullet shot through his leg.

He instantly cringed, squeezing my hands as I tried to hold onto him, pushing him forward to maintain the arch. My arms burned. I forced my joints to retain their hold. The volley of bullets below continued. Fear overwhelmed him.

My arm cramped.

My elbow unbuckled.

He tried to stabilize us, but it didn't work.

We fell.

Just as the bullets moved to the next stall.

I felt the floor shake.

The gunfire was sending shockwaves through the floor.

The bullets still rang out, and I looked down at the arm which had burned. A bullet had grazed me.

His wound was not a graze.

His fingers tightened around mine, his face contorted in pain. He unclenched one to cover his mouth the instant the bullets stopped.

His eyes turned away. I managed to squeeze back hard enough to get his attention. We couldn't move. I felt the friction of the broken tile when we had landed. Any sound the shooter heard would be proof of life. Alex was trying to mouth something...

"Not over."

My ears were ringing. All I could hear was ringing. I realized I couldn't judge my breath, my voice, my movement based on what I could hear. What would I hear?

And then I heard it. I reacted for a short moment, but then froze. The bullets were going into the air, but stopped as soon as they started, meant to spook any survivor.

I didn't breathe. It was easy. I looked at Alex's leg. The bullet had hit muscle, not bone. Straight through. But it was bleeding.

The shooter was still there, though I could barely hear his footsteps over the ringing.

I met Alex's eyes, then looked significantly at his wounded leg.

Alex mouthed, "No."

I needed to stop it. He was bleeding too much.

I reached out to put pressure on the wound, but then I realized why he had refused. He would squirm. It would give us away.

Why wouldn't the shooter leave? What was he waiting for?

Then I heard it over the walkie-talkie. "88, 65, 9, 4. Code in."

"7," rang out in the presumably empty room. He shot again, just three bullets. I was ready this time. I didn't move.

"Way to be thorough." I heard the sarcastic jab on the radio.

"Yeah, well, you know me…"

They were still outside, but I heard the door slam. They were on the move. Their laughter echoed down the staircase.

They wouldn't hear. I touched his head first.

But he nodded, whispering, "Do it."

I placed my hand over the exit wound, which was soaked with blood. I looked to make sure Alex wasn't going to pass out or scream. I heard a grunt, and then a moan.

At least we were alive. But I remembered being shot. You can't think. You can't remember. The world is on fire.

I risked a whisper. I heard the transport leave, not even sure if he could hear me. I reached in close enough for him to feel my breath on his ear.

"Alex."

His teeth were gritted. The ringing in my ears subsided slightly. I reached out one hand to his. His hands had scratches from landing on the tile. I noticed mine did, as well.

I pressed on the wound for three minutes. There was silence, except for when he moaned in pain. Until they checked the other two buildings, there was no chance of us moving out. The bleeding hadn't stopped, so there was no point in displacing now.

I flinched. I couldn't stop the bleeding until I had made his pain worse.

I had to cauterize the wound.

I broke from our gaze for a second, touching my hand to his forehead, and then running my fingers through his hair. He must have known, because he reached for his belt.

He muttered, "Aislyn, do you need my knife?"

I found the knife on a strap attached to his leg. There was also a lighter and another tool. I thought maybe it would help my confidence. But it didn't. As soon as I had a hand on the lighter, my hand started to shake. I scolded myself for shivering. He needed this. But I was terrified I couldn't do it. My hand must have been moving slowly, because he had enough time to grasp it.

My eyes moved from the lighter to his face.

"You've never cauterized a wound before, have you?"

I shook my head.

He nodded, closing his eye for an instant, "I trust you."

He slowly lifted the lighter out of my hand and held it under the knife. I moved my knee to where my hand had been on his wound. I didn't want to lose pressure for a second. He grunted as I pressed my knee down, even as I saw the blade start to cast a glow. This blade I would place on his flesh to ensure the bleeding would stop. I watched his eyes focus on the flame. I couldn't imagine what he was thinking as he stared at it, knowing what was coming as the blade became orange.

He didn't even try to look at me now. He turned his body to be on his abdomen. Both his elbows and forearms lay flat on the ground. I could see the tile dust spread as his breath hit the floor.

He must have sensed me hesitate. I had put the flat of the blade about an inch above his leg. He must have felt the heat radiating off of it.

"Aislyn, do it now."

I finally leaned in. The knife made contact.

His leg shuddered instantly, almost seizing underneath the heat. I started to press in a bit more, and leaned onto his leg to keep it still. He didn't scream. Heaven knows how. He shot out breaths, the dust blowing out from him like smoke. He was gripping the tile, even though it made his hands bleed.

I tried to keep my hands steady, but more out of desperation than focus. This needed to work. He needed to live.

I had counted to ten, hoping it was enough.

The bleeding had stopped. I discarded the knife and reached out for him.

They were shooting up another building in the distance. I reached out for his forearms. They were shaking, but I managed to lift him up. He was clinging to me.

I couldn't say anything, though it was probably safe enough to talk. The gunfire in the distance rattled through my brain.

My forehead touched his. I still held onto his arms, crouched down, curled up in the safety of the moment. Only a moment.

Only always a moment.

"We need to move, Alex."

"I know," he said, grimacing.

"I don't know if you heard. I'm pretty good at saving invalids."

He dropped his head to his chest, smiling a dry smile.

"Yeah, I heard."

I pulled his head in and stroked his brow, holding him a few more minutes before I risked checking my phone. It had no signal, but the display had a little light. I attempted to signal Brie that Alex had been hit, but I could only hope it went through.

We were moving down the stairs, about to pass the floor I had been on earlier. It struck me that neither of us had been in this building without bleeding.

That realization made another memory creep in.

"Alex, can you hang on a second?"

I wasn't sure if it was the adrenaline, or the smell of blood, but I remembered clearly what I couldn't understand about the words then: the words written on the box I hid behind after he shot me.

I had thought the box was abandoned. I had thought Unnecessaries had written on it. But I now recognized the language.

I found the box over by the dried blood I had left behind three months ago: the box with the logo of Mavory's company.

"I think," I said, now turning the box around to explain, "no one recognized it as a language. I'm sure the security doesn't know Elite language. They didn't catch…what it says. What does it say?"

Alex was wincing in pain, and yet the second I showed him the box, he stood up straight, supporting himself in the doorway. No one must have known the Elite language to notice the scribblings of a slave, but Alex could read it.

He didn't speak at first.

"Alex, what does it say?"

He paused, shifting slightly to breathe.

"*Find us. Where the food grows. Before we die.*"

CHAPTER 36

There was a creek. It felt almost too cold to put my legs in, as the breezes started to grow colder in the morning and late night.

But I put my feet in. Because I was alive to feel the cold.

We were miles from the warehouse with the box that haunted me. We had waited until the officers had tried another buildings, and then made a run for it. We had trudged through forest and fields.

We'd walked ten miles when he said, "What happens now?"

"We try to get to a station," I said, nervously. I didn't know what to do. "I want to treat your wound a little bit more."

I said it as an afterthought, but then turned.

I saw him wincing. I asked him again.

"Are you okay?"

"Yeah. What about your arm?" he asked.

"It's fine," I lied. The truth was, the bandage was stopping it from looking horrible. It was all purple, and I had no clue why.

Only I had the distinct impression he was lying, too.

The wound stung, and not from being sore. I stood up, even as he shook his head to deny his pain again. "It's nothing."

"No, Alex, it's something…you just–"

His reaction interrupted me as he gripped his leg. He cursed, and then said something under his breath. He looked afraid.

"Aislyn, be honest. How does your arm feel?"

I stopped, wondering if I could just stare at some leaves with him again and not jump back into panic.

"It's stinging. Bad. It's purple," I answered.

"It might have been…do you have a med station?"

"It's still five miles off," I said.

He said something, but trailed off. The further we went, the harder he found it to talk. His leg started shaking when we were on mile three. He eventually had to lean on me to continue to walk. It had been hours, but we had barely made any progress. I wasn't able to talk; all of my energy was spent on helping him.

He kept repeating something. He would say something. Mostly I just let him lean on me, drenched in sweat. I was wondering if he was going through withdrawal again.

It had darkened, the moon casting beautiful shadows that I pushed out of my mind. I almost wanted to stay there, with him. Maybe that was our destiny, to curl up on the leaves, under the moon, and remain shadows in its light. He opened his eyes. He knew what I was thinking.

Even though he hadn't talked in hours, he said, "Keep going."

I shook my head, paralyzed by fear. By then, the clouds parted. The starlight hit my eyes. It could have blinded me.

He whispered, "Keep going. For Emmy. Please…"

And I found the will to do what I needed to do.

No one else was going to die for me.

I kissed his forehead, and left him. I left, for a chance to save him.

I ran for the med station. Faster than I thought I could, for about half a mile. I was determined to run longer, faster even, when I heard a sound of footsteps. Then a voice saying, "Nature, I despise you."

I stood up, shouting his name.

"Liam?"

It was the first time I had spoken in hours. Though I had meant to scream, the word barely choked its way out. But then I screamed it, repeating it in a flurry of desperation.

Liam saw me, from far off, and he started running down the hill. He reached me, grabbing and pulling me into a hug. He was still winded when he started talking.

"I kept praying that since I found you once, I'd find you again. I found you again. Oh my–"

I closed my eyes, taking in the significance of the last time I saw him. But I needed...

"Where is Brie? Lydia? Someone medical."

"What happened?" he looked confused, then looked at my arm. Footsteps came crashing behind him.

"Where's Alex?" Michael asked, running up from behind Liam. He must have noticed the panic in my eyes.

"I couldn't carry him–"

He cursed, and spoke into his watch. "Collin? We need you!"

"Did you find her? What's going on?"

"She's fine, but I think Alex..."

"Something's wrong. With the wound. I think it's poisoned."

I was talking to them, but not looking at them, and I started to feel dizzy suddenly. Michael grabbed my head, grabbing my focus by forcing myself to stare at him.

"Where is he, Aislyn?"

We started to run. I gave them my MCU that traced my steps. I barely noticed any of my own wounds or any scratches on my body as I ran through the brush. Brie was asking what happened over the comm, her first questions about injuries. Slowly the story worked backward, like a reverse debrief. I heard George's voice, and then felt even more shocked when I heard Will's.

When we reached Alex, he looked still, almost eerily still, and then he started to seize. I reached out to grab him.

"No, don't hold him. Just let him go."

It ended after only a few seconds. Liam was able to come back, and they tried to lift him.

"He has clear airways. The shuttles are already…" Liam said.

A few seconds later, two shuttles came plowing through the thick forest. The air from both of them almost created a vortex, strewing leaves everywhere. Alex stirred, but couldn't move.

And then I heard Collin's voice calling out to Michael.

But Collin didn't reach me first.

"Aislyn!" Eva screamed, throwing her arms around me.

I wanted to protest. She was yelling the wrong name. No one was worried about who was actually in trouble.

Why was no one shouting his name? Where was Brie, or someone that could save him?

But the person who always knew me best didn't call my name. He did what I needed him to do.

I heard Collin yell something to Liam and then curse as he fell to his knees, checking the wound with a much better light than we had. He began to call Alex's name, trying to wake him.

"The bullet went through. I saw, I checked. There's an exit…"

"No, this exit wound is too small," Collin said, panicked. "Sam said they've been experimenting with new bullets. They separate, especially when hitting bone. They don't even split the bone. The hope is that they'll do more damage in his body. "

"Why is he seizing?" I asked in desperation.

"It's poison. Each piece is poisoned…"

"Alex? Alex? Can you hear me?" Michael was calling his name as he was injecting him with something.

Brie came running down the hill, a wave of newly fallen leaves sticking to her. She ordered those around Alex's leg to move.

Collin was yelling, "Sam told you about this, right, Brie?"

I was holding Alex's hand. Collin was holding the other one. I barely had time to see him, but he looked determined, as if his eyes could make me believe they could save Alex.

"No one else is going to die for this. No one else, Aislyn."

Collin kept repeating it. And without asking the question, I knew the details of the intel had been received.

Brie checked the wound, making Alex moan in pain. His eyes still wouldn't open. Collin kept repeating his words, so maybe if Alex died, he would know he didn't die for nothing.

Had we done this for nothing?

"You told them? The intel?" I asked Brie.

"I told everyone. Sam got me on every screen in Central Command. There were teams coming out to get me. I hadn't heard from you. I got baby Emerson on one of the shuttles. Then we headed out here," she said, sounding nervous. "Is he–?"

Michael said, "Conscious! Just opened his eyes and his BP is rising a bit."

Collin looked at his eyes. "Alex, you can't move. We don't want the poison spreading anymore."

Then Collin turned to me. "Did you get hit at all?"

I nodded. Liam began checking me, pulling at my arm as we headed back to the shuttles, working furiously to get them online.

"Alex, Alex…my name is Collin. This is Michael and you know Eva. Okay, I know you don't know who we are…"

"I know…who you are." Alex looked at Collin. He looked strangely more at peace in that moment. "Is she safe?"

Collin nodded. "She's right here. She's not giving up. We aren't either."

Alex asked, "Do you need to know anything, in case I d–"

"No, no, no…not yet. We aren't going there yet," Collin said hurriedly. "Listen. We think your bullet was a splinter. Are you familiar with them?"

Alex closed his eyes in anguish and nodded.

"What poison is in the bullets?" Collin asked. "Do you know?"

Alex was straining his memory, fighting seizing again. The relaxant was working; Collin yelled to Brie to give him more.

"Is he bleeding out?" Collin asked. "That'll rule out anti-coagulating poisons."

I shook my head, and for the first time looked at my own poisoned area, growing blue. It was sucking out the air in my body, one cell at a time.

Michael took over talking to Alex. "Collin, there's only so much he can do, he can't speak…"

Collin interrupted him, looking back at him. "Blink. Blink if you think it might be arsenic."

Alex held his eyes open.

"Monkshood. Tylithyium. Um…what other poisons?"

Eva, who looked like she was lost in concentration, yelled out suddenly, "No, it couldn't react with the bullet, it would deteriorate it over time. It would have to be…" Eva closed her eyes in concentration, naming off ten chemicals. Alex blinked.

Collin yelled, "Eva, again…slower."

Eva came over to him, looking at my wound as she squeezed by me. She leaned over him.

He blinked, and Eva said, "okay" and she put her hand on his forehead.

This time Alex clearly blinked at two specific names. Eva sighed. "Okay, I can get it out. I just did a local." She ran a few more directions by Collin, who unrolled the surgical kit.

"Alex, we're injecting you with something that should help. Brie saw the fragments from the splinters. We need to give you some painkiller—"

Alex instantly shook, and looked at me desperate for them to understand. It was Brie who reached out to him.

"Alex, it's not the one you usually take, okay? We know what you're trying to do, but we need you lucid. Besides," Brie paused as Alex grunted as she stuck the needle in.

"It's already done."

His first words that he spoke in hours. "You know, being compassionate and sadistic are kind of opposites, Brie."

"Yeah, like you should talk," she said, pulling out a scalpel and concentrating on his wound. He grunted as she cut his knee open, revealing a few tiny pieces of shrapnel encased in purple flesh.

Collin kept repeating, "Hold on." He glanced at his MCU, just as Will did. Then both looked very uncomfortable all of a sudden.

"Just ignore it. I'm not…" Will started, but Alex interrupted.

"No, it's okay. Ask me whatever your leaders want to know."

Collin shook his head. "I can't. Just concentrate–"

Alex finally spoke. "What, on the pain?" Then he cursed.

I was about to protest, but I realized that it might distract him.

"Aislyn and you sent the info to Brie. There were two files, and we can't understand the code on one. That one that says X45-2R."

"The tech. That's the tech I.D. number of who writes the file; there's a tag. It's like a signature. You can find them. It makes a good target to ask questions…especially if we get it to…Lynn."

His eyes squeezed in pain. I squeezed his hand, and Collin said, "She's almost got it. She got four already. You're doing great. What is the significance of the order of the numbers in the second manifest? They look alphabetically ordered, then they start over?"

He nodded. "My guess…Elites, Citizens…."

"Rank?" Collin asked. Alex nodded.

"Can you stop?" I didn't know if he heard my whisper.

"Yes, I can. That's the only two things–"

Brie interrupted. "Alex, one's pressed up against a nerve."

"Just do it, don't tell me," he said. "The baby? Becca's baby?"

"She's safe, Alex. She's…"

What she was about to say was stopped by a bloodcurdling scream. I didn't know if he could hear me or Collin saying his name, or see Will hold his leg down.

I breathed relief as the last piece came out. But was jolted by the yell in the distance.

"We have incoming."

There was another shout from George. Before I could even react, Collin and Michael were picking Alex up.

Brie was grabbing my arm and shoving me forward.

"There's an old Q station, but they'll know we're here."

"We'll have to risk it, we don't have a choice," Collin yelled.

We were driving in the shuttle in only a minute when someone yelled out the name of a drone. I was still staring at the shuttle floor. It was clean. I wondered if blood would be on it again soon.

We screeched to a halt and Brie and Eva helped Collin and Michael get Alex out. I heard someone yell my name, but their plea didn't move me. I heard the drone. Collin pulled me out, grabbing my arm, throwing it around him, and running with me.

"Stay with me, Aislyn. Please."

I stumbled down the last of the stairs of the Q station when it hit. The whole structure shook, the concrete ceiling cracked, and it felt like a hammer had hit my ears. Collin had caught me, clinging to me as he yelled to Will.

A light flickered. An echo of rock grinding together. Silence.

Everything fought the void darkness.

I struggled to open my eyes. I breathed enough to keep living. I felt enough fear to keep fighting. But not today.

Today I was done.

Alex was alive. They were all alive.

Thousands of people were still alive.

Maybe despite everything, the light still had a chance.

But the darkness of sleep stole me from Collin's worried scream, calling my name.

And I left the light and the dark for oblivion.

CHAPTER 37

I had passed out. Or at least that was what my headache told me. Maybe I'd hit my head on something on the missiles impact, and didn't recognize it. But it wasn't an easy sleep. It wasn't home.

I woke up on the table. I felt a hand beside me, taped up, most likely with an IV on it.

And then, as I opened my eyes, another hand grasped mine. The first hand I had ever held after being named a Protector.

That hand squeezed. There was a sharp intake of breath.

"Collin?"

"Yeah, Aislyn," he leaned in. "I'm here."

I pulled up, even as he said, "easy, easy" to try to keep me slow. But I was fine. I felt fine. But desperate.

"Eva? Brie? Are they okay?"

Brie answered, "I'm over here. Eva's upstairs, keeping watch. I stayed with you and Alex. Liam, Michael, and Will are looking for what survived from the shuttle. The drone obliterated everything. Emily's on a bit of a mission with George. She went back to try to cover your trail, wipe up Alex's blood. Alex is really weak, but otherwise, he's doing a lot better."

"Are you sure?"

But it wasn't Brie who answered.

"She's sure."

I turned to see Alex, who was smiling nervously on the other med table. His eyes were still closed, opening a little after he spoke. His bandaged leg dangled off the table. He looked pale.

He moved to get up. Collin swung around to help him, but Brie got there first. She leaned over him to look at the wound, and then checked his eyes. As she was checking, Alex looked at Collin.

"So, what happens now?"

Collin sighed, moving his hands to the edge of the table to lean on it. "The Council ordered me to take you back to the Territory. I don't agree with that decision. So…I argued that I was going to wait for an order from Patterson."

"But I don't know…I don't want to go back to the Republic."

Collin shook his head, "If you go to the Territory, you'll have to stand trial. In the end, it will just be a waste of time, and I'm not sure…what the outcome would be. This is a field mission, so Patterson has the authority to make the call. I'm going to send him our renewed agenda, based on what we're going to decide when everyone gets back. It's his decision, I'm sorry. I know that you can barely trust anyone. I know you trust her. I want you to be able to trust me."

Alex nodded, and without saying anything more, Collin continued to look at him, and then nodded to Brie.

"Brie? Vitals?"

"I would rather give him a little more pain meds–"

He shook his head. "No. Please don't. Brie…"

Collin was about to say something, but Brie said, "Okay."

I thought she would put up more of a fight, but she added, "I have something else, then. To help you."

He looked at her curiously, and then at me. I shrugged my shoulders, still feeling relieved that at this point, Alex was safe.

"What?"

"Something...I should have shared with you...before," Brie stumbled out, making me stare because it was so rare to see her stutter. She took a breath before starting again, "You see, the Unnecessaries we save? They inspire us. You have earned the right to be inspired. And I shouldn't have taken that away from you. They took her away from you. I want you to know I'm not doing this so you'll feel guilty. I'm doing this. To give her back."

She took out her MCU, and on the main screen, an image of an infant popped up.

"Caleigh first weighed in at six pounds, nine ounces. She was given no vaccinations because of her tense birth, but was declared healthy, despite struggling for the first few hours. When I held her..." Brie swallowed, and then went to the next image.

Images flew for the next ten minutes. Slowly everyone returned, watching him watching Caleigh. He would smile at times, and then there were moments he would look like he was suppressing other emotions that threatened to rise.

Will was about say something when Alex interrupted.

"Wait! Who is that? Behind her, in the picture?"

"You should know, Alex," Collin started. "You should know that there was a reason that Michael, Liam, and I came out her.

We realized something that no one else had ever discovered." He paused, sounding a little shaky. "The day after we sent Brie and Eva out, we were in the yard, discussing what you all would do next. Gabriel found me. You see, he told us something after Erica brought the girl who needed the contacts. She started playing a game with them. And he didn't know how to play the game, but he said it was so strange that so many of them knew how to play."

"What game?"

"They call it 'coffee cups'," Will said. "It's like tag. If you're touched, you're on the ground. But if someone brings you a coffee cup, you're free."

Brie moved closer to Alex. "The girl behind Caleigh. She was saved last year by Tessa. She lived in an alley, on the…"

"Corner of Market," Alex's voice shook. "She had breathing issues. Then she disappeared. I thought she was dead."

Collin said, as he moved over to him, "So, we pulled all the older kids together and asked them questions. Michael started tracing your patterns. When Sam and Liam got out of prison, they ran through this trail of surveillance and pictures for an hour."

Alex looked at Liam, who rose his eyebrows.

"Yeah, prison. It's a long story."

Alex took a sharp breath. "They all played 'coffee cups' because of the few kids I helped?"

Collin smiled. "Yeah…just a few."

In the next instant, another picture took its place. Alex put his hand over his mouth, total shock filling his eyes.

"She…that was eleven months ago. I thought she…"

The picture changed again.

"And we found that when we asked them about it…"

The pictures kept going. Brie's eyes turned to Collin in shock.

"Collin, how many?"

"Thirty of them. Thirty said a coffee cup saved their life."

I reached out to touch Alex's shaking hand. Collin reached out and touched his shoulder. Something in Alex finally released, even as he removed the fist from his mouth. He turned to me, and smiled against tears as he spoke.

"You were right. It's the part of the story we can't see that might, in the end, give us hope."

There was a silence that followed that felt thick, as if God had silenced all of us for the moment he had been waiting for: setting a soul free from guilt and affirming every risk he had every taken.

Eva was the one to break the silence, if only because she heard that sentence and thought of our other, more pressing issue.

"Speaking of those parts of the story we couldn't see…we all just saw quite lot. What do we do with this intel? Where do we even start?"

"We don't start," Brie said. "Not now."

"She's right," Collin said. "We wait for Patterson's orders. We comb the intel, and try to decide what else we need to determine while Alex is here, just in case you can't stay. If they try to arrest Alex, Will and I have a window to help him escape. Be ready to take it."

Alex shook his head. "You don't need to…"

"It's done," Collin said with a loyalty Alex didn't expect. "As for the intel, I'm worried we're still missing some crucial pieces of information: where all the Unnecessaries go, how they get there, and how to even start to plan on rescuing them."

"Are we going to rescue them?" Liam asked.

"What else would we do? Just go back to protecting Vessels and Unnecessaries while there's thousands, maybe a million people who are, essentially, in slavery?" Eva commented.

"No, I think we just said we need a plan," Michael argued.

Then, to my surprise, everyone in the room looked at me. "What?"

"What do you mean, 'what'?" Liam said. "You're the planner. You're the storyteller, spy, dancer, and all-around crazy person. Come up with a plan. Let's hear it."

I stared around the room, hoping to be inspired by the people I loved around me. But instead, I was terrified.

"The last plan I had…got Megan killed," I said.

"Um…last time I checked…" Eva got up and stood in the center of the room, looking uncharacteristically intimidating. "The last plan you had got a baby safely delivered, got intel no one else could have, and got us a chance to save thousands of lives. But by all means, have that 'failed' mission define you."

I shook my head, even while smiling at her. I was trying to ignore Alex, who was looking like he was about to challenge me.

"Eva, that's not the point. The point is that I can't ask anyone to follow any plan I create. I can't even ask you, I–"

I didn't continue. I stared at Brie, who I didn't expect to talk first, but she said, "I think…you're forgetting, Aislyn, you don't need to ask us. We can say it, and mean it, before you have a chance to ask. You would never need to ask me. I'm with you."

"I'm with you," Eva said, without hesitating.

"I'm with you." Alex smiled slightly.

One by one, each of them said the words I hadn't earned. There was silence, but my head was still spinning.

I stared, wondering what to do before I realized I had nothing yet, but maybe...

"Okay. Give me twelve hours, and I need...I some air."

Collin nodded upwards.

"I have to send Patterson a message. I'll come up, too."

I slowly released Alex's hand, and walked up the stairs. Collin was already plugging in his MCU to the cable in the ground. I smelled the charred wood, staining the purity of the late summer air. I was only a few steps away from me when he stood up.

He stared at the MCU, and then shut it down as he turned to me. Something about the way he looked at the screen made it feel significant.

"What was it?"

"What Patterson needed to know about Alex and the intel details. And something else...that he needed to know."

He stopped too suddenly. He looked strangely determined.

"If this is going to be awkward for you, you should know that Alex and I..."

I stopped myself. I still felt torn. And Collin saw it.

"We're not as together as you might think, Collin. I'm still as confused as I was. I know, you might be jealous, but I'm—"

He interrupted, "I don't expect you to explain. And I don't need you to pity me. I made a mistake ever letting you think I didn't love you. But that mistake…has just been rectified."

There was a moment when I had no idea what he could mean, but then I looked at his MCU as he continued to speak.

"At least this way…you'll know."

I began to shake my head in shock.

"Collin, what did you send him?"

"My revised A-42. If Hannah doesn't approve it, I'll face immediate dismissal. And I don't care."

My lungs struggled to capture the air; it seemed too thin. I found myself struggling to ask him what he meant. But then, he turned to face me. His eyes avoided mine.

"I know, it's not really good timing. But I needed to do it. It's not about jealousy. I'm done lying."

While my head was spinning, my need to know was more urgent than his willingness to reveal it.

"So, the part you revised was…the question. Is it your intent to continue as a trainer of the 189th generation?"

"That is the question. The revision specifically stated that I will not be renewing my right to be a trainer."

Confusion made it hard to speak. There was only one word that came out. "Why?"

"What? The official reason I just sent?"

"Yes!" I screamed, desperate to understand.

He moved one step closer, his head slowly looking up from the ground.

He had never looked more vulnerable. More wounded.

But he had never spoken with more conviction.

"Despite all efforts to subdue or combat my feelings, I am, and will always be, irrevocably in love with the 27th Protector. I have lost the strength and will to deny it. I now tie myself to her fate in every way imaginable."

I could feel my lip quivering. I bit it down as he continued.

"What I didn't write was that…even if she never kisses me again, if she never holds me again, if she never loves me again, I will follow her. I will risk everything. I just need her to know the truth; because the lie destroyed her. The lie destroyed me."

"Collin, I–" My disbelief caught me. I felt urgent to tell him how I felt, but I couldn't figure it out quickly enough to find words. He must have known that, because he quickly cut me off.

"I don't need you to try to make sense of it. I don't deserve forgiveness. But as I stood in a room a few minutes ago, and heard everyone say something. I knew that I couldn't say it truthfully until I had done this. And I know that my decision to love you will lead to either the most beautiful or the most tragic end we could imagine. Those three words would mean far more than any words I've ever spoken to you. So hear them, Aislyn. These three words are infinite, blaring, and eternal."

I could hear my heartbeat echoing in my ears as he whispered it: in a way, that made it the loudest thing I had ever heard him say.

"I'm with you."

Epilogue

Emily was strong. She figured that was why they sent her to clean up Alex's blood. They didn't know that she hated blood.

George did. Maybe that was why he volunteered to drive.

She was almost done, trying to spray all of the broken shards of tile with the liquid that was meant to make the blood impossible to identify. But she knew whose blood it was. That was both scary, confusing, and exhilarating. She went down a few flights of stairs, but she stopped.

"George? What are you doing in here?" she said, annoyed.

"They said to be thorough. Alex left a trail through here."

George had followed the trail and was now staring at the box that Aislyn had described. Emily stared at the words, the meaning behind them sent a chill up her spine.

"What is it?" she asked. He didn't look terrified, but sick.

He didn't say anything; he just turned the box until they could see the bottom. There was a date. And a name.

George asked, "It's about four years ago. Her name…it was in the debrief from Aislyn. Gabriel said she was–"

"I read the debrief, George. Gabriel thinks she's dead. And we can't even tell him she's alive. She might not be anymore."

George grazed his fingers along the letters in the name which glowed in the light of his MCU.

"Kieri." George spoke it, like bringing someone back to life.

Emily moved forward, leaning on his shoulder as she spoke.

"We'll find you. Where the food grows. Before you die again."

Acknowledgments

This book exists because of courage, but it wasn't all mine. Any courage I had, God gave me.
Any persistence I had was because my husband wouldn't give up on me. My girls gave me a reason to write, and a reason to stop writing and play in sand for hours. I needed both their applause for my dedication and their distractions.
But there were so many gifts given to me.
Some people gave me inspiration. They don't even know my name, or that I exist. They were speaking, screaming sometimes, but they kept me going. Thank you, Jennie, Craig and Steven.
A band gave me a soundtrack to write and hope. Thank you, For King and Country.
A dear friend gave me a sounding board. Thank you, Jewell.
Two brave editors gave me all my mistakes…and ways I could fix them. Thank you, Gretchen and Anna.
An artist gave me a cover: Thank you, Bo.
A few brave souls bought my first book, read it, and helped to cover the costs with this book: Thank you, Becca, Mike, and Jen.
Others rejected me. This was the hardest gift to receive, but in the end, I'm glad I opened it. It led to understanding my own emotions in a way I hope will enhance my writing in the future.
Other gifts I could never count. They were everyday things, full of love and support. I'm afraid I've forgotten too many of them. I'll try to tell you thank you, when I see you and your words echo. Until then, thank you.

www.the27Protector.com
#NoUnnecessaries

Made in the USA
Lexington, KY
07 March 2016